THE MIDDLE OF THE JOURNEY

THE
MIDDLE
OF THE
JOURNEY

❯❮❯❮❯

LIONEL TRILLING

with a new Introduction by the author

AVON
PUBLISHERS OF BARD, CAMELOT AND DISCUS BOOKS

AVON BOOKS
A division of
The Hearst Corporation
959 Eighth Avenue
New York, New York 10019

Copyright © 1947, 1975 by Lionel Trilling
Published by arrangement with The Viking Press
Introduction © 1975 by Lionel Trilling
Published by arrangement with Author's estate.
ISBN: 0-380-00520-4

First Avon Edition, February 1976
Third Printing

AVON TRADEMARK REG. U.S. PAT. OFF. AND
FOREIGN COUNTRIES, REGISTERED TRADEMARK
MARCA REGISTRADA, HECHO EN U.S.A.

Printed in the U.S.A.

To Diana

INTRODUCTION

The re-issue of *The Middle of the Journey* so many years after it was first published makes an occasion when I might appropriately say a word about the relation which the novel bears to actuality, especially to the problematical kind of actuality we call history. The relation is really quite a simple one but it is sometimes misunderstood.

From my first conception of it, my story was committed to history—it was to draw out some of the moral and intellectual implications of the powerful attraction to Communism felt by a considerable part of the American intellectual class during the Thirties and Forties. But although its historical nature and purpose are attested to by the explicit reference it makes to certain of the most momentous events of our epoch, the book I wrote in 1946–47 and published in 1947 did not depict anyone who was a historical figure. When I have said this, however, I must go on to say that among the characters of my story there is one who had been more consciously derived from actuality than any of the others—into the creation of Gifford Maxim there had gone not only such imagination as I could muster on his behalf but also a considerable amount of recollected observation of a person with whom I had long been acquainted; a salient fact about him was that at one period of his life he had pledged himself to the cause of Communism and had then bitterly repudiated his allegiance. He might therefore be thought of as having moved for a time in the ambience of history even though he could scarcely be called a historical figure; for that he clearly was not of sufficient consequence. This person was Whittaker Chambers.

But only a few months after my novel was published, Chambers' status in history underwent a sudden and drastic change. The Hiss case broke upon the nation and the world and Chambers became beyond any doubt a historical figure.

The momentous case had eventuated from an action taken by Chambers almost a decade earlier. In 1939 he had sought out an official of the government—Adolph Berle, then Assistant Secretary of State—with whom he lodged detailed information about a Communist espionage apparatus to which he himself had belonged as a courier and from which he had defected some years earlier. What led him to make the disclosure at this time was his belief that the Soviet Union would make common cause with Nazi Germany and come to stand in a belligerent relation to the United States. As a long-belated, circuitously reached outcome of this communication, Alger Hiss was intensively investigated and questioned, a procedure which by many was thought bizarre in view of the exceptional esteem in which the suspected man was held—he had been an official in President Roosevelt's administrations since 1933 and a member of the State Department since 1936; he had served as adviser to the President at Yalta, and as temporary Secretary General of the United Nations; in 1946 he had been elected president of the Carnegie Endowment for International Peace. The long tale of investigation and confrontation came to an end when a Federal grand jury in New York, after having twice summoned Hiss to appear before it, indicted him for perjury. The legal process which followed was prolonged, bitter, and of profound moral, political, and cultural importance. Chambers, who had been the effectual instigator of the case, was the chief witness against the man whom he had once thought of as a valued friend. He was as much on trial as Alger Hiss—people commonly spoke of the Hiss-Chambers case—and his ordeal was perhaps even more severe.

At the time I wrote *The Middle of the Journey*, Chambers was a successful member of the staff of *Time* and a contributor of signed articles to *Life* and therefore could not be thought of as having a wholly private existence, but he was not significantly present to the consciousness of a great many people. Only to such readers of my novel as had been Chambers' college-mates or his former comrades in the Communist Party or were now his professional colleagues would the personal traits and the political career I had assigned to

Gifford Maxim connect him with the actual person from whom these were derived.

In America *The Middle of the Journey* was not warmly received upon its publication or widely read—the English response was more cordial—and some time passed before any connection was publicly made between the obscure novel and the famous trial. No sooner was the connection made than it was exaggerated. To me as the author of the novel there was attributed a knowledge of events behind the case which of course I did not have. All I actually knew that bore upon what the trial disclosed was Whittaker Chambers' personality and the fact that he had joined, and then defected from, a secret branch of the Communist Party. This was scarcely arcane information. Although Chambers and I had been acquainted for a good many years, anyone who had spent a few hours with him might have as vivid a sense as I had of his comportment and temperament, for these were out of the common run, most memorable, and he was given to making histrionic demonstration of them. As for his political career, its phase of underground activity, as I shall have occasion to say at greater length, was one of the openest of secrets while it lasted, and, when it came to an end, Chambers believed that the safety of his life depended upon the truth being widely known.

That there was a connection to be drawn between Whittaker Chambers and my Gifford Maxim became more patent as the trial progressed, and this seemed to make it the more credible that my Arthur Croom derived from Alger Hiss; some readers even professed to see a resemblance between Nancy Croom and Mrs. Hiss. If there is indeed any likeness to be discerned between the fictive and the actual couples, it is wholly fortuitous. At no time have I been acquainted with either Alger Hiss or Priscilla Hiss, and at the time I wrote the novel, we did not, to my knowledge, have acquaintances in common. The name of Hiss was unknown to me until some months after my book had appeared.

It was not without compunction that I had put Whittaker Chambers to the uses of my story. His relation to the Communist Party bore most pertinently upon the situation I wanted to deal with and I felt no constraint upon my availing myself of it, since Chambers, as I have indicated, did not keep it secret but, on the contrary, wished it to be known. But the man himself, with all his idiosyncrasies of personality, was inseparable from his political experience as I conceived it, and in portraying the man himself to the extent I did I was conscious of the wish that nothing I said or represented in my book could be thought by Chambers to impugn or belittle the bitter crisis of conscience I knew him to have undergone. His break with the Communist Party under the circumstances of his particular relation to it had been an act of courage and had entailed much suffering, which, I was inclined to suppose, was not yet at its end.

Such concern as I felt for Chambers' comfort of mind had its roots in principle and not in friendship. Chambers had never been a friend of mine though we had been in college at the same time, which meant that in 1947 we had been acquainted for twenty-three years. I hesitate to say that I disliked him and avoided his company—there was indeed something about him that repelled me, but there was also something that engaged my interest and even my respect. Yet friends we surely were not.

Whether or not Chambers ever read my book I cannot say. At the time of its publication he doubtless learned from reviews, probably also from one of the friends we had in common, that the book referred to him and his experience. And then when the trial of Alger Hiss began, there was the notion, quite widely circulated and certain to reach him, that *The Middle of the Journey* had evidential bearing on the case. In one of the autobiographical essays in his posthumous volume *Cold Friday*, Chambers names me as having been among the friends of his college years, which, as I have said, I was not, and goes on to speak of my having written a novel in which he is represented. He concludes his account of my relation to him by recalling that when "a Hiss investigator" tried to induce me to speak against him in court, I had refused and said, "Whittaker Chambers is a man of honour." I did indeed use just those words on the occasion to which Chambers refers and can still recall the outburst of contemptuous rage they evoked from the lawyer who had come to call on me to solicit my testimony. I should like to think that my having said that Chambers and I were not friends will lend the force of objectivity to my statement, the substance of which I would still affirm. Whittaker Chambers had been engaged in espionage against his own country; when a change of heart and principle led to his defecting from his apparatus, he had eventually not only confessed his own treason but named the comrades who shared it, including one whom for a time he had cherished as a friend. I hold that when this has been said of him, it is still possible to say that he was a man of honour.

Strange as it might seem in view of his eventual prominence in the narrative, Chambers had no part in my first conception and earliest drafts of *The Middle of the Journey*. He came into the story fairly late in its development and wholly unbidden. Until he made his appearance I was not aware that there was any need for him, but when he suddenly turned up and proposed himself to my narrative, I could not fail to see how much to its point he was.

His entrance into the story changed its genre. It had been my intention to write what we learned from Henry James to call a *nouvelle*, which I take to be a fictional narrative longer than a long short-story and shorter than a short novel. Works in this genre are likely to be marked by a considerable degree of thematic explicitness—one can usually paraphrase the informing idea of a *nouvelle* without being unforgivably reductive; it needn't be a total betrayal of a *nouvelle* to say what it is "about". Mine was to be about death—about what had happened to the way death is conceived by the enlightened consciousness of the modern age.

The story was to take place in the mid-Thirties and the time in which it is set is crucial to it. Arthur and Nancy Croom are the devoted friends of John Laskell; during his recent grave illness it was they who oversaw his care and they have now arranged for him to recruit his strength in the near vicinity of their country home. Upon his arrival their welcome is of the warmest, yet Laskell can't but be aware that the Crooms become somewhat remote and reserved whenever he speaks of his illness, during which, as they must know, there had been a moment when his condition had been critical. To Laskell the realization of mortality has brought a kind of self-knowledge, which, even though he does not fully comprehend it, he takes to be of some considerable significance, but whenever he makes a diffident attempt to speak of this to his friends, they appear almost to be offended. He seems to perceive that the Crooms' antagonism to his recent experience and to the interest he takes in it is somehow connected with the rather anxious esteem in which they hold certain of their country neighbours. In these people, who, in the language of the progressive liberalism of the time were coming to be called "little people", the Crooms insist on perceiving a quality of simplicity and authenticity which licenses their newly conceived and cherished hope that the future will bring into being a society in which reason and virtue will prevail. In short, the Crooms might be said to pass a *political* judgment upon Laskell for the excessive attention he pays to the fact that he had approached death and hadn't died. If Laskell's preoccupation were looked at closely and objectively, they seem to be saying, might it not be understood as actually an affirmation of death, which is, in practical outcome, a negation of the future and of the hope it holds out for a society of reason and virtue. Was there not a sense in which death might be called reactionary?

This was the *donnée* which I undertook to develop. As I have said, the genre that presented itself as most appropriate to my purpose was the *nouvelle*, which seemed precisely suited to the scope of my given idea, to what I at first saw as the range of its implications. After Chambers made his way into the story, bringing with him so much more than its original theme strictly needed, I had to understand that it could no longer be contained within the graceful limits of the *nouvelle:* it had to be a novel or nothing.

Chambers was the first person I ever knew whose commitment to radical politics was meant to be definitive of his whole moral being, the controlling element of his existence. He made the commitment while he was still in college and it was what accounted for the quite exceptional respect in which he was held by his associates at that time. He entered Columbia in 1920, a freshman rather older than his classmates, for he had spent a year between high school and college as an itinerant worker. He was a solemn youth who professed political views of a retrograde kind and was still firm in a banal religious faith. But by 1923 his principles had so far changed that he wrote a blasphemous play about the Crucifixion, which, when it was published in a student magazine, made a scandal that led to his withdrawal from college. He was subsequently allowed to return, but in the intervening time he had lost all interest in academic life—during a summer tour of Europe he had witnessed the social and economic disarray of the continent and discovered both the practical potential and the moral heroism of revolutionary activity. Early in 1925 he joined the Communist Party.

Such relation as I had with Chambers began at this time, in 1924–25, which was my senior year. It is possible that he and I never exchanged a single word at college. Certainly we never conversed. He knew who I was—that is, he connected me with my name—and it may be that the report I was once given of his having liked a poem of mine had actually originated as a message he sent to me. I used to see him in the company of one group of my friends, young men of intimidating brilliance, of whom some remained loyal to him through everything, though others came to hold him in bitterest contempt. I observed him as if from a distance and with considerable irony, yet accorded him the deference which my friends thought his due.

The moral force that Chambers asserted began with his physical appearance. This seemed calculated to negate youth and all its graces, to deny that they could be of any worth in our world of pain and injustice. He was short of stature and very broad, with heavy arms and massive thighs; his sport was wrestling. In his middle age there was a sizable outcrop of belly and I think this was already in evidence. His eyes were narrow and they preferred to consult the floor rather than an interlocutor's face. His mouth was small and, like his eyes, tended downward, one might think in sullenness, though this was not so. When the mouth opened, it never failed to shock by reason of the dental ruin it disclosed, a devastation of empty sockets and blackened stumps. In later years, when he became respectable, Chambers underwent restorative dentistry, but during his radical time, his aggressive toothlessness had been so salient in the image of the man that I did not use it in portraying Gifford Maxim, feeling that to do so would have been to go too far in explicitness of personal reference. This novelistic self-denial wasn't inconsiderable, for that desolated mouth was the perfect insigne of Chambers' moral authority. It annihilated the hygienic American present—only a serf could have such a mouth, or some student in a visored cap who sat in his Moscow garret and thought of nothing save the moment when he would toss the fatal canister into the barouche of the Grand Duke.

Chambers could on occasion speak eloquently and cogently, but he was not much given to speaking—his histrionism, which seemed unremitting, was chiefly that of imperturbability and long silences. Usually his utterances were gnomic, often cryptic. Gentleness was not out of the range of his expression, which might even include a compassionate sweetness of a beguiling kind. But the chief impression he made was of a forbidding drabness.

In addition to his moral authority, Chambers had a very considerable college prestige as a writer. This was deserved. My undergraduate admiration for his talent was recently confirmed when I went back to the poetry and prose he published in a student magazine in 1924-25. At that time he wrote with an elegant austerity. Later, beginning with his work for the *New Masses*, something went soft and "high" in his tone and I was never again able to read him, either in his radical or in his religiose conservative phase, without a touch of queasiness.

Such account of him as I have given will perhaps have suggested that Whittaker Chambers, with his distinctive and strongly marked traits of mien and conduct, virtually demanded to be coopted as a fictive character. Yet there is nothing that I have so far told about him that explains why, when once he had stepped into the developing conception of my narrative, he turned out to be so particularly useful—so necessary, even essential—to its purpose.

I have said that he entered my story unbidden and so it seemed to me at the time, although when I bring to mind the moment at which he appeared, I think he must have been responding to an invitation that I had unconsciously offered. He presented himself to me as I was working out that part of the story in which John Laskell, though recovered from his illness, confronts with a quite intense anxiety the relatively short railway journey he must make to visit the Crooms. There was no reason in reality for Laskell to feel as he did, nor could he even have said what he was apprehensive of—his anxiety was of the "unmotivated" kind, what people call neurotic, by which they mean that it need not be given credence either by him who suffers it or by them who judge the suffering.

It was while I was considering how Laskell's state of feeling should be dealt with, what part it might play in the story, that Chambers turned up, peremptorily asserting his relevance to the question. That relevance derived from his having for a good many years now gone about the world in fear. There were those who would have thought—who did think—that his fear was fanciful to the point of absurdity, even of madness, but I believed it to have been reasonable enough, and its reason, as I couldn't fail to see, was splendidly to the point of my story.

What Chambers feared, of course, was that the Communist Party would do away with him. In 1932—so he tells us in *Witness*— after a short tour of duty as the editor of the *New Masses*, he had been drafted by the Party into its secret apparatus. By 1936 he had become disenchanted with the whole theory and ethos of Communism and was casting about for ways of separating himself from it. To break with the Communist Party of America—the overt Party, which published the *Daily Worker* and the *New Masses* and organized committees and circulated petitions—entailed nothing much worse than a period of vilification, but to defect from the underground organization was to put one's life at risk.

To me and to a considerable number of my friends in New York it was not a secret that Chambers had, as the phrase went, gone underground. We were a group who, for a short time in 1932 and even into 1933, had been in a tenuous relation with the Communist Party through some of its so-called fringe activities. Our relation to the Party deteriorated rapidly after Hitler came to power in early 1933 and soon it was nothing but antagonistic. With this group Chambers retained some contact despite its known hostility to what it now called Stalinism. Two of its members in particular remained his trusted friends despite his involvement in activities which were alien, even hostile, to their own principles.

Although I knew that Chambers had gone underground, I formed no clear idea of what he subterraneously did. I understood, of course, that he was in a chain of command that led to Russia, by-passing the American Party. The foreign connection required that I admit into consciousness the possibility, even the probability, that he was concerned with something called military intelligence, but I did not equate this with espionage—it was as if such a thing hadn't yet been invented.

Of the several reasons that might be advanced to explain why my curiosity and that of my circle wasn't more explicit and serious in the matter of Chambers' underground assignment, perhaps the most immediate was the way Chambers comported himself on the widely separated occasions when, by accident or design, he came into our ken. His presence was not less portentous than it had ever been and it still had something of its old authority, but if you responded to that, you had at the same time to take into account the comic absurdity which went along with it, the aura of parodic melodrama with which he invested himself, as if, with his darting, covert glances and extravagant precautions, his sudden manifestations out of nowhere in the middle of the night, he were acting the part of a secret agent and wanted to be sure that everyone knew just what he was supposed to be.

But his near approach to becoming a burlesque of the underground revolutionary didn't prevent us from crediting the word, when it came, that Chambers was in danger of his life. We did not doubt that, if Chambers belonged to a "special" Communist unit, his defection would be drastically dealt with, by abduction or assassination. And when it was told to us that he might the more easily be disposed of because he had been out of continuous public view for a considerable time, we at once saw the force of the suggestion. We were instructed in the situation by that member of our circle with whom Chambers had been continuously in touch while making his decision to break with the apparatus. This friend made plain to us the necessity of establishing Chambers in a firm personal identity, an unquestionable social existence which could be attested to. This was ultimately to be established through a regular routine of life, which included an office which he would go to daily; what was immediately needed was his being seen by a number of people who would testify to his having been alive on a certain date.

To this latter purpose it was arranged that the friend would bring Chambers to a party that many of us planned to attend. It was a Hallowe'en party; the hostess, who had been reared in Mexico, had decorated her house both with the jolly American symbols of All Hallowmas and with Mexican ornaments, which speak of the returning dead in a more literal and grisly way. Years later, when Chambers wished to safeguard the microfilms of the secret documents that had been copied by Hiss, he concealed them in a hollowed-out pumpkin in a field. I have never understood why, when this was reported at the trial, it was thought to be odd behaviour which cast doubt upon Chambers' mental stability, for the hiding-place was clearly an excellent one. But if a recondite psychological explanation is really needed, it is perhaps supplied by that acquaintance of Chambers—she had been present at the Hallowe'en—who easily connected the choice of hiding-place with the jack-o'-lanterns of the party at which Chambers undertook to establish his existence in order to continue it.

Chambers was brought to the party when it was well advanced. If he had any expectations of being welcomed back from underground to the upper world, he was soon disillusioned. Some of the guests, acknowledging that he was in danger, took the view that fates similar to the one he feared for himself had no doubt been visited upon some of his former comrades through his connivance, which was not to be lightly forgiven. Others, though disenchanted with Communist policy, were not yet willing to believe that the Communist ethic countenanced secrecy and violence; they judged the information they were given about Chambers' danger to be a libelous fantasy and wanted no contact with the man who propagated it. After a few rebuffs, Chambers ceased to offer his hand in greeting and he did not stay at the party beyond the time that was needed to establish that he had been present at it.

In such thought as I may have given to Chambers over the next years, that Hallowe'en party figured as the culmination and end of his career as a tragic comedian of radical politics. In this, of course, I was mistaken, but his terrible entry upon the historical stage in the Hiss case was not forced upon him until 1948, and through the intervening decade one might suppose that he had permanently forsaken the sordid sublimities of revolutionary politics and settled into the secure anti-climax of bourgeois respectability. In 1939 he had begun his successful association with *Time*. During the years which followed, I met him by chance on a few occasions; he had a hunted, fugitive look—how not?—but he was patently surviving, and as the years went by he achieved a degree of at least economic security and even a professional reputation of sorts with the apocalyptic pieties of his news-stories for *Time* and the sodden profundities of his cultural essays for *Life*. Except as these may have made me aware of him, he was scarcely in my purview—until suddenly he thrust himself, in the way I have described, into the story I was trying to tell. I understood him to have come—he, with all his absurdity!—for the purpose of representing the principle of reality.

At this distance in time the mentality of the Communist-oriented intelligentsia of the Thirties and Forties must strain the comprehension even of those who, having observed it at first hand, now look back upon it, let alone of those who learn about it from such historical accounts of it as have been written.* That mentality was presided over by an impassioned longing to believe. The ultimate object of this desire couldn't fail to be disarming—what the fellow-travelling intellectuals were impelled to give their credence to was the ready feasibility of contriving a society in which reason and virtue would prevail. A proximate object of the will to believe was less abstract—a large segment of the progressive intellectual class was determined to credit the idea that in one country, Soviet Russia, a decisive step had been taken toward the

* The relation of the class of bourgeois intellectuals to the Communist movement will, I am certain, increasingly engage the attention of social and cultural historians, who can scarcely fail to see it as one of the most curious and significant phenomena of our epoch. In the existing historiography of the subject, the classical document is *The God That Failed*, edited by Richard Crossman (New York, Harper, 1949; London, Hamish Hamilton, 1950) which consists of the autobiographical narratives of their relation to Communism of six eminent cultural figures, Arthur Koestler, Ignazio Silone, Richard Wright ("The Initiates"), and André Gide, Louis Fischer, Stephen Spender ("Worshippers From Afar"). The American situation is described in a series of volumes called *Communism in American Life*, edited by Clinton Rossiter (various publishers and dates), of which the most interesting are the two volumes by Theodore Draper, *The Roots of American Communism* (New York, Viking, 1957; London, Macmillan, 1957) and *American Communism and Soviet Russia* (New York, Viking, 1960; London, Macmillan, 1960), and Daniel Aaron's *Writers on the Left* (New York, Harcourt, Brace & World, 1961). The most recent and in some respects the most compendious record of the relation of intellectuals to Communism and the one that takes fullest account of its sadly comic aspects is David Caute's *The Fellow Travellers* (London and New York, Macmillan, 1972).

establishment of just such a society. Among those people of whom this resolute belief was characteristic, any predication about the state of affairs in Russia commanded assent so long as it was of a "positive" nature, so long, that is, as it countenanced the expectation that the Communist Party, having actually instituted the reign of reason and virtue in one nation, would go forward to do likewise throughout the world.

Once the commitment to this belief had been made, no evidence might, or could, bring it into doubt. Whoever ventured to offer such evidence stood self-condemned as deficient in good will. And should it ever happen that reality did succeed in breaching the believer's defenses against it, if ever it became unavoidable to acknowledge that the Communist Party, as it functioned in Russia, did things, or produced conditions, which by ordinary judgment were to be deplored and which could not be accounted for by either the state of experimentation or the state of siege in which the Soviet Union notoriously stood, then it was plain that ordinary human judgment was not adequate to the deplored situation, whose moral justification must be revealed by some other agency, commonly "the dialectic".

But there came a moment when reality did indeed breach the defenses that had been erected against it, and not even the dialectic itself could contain the terrible assault it made upon faith. In 1939 the Soviet Union made its pact with Nazi Germany. There had previously been circumstances—among them the Comintern's refusal to form a united front with the Social Democrats in Germany, thus allowing Hitler to come to power; the Moscow purge trials; the mounting evidence that vast prison camps did exist in the Soviet Union—which had qualified the moral prestige of Stalinist Communism in one degree or another, yet never decisively. But now to that prestige a mortal blow seemed to have been given. After the Nazi–Soviet pact one might suppose that the Russia of Stalin could never again be the ground on which the hope of the future was based, that never again could it command the loyalty of men of good will.

Yet of course the grievous hurt was assuaged before two years had passed. In 1941 Hitler betrayed his pact with Stalin, the German armies marched against Russia and by this action restored Stalinist

Communism to its sacred authority. Radical intellectuals, and those who did not claim that epithet but modestly spoke of themselves as liberal or progressive or even only democratic, would now once again be able to find their moral bearings and fare forward.

Not that things were just as they had been before. It could not be glad confident morning again, not quite. A considerable number of intellectuals who had once been proud to identify themselves by their sympathy with Communism now regarded it with cool reserve. Some even expressed antagonism to it, perhaps less to its theory than to the particularities of its conduct. And those who avowed their intention of rebutting this position did not venture to call themselves by a name any more positive and likely to stir the blood than that of anti-anti-Communists.

Yet that meeching phrase tells us how much authority Stalinist Communism still had for the intellectual class. Anti-anti-Communism was not quite so neutral a position as at first it might seem to have been: it said that although, for the moment at least, one need not be actually *for* Communism, one was morally compromised, turned toward evil and away from good, if one was against it. In the face of everything that might seem to qualify its authority, Communism had become part of the fabric of the political life of many intellectuals.

In the context, *political* is probably the mandatory adjective though it might be wondered whether the Communist-oriented intellectuals of the late Forties did have what is properly to be called a political life. It must sometimes seem that their only political purpose was to express their disgust with politics and make an end of it once and for all, that their whole concern was to do away with those defining elements of politics which are repugnant to reason and virtue, such as mere opinion, contingency, conflicts of interest and clashes of will and the compromises they lead to. Thus it was that the way would be cleared to usher in a social order in which rational authority would prevail. Such an order was what the existence of the Soviet Union promised, and although the promise must now be a tacit one, it was still in force.

So far as *The Middle of the Journey* had a polemical end in view, it was that of bringing to light the clandestine negation of the political life which Stalinist Communism had fostered among the intellectuals of the West. This negation was one aspect of an ever more imperious and bitter refusal to consent to the conditioned nature of human existence. In such confrontation of this tendency as my novel proposed to make, Chambers came to its aid with what he knew, from his experience, of the reality which lay behind the luminous words of the great promise.

It was considerably to the advantage of my book that Chambers brought to it, along with reality, a sizable amount of nonsense, of factitiousness of feeling and perception. He had a sensibility which was all too accessible to large solemnities and to the more facile paradoxes of spirituality, and a mind which, though certainly not without force, was but little trained to discrimination and all too easily seduced into equating portentous utterence with truth. If my novel did have a polemical end in view, it still was a novel and not a pamphlet, and as a novel I had certain intentions for it which were served by the decisive presence in it of a character to whom could be applied the phrase I have used of Chambers, a tragic comedian. I had no doubt that my story was a serious one, but I nevertheless wanted it to move on light feet; I was confident that its considerations were momentous, but I wanted them to be represented by an interplay between gravity and levity. The frequency with which Chambers verged on the preposterous, the extent to which that segment of reality which he really did possess was implicated in his half-inauthentic profundities made him admirably suited to my purpose. If I try to recall what emotions controlled my making of Gifford Maxim out of the traits and qualities of Whittaker Chambers, I would speak first of respect and pity, both a little wry, then of intellectual and literary exasperation and amusement.

It was not as a tragic comedian that Chambers ended his days. The development of the Hiss case made it ever less possible to see him in any kind of comic light. The obloquy in which he lived forbade it. He had, of course, known obloquy for a long time, ever since his defection from Communism and the repudiation of the revolutionary position. Even gentle people might treat him with a censorious reserve which could be taken for physical revulsion. Such conduct he had met in part by isolating himself, in part by those histrionic devices which came so easily to him, making him sometimes formidable and sometimes absurd. But the obloquy that fell upon him with the Hiss case went far beyond what he had hitherto borne and there was no way in which he could meet it, he could only bear it, which he did until he died. The educated, progressive middle class, especially in its upper reaches, rallied to the cause and person of Alger Hiss, confident of his perfect innocence, deeply stirred by the pathos of what they never doubted was the injustice being visited upon him. By this same class Whittaker Chambers was regarded with loathing—the word is not too strong—as one who had resolved, for some perverse reason, to destroy a former friend.*

The outcome of the trial did nothing to alienate the sympathy of the progressive middle class from Hiss or to exculpate Chambers. Indeed, the hostility to Chambers grew the more intense when the verdict of Hiss's guilt became a chief ground upon which the unprincipled junior Senator from Wisconsin, Joseph McCarthy, based his notorious anti-radical campaign.

So relentlessly was Chambers hated by people of high moral purpose that the news-letter of his college class, a kind of publication which characteristically is undeviating in its commitment to pious amenity, announced his death in 1961 in an article which surveyed in detail what it represented as his unmitigated villainy.

If anything was needed to assure that Chambers would be held in bitter and contemptuous memory by many people, it was that his destiny should have been linked with that of Richard Nixon. Especially because I write at the moment of Nixon's downfall and disgrace, I must say a word about this connection. The two men came together through the investigation of Hiss which was undertaken by the Committee of the House of Representatives on Un-American Activities; Nixon, a member of the Committee, played a decisive part in bringing Hiss to trial. The dislike with which a large segment of the American public came to regard Nixon is often said to have begun as a response to his role in the

* A psychoanalyst, Dr. Meyer Zeligs, has undertaken to give scientific substantiation to this belief in *Friendship and Fratricide* (New York, The Viking Press, 1967; London, André Deutsch, 1967), a voluminous study of the unconscious psychological processes of Chambers and Hiss and of the relations between the two men. In my opinion, no other work does as much as this one to bring into question the viability of the infant discipline of psycho-history.

Hiss case, and probably in the first instance it was he who suffered in esteem from the connection with Chambers. Eventually, however, that situation reversed itself—as the dislike of Nixon grew concomitantly with his prominence, it served to substantiate the odium in which Chambers stood. With the Watergate revelations, the old connection came again to the fore, its opprobrium much harsher than it had ever been, and as discredit overtook the President, partisans of Hiss's innocence were encouraged to revive their old contention that Hiss had been the victim of Chambers and Nixon in conspiracy with each other.

The tendentious association of the two men does Chambers a grievous injustice. I would make this assertion with rather more confidence in its power to convince if it were not the case that there grew up between Chambers and Nixon a degree of personal relationship and that Chambers had at one period expressed his willingness to hope that Nixon had the potentiality of becoming a great conservative leader. The hope was never a forceful one and it did not long remain in such force as it had—a year before his death Chambers said that he and Nixon "have really nothing to say to each other". The letters in which he speaks of Nixon—they are among those he wrote to William Buckley*—are scarcely inspiriting, not only because of the known nature and fate of the man he speculates about but also because it was impossible for Chambers to touch upon politics without falling into a bumble of religiose portentousness. But I think that no one who reads these letters will fail to perceive that the sad and exhausted man who wrote them had nothing in common morally, or, really, politically, with the man he was writing about. In Whittaker Chambers there was much to be faulted, but nothing I know of him has ever led me to doubt his magnanimous intention.

Lionel Trilling

---

* See *Odyssey of a Friend. Whittaker Chambers: Letters to William F. Buckley, Jr. 1954–1961*, edited with notes by William F. Buckley, Jr. (New York, privately printed, 1969).

THE MIDDLE OF THE JOURNEY

1

WHEN the train reached Westport, Gifford Maxim gave not the slightest sign that he had come to his destination. He waited until the aisle was empty of all the other passengers who were getting off. Then he said suddenly, under his breath, "I get off now. I hope you'll be feeling all well soon."

He looked straight ahead as he said it, not turning his head to John Laskell. He laid his great hand for an instant on Laskell's forearm and said, "I won't forget this, John." He said it with quiet certitude. It was the firm, convinced promise of the exile who knows that some day, in some way, he will come to power and then he will not forget the friends who helped him in his adversity.

Without another word or look, Maxim got up and left the car.

John Laskell saw him on the station platform. Maxim looked first to the right, then to the left. He turned abruptly to the left where the rank of taxis was. Laskell saw that he was making a point of not walking too fast, as if he feared that haste would attract attention. How full of moral charm that conspiratory caution of Maxim's would once have seemed—how craven and sad it was now! Seeing Maxim exercise the foolish care that was part of his delusion, Laskell was smitten with sorrow for this friend who believed that he did not exist, who was now on the way to make arrangements about acquiring an existence. It did not matter that Maxim's fear was an absurd one. It was the measure of the world's sickness that a man like Maxim should have such a delusion.

He saw Maxim get into a taxi and shut the door. As the taxi drove off, the train began to move. At these simultaneous movements of separation, he going his way, Maxim going his, Laskell felt a desperate loneliness. And he felt not only alone—he felt quite

3

unsafe. Something untoward might happen. At first he did not know what that might be, and then a possibility occurred to him—suppose the car he was riding in were to be cut off at some junction. If any car were cut off, it would be the last one. Maxim had chosen the last car for them, and then the last seat in this last car, because he wanted—it was part of his delusion—to lessen the chance of being approached and attacked from behind.

Perhaps, Laskell thought, the conductor had announced that the car was to be cut off and he had not heard.

It was nonsense, of course. But when the conductor passed through the car to collect the Westport tickets, Laskell had to ask the question. No, the car would not be cut off, it went through to Hartford and beyond. Laskell was reassured not only by the answer but by the conductor's friendliness and by his seeming to think that the question was a perfectly reasonable one. After all, cars were sometimes cut off.

Laskell's vague uneasiness did not wholly vanish, but he was able to look at it now with some irony. A little irony was surely called for—the idea of traveling as "protection" for Gifford Maxim had so distressed him, yet now he had to see that Maxim's company, forced on him as far as Westport, had been something very like a protection for himself. His illness had weakened him more than he had known if he could find any comfort at all in the presence of this new ruined Maxim, this probably treacherous man who had been disowned by his Party, and who had sat yesterday in Laskell's room slandering the cause for which he had fought so long.

Illness had surely touched Laskell deeply if he could think about the need for protection at all. And yet—he tried to be fair to himself —it was not unnatural that he should have a dim sense of vulnerability. For quite a time now his everyday life had been beautifully taken care of by someone else; it was not so very strange that he should be aware of a vague danger when his life was again his own responsibility. Possibly he had accepted illness with too much willingness, but even that was not beyond understanding—a man at thirty-three might find advantage in an enforced momentary retreat. It was nothing to be ashamed of, not unless it were allowed to go beyond its proper term. But its proper term had most certainly been reached, Laskell thought, and he settled his shoulders back against the seat and organized within himself a firm and sensible resistance against his foolish anxiety.

In the Hartford station, in the half-hour between trains, John Laskell found that he was entirely at ease. He had really not liked the idea of being alone and unknown in a strange city. But as he drank a cup of coffee at the restaurant counter he experienced no discomfort at all. He even had a gay sense of adventure—health, he thought, was quite as much of an adventure as sickness had been.

It would never have occurred to anyone who chanced to notice John Laskell drinking his coffee that he was a man likely to be troubled by an anxiety about not reaching his destination by rail-road, or likely to find adventurousness in so ordinary an act as drinking a cup of coffee at a station counter. He took his hat off when he sat down at the counter, and now he was perhaps rather noticeable, for he was strikingly pale and his hair was cut very much shorter than is usual with a man of his general appearance, a man who was well and casually dressed in gray flannel and white oxford shirt and bright striped tie. It was cut as short as hair could be without being actually shaved. This, at first glance, might have made his place in the world uncertain, though actually it confirmed it, for it brought out the shape of his skull, which was clearly the result of an infancy of careful middle-class nourishment. And all of Laskell's face and manner suggested that he was a person for whom the world might perhaps have absorbing doubts but certainly not any fears. His gray eyes were serious, possibly even sad, but they looked about with the expectation of finding some matter of interest and humor. If his rather wide mouth was almost too mobile and not wholly sure of itself, that was only a pleasant modification of his air of maturity and responsibility. A friend seeing him now would have found his appearance some-what changed from the usual, the nose more salient, the eyes deeper set, the cheekbones more in evidence, and would have put this down to Laskell's loss of weight during his illness, to his pallor and to his odd haircut, which had been intended by way of therapy, for his hair had begun to fall out as a result of his fever. But the change from his usual appearance did not diminish the impression of a man who took life in the sensible, normal ways.

As he drank his coffee, paid for it, left a dime for the waitress and exchanged a smile and a word or two with her, and went out to the platform again, a man not tall but well set up, almost handsome but fortunate in being just short of that, he appeared to be surely a person for whom the world was a place to be familiarly at home in, for whom trains were run and timetables kept accurate, for whom illness was not usual but who, having once been ill, recovered as fast and as simply as possible, and then, as a most natural thing, traveled to spend a month in the country with friends.

The little train for Crannock made up here at the station. There were plenty of seats, there was a place for his luggage, the two bags and the rod and creel which had made such an issue between his nurse and himself just before his departure. He scarcely questioned whether it was really the train for Crannock. Everything was in order. Still, it was two o'clock, the empty time, the time when he had been in the habit of taking his nap, and he felt rather tired. It was hot in the train, the windows leaked cinders and his mouth felt gritty and dry. The faces of the passengers were local and countrified. The conductor greeted many of them with some word of recognition, but naturally he did not greet Laskell. And Laskell foolishly felt that he could by no means be sure of the good will of these people with whom he was traveling. He was the stranger, the outlander, the foreigner from New York. But he held before his mind what it would be like to see Nancy and Arthur Croom on the station platform, waiting for him according to plan. They would be sunburned and healthy and full of affection. They would be even fuller of affection than they always were, because of the dangerous illness he had been through. And Laskell felt the warmth of his own feeling for the Crooms as he thought of the welcome they would give him. He had much to tell them. His picture of them became even livelier as he thought of them listening to his news. First there was the adventure of his having been so near death. Then there was the quite momentous news about Maxim—the grotesque story of his break with the Party.

Laskell did not catch sight of the Crooms when first he got off the train at Crannock. Nor did he see them when he had recovered from this disappointment and looked around him.

There was a little row of cars toward which the other passengers who got off were heading. From each car there had come some welcoming person to take a suitcase or an arm or to give a kiss or to utter some fond, welcoming cry. But no one came toward John Laskell. He was sure that it was some trick of his mind that prevented him from seeing the people he was looking for. The Crooms were not there.

Then they would be here in a moment. There was the road, and Laskell was so certain of their immediate arrival that he almost saw them materialize, driving up the road, waving him their welcome and their frantic regret for the delay. Meanwhile all the cars had driven away. Now the express agent came out with his hand-truck. He collected the packages that had been discharged from the train. The train left. There was a bench and Laskell sat down on it.

He looked at his watch. The train had not been more than five minutes late—it was impossible that the Crooms could have come and gone. There was no sound save the chatter of the telegraph machine in the office and then the wirelike sound of cicadas rising and falling in the late afternoon, a sound like a mode of silence. The sky was blue and immense. The sun was hot. Laskell saw a little knot of houses and stores, not far from the station, and a row of red filling pumps. He saw a man at the pumps, but the man went away.

The vertigo of fear began in his stomach and rose in a spiral to his brain. He did not know what he was afraid of. He was not terrified by anything, he was just in terror. It had the aspect of movement, of something rushing at him, or in him, like a brown wind. Some alien intelligence wanted desperately to shriek, yet knew that if it should utter a sound, it would be lost; and wanted blindly to clutch, yet dared not move.

Afterward Laskell was not really able to recall what had happened to him during those terrible moments. There was no way of reconstituting the occurrence. It was so apart from his busy and fortunate life that he had nothing to connect it with. When he tried to remember, there were certain images that came to his mind to point to the quality of the event. He did not think of these things on the station platform, but the images came unbidden when he tried to remember, and they were in the direction of what he had felt. There was the image of the Mexican politician lying on the ground, unconscious, while his enemy administered a hypodermic and cut his tongue out. This was something that Laskell had read about in a newspaper in his boyhood in the time of Huerta. There was the image of Chinese torture in which a man was shut in a narrow position in a box and fed at intervals and left to endure like that. This also came from something he had read in his boyhood. And from a newspaper item he had read quite recently there came the image of the man who had spent six days ill in his automobile in a thickly populated street in New Haven, able only now and then to ask children to fetch him water; the children had not spoken of his plight, and he lay there unable to move until on the sixth day a woman noticed him.

It could not have lasted long, although it was not commensurate with time. Perhaps it subsided almost immediately it reached its climax. Laskell sat there, sweating and trembling, but able now to find a difference between his mind and his terror. Then he was able to look at the fear with a curiosity that was horrified but nevertheless an act of intelligence, and then able to think about the incongruity of this happening to him, a man so much in control of his life. At last he was able to ask himself, strictly and with an educated man's knowledge of the devious craft of the mind's unreasoning parts, what effect his weeks in bed could have had that, like an infant deserted, he had been overwhelmed by hysteria because the Crooms, for some reason they could not help, had not met him.

The man at the filling station did not know of the Crooms. But then Laskell remembered the name of Folger, and the man recalled that the Crooms were the summer people who had bought the place up the hill from the Folgers. It was not more than seven miles and he was willing enough to taxi Laskell.

There was certainly nothing lacking in the intensity of the Crooms' distress when they saw John Laskell drive up with a stranger. They were out on the road, waiting, so anxious were they about their friend's lateness. Arthur paid the driver before Laskell could do anything about it and Nancy kissed him fondly on the cheek and said, "I'm terribly sorry, John dear. Are you all right?" She took Laskell's hand and led him to a long chair in a shady place.

There was a pitcher of lemonade, all dewy with the chunks of ice in it, and Nancy at once poured him a large glass and made him put his feet up on the footrest of the deck chair. She was wearing a long house-coat of delicately printed cotton, but the hand that emerged from the sleeve as she poured the lemonade was strong and brown. Nancy was not exactly a pretty girl, but she was remarkably good-looking in a modern way, with her clear eyes that showed a child's wonder but could also show a child's strong, demanding anger. Her pregnancy, about which she had written him, was not yet apparent and she was slim and supple.

Laskell took the glass and sipped the lemonade. He had stopped trembling and sweating before taking the taxi, before he had even gone to inquire about the taxi. But he still felt deeply shaken, as if his emotions were not quite in their accustomed places. But they would soon be put to rights in the company of his friends. He hoped there were no betraying signs, in his manner, of the terror he had experienced.

He looked around him, at the house, which was a small but very sturdy clapboard house, at the lawn that lay between the house and the road, at the remarkably fine maples that bordered the road and cast their shade over lawn and house, a shade so thick that it kept the lawn rather sparse and mossy. He made a gesture with his glass to include all the Crooms' little domain and said, "Nice!"

Arthur came up carrying Laskell's luggage from the road. "Damn that Duck!" Arthur said. "I'll wring his neck for him when I see him." And he stood there in anger, still holding the two bags, the rod and the creel.

Nancy said to Laskell, "He's the man who works for us. We let him take the car to Hartford this morning. He was supposed to get back here in time for us to meet you. And we arranged that if he couldn't do that he was to pick you up at the station himself. He had plenty of time, but he's so unreliable."

She turned to her husband. "Really, Arthur, Duck just can't be trusted. Imagine letting John wait there at the station, in that broiling sun! And he's been so ill. John, you look so pale. And they cut your hair all off."

"It's all right," Laskell said. "No harm done."

Here was the shade of the maples, and the glass of lemonade, and his friends. He would rather not think of the moment when the vertigo of fear had reached its climax. After all, it had passed. And for what that moment contained he could blame no one. What that moment contained was given by life itself or by the mind itself. Certainly he did not want, merely in order to fix "blame," to have to hold in his mind a terror that was greater than any terror of death could ever be. After all, it had passed. He had come to himself and found the man with the car who had agreed to drive him to the Crooms'. And at the Crooms' he now was, perfectly safe. Already the experience seemed to be receding from reality. He was glad that it was not Nancy and Arthur who had failed him, that the "blame" rested with someone so unrelated and anonymous as this odd-job man, Duck.

"Are you all right, John?" Arthur asked, still holding the luggage.

"Oh, perfectly." Laskell made it as final as he could.

"I'm terribly sorry," Arthur said. His face was miserable at there being nothing he could do about what had happened.

"Forget it," said Laskell.

Arthur set down the suitcases and leaned the rod against one of them. "It's my fault really."

It was exactly what Laskell did not want to consider. Best to drop the whole matter of fault and blame, else he would have to ask why the Crooms had lent the car for Duck's Hartford trip on this particular day.

"I should have known better than to let Duck take the car," Arthur said. "He's a wonderful workman, you should see the fireplace he built for us, but he's quite unreliable. He promised me faithfully that he'd pick you up himself." He said to Nancy in mournful speculation, "I suppose he got drunk."

"Yes, I suppose so," Nancy said, equally gloomy. She shook her head unhappily. "It isn't that he drinks much," she said to Laskell, "but he's so easily affected by it. It must be a physiological weakness, something constitutional. Two glasses of ale and he's not himself. He drinks ale. It's really been the ruin of him, he could have amounted to a great deal." She contemplated the ruin of Duck, frowning sadly. "Of course," she mused, "he's very unhappy."

Laskell noted a brooding solicitude for Duck which seemed to him inappropriate. If he did not want to see blame attached to anyone, neither did he want what this Duck had done—since it was Duck who had done it—to be passed over or explained away by a constitutional weakness or by his unhappiness.

He was now feeling nothing more than a physical disorientation —he did not quite know whether the east was on his left hand or his right, or before or behind him. He no longer had any fear, but he felt a delicate emptiness, as if all his knowledge of himself had been evacuated. It would fill up, this emptiness. It would be helped to fill up if things were kept quite clear—if, for example, it were understood that Duck had been quite simply at fault, if he were regarded not with this commiseration but with a simple suitable anger.

"Here's Micky," Arthur said.

The child was approaching uncertainly but gamely. The last time Laskell had seen him he had still been toddling: it was a great advance. He lurched toward Laskell with large curious eyes. A young girl walked behind him, very pale, presumably in charge of him.

"John's tired—he doesn't have to bother with Micky now," Nancy said.

But Laskell leaned forward in his chair and said, "Hello, Mick!" and held out his hands for the child.

Micky looked at the guest and let out a long gurgling crow, which could scarcely have been of real recognition but might have been of pleasure, and then tacked sharply to the right. He looked at Laskell with a coquettish doubt and then came running, shoulders back and belly out. When he got within a few feet, he pulled up sharply and then suddenly doubled over. It was as though he were making a bow of great significance, and its suddenness made it comically like one of those bows that one character in a Dostoevski novel makes to another in recognition of his crisis. But Micky had only gone down to pick up a large moldy maple leaf, and this he held out to Laskell at full stretch. He took a few tentative steps forward, still holding the leaf as far out as possible from himself.

It was a gift, and Laskell leaned forward to accept it. But the nursemaid now came from behind, caught the child's wrist firmly, removed the leaf and scrubbed his palm with her clean handkerchief. The little boy thrust out his lower lip. Nancy said quietly,

"He may have it, Eunice," and offered him another leaf, a fresh green one. Micky took it, looked at it, and dropped it. He abandoned his intentions and moved off to play with the handles of the suitcases.

Nancy took Eunice's arm and presented her to Laskell. "This is Eunice Folger, John. You're going to stay with her mother and father." To the girl she said, "This is Mr. Laskell, Eunice." The girl, who was about eighteen, smiled wanly and looked away. She seemed remote rather than embarrassed. Laskell felt that he was looking at her coldly, but it was only because she did not fit into the place in his mind he had got ready with such speed for the reception of Micky.

"You'll love Eunice's mother and father," Nancy said. "Won't he, Eunice?"

"What?" said Eunice.

"Love your mother and father. Won't Mr. Laskell love your mother and father?"

There was a flicker over Eunice's face as if she were being teased. Nancy was assuming that she would understand this way of talking—it was the slightly affected make-believe that you were beyond modesty and could be objective about the people and things that belonged to you. But Eunice only looked a little stubborn. Nancy turned from her and said, "You will, John. They're wonderful." And as Eunice moved away, Nancy added in an undertone, "The real old stock. You know, Benjamin Franklin had Folger ancestors."

Arthur came up and looked down at Laskell with the whole of his fine ugly face. He planted himself before his friend, would not budge until he got the answer he wanted. "John," he said urgently, "how do you feel? Are you all right? You look pretty pale."

It was the Crooms who had arranged for Dr. Graf and the nurses, Paine and Miss Debry, that whole significant entourage of his illness. It was the Crooms who had shopped for his extra sheets and pajamas, who had sent the crate of oranges. This was the moment to tell them of their part in his illness, and then of what his illness had been like, with its closeness to death, of what a strange and illuminating experience it had been. He wanted to tell them about it to discharge, not his gratitude—he did not want to discharge that—but his involvement with that long new experience. He wanted, as it were, to lay his near experience of death at the feet of life, to put it at the service of life, and life could have no better representatives than the Crooms. They were standing before him, close together, almost unconsciously letting their shoulders touch, unconsciously aglow from their proximity to each other. More than most people they were committed to life. Their commitment was expressed in their youth, their vigor, their unquestioning attachment to each other, the child they had and the child to come; but it did not stop there, as Laskell knew—it went beyond, expressing itself in their passionate expectation of the future, an expectation that was at once glad and stern, in their troubled but clear sense of other people all over the world, suffering or soon to suffer. Life could not reach further, could not pitch itself higher, than it had in these young Americans.

They stood there looking down at him in his canvas chair, waiting for him to answer Arthur's question.

"I'm really quite well now," he said. He spoke quietly, for the story that he was beginning was a long one. There was not only the account of his illness, which had elements in it that would not be easy to explain, but also the story of Maxim's visit. By some logic that Laskell did not wholly understand, the story of Maxim's visit came as the natural sequence to the story of his illness. He had a kind of pride in being the one person in the world who could give them a really circumstantial account of Maxim's defection from the Party.

He said, "I've never thanked you, you know, for everything—"

"Oh, John, don't be a *fool*," Nancy cried passionately. "You had us so frightened there for a while, you were *so* sick. We thought at one point— Dr. Graf told us that you—"

She stopped. She had no language for it. But she had indicated the thing and now they all contemplated it. If Laskell had died, it would have been the Crooms' first immediate experience of death. They were so very young. Sometimes Laskell did not remember the difference of age between himself and the Crooms. At other times he was much aware of it. Now they seemed very young indeed. Actually, as Laskell sometimes reminded himself, there was no such very great difference between them as he was in the habit of thinking. He was thirty-three. Arthur was twenty-eight, Nancy twenty-six.

Nancy was still trying to say it. "Dr. Graf told us that you almost— He said that you nearly—"

"Died?" said Laskell helpfully.

"Yes," Nancy breathed. She accepted the word that had been supplied to her, yet drew back from it, looking at Laskell almost with a kind of rebuke, as if he had forced her to say more than she intended.

She made an effort to recoup. "He said that the infection was so virulent that it—that the condition was so far advanced, had progressed so far that—"

Then she surrendered and seemed with the little gesture of her hand to accept the word that Laskell had suggested. It went against the grain, but she saw that it was hopeless to struggle against it, there was no other word, and she gave up with as much grace as she could muster. She smiled and laid her hand on Laskell's arm. She said, "It's wonderful to have you with us here."

Her tone was most intense. It was charged with love but it was charged also with finality—she brushed away as unthinkable all the intervening time since she had last seen her friend.

They were all drawn together into a family by the thought of the danger that Laskell had escaped. The sun was setting, the little New England hills were drowsy. A breeze came up and stirred the trees under which they were sitting. The peace that Laskell felt was not the white empty peace of illness which he had so much loved while it lasted. It was rather the populated, various, living peace of affection and houses, of words and touch. This peace was better than the other. And yet, having known the other, it seemed important, even necessary, to tell about it. But the moment for telling had passed. Nancy's gratification at his being here and safe had somehow made it impossible for him to tell how he had got here and how he had become safe.

"Is it lovely to be here with us?" Nancy asked when Laskell seemed to have nothing to say.

"Lovely," he answered. And it was. He tried to give himself wholly to the loveliness of being here, to submit to this new and better peace that had been beneficently imposed upon him. He got up from his chair to help dismiss from his mind the sense of disappointed urgency.

He did not wholly succeed. It was all very well to say that his life of illness was over and very properly over—the fact was that John Laskell had never in his whole life been so happy as during the days he had spent in bed. He had never been so entirely without self-reproach. Some remarkable thing had happened to his mind and will. The perfect peace that resulted had seemed to him to be a kind of virtue and a kind of wisdom. It was this that he would have liked to tell the Crooms about. For example, during the latter part of his time in bed he had been able, for quarter-hours at a time, to stare at a rose that had survived the death of eleven other roses that had been sent to him. For as many days as the rose lasted, Laskell had kept it on a little table near his bed, handy for contemplation. He could become lost in its perfection, watching the strange energy which the rose seemed to have, for it was not static in its beauty, it seemed to be always at work organizing its petals into their perfect relation with each other. Laskell, gazing at it, had known something like desire; but it was a strange desire which *wanted* nothing, which was its own satisfaction. He had been so very much involved, was so quick to ask for it every morning of the three days it continued to bloom, that his nurse Paine had teased him about it. She had said dryly, "Well, you're having quite a love affair with that flower." That had delighted him, it had been so apt; and really, when he had asked Paine to put the rose on the table his voice had been quite shy. Yet what a strange love it was that was satisfied by its own desire and wanted nothing. It puzzled him, but even the puzzle was a happiness—for it was a puzzle that did not need solution and he did not try for one. He rested content with the contentment that this harmless activity gave him, a kind of fullness of being, without any of the nagging interruptions of personality.

Arthur and Nancy looked at Laskell with a glow of approval for his great good sense in being safe and here. And no doubt that was the main point. The account of how he had become safe and had got here could very well wait. And perhaps he would even find that it could be left out altogether.

Out on the road the little boy was exploring, Eunice walking

behind him with outstretched cautionary hands. Suddenly the
child turned to them with a beaming face and let out that strange
chortling crow of his. It came so suddenly and with such an ecstasy
that they all laughed and Laskell said, "Hurray!" Eunice came
from behind and thoroughly wiped the corners of Micky's mouth
with her handkerchief, for a quantity of saliva had come out with
his joy. He resisted her, trying to keep something in view on the
road, trying to get to it.

It was a charming sight, so charming as to seem for the moment
unreal, the couple that now appeared on the dusty road. Before a
tall woman walked a tall girl of about eleven, dressed in a kind of
blue romper suit which had been pulled up to the top of her long
thighs. She walked alert on fawnlike legs, her head high and conscious. Her light hair had been turned up in a topknot which gave
her a somewhat grown-up air. The age of the woman was hard to
determine. Her beauty—for at the distance she had a kind of
beauty—was that of maturity, but a young maturity. Her bright
dress, cut in the "peasant" style which had been popular among
the women of the painting colony at Provincetown, showed a firm
bosom and strong hips. Her hair was done in a coronet of great yellow braids. Her bare legs were neat and nervous. She carried a
heavy pail in each hand, and the weight of the pails on the down-
grade of the road made her brace her shoulders and throw her hips
forward. The dust of the road rose about her in a golden haze.

It seemed to Laskell that the pair had the quality that, vaguely
and no doubt pointlessly, people have a desire to call Greek. There
was water in the pails and Laskell thought of wells at sunset, of
sacred serpents, of bread and cheese and honey and milk, of days
lived out in growth, fertility, and then gentle decay. And because,
if his mind took this direction from the sight of the mother and
child, it was inevitable that Demeter and Persephone should be
on its path, he thought also of violence and sorrow.

The woman set down her pails and knelt to talk to Micky, upon
whose shoulder the watchful Eunice placed a protective hand. The
little girl was chattering to Eunice, her head cocked. She seemed to
assume that she was quite as grown-up as Eunice. Perhaps that was
why Eunice seemed to be discouraging the conversation, looking
off into the distance.

Nancy got up and started toward the house. "Arthur, show John the house, he'll want to see it," she said, "and I'll put on a dress and then we'll take John to the Folgers'. Duck *can't* be much longer with the car."

Laskell would have liked to stay to watch the woman and the girl. They were very bright there in the late sunlight and they engaged his whole mind and rested it. But Nancy was waiting at the door.

The woman called from the road, "Do you mind if I keep the book a little longer?" She had a pleasant, throaty voice.

"Don't have it on your mind, Emily—keep it as long as you like," Arthur called back.

"Thank you!" she said. "Just a few days more."

"Don't hurry," Arthur insisted.

Nothing in the Crooms' house was quite finished. There was still carpentry to be done and plastering and all the papering. But already the rooms were arranged for living and bore the mark of life, expressing the Crooms entirely, for they showed Arthur's interest in comfort and casualness and Nancy's feeling for elegance and neatness. And looking at the brightness and cheerfulness of the rooms, their compact privacy, Laskell thought how much the great urban housing developments, for all the clear need of them and his own commitment to them, were at best poor makeshifts for the traditional idea of a house, sentimentalized though that had been.

"Do you like it, John dear?" Nancy came down the stairs buttoning the collar of her dress. "Do you like it very much?"

She came down into the living-room, bringing into it even more life than it had had before, entering not only into the room but into the special, sexually charged relationship of a young woman with the room she is contriving. She was so full of loving pride in the room and so full of expectation of his approval of it that although Laskell only said, "Very much indeed," he said it in such direct response to the way she felt and the way she looked that it satisfied her completely.

"There are so many things to be done," Nancy said. She frowned. Now that she had received Laskell's praise, she permitted herself the luxury of being overwhelmed by all the practicality that yet remained to be conquered. "It's so bare still—no pictures, no books yet. All the books are piled up in stacks in Arthur's study."

But on the table two books stood between a pair of heavy glass blocks. One was Arthur's book on business cycles, the work that had made his young reputation. The other was Laskell's own little book, *Theories of Housing.* They were the only two books in the room and they stood there in that special and almost consecrated way between the cubes of green glass. Laskell was deeply touched that his book, that he himself, should have such a place in the Crooms' house.

On the flyleaf of Laskell's book was written, "To Nancy and Arthur with my dearest love." When Laskell had written the inscription he had been at first troubled by the thought that it was an excessive sentiment. He had then known the Crooms only two years and he thought that perhaps "dearest love" was too much to express what he felt toward them. He even wondered whether so full an expression of feeling might not be a burden to these young people, a responsibility of emotion that should not be forced on them, though really he forced nothing on them, it had been the Crooms themselves who had first insisted on the friendship. And Laskell had gone so far as to pick up another copy of the book to write a more measured inscription. But with his pen almost on the new flyleaf, his sense of fact asserted itself—like many men, Laskell thought that written words should be very precise in the expression of one's feelings and he asked himself whether it was not simply and literally true that the Crooms were the people in all the world he loved best. And he had turned the flyleaf and the title page and, on the dedication page, saw the initials E.F. standing alone. He had not been able to put Elizabeth's full name on that page; he had not even been able to put "To the memory of E.F."; nor even "To E.F."—the dedication stood only as her initials. If Elizabeth Fuess had been still alive, he would have written a most affectionate inscription in the Crooms' copy, but not the particular one he had already written. But now there was no Elizabeth, and the simple literal fact was that he gave the best of what love he had to Nancy and Arthur.

And now he was glad indeed that he had written as he had. It was the mark of their return of his love that he was here now, the Crooms' first guest in their unfinished house, and that it seemed right to them that his book should stand with Arthur's between the massive glass blocks.

"I'm so happy you're in it," Nancy said, and took Laskell's hand. "And next year when you come, we'll really be able to put you up."

A car drew up on the road. "There's Duck now," Arthur said. He spoke grimly and went out to deal with the offender. His face was quite stern.

Nancy watched him go. Then she seized Laskell by the arm and drew him with her to follow Arthur out of the house.

"Arthur!" she called. Arthur, already halfway across the lawn, turned around. Nancy waited for him to start back toward them, and when he came near enough she said, "Tell him we're very an-gry—*very* angry."

Arthur nodded. It was clear that he would tell Duck something about his anger but that he would not be very angry. Nancy's injunction had made real anger impossible.

"He's a scoundrel," Nancy confided to Laskell. There was a touch of modest pride in her voice. "A dreadful scoundrel. But he is so *real*—just as real as Emily is unreal. That's the woman you just saw on the road."

"Are they connected with each other?" Laskell asked.

"Oh, they're married," said Nancy, as if he should have known. "Emily came here one summer and she made him marry her after he got her pregnant. He comes from around here, his family were among the first settlers. It seems there was an awful scandal with Emily. She was a distant relative of Miss Walker—Miss Walker is an old Boston lady who has a lovely house over that way." And Nancy waved into the unspecified distance. "I guess she had some kind of Lady Chatterley business in mind; Duck does have a kind of gamekeeper look. But that was before the book, of course. She was a schoolteacher with advanced ideas, or maybe a librarian, I forget. They're very poor and they live in a remodeled tool house just down at the corner of the road. Duck made it. You'll see it on the way to the Folgers'. Goodness!" she concluded breathlessly, "how much gossip I've picked up in these weeks." And she stood there, a confessed gossip, her eyes shining with the pleasure of it.

Duck had got out of the car and stood with a foot on the run-ning board. He was a dark, slim, compact man. He was talking easily, looking down at his foot on the running board and then suddenly up at Arthur, as if making swift decisive points after close thought. From the distance Laskell could see that some of his teeth were missing. This did not keep him from smiling easily. At last he took his departure down the hill. He waved to Nancy as he went and Nancy waved back.

Arthur, as he walked toward them, shrugged his shoulders in humorous defeat. "What's there to do with him?" he said. "He says they told him at the station that the train would be half an hour late."

Nancy said primly, "I hope that at least you didn't let him think you believed that?"

"No. But what can you possibly do with Duck? He lies so ele-gantly. And as Emily likes to say about people, he's not so much *im*moral as *a*moral."

It was as if they were talking about a young poet of their ac-quaintance whose gifts excused such faults as coming much too late to dinner.

Arthur put the bags into the back of the car and they all three got in the front. Just as they were about to start, Nancy spied Las-kell's rod and creel on the grass. "Oh, your fishing things," she cried, "you've left them!"

"Leave them for now," he said.

Where the Crooms' steep dirt road turned off to the asphalt road, Nancy said, "There's the Caldwell place I was telling you about." And Laskell had a glimpse of a tiny structure like a playhouse built for a child, curious in shape and very gay with red and green paint. He saw bright window sashes and bright curtains and a patch of flowers which must have been difficult to grow, for the soil around the house was virtually all sand.

"Duck built it, but the color scheme is Emily's. You'll have to be on the lookout for her when you walk to see us—she's the waylay-ing kind. There's the church!"

It was New England white, with a rather short steeple, not a very distinguished church.

"Handsome," said Laskell, responding to Nancy's local pride.

Then in a moment they were at the Folgers' place.

It was a large house on a broad clean lawn, a most attractive house, square and firm-set. There was a graceful doorway at the front, but no path led up to it. Arthur turned into the driveway alongside the long, low, unrailed porch, and it was obvious that all life came and went by the side door.

It was very still. Hens pecked about the lawn and three fat hounds came up in the most amiable way to nose the visitors. On the low veranda sat an old man in a rocker. He was asleep with his toothless mouth open, but he woke when they came onto the porch and he closed his mouth and nodded to them. Nancy said, "Hello, Mr. Folger. Nice day," and nodded vigorously.

"Mr. Folger's father," she said to Laskell. "Ninety-two years old."

She did not have to whisper, the old man was deaf. He was a very clean old man in a blue shirt buttoned up to his neck and a felt hat. He said something, perhaps friendly, but it was a mumble under his mustache and could not be understood. Laskell was dismayed. He felt uncomfortable before this old man with his watery eyes and vanishing faculties. He wondered how Nancy had arranged for the meals to be served—the idea of having to eat with the family at table with this old man filled him with a chilled, helpless revulsion.

A woman came to the screen door, smiling and holding the door open for them to enter. They came into a cool, dark dining-room.

"This is our friend John Laskell," Nancy said, and Mrs. Folger held out her hand.

She was a pale, drawn woman, notably wide at the hips, narrow in the shoulders, and cheerful about the eyes. Laskell liked her immediately. She had a quick social suspicion of him, a desire to make an impression on him and to keep him from making an impression on her. She appeared to consider herself at a disadvantage with these three people, city people, with their way of talking, strangers to her, friends among themselves. But she controlled these emotions and made herself a pleasant hostess under difficulties. She made a good deal of verbal fuss about her being in an apron to receive them, and about the flour that had got into the cracks of her hands and under her nails. But at the same time she was aware that these were things that gave her standing with her visitors.

She turned to Laskell and wrinkled her brows into a frown and said, "So you've gone and got yourself sick, a big boy like you! You ought to know better than that." She looked at him. "Pale as a ghost," she said. "Well, we'll just have to make you well again, that's all." She appealed to Nancy, "Won't we, Mrs. Croom?"

The pleasure rose girlishly in Nancy's face. "I suppose we'll have to, Mrs. Folger, or he'll just be a nuisance."

"That's right, just be a nuisance," said Mrs. Folger.

It was the conspiracy of all women to keep men from being a nuisance, the loving, ironic, unsatisfactory conspiracy. Nancy loved being in it. Her cheeks were flushed and her gray eyes were merry. "And we'll not have you being a nuisance," she said, and shook her head and her finger at Laskell.

"But this boy must be tired, we'll just show him to his room." If for a moment Nancy had seized the leadership of the female conspiracy by her contribution of the idea of the nuisance, Mrs. Folger was now again entirely in command and Nancy was quite content to have her there. Mrs. Folger led the way upstairs. Laskell followed with Nancy, and Arthur went out for the bags.

They passed through a little dark front hall, cool and even chilly, smelling not unpleasantly of damp, and climbed the steep and narrow stairs. The room was large and light. On one side it faced into a full spreading tree and on the other side toward the fields and hills. The furniture was the old commonplace yellow furniture of forty or fifty years before, giving off a smell of wood and varnish. There was a washstand with a pitcher and bowl and slop jar, and there was a dresser and a table, both covered with clean white linen tidies edged with tatting. The big bed was of brass.

Nancy said, "Isn't it nice?"

It was nice and Laskell said so.

Arthur came in with the bags. "Well, here you are!" said Arthur.

They both smiled to Laskell in that bright, clean, worn room with its tree and its view. In their pride at what they had provided for him and in their welcome, in Mrs. Folger's honest, wry satisfaction at his approval of the room, Laskell felt happy too.

And yet beneath the happiness there was still moving a something lost, a part of himself, a dull part or a bad part, some little dark worm of a thing, sullen and lost and not yet comforted, sending into all this brightness dumb messages of unease.

"And now," said Nancy, "you get yourself settled and take a rest and we'll pick you up for dinner in an hour. I did tell you, didn't I, that you're having dinner with us this evening?"

As soon as they left him, Laskell went to look out of the window at the strong, unspectacular dips and rolls of the glacier-cut landscape. Each field was a different color, brown or yellow or varying greens, rolling steeply. It was very quiet, except for the repeated crow of a rooster. He saw Nancy and Arthur get into their car and drive away, and though they were to return for him in an hour, he wished they hadn't had to go.

The countryside was so still, so without people, though bearing everywhere the signs of human work, there was so much silence around the house, that Laskell began to feel large and obtrusive and embarrassed by himself. He had the feeling that not everything had been settled, that there was some other thing, some one other thing, not accounted for.

He opened his two bags and began to arrange his belongings. On the dresser he made a little row of the few books he had brought. This he flanked by a precise stack of notes for the book he was writing about the planned cities of antiquity. He took out the waders, which almost filled one of the bags, and hung them up. He put his tackle-box on a shelf in the closet, and wished he had not left the rod and creel at the Crooms'. He was glad to have his fishing things with him. He remembered the absurd squabble with Paine about taking them. She had said "Yes," and he had said "No." Now he was glad that she had won. He put his shirts and underwear into a drawer of the dresser. He placed two cartons of cigarettes very exactly beside his books.

All this helped a little. But he could not go on arranging things, for now he had no more things to arrange. So the apprehension grew, the sense of his size, of his exposure, of how dangerous this empty new world was. And there came to him, at first dim and un-recognized, then increasingly heard and more and more charged with nostalgia, like a strain of known music coming nearer, the sense of his vanished life of illness, of the beauty and truth of that life.

He stood there suddenly desolated by the loss.

He called nothing to his aid to check the deprivation that flooded over him, not reason, not pride, not shame. Nothing that he had now and nothing that he was likely ever to have could have anything like the value of the peace, the strength and integrity he had known in his ill-health. He thought with a cold and justified anger of all that happened to him in the short time since his illness —he thought of Paine's impatience to desert him, of Gifford Max-im's visit, of Maxim's madness and treachery, hating Maxim, but hating almost as much the cause that Maxim maligned and be-trayed, for that cause, as much as Maxim, seemed now to be a part of the irrelevant world of non-illness. Of non-illness, for it was surely not the world of health. He thought of his fears on the train and of the justification of those fears in those hideous moments on the Crannock station platform, and he thought of his sense of frus-tration at being unable to tell the Crooms the story of his illness and what it had meant to him.

Standing there alone in his bright strange room, Laskell hated the room and he hated Mrs. Folger's cheerful busyness. And then he felt what he would never have believed it possible to feel—he felt a bitter anger at Nancy Croom. Without any love at all he saw her as she stood on her lawn trying not to say what was the simple fact.

"That you almost— That you nearly—" she had said.

"Died" was the word, and Nancy's face, now that no love showed its charm, appeared to Laskell in its stark irritability as he gave her the word. He saw in it all her dislike of having to accept the word—yes, even her momentary dislike of him because he had given it to her. And then he remembered, or thought he remem-bered, that he had seen that look before. It was when he had given the Crooms their copy of *Theories of Housing* and Nancy had glowed with pleasure at the inscription he had written in it and had impulsively kissed him. Then she had begun to examine the

book with a childlike intensity, considering the jacket, the bind-
ing, the title page, and then had come to the initials E.F. on their
page by themselves. She had looked at Laskell with the happiness
gone from her face. He had smiled at her reassuringly to show that
he was quite all right, that his grief at Elizabeth's death was not
being awakened by a friend's looking at the initials. But now he
knew that it was not in sympathy and sorrow that Nancy had
looked at him but in something like disapproval. It was the way
she had looked at him when, on the lawn, he had given her the
simple word "died."

It did not put Nancy in a very pleasant light, his sudden awareness of her disapproval of death. But the perversity did not last
long. There came to Laskell's mind, unbidden but welcome because it checked his anger at Nancy, the very sound of his voice as
he had said to Dr. Graf, "Do you mean that I could have died?"
And Dr. Graf, with that dryness of his, had answered, "Yes, you
could have, and if it gives you any satisfaction, I thought you
would."

Dr. Graf had apparently heard "satisfaction" in Laskell's voice.
And no doubt Nancy, with her commitment to life, had heard in
his voice that same satisfaction. Laskell shook his head in annoyance with himself. No, Nancy had not been evasive of death any
more than she was evasive of life. She had only been even more
perceptive than Laskell had always thought her and she had read
his secret mind.

And, after all, how much perception did it take? For it was not
only Dr. Graf who had caught on to his satisfaction at being ill;
there was Paine too. He seemed to be quite a transparent case. "I
think," Paine had said, rather archly, for although she was the most
remarkable of nurses, like any nurse she was likely to speak archly
and to talk to her patient as if he were in the third person as well
as in the second, "I think he doesn't want to get well."

Laskell had taken a kind of pride in the strange new emotions of
his illness, especially in that odd little experience with the flower,
but he had no pride now as the real meaning of that rose-business
broke in upon him. Quite a love affair with that flower, Paine had
said. Quite a love affair with non-existence. That involvement with
the rose, that desire that wanted nothing—what was it if it was not

the image of death? Or, if not of death, then of not being born, which is but the gentler image of death? It was not quite extinction that he had taken such a fancy to, but it was something just short of extinction. It was the removal of all the adverse conditions of the self, the personality living in nothing but delight in itself. It was what the philosophers used to suppose of the existence of God and of the union of the self with God, and it was much like what the psychologists now imagined of unborn children laid up in the encompassing heaven of the womb, unwilling to be dragged forth.

Quite a love affair with that flower, quite a love affair with death! It was something for a man like John Laskell to have to face. He had committed himself to the most hopeful and progressive aspects of modern life, planning their image in public housing developments, defending them in long dull meetings of liberals and radicals. And yet he had been able to practice this large deception on himself, had been willing to think of his days in bed as having some large value because they had so completely rested his mind and will. All Nancy had done to arouse his unjust anger at her had been to see through the deception and refuse to be a party to it. It was something for a man like John Laskell to have to face. But he did face it.

Then, with this much self-knowledge gained, Laskell began to get what seemed like a clue to his terror on the station platform. Was that not the other side of the image of death or of not being born?—the moment when the foetus conceives of the womb no longer as the perfect place where desire and gratification are one, but as a hideous imprisoning box; it struggles to escape from the living death which that enclosure is, where it must lie silent and tongueless; the cry of anguish that it gives, the expression of suffering on its face, are not its resistance to being born into the light, but rather its inexpressible terror of the danger it has just escaped. What had happened to him on the station platform was perhaps the painful end of that pleasant illness of his, his sudden terror that he would not escape the state of being unborn.

It could be thought of that way, and Laskell decided that that was the way he would think of it.

He filled the washbasin from the big white pitcher of tepid water and washed his hands. He poured the dirty water into the large crockery slop jar. He rinsed the basin and poured out the rinsing water. He took off his sweaty shirt and his undershirt and hung them in the closet. He laid out a fresh shirt and undershirt. He filled the basin again and soaped his face and neck, his chest and his armpits. He did all this with a pedantic thoroughness. He was insisting to himself that life was really a matter of routine, of clean face and neck and ears and shirts, not of such betrayals of the mind as led to being in love with death or to such things as the madness and treachery of Gifford Maxim. He looked at himself in the mirror, a familiar enough sight. But the face was not wholly familiar. He could not make his own usual objection to it, that it was not serious or firm enough, for the eyes seemed to be looking out of the mirror with a kind of anger.

It was while he was washing and trying to prove the world reasonable that Laskell's blood froze with the voice he heard.

It came from directly below his window, from the porch. Laskell stood with his face covered with suds and his hands still about his neck, his scrubbing suspended. He listened to the sound and followed it. For it could be followed. It began very low, a human voice beginning very low and reasonable, a colloquial utterance, very social, extremely polite. And then it rose to a high pitch of querulousness, going fast at first and then much slower, as if it were arguing, explaining, asking, deprecating.

But it said nothing. For the sounds were not words although they fell just short of words. Laskell stood there with the suds itching as they dried on his skin. His heart was frozen. The voice was terrible in its imitation of human reason. It was sad and grieved, it did not complain but simply communicated its grievance to all the world, and what made it so much more frightening was that Laskell believed that he could detect more than grievance in it. It almost seemed to him that the voice was expressing the grievance of others, was commiserating with others, speaking of their sorrow, for the sorrow of other deprived minds. And this power of generalization, this appeal, as it were, to justice, was more terrifying than anything else.

The voice rose and fell, making its explanations, sometimes inaudible, sometimes very loud and full. It expected no answer.

But in a while it received an answer. There came the whining of hounds, puzzled, miserable, then a deep growling that broke out into a long full-throated baying, interrupted by sharp little barks. The voice rose and fell, rose and fell in its imitation of human reason, and the hounds mingled their voices with it. The hounds were, in a manner, speaking—and it seemed to Laskell that they were uttering their deep unhappiness at their condition of being hounds, as if, hopelessly, desperately, they, together with the mad person, were struggling to be human.

Laskell knew whose voice it was. And again he felt a hard rigid anger at Arthur and Nancy. For they must have known that the old man was mad, that his faculties were gone, reduced to this vocal idiocy. And yet they had allowed their admiration for the Folgers to lead them to forget what the old man was like and had arranged for their friend to live with this horror. There had been too much horror in the day for him. It was only twenty-four hours ago that Gifford Maxim had sat in Laskell's room and spoken about the necessity for him to establish an existence, a man who, once shining with reason and morality, was now bereft of loyalty and mind; it was only an hour ago that Laskell himself had had that shocking experience on the station platform.

With the speed of fear Laskell rinsed his face of the soap, dried it, and put on his shirt, his fingers scarcely able to manage the buttonholes. The voice was keeping up its insane exposition of grief and injustice, its effort to comfort those who shared in the suffering of this injustice, and the hounds were joining in with their deep voices.

Laskell went down the stairs and found his way through the little hall to the dining-room where he had first been received here. He looked out through the screen door. The old man was indeed sitting there, but he was just sitting there, rocking quietly in his rocker. All that he was doing with his mouth was smiling a little as he watched the three hounds lift their muzzles to his companion, a big heavy man sitting on the edge of the porch.

This man was talking to the hounds, and the hounds were listening enthralled, and were answering him as best they could. Their feet were braced and their throats were tense. And as the man's voice sank they growled a little, and as it rose they began to whine, and then they yelped delicately as the voice rose louder still, until from their throats came a deep melodious howl which would then sink back to an anticipatory growl, and then the gamut would be run again. The man was making a sound like a dog, a good-natured and even witty dog who had somehow just been learning human speech and was using it to the other dogs, who understood it but could not themselves quite use it.

"Wurra marra," the man growled. "Wurra marra, huh? Wurra marra wirra dirra? Warra dirra, warra dirra? *Way*-ra dirra, *way*-ra dirra, *way*-ra dirra forra poo–oo–oo–oo–rrr boys?" He was speaking to them about their dinner, as they well knew. "What's the matter?" he was saying. "What's the matter, huh? What's the matter with the dinner? Want your dinner, want your dinner? Where's the dinner, where's the dinner, where's the dinner for the poor boys?" And as he growled and bayed at the poor boys, he pulled their long ears and chucked their heads about, and they answered him with their ecstasy of affection, communication, and hunger, their rumps and their tails never still.

In the weeks that Laskell was to spend with the Folgers he would come to listen to this "mad" conversation with the greatest pleasure. Alwin Folger talking to his dogs, to his old horse Harold, to his cows, was something that would never fail to delight him. He would hear it from the barn at the morning milking, that endless conversation that had in it the perfect comic belief that all the animal creation could be communicated with. The mornings were quite cool, almost cold, and Laskell would lie half awake under the blankets and quilts listening to that strange cheerful talk.

Mr. Folger looked up as Laskell came out of the house. Then he went back to his conversation with the hounds, although he somehow managed to carry it on with a recognition of Laskell's presence. But the hounds were divided in their interest now, looking with mild shifting glances at the stranger and back to their master. "I'm John Laskell," he said, with the sense that the hounds had made the introduction.

"How are *you?*" said Folger, not as a question but as a greeting. He was a large man with a mild firm face touched with irony. "Glad to know you," he said. He did not offer to shake hands but there was acceptance in his manner and Laskell sat down beside him on the edge of the low porch. Folger suddenly shot out a hand

and caught one of the hounds by its dewlap and drew it gently toward him. He looked into its eyes.

"Wurra marra, huh?" he demanded peremptorily.

The hound wriggled its rump and tried to disengage its head to avoid the human gaze. He was divided between happiness and unhappiness, caught and held, yet loving the game that was being played with him. "Wurra marra?" Folger repeated, pressing the point.

Already Laskell felt comfortable sitting there and listening. The two other hounds watched their captive comrade half with pleasure, half with apprehension, mouths open, tongues out, seeming to grin. Laskell lit a cigarette. The old man in the rocker behind him said something that he could not understand, something in reference to the hounds, and Mr. Folger turned to his father and nodded a notice of the remark and smiled. Laskell saw the fading light over the low hills. He shivered comfortably in the cool of the early evening. All the fears and tensions of the day, all the ideas and all the fantasies, were laid at rest.

2

JOHN LASKELL'S friends understood very well a certain course of action and they had a name for it. They called it "the mechanism of escape"—when the going got rough, one was tempted to turn from the hard reality to some pleasant illusion. Under some circumstances even illness could be an escape, and if Laskell's friends had known how happy Laskell was in his illness, they could not have failed to understand that he was evading something. In the middle thirties people watched each other very closely for signs of weakness.

To be sure, Laskell had never given any indications of a tendency toward evasion. When it came to reality, he seemed to be able to face it as well as the next one, perhaps even better than most. Nothing could be more real, for example, than his profession. An expert in public housing deals with the basic needs of poor people. He deals with the shape of houses, with steel and brick and with what is even more impenetrable and resistant, the interests of owners of land, of real property, as it is called. And so far as politics went, his friends knew that Laskell was quite as "conscious" as they were. Many of Laskell's friends were connected with one or another of the radical political parties, either as members or as sympathizers—such was the name then used. Laskell himself was committed to no party, but he nevertheless faced reality in the busy life of committees. He was what was then known by radicals as a "sincere liberal"—the phrase was at least in part meant to be kind—and he had gained for himself a good deal of respect by hard work. Certainly he did not give the impression of a man inclined to run away from anything.

And it would have been hard for his friends to name anything he might be running away from. For, as lives go, John Laskell's life was most fortunate. Certainly its material aspect was very lucky: Laskell had an income. It was not a large income. It was of the size that financial people call a backlog, but in those cheap and rather frugal days of the thirties, it made, for an unmarried man of modest tastes, a comfortable little financial glow all by itself.

The times being what they were and the social world in which he moved being what it was, Laskell often had occasion to feel ashamed of his income. For although among his friends there were many intelligent people who were financially very well fixed, there were also many who were either quite poor, or, if they were well off, put to the necessity of making money by means they despised. They worked in advertising agencies or publishing houses by day and did what they could in the evening. And yet the income may well have had a good effect on Laskell. It preserved him from the very beginning from the brunt of those problems of "integrity" which, although they had always been of importance in American careers, were just now of more importance to men of talent than ever before. Laskell, with only a little caution and not much sacrifice, could manage to live without a salary. The alternatives to doing what he thought right did not present themselves, as they did to many of his friends, as "selling out" or as "corruption." He did not have to think of himself in such heroic and tragic language and this suited his reasonable temperament.

He was thirty-three years old, he was getting rather better looking as he got older, his dark hair had not thinned at all, and until this juvenile disease of scarlet fever struck him, he had never in his adult life been ill.

Laskell had come to his profession rather late and perhaps for that reason was the more attached to it. Until he was twenty-four he had planned a literary career. He wrote quite well and he had been in revolt against the culture of his affectionate and comfortable Larchmont family. He had wanted what young men of spirit usually want, freedom and experience, and literature was the way to get them. Literature was the means by which one became sentient and free. But the literary career somehow did not develop. Perhaps it was a kind of modesty that kept Laskell from writing, a diffidence about imposing himself or about looking into himself. From literature to the study of philosophy had been an easy step, scarcely looking like a retreat. But the change did not settle him, and it might have seemed that having an income was going to mean that he would fritter away what talent he had.

But when Laskell was twenty-four a chance encounter resolved his uncertainties. He was visiting one of his liberal, well-to-do friends, and among the company there was a man who insisted on talking about public housing. Between this man and John Laskell there flared an immediate hostility. It was one of those antagonisms that give great moral satisfaction to both parties. Laskell was willing to have the man talk about anything that could be contradicted. And contradict he did, with a kind of cool persistence that surprised him, for he had never been a contentious person. He did not know where he got the ideas he used for his arguments. No doubt they came from his opponent's own laboriously acquired store, needing only to be turned upside down. He was pleased when the man became abusive and denounced not only Laskell, but what he called Laskell's "whole school of thought." Suddenly there he was, a member of a school of thought in a profession he had never before considered. It was, the man said, a brilliant but unsound school. The ideas that Laskell had produced only to be contrary seemed to him to be suddenly right and important.

The chance debate made up Laskell's mind. Through his years of study in America and Europe, the interest so fortuitously aroused that evening never flagged. Laskell discovered in himself gifts for practicality and detail which, in his dream of literature, he had never suspected. He could deal, he found, not only with social theories, but also, as was necessary, with rents and rules and washing machines.

Now and then Laskell remembered with a kind of regret that he had once dreamed of fame, even of immortality, where now he was concerned only with a sound professional reputation. But his willing sacrifice of his young ambitions—which, after all, could never have been fulfilled—made the work he had chosen all the more valuable to him. Now that he had lost the vague rebelliousness which he had once attached to his notion of the life of the mind, he found that he enjoyed his mind far more and used it much better. He discovered that nothing was irrelevant to his profession. Every aspect of culture bore upon it, economics, sociology, history, technics, art. Now when he wrote—for technical journals and occasionally for the liberal magazines—it was with none of the self-doubt that had impeded his early literary efforts. His book, *Theories of Housing*, was much respected. One reviewer even called it "a little classic." He was taking great pleasure in the collection of material for his book on the planned cities of antiquity. He knew that he would never be great, he was reconciled to being useful.

Despite the nature of his profession and despite his hard work on semi-political committees, Laskell was not really a political person. The picture of the world that presented itself to his mind was of a great sea of misery, actual or to come. He did not think of it as forces in struggle. And the sea of misery often washed around the feet of his own existence. There were days when he was meaninglessly depressed, when there seemed no point to his busy life. Such days had been frequent in Laskell's youth. They had seemed proper to the literary temperament. They did not seem proper to the life of useful activity he now led. But they always passed and Laskell did not attach much significance to them. He understood that they were part of the difficulty of being a modern man. It was a difficulty he heard much discussed among his friends.

Although John Laskell's life was fortunate, it had been touched, once, by tragedy. There was no ascertainable reason why Elizabeth Fuess should have died. She was a very healthy girl and she had had in her illness the best doctors, the best pneumonia nurses, the best equipment that the money of her comfortable parents could provide. Laskell had been with her when she took the chill with which her illness began. They were playing tennis on an east-side court. It was a Sunday late in September, a hot day that had suddenly, toward the end of their last set, become cloudy and windy. They had been playing well, in the way they usually played—they considered that they were playing well when their rallies were long and they gave each other the opportunity for well-stroked shots; they said that this spoiled them for playing with anyone else and they often resolved to change their ways and really to try to keep the ball out of reach. Laskell came off the court that day and went to the bench where Elizabeth was putting on her sweater. He was always aroused by Elizabeth after tennis—he liked her dampness and the way she smelled, her disheveled hair, the redness of her face, the moist clay-dust on her legs and forehead. She liked the same things about him, and so they usually came off the court in an erotic glow, tired as they might be. But that day he saw that she was not as usual, not happily fatigued and consciously physical, but pinched and white in the face and shivering violently. She looked almost frightened, the chill had been so sudden. He took her back to her apartment in a cab, got her into a hot bath, lighted a fire, and gave her whisky. She felt better, the chill passed, but she was so very far from wanting to make love that she asked him to leave. When he telephoned the next day, it was her married sister who answered. She had been called in the night by Elizabeth.

Elizabeth had died ten days later in a hospital. No one in grief could have been more civilized to Laskell than were Elizabeth's parents and her sister. They liked Laskell and they had always shown only a little edge of disapproval of the affair, if affair was the word for it—Laskell himself knew enough of affairs to believe that the relation of Elizabeth and himself was something much more. They tried to suggest to him that their feelings toward him were good, and they were able to do so with only a little awkwardness. They had rather supposed that some day John and Elizabeth would marry and that it was only some modern way of doing things that had kept them from marrying at once. Elizabeth was the spirited daughter and she was taken to be modern even though she did not write or paint or hold a job. She lived alone in an apartment in Greenwich Village and spent much of her time reading books that her parents were not interested in, but the apartment itself was very decorous and neat and Elizabeth dressed in a way that her mother admired and they had good hopes that she would soon marry and settle down. They were encouraged in these hopes when they met John Laskell and guessed the relationship between him and their daughter.

John Laskell and Elizabeth Fuess knew that they were going to marry. They took their relationship now as seriously as a marriage, did they not? They lived close to each other in the Village and they were always in and out of each other's apartment, each taking possession of the other's, moving around in it with a complete sense of ownership. They went on long week ends together. They had no reasoned objection to marriage, they talked of "When we're married." But the idea just seemed superfluous at the moment. Both of them were sufficiently of the middle class to be unable to think of marriage as an impossibility, but both were sufficiently of their time to be astonished at their being in love. It went against many of the things that their culture held were possible to fully conscious people. They were very fully conscious and they regarded with wonder and uncertainty the devotion they had for each other. But they spoke of marrying in the spring. When they talked of marriage, it was as if they had invented the institution for their own special purpose.

Laskell found Elizabeth's death beyond the powers of his thought. He believed that this was because it was impossible to judge the event, and without judgment there was no way of thinking about it. She had been, simply, alive at one moment, twenty-six years old, a young woman of more than usual intensity of life, and then she was dead. No fact, no segment of reality, could be more definite, more self-defining. To think about it at all meant to be involved in questions such as that of the injustice of the event. But that would have implied the idea of justice, and Laskell knew that that question was an impossible one. There was nothing to think about, he found, except the picture that somehow stayed with him of Elizabeth shivering on the tennis court. He saw how much they had been right in feeling that their love had been a kind of exception, a lucky chance snatched from the way things were in the stern modern world, a piece of feeling fortunately left over from the gentler past. He saw that the more clearly when he knew that he could not act as lovers had once acted, he could not weep and curse, but only feel a kind of hard empty sternness to meet the sternness of the world. When, at the suggestion of Elizabeth's sister, he went to Elizabeth's apartment to take something of hers to keep, he took two or three of her favorite books with her name in them. He considered taking something more personal, but when he thought of taking the Monet pastel of which she had been fond, he realized it was too valuable, that everything in the apartment, which he once felt he possessed together with her, belonged *legally* to Elizabeth's parents. He looked into the box where she had kept her careless jewelry, to take perhaps a pin or ring she had often worn, but he took nothing as a keepsake.

His friends had the good sense or the good taste not to try to say anything to him. There was, of course, nothing to say. Perhaps if Elizabeth had been his wife they would have had some form of words, some way of philosophizing or offering comfort. But Elizabeth was not his wife, no matter how close they had been, and that fact was borne in on him whenever he remembered, with no resentment at all, that it was her sister whom Elizabeth had called in the night, not him. At that time he knew the Crooms only slightly; their warm friendship had not yet begun and it was Gifford Maxim who gave him what companionship he looked for. This was odd, when one thought of Maxim's philosophy, of the views he would naturally have about death and personal sorrow. But Maxim, though always enormously busy with his Party activities, would drop in almost every day in the early evening and take Laskell to dinner in the neighborhood and come back to sit with him for an hour or so. Maxim had been strangely fond of Elizabeth, although she had always regarded him with friendly irony. Laskell found that Maxim's presence, his great, scarred, silent face, gave him fortitude and comfort.

But if grief had touched Laskell's life, after all it sooner or later touches every life and Laskell's had scarcely been shattered. Laskell had met Elizabeth's death with mature courage, as his friends all agreed. He had a considerable amount of good sense about himself. He believed it wrong to let the present be shadowed by the past and he tried in a sincere and simple way to enjoy his life and to make it useful. And for the most part he had succeeded. He could not honestly have said that these last three years had been unhappy. Yet here he was in bed with scarlet fever—an absurd disease at thirty-three—taking a profound pleasure in being ill.

But that did not put it accurately. His pleasure was not in being ill but in being well, in his wonderful clarity, in his sense of lightness and grace, his feeling of perfect order.

It had begun as soon as the delirium had passed. He had opened his eyes and seen the woman sitting in the armchair by the window. The lamp beside the chair was the only light in the room and it shone down full upon her white lap, but he could not see her face.

"I am pain," she said.

John Laskell heard it clearly, but he lay still, thinking it best not to say anything at all.

She had spoken, making that astonishing remark, as soon as Laskell had opened his eyes. She said it again, "I am Paine, Miss Paine. Isn't that a dreadful name for a nurse?"

Her voice was English. She said "nuhss" with a mere little breath of sound where the *r* should be. It made Laskell feel safe.

She had not been occupied with anything as she sat there, not reading or sewing or knitting but wholly engaged in watching her patient. She had introduced herself without getting up. Now she came and stood by the bed.

"But *you* have a nice name," she said quietly. " 'John Laskell.' "

It was as if she were telling him his own name. It was a thing one often did with children, make conversation about their names. The sound of his name, the substantial mystery of identity, gave Laskell all the pleasure he could as yet feel. Later he remembered her cleverness in giving him something to hold on to.

"It sounds quite English," Miss Paine said. She spoke it again, as if testing it. " 'John Laskell,' " she said. "It sounds like a Lancashire name. Are you English?"

Laskell thought that it was by choice that he answered her with only the merest shadow of a smile. It was to be his belief through the next few days that he did everything at a minimum for reasons of his own, because he chose to do just that much and no more. Miss Paine seemed to understand that the smile meant, No, he was not English. There was a modification he might make—his mother had been born in the first year of his grandparents' long English visit. But that did not make her English, or him. He added nothing to his dim negative smile.

"I thought you might be. You talk as if you might, not like most Americans."

He could just about gather that it was meant as a compliment. But it seemed to Laskell that he had not yet said a word. Miss Paine said, "And you've been talking a great deal, my dear man." And she explained with a precise little nod, "Delirious."

Laskell understood then that the ultimate confrontations which had been forced upon him for so long were the fantasies of delirium. He had been undergoing something that had the character of a perpetual examination in mathematics, on the result of which much more than life itself depended. Those infinite abstractions were in some way connected with the terrible pain in his throat. They were not real. He felt grateful to Miss Paine for having explained everything so precisely.

Miss Paine put a thermometer under his tongue and took his wrist between firm fingers and thumb. She consulted her watch, which was a rather large one pinned to her blouse; Laskell looked at her, not turning his head but only his eyes. His eyes hurt as they moved. As she looked at her watch her face was abstracted, but she noticed his glance and smiled down to him, still counting. She had a chart on a clipboard and on it she wrote what his pulse was and then stood waiting for the thermometer.

Laskell saw that the bulb of his lamp had been covered with a piece of the blue paper that is wrapped about absorbent cotton. He understood this device at once. It was what had been done when he had been ill as a child. And then it had been done again by the nurse when his mother was very ill. The cone of light and the great shadows on the wall were just as he remembered them all those years ago. The blue paper around the bulb meant that things were at rock-bottom where there was nothing you could do.

The single window of the bedroom was open—it was a hot night. It was very late. There were no intimate noises coming up from the street. But Laskell could hear the whistles on the river, the chuffing of locomotives and their bells, the clop-clop of the hoofs of horses coming down from the north of the city. These sounds had for him the very meaning they had had in sleepless nights of his childhood when his mother had sat up with him. It was an illimitable unknowableness, space dissolved into time, huge areas and vistas never to be inhabited by his consciousness, although when he had learned about the constellations and the signs of the Zodiac, he had dimly understood those spaces to be inhabited by the brooding minds of the Water-Carrier, the Archer, the Fishes, the Maiden, the Crab, the Twins, and the Bull. From all this he was precariously fenced, but fenced nevertheless, lying in a delicate balance between danger and safety. He dozed as Miss Paine sponged him, but he could smell the alcohol and feel that tepid washcloth on his face, the returning identity as his face was cleaned.

Miss Paine said, "Just stay awake long enough to drink this juice." She was lifting up his pillow, with an arm beneath it, and holding to his lips a glass with a bent glass tube in it. He carefully turned away his head as the diluted orange juice burned his throat. "You must try to drink quantities," she said. "With scarlet fever we flush the kidneys."

The naming of the disease set a good many things to rights. He sank back to sleep with the comfortable assurance that soon his universe would have its familiar order, that all he had to do was endure.

When Laskell woke again at daybreak, it was with a clear sense of the difference between the world of his bedroom and the unencompassable world of the delirium he had just passed through. He noted the familiarity of the big mahogany dresser, the bookcases, the photographs on the dresser. He saw the nurse in his armchair, asleep. He remembered her name and what she had first said to him. "I am pain. Isn't that a dreadful name for a nurse?"

He was a man of rather humorous habit, which now asserted itself. He thought of Paine with amusement, of her life spent entering one sick-room after another, her opening words always known to her and never varied. She presented this poor little product of her wit to the old and the young, to the despairing and the hopeful, to the clever and the dull, certain that it would succeed equally with them all in their common need of her. "I am Paine. Isn't that a dreadful name for a nurse?"

She was craggy, this Miss Paine, thin and angular and vaguely middle-aged, and her meager dull hair was a little disordered and her tiny cap was awry. Laskell lay there and looked at her in the gray, growing light. And then she awoke and saw him watching her. She smiled to him, not immediately moving from her huddled position of sleep. Then she rose and set her cap and her hair straight before the mirror and was neat again, or at least as neat as she ever would be, for she could never rise above a respectable dowdiness, no matter how newly laundered her uniform was.

She stood beside the bed and looked down at her patient. "You're better," she said quietly, stating a fact and not congratulating him on it. Laskell became aware of his ability to swallow with much less effort.

Miss Paine looked at the watch on her chest and said, "It's too early to get you ready for Miss Debry, but you'd like a little sponge."

"Who?" Laskell said with some intensity. It was his first word spoken in consciousness. It came out hoarse and rusty and far-off.

"That's the day nurse."

Miss Paine answered Laskell's look of perplexity and unhappiness by laying a hand on his shoulder. "I'm not deserting you. I'll be back tonight," she said. She spoke with a touch of coy professional reassurance, but she seemed to mean what she said.

Laskell hoped she knew that it was not merely that he wanted her to be loyal to him. He wanted to be loyal to her. He felt a very direct, simple, and complete connection with her and he did not want it disturbed by the introduction of anyone else.

She went for the basin and the cloth. As she sponged his face and neck she said, "Just you wait until you peel. Now *that's* a *real* cleaning up, skin as soft and clean as a baby's."

At seven o'clock she woke him from a light doze and began to "get him ready for Miss Debry." She used these words again and Laskell found them quite natural. He even found them rather pleasant. He understood that he must have been got ready and handed around a good deal in the last few days.

"You haven't many suits of pajamas," Miss Paine said. "But Mr. Croom is attending to that. And you haven't nearly enough sheets, but Mrs. Croom is attending to that. Lovely people the Crooms are, I do think. Both of them." Laskell found it a little surprising, this relationship between Miss Paine and the Crooms, developed, as it were, over his insensate body.

And then, as if reminding him of his duty of gratitude, Miss Paine said with great severity, "Your friends Mr. and Mrs. Croom have been wonderful to you. They have taken care of everything."

She might well have spoken with severity, for there was no gratitude in Laskell. At this time of his life no one in the world meant more to him than young Arthur and Nancy Croom. No one meant as much. Ordinarily he would have liked nothing better than to hold affectionately in his mind another proof of the Crooms' goodness. He smiled to Miss Paine, but it was not in recognition of what his friends the Crooms had done but simply out of his vast contentment that whatever needed to be done had been done. Someone, after his thick-voiced, incoherent telephone call, had "taken care of everything."

"How long will this last?" Laskell asked.

Miss Paine was gathering the discarded sheets and pajamas from the floor and she answered over her shoulder and still stooping. "Scarlet fever? Oh, if you're good," she said, "three weeks, perhaps four. *If* you're good."

Her tone was notably indifferent. It was clear that she did not want to give weight to his question, would not consent to his believing that he was very ill.

Laskell understood that it would be a good six weeks and that he was very ill. And when Miss Paine turned to look at her completed work, at the neat bed, at Laskell's precisely parted hair—as he now knew from her telling him, it was parted on the right side, the same side as the Prince of Wales parted his hair—at Laskell's arms in the fresh blue pajamas nice and quiet and symmetrical by his sides, Laskell met her professional pride with a motionless answering pride at his beautiful readiness for Miss Debry.

He was quarantined. Miss Debry told him with a kind of religious awe that the Board of Health had pasted a sign on the door of the apartment. No one could come in to see him. He lay secure in the strength of the taboo.

One day was like another. This made time go fast and not, as Laskell would have thought, slow. Each day was like a fresh sheet on his bed, spotless and exactly like every other sheet. And just as the thing he lay on was not *a* sheet but *the* sheet, no matter how often it was changed, so the thing he lay through was *the* day. Whatever time might be, it was not what so many people said it was, a stream. Questions like that of what time was presented themselves to Laskell and he did not so much think about them as regard them with pleasure.

There was one part of the day that was perhaps less pleasant than the rest. This was the few hours after lunch, when the city, already baking in the late June heat, seemed to have lost its energy. Then Laskell remembered himself as a boy in the great empty afternoons of summer in a seaside resort, moving alone with the sense that in all the world everyone but himself had a happy occupation;

one day, he recalled, he had come on a dead dog, blackly festering in the sun, and suddenly felt he knew what it had been like to be the Greeks in their camp on the beach before Troy when the pestilence had stricken them because they had offended Apollo. Had he really thought that? He was not sure. But he was sure that he had seen the dog with a kind of terror and he was sure that he had read the *Iliad* when very young, beginning with excerpts from a set of books called *The Children's Hour,* and had been frightened in his dreams by the fierceness of Achilles. But he was not sure that he had as a child brought the two things together.

Laskell learned to take his longest nap in that empty time after lunch. He slept in the morning too, after the routine of breakfast, bath, and change of bed linen, and then he would lie content until noon. In the late afternoon, after the long nap, he would lie quiet, aware of the city moving toward the mystery and eroticism of the evening.

He kept books by his bed, those he asked for from his shelves and those his friends sent him as gifts. But he did little more than sift through the pages. He was rather amused by the ignorance of friends whose health hid from them the knowledge of what a sick man would want. He was even annoyed by his friend Kermit Simpson who sent him Dostoevski's *The Possessed* because, as Kermit's card said, Laskell had never read it and now had the leisure to do so. Nothing could have been kinder than Kermit's gift, for Kermit had had the big book cut up and stitched into four separate volumes to make it easier for a sick man to hold. But Laskell could not keep the characters in their places and the intensity of the emotions alienated him not only from the book but also, most irrationally, from the giver. On the other hand, he experienced great pleasure from gifts of flowers and fruit. His annoyance with Kermit Simpson passed as irrationally as it had come when Kermit sent him a large basket of figs and pomegranates.

What John Laskell chiefly felt as he lay there in his wide bed was awareness. He did not know, really, what he was aware of. He did not even know what awareness was, except that it was different from consciousness or thought. He had no real thoughts and no wishes. He did not think about his work nor did he think about himself at all. Yet his awareness was an awareness of himself. He lay through the day, drinking in the light that filled the room, and experienced something just short of an emotion. It had great delicacy and simplicity, as if the circulation of his blood had approached the threshold of his consciousness and was just about to become an idea. It was as if being had become a sensation.

Laskell did not try to understand this. But he remembered a moment when one of his professors of philosophy at Columbia had leaned half his short body across the table in the passion of his question and had asked, "Gentlemen, what does it mean to *be?* Not to be a man. Not to be a bird. Not to be a stone. *Or* a tree. *Or* a house. But gentlemen: What does it mean—just—to—BE?"

Woodbridge, of course, had been talking about a technical problem in metaphysics, yet this question and its intensity were now, suddenly, memorable to Laskell.

If there was one thing that marred his existence in these days of illness, it was Miss Debry.

Miss Debry, as Laskell began to understand, was beautiful. The understanding was late in coming. Much before it came had come the understanding that Miss Debry was unendurable. But late one afternoon Laskell saw her standing in profile before the window, writing her last entry of the day on the chart. She held the clipboard against her, just under her breast, and her head was bent over it. If Miss Paine's uniform could never look fresh, Miss Debry's always gleamed with whiteness. Some process of starch that Miss Paine perhaps forbade at the laundry and Miss Debry insisted on made Miss Debry's skirt stand out. Miss Paine's cap was tiny and it perched on the top of her scant hair and it could not look really white because it was of such thin material that the hair showed through it. But Miss Debry's cap was large and winged and made of a heavy material, and across it was fixed a band of dark blue ribbon, so that she was very nearly wearing a hat, a small white hat of considerable elegance, chosen to set off her dark hair.

It was in their appearance as nurses that Laskell first compared the two women. Having begun so, he then observed the quality of Miss Debry's more personal appearance, somewhat as if it were the inescapable next step in logic which he had to take. She was neither short nor tall. She was not slim but certainly not to be described by a word so heavy as plump. Outside of paintings, Laskell had never seen a woman contrived in these proportions. Her skin was superbly white, her hair superbly dark, and she had fishpool eyes. The late light poured in at the window and Miss Debry was willing to stand full in it. It made her very beautiful, very much to be observed. Laskell was glad that it was the late light. Soon after the sun set Miss Debry would be gone, giving place to Miss Paine. He lay there watching her. He hated her.

She put down the chart and stood at the foot of his bed. "Now then," she said, "we'll get you ready for Miss Paine. All right?"

Laskell, now that his mind had turned to the matter of her beauty, remotely observed her fine, heavy neck and the pretty way her hair grew at the nape.

"All right?" Miss Debry insisted. She always wanted Laskell to declare his assent to every detail of the routine. He had no wish to assent, but he knew that she would insist. He nodded.

"Don't you want to talk? Are you tired? I suppose all that fever *could* make you tired. Well, I'll get the basin."

She washed his face and neck and then unbuttoned his pajamas. "You haven't begun to peel yet, have you? You will soon though. You have a lot of hair on your chest, haven't you? Do you know what they say about hair on the chest? Do you know what they say?"

She expected an answer. Laskell gave it and hoped that he would be rewarded with a Canadian version of the meaning of hair on the chest. "No," he said.

"They say it shows you're strong."

"Oh, do they?"

"Yes, that's what they *say*."

She washed his back and dried it and rubbed it with alcohol and then with talcum. "You have a nice little apartment here. It's very tasty and cozy. Will your wife be back soon?"

Into the pillow Laskell said, "Not married."

"Oh! I thought you were!" she said insincerely. "Because it is fixed up so nice. Are you an artist? You have so many pictures."

"No."

"What are you then, a writer? Is that why you have so many books? Are you a writer?"

"Yes, a writer." Laskell thought it was simpler that way.

"Oh, a writer. And living here alone in Greenwich Village. My, you must have times!" Her voice became naughty. "This is Greenwich Village, isn't it? I used to know a painter in Montreal who lived alone in a studio and my, what times we used to have there, a whole bunch of us." She held the fresh pajama coat for Laskell to put his arms in.

"Wild," she said. "He's famous, do you know him—Walter Capper?" Now she was at the foot of the bed. She reached under the covers and drew down the trousers of his pajamas.

"Did you ever hear of him? He's famous."

"No."

"He paints nature," she explained.

She washed each of his legs and thighs, using the elaborate technique that preserved modesty by exposing only part of the body at a time. Then she handed him the washcloth with the phrase she had been taught, "Now will you bathe yourself?"

Laskell obediently washed between his thighs. Miss Debry said, "My, the old priests in the Montreal hospital, they could never get over the idea of a woman's giving them a bath. Goodness, how embarrassed they'd be. It was all you could do—are you finished? Give me the cloth. Now I'll make your bed. All right?"

Laskell saw the old priests in their Montreal beds and he felt very sorry for them.

But at least, every day, she would be gone. She was the one thing in the world that troubled his peace. The late June days were glaring and bright and in the brightness stood Miss Debry in her white uniform with her white skin. Laskell loved to sleep and he loved to lie motionless in the bright room when she was not there. He looked forward to her leaving the room to make his lunch or to eat her own.

Miss Paine came at seven o'clock and there were two hours of summer dusk in which she would sit knitting socks for her nephew in Australia. As the night came on, the beautiful peace would envelop Laskell more completely than ever. The noises in the street, the conversations of his Italian neighbors sitting on their stoops, the calls sent out to bring the children in to bed, and then just the indistinguishable, undifferentiated sounds of life—these seemed to Laskell at once full of sadness and of delight. Quite often, after

Miss Debry had mentioned them, he would think at this time of day about the ailing priests in the Montreal hospital, old men soon to be finished with life.

He learned to call her Paine, dropping the Miss. Her first name, as she shyly told him, was Nerissa. She would talk whenever Laskell seemed to want her to, telling him stories of her life, and in the stories she was always called Paine with no Miss. It made her seem to Laskell that much more English. She was what he knew so well from all the English books he had read. She was the family nurse or housekeeper, she was the nanny or the governess you went to visit when you were grown. She was a deeply connected person, willful and self-respecting and loyal, and she was the repository of all your childhood. In her eyes you were never innocent but you were never more than naughty or wild or inconsiderate.

Paine had nursed in a hospital in 1917 and 1918, an officers' hospital, a great country house incredibly named "Lances," and she had many stories about Splendid Fellows. Each one of the young officers who figured in her stories was a splendid fellow. She had a general admiration for manhood that followed tradition and built empire, and with it went a special interest in that manhood when it was in sickness or pain. Laskell had only to lie there with Paine in attendance to be himself a splendid fellow with full license to be in bed.

She taught him cribbage, bringing her own little board and pegs for the scoring, and he learned to say "one for his nobs." At his direction she dug up an old box of chessmen and they played what she called "bumble-puppy chess." It was really not much more than a sedate and varied kind of checkers. "There are people to whom it is practically a science," she explained. One of her patients had so regarded the game and it was he who had taught her the elements, but he had not been able to teach her more than these. "He could usually mate me in five or six moves unless he helped me," Paine said. "But we have our own fun, don't we?" And Laskell gravely agreed.

The doctor was the Crooms' Dr. Graf, a grave, broad, comfortable man, mature and Jewish and apparently humorless. It was a strange thing about him that he owned, as he told Laskell, a large bulldog. He now came only once a day, but he did that with such regularity and examined so thoroughly that Laskell began to ask questions.

"It's never a light thing at your age," Dr. Graf answered, "and we have to watch out for secondary complications now that the danger is over."

"Danger? What do you mean by danger?" asked Laskell.

"What do I mean by danger? Why, what do we ever mean by danger?" said the doctor.

"You mean I could have died?"

"You could have died, and if it gives you any satisfaction, I thought you would," Dr. Graf said, and his voice was so dry that Laskell understood that he would have to revise his opinion of Graf's humorlessness.

The doctor went on. "Your ears are all right and your heart is all right. Perfectly. Your hair may start falling out, but it may then come back after a while." He spoke with the casualness of a man himself long established in baldness. "What we must watch is the kidneys. I think they're clear but I'm going to use a catheter tomorrow."

Laskell did not know what that was.

"We tap the bladder directly, with a thin rubber tube," the doctor said.

When the doctor had gone, Miss Debry said, "It hurts. It hurts to be catheterized." Laskell hated to have the information from her, at once so heedlessly and with such a note of childish awe at pain.

"I'm to be catheterized tomorrow, the doctor says," he told Paine that evening.

"Yes, naturally. I've wondered why he hasn't done it before."

"It must be awkward. Does it hurt?"

"Nuisance, yes. Yes, it does hurt rather. Stays with you too a while."

It did hurt and it stayed with him quite a while and he felt limp and humiliated.

"That's to make sure there are no germs," Miss Debry explained when the doctor had finished and left with his specimen. "Did you ever *see* a germ?"

"No."

"I did—I saw one once. A doctor showed it to me in the hospital, through a microscope. But I can't say what kind it was."

Laskell kept silent.

"I can't say what kind it was," said Miss Debry.

Laskell said fretfully, "Why not?"

"I can't."

"Didn't he tell you what kind it was?"

"Oh, yes. He told me."

"Don't you remember?"

"Oh, yes. But I can't say." And she busied herself with her paraphernalia at the table.

"You mean you won't."

"Yes, I won't."

"Why won't you?"

"Because. Because it wouldn't be nice."

Laskell wondered about the depths of a mind that grew coy about saying *spirochete* or *gonococcus*. "Oh, don't be silly," he said in exasperation.

She had been waiting only for a little show of force and she yielded at once. "Well, then—it was a *baby* germ." And she blushed, really embarrassed by having said it.

Laskell's mind sank at the contemplation of her foolishness. It was no doubt her being Canadian, in conjunction with her mention of the sperm, that made him think of salmon, of the round translucent red eggs, of the great fish themselves with the firm pink flesh organized into one wonderful muscle with one sure instinct, of the spawning millions of salmon with their incredible redundancy of eggs, returning from the sea to the upper reaches of their home waters in a blind culminating energy in which love and death were one.

Miss Debry was as beautiful and complete as one of those great fish. Or she would be, if she did not have her foolish little social mind that had to be served by her powers of conversation. She was wonderfully beautiful as she stood there with her neck still touched by the pink of her blush and her deep dark eyes lowered in the mild unimportant shame she had contrived for her own purposes. But Laskell simply did not have the violence to fix on that

superb physical being of hers and pass over the foolish triviality of
a mind acquired in provincial schools and hospitals. Even in health
he had never had that much violence and simplicity.

But there she was, now brought into the sexual ambit and beginning to glow with it. And Laskell himself was now enough in it
for him to have to say something. "Your cap is very pretty," he said
crossly.

It was the first personal notice she had had from him and she
turned toward him to take it with the practiced self-consciousness
of a small-town belle. "Do you like it?" she said. "It's the cap of St.
Michael's Hospital. Every hospital has a distinctive cap," she said
as if she were repeating a lecture she had heard on the etiquette
and ritual of her profession. "And St. Michael's is by far the pret-
tiest, I think." She turned her head this way and that to let Laskell
see it from all angles. "They give it to you when you graduate.
'Capping,' it's called." She bent her head for him to see how it was
fashioned on top. "And they give you this pin, too."

The bodice of her uniform was fastened with a large round pin
of blue enamel and gold. She sat down beside him on the bed so
that he could see the emblem and device on the pin, leaning forward for him to examine it. She unfastened the pin and gave it to
him. The V of her bodice opened somewhat wider.

It was at that moment that Paine put her head in at the door
with a chirpy "Good evening."

"One of the first rules," Paine said as she put the thermometer
into Laskell's mouth just before his supper, "one of the first rules is
that you do not sit on the patient's bed, unless to raise the head for
feeding. No Edinburgh-trained nurse would any more think of it!
It's an ill-conditioned Canadian thing to do. *Put* that thermometer
back in your mouth."

She whisked out to fetch the tray. She came back with the tray
and set it down on the dresser, read the thermometer and entered
the reading on the chart.

"She wanted to show me her hospital pin," Laskell said.

Paine stood holding the tray, looking down at him. "Show you
her pin!" she said with a finality of scorn.

And then a rich and wicked smile broke over the dutiful face.
She said with a large concessive admiration, taking in, in a broad

and more than tolerant view, the way of the world, "Well, I've got to admit that they looked as if they were worth showing."

And she laid the tray across his knees.

It was so. Miss Debry's breasts seen under the too elaborate lace beneath the starched white cotton bodice, seen when the neck of her dress was unfastened, these were the objects of Paine's judgment. It was a judgment made without any bitterness or jealousy. It did not bring into question or comparison Paine's own meager bosom. She made it without reference to anything but Laskell. She was judging as a young man judges. She knew what young men thought worth looking at, what the splendid fellows liked. It was a natural part of their being so splendid. And they ought to have what they wanted—it was as if she had made Laskell the free offer of Miss Debry's remarkable charms. The offer made, it was permanent, and therefore Laskell felt no need to accept it for the present.

If Laskell woke thirsty in the night, Paine knew it at once, as if she could hear his eyelids parting. When she had given him the drink, holding up his head with her arm beneath the pillow, she would ask, "Enough?" as though she wanted him to consider before he answered. He would think carefully whether he had enough before he said, "Yes, thank you, Paine." She always took the occasion of his waking to sponge his face and neck with a tepid washcloth. It felt like a mask being removed and he would murmur contentedly, "Thank you, Paine," asleep before she had finished toweling his face.

Laskell's kidneys, said Dr. Graf, would need watching for some time, but at present they were clear. There was no longer need for two nurses. One nurse on duty through the twenty-four hours would do.

"And so you can let Miss Paine go," said Dr. Graf.

"Why let Miss *Paine* go?"

Dr. Graf shrugged. "Just the usual way. The usual thing is to keep the day-nurse and let the night-nurse go. But if you prefer—"

"I'd rather keep Miss Paine."

"She's more efficient?"

"Yes. And quieter."

"The other one talks too much?"

"Incessantly."

"I'll see if I can manage it without tears," said Dr. Graf.

Laskell noted what seemed to be an expression about the doctor's eyebrows. It perhaps meant that Dr. Graf thought it odd that Laskell should prefer to spend the days of his convalescence with Miss Paine rather than with Miss Debry. It even seemed as if the doctor, had he been in the same situation, would have chosen Miss Debry. Laskell tried for a moment to think of Miss Debry as she might appear to him when health returned. But having thought, he said to Dr. Graf, "I'd be very grateful if you would."

Dr. Graf was not successful in managing it without tears. Miss Debry departed with scarcely a good-by said and Laskell was left with Paine.

He had no visitors. The quarantine sign was still on the door of the apartment. Those of his friends who had children could not, of course, think of coming. Paine reminded him of this when she thought he might be feeling lonely and neglected. A few of his friends who had no children did try to brave the sign, but Paine would not let them see her patient. At most she would let them enter the tiny vestibule. "You may call in to him from here," she would say, and a friend would call in an embarrassed voice, "Hello, John, how are you?" And Laskell would call back in a formally cheerful way, disliking the situation, "Oh, fine, fine." Then the summer deepened and there were fewer people in town and no visitors.

If Laskell ever had daydreams or thoughts of the future, they were about Paine. He thought of how he would keep his connection with her even when he was well. He would send her a present every Christmas. Now and then, say twice a year, he would take her to dinner and then to a theater. These evenings would be pretty dull evenings, relieved only by the shrewd things Paine would now and then say. But Laskell looked forward to them despite, or even because of, this dullness. Surrounded by the bustle and inclemency of winter—he always saw the scene with a wet snow falling—they would be quiet and restorative, a part of his life that his clever friends would not understand or know about, and so much the better for that.

Most of the time he lay there in his new sensation of awareness, the delicately pulsating apperception not of his mind only but of his whole being. This strange sensation was unlike anything he had ever felt before, although he sometimes thought it might have much to do with everything he would feel in the future.

It was Paine who led him to think that what he felt was love. She did not suggest this directly. But love, she said, was what he felt toward the remarkable flower which, at the end of his time in bed, so engaged his attention.

"You seem," Paine said dryly, "to be having quite a love affair with that flower."

Her dryness was a sympathetic one, as if the flower were a girl. It was the dryness with which people point out the natural weakness of human nature without reproving it, a tone often used about love. She was getting him ready for the night and she transferred the glass with the flower in it from the bed-table to the dresser with the same brusque but friendly air that she might have used to an attractive and very well brought up girl-visitor who, however charming she was, must now be sent packing so that the routine of the sickroom could go on.

The rose, like the others it had outlasted, was not red, nor yellow, nor the "tea" color, but a strange new tone, a flushed and dusky pink, tawny and bronze. It drew Laskell as he had never been drawn by anything before. The dryness of Paine's tone, together with her expressed admiration for the splendid fellows, suggested at first that she was mocking him. A high and continued regard for a rose was probably not to be considered manly. But from Paine's manner it would appear that an involvement with a flower was quite the expectable thing in a splendid fellow. It was apparently an amiable weakness, as easily to be understood as gambling away a month's pay or kissing a pretty probationary nurse or getting drunk.

It was, of course, a very feminine-looking flower with its depths and involutions of shape, with its color of tawny-pink. It seemed to have some secret to which he could penetrate. But of course there was no secret. There was nothing within or behind or beneath what he saw. The strength and continuity of his feeling was all the knowledge he would get. Part of the knowledge was the sense that the knowledge was limited. And eventually the flower died, and it amused and pleased Laskell that Paine announced the event by saying, "Well, Rosenkavalier, your days are ended." She had a certain small store of surprising references which he could not account for in her general lack of education.

Now and then the world broke in on Laskell by way of the telephone. Arthur Croom called from the country to see if things were going well, and Paine came in beaming from her conversation to tell him about it.

"Oh, I do like that Mr. Croom," she said. "He's so lively and straightforward. What is his line of work?"

"He's a professor of economics," Laskell said.

"A don!" said Paine. "But he seems so young."

Don was scarcely the word for Arthur. Arthur quite destroyed the notion of donnishness with its meaning of retreat and isolation. As for his being young and a professor, that was at present one of the great things about Arthur. At twenty-eight, Arthur Croom was the political man whom the nation had not had in sufficient numbers. He was the man in whom the drive for power did not destroy intelligence and character. Henry Adams would have understood Arthur Croom and envied his chances. His political nature was not signalized by anything proconsular or hard or merely executive. On the other hand, he had a resistant toughness about the way of the world. But this was not cynicism; rather, it was the armor of idealism. Of Arthur's idealism there could be no doubt, though it did not go with a lively sensibility, and among Laskell's friends idealism and sensibility were usually found in company. There was strong talk of a Washington job for Arthur Croom, and this was not surprising. Laskell thought of his friend as the kind of man who was going to dominate the near future—not the far future when the apocalyptic days would come, but the time now at hand before things got very bad.

He tried to tell Paine something about this remarkable friend of his. He succeeded fairly well, for Paine was ready to appreciate the kind of person Arthur Croom was. "And so devoted to you!" she said. It was not possible to misinterpret the remark. She did not mean that it was surprising that Arthur Croom with all his gifts and promise should be devoted to Laskell. What she probably meant was that devotion was another of Arthur's gifts, for she added, "Ah, *he'll* not be a don for long." She loved action above all things.

On another day Paine said, "A man, name of Maxwell, just phoned and said he had to see you at once. I said he couldn't come, of course."

"Maxwell? Are you sure?" Laskell said. "Was it Maxim?"

"Yes, Maxim, that's right. He said it was important, but when I asked if he wanted me to give you a message, he said no."

If Arthur Croom was the man of the near future, Gifford Maxim was the man of the far future, the bloody, moral, apocalyptic future that was sure to come. Once Laskell's sense of the contradiction between his two friends had been puzzling and intense. But now it was possible to hold Gifford Maxim and Arthur Croom in his mind with no awareness of contradiction at all. He was able to see them both as equally, *right* was perhaps not the word, but valid or necessary. They contradicted each other, the administrator and the revolutionary, and perhaps, eventually, one would kill the other. Yet now Laskell saw how they complemented each other to make up the world of politics.

So effective was Laskell's new way of seeing things that he felt no uneasiness at not being available when Gifford Maxim wanted him. And more than that: he now felt none of the unhappiness which had overwhelmed him whenever he thought of how he had failed Maxim at their last meeting.

There had been a Negro cleaning woman in the apartment when Maxim had paid his last visit and Maxim had said, under his breath but sternly, "Get rid of her, will you? Tell her to go home." It seemed a foolish and melodramatic thing to say. But Maxim knew his business, and Laskell was glad the woman was just leaving anyway. Then, when she had gone, Maxim had asked a favor of Laskell: if there were certain letters that came addressed to Laskell but addressed in a certain way that would distinguish them from his other mail, would Laskell receive these letters and keep them unopened until they were asked for by Maxim or by someone Maxim would send? And would he without asking any questions just simply say yes or no? Laskell had said no, and ever since he had felt ashamed.

Laskell did not exactly know why he had said no. When Maxim had asked him to stand as surety in the leasing of certain offices he had said yes. When Maxim had asked him to serve on certain committees, he had said yes. He had at Maxim's request endorsed a note and had even made outright a sizable cash contribution to a tottering periodical, all with the sense that, although he did not wholly agree with Maxim and Maxim's political party, he wanted them to exist because of their clear relation to the future. When he had said yes to Maxim's requests, he had a strong feeling of hope. But he had said no to the request about the letters. He had felt tired and depressed after the refusal. In the year that had passed he had often been puzzled and unhappy about it. Now, as he was reminded of Maxim, none of these feelings recurred.

When Laskell began to peel, Paine made a great thing of it. The old skin began to flake and then to come off in strips and patches, leaving the skin beneath fresh and soft. "You'll be as soft as a newborn babe!" Paine said. "And clean!—the cleanest man in New York."

Laskell grinned and took a great interest in his new clean skin and in the discarded old one. The calloused skin of his heels came off in single pieces, like cups, and he regarded them half with pride, half with revulsion. His feet were fresh and elegant now, without any mark to show that he had ever worn shoes.

"Well," said Paine, "this is the beginning of the end. You'll soon be thinking of getting up, my hearty!"

Laskell politely agreed. But he thought there was still no hurry.

But at last he began the routine of getting up—feet dangling over the side of the bed, a half hour in the armchair, an hour in the armchair, a tour of the apartment on Paine's arm, two hours in the armchair in the other room.

He had put off the move as long as he could, for he foresaw no advantage from it. And he was right—the great quiet wisdom of the bed vanished as soon as he got up. His body, recently so light and ordered, felt depressed and grim. In bed he had been young, or ageless, and now he felt old. He tried not to think about his hair. As the doctor had predicted it might, it began to fall out.

Paine applauded each forward step but he was a little sulky.

"I think," said Paine with professional archness, "I think he doesn't want to be well again."

Laskell digested his bitterness as best he could. The white endless peace of the bed was over. There was no getting back the existence in which he understood so much. And Paine, who had been so important in that peace, she too was on the way to being over. She had become casual with Laskell. He was no longer the center of her regard. She was restless. Her function had departed and she too wished now to depart. She lived for the moment when she could enter a new sickroom and say, "I am Paine. Isn't that a dreadful name for a nurse?"

Her desire to go made Laskell stubborn. She pointed out that he was wasting money keeping her and Laskell replied sharply with a phrase he had never used before in all his life. "I'll be the judge of that," he said. She said that she had become nothing more than a cook. Certainly she was not a good cook. Now that the connection between them was broken, she was fussy and demanding. She bought expensive cuts of meat for herself and ate them while he picked joylessly at the vegetables to which his diet was limited and which she reduced with a fierce thoroughness to tasteless pulp.

"You don't need me," Paine said. "You can do for yourself now."

"I can't cook for myself and you don't expect me to run around to restaurants yet, do you?"

"I'll get a maid for you. That's all you need."

"I don't want a maid."

"You ought to go away. The doctor said you ought. You need country air."

"I have no place to go."

Laskell did not say this only for argument. He really had no place to go. It seemed impossible to imagine even a kind of place, let alone a particular place. And he had to face the fact that whenever he thought of making a train trip alone he was filled with an intense irritation. It was as if someone were insisting that he do a thing which was not actually dangerous but had some element of danger in it, like riding on a roller-coaster or climbing a very tall ladder. Nothing would happen, but he preferred not to do it.

"Couldn't you go to Mr. and Mrs. Croom? They're great friends of yours. Wouldn't they have you?"

"Yes, of course. They've written to ask me." For he did not want Paine to think he was not wanted.

"Well, then?"

Laskell shrugged. He despaired of making her understand, although only a short time before she had understood so much. He thought that she was being stupid and even vulgar.

But he got out the letter from Nancy Croom and read it over again.

"You must not stay in that hot apartment of yours," Nancy wrote. "You must come to us. The new little house is delightful, but it is still in such a mess that we cannot put you up. Besides, I am not very good company these days because—surprise!—I'm going to have another baby. But just about ten minutes on foot live the Folgers and the Folgers have a beautiful light room which they are willing to rent. Mrs. Folger is a wonderful cook—wins all the prizes at the bazaars and fairs. You can have this room and cooking for ten dollars a week. And you can have or shun company just as you wish. You will have the society of the Folgers, which is a kind of salubrious influence in itself. We have forgotten that there are such people in the world, growing right out of their soil and developing a kind of spirit which in our absurd city life we never see. I know, of course, that the progressive movements are likely to come from the city, but although you will scarcely believe it, Mr. Folger is a socialist! Not that I think much of socialists as such, but it does mean something, doesn't it, for a farmer to have come even so far? I'm sure you'll love them as much as we do. Please come. You know how much we want you."

Laskell read the letter over many times. He did not know why he did not respond to it. He understood from this how sunk in perversity he was, how much the debility of his convalescence was distorting his emotions. He had never before resisted an invitation or an appeal from Nancy. He was not even pleased by the Crooms' expectation of another child.

When Paine saw him with the letter, she picked up the large framed photograph that stood on Laskell's dresser and said, "Is this by any chance Mr. and Mrs. Croom?" For all her interest in the Crooms, she had never so far presumed to ask. Her intention was perfectly transparent. She was trying to interest him in the Crooms. He put out his hand for the photograph.

"Lovely looking people," said Paine. And they were, Nancy with that wonderful modern face of hers, Arthur with his fine ugliness that was not only his beauty but his good fortune, for it somehow indicated all the goodness and intelligence he had.

"She looks so *very* charming," said Paine, and for a moment her voice indicated her old accuracy of perception. For she spoke of Nancy's charm with a sense that it meant something special to Laskell, yet there was no commonplace banter in her tone. She was paying Laskell a compliment on his friend, but she seemed to know very well what the nature of the friendship was, she implied nothing flirtatious.

As if at Paine's bidding, Laskell thought about the Crooms, about Arthur's subtle vigor and Nancy's charm, her fine moral clarity. They seemed to him like all of affirmative life. And affirmative life was no doubt what he needed now, sunk as he was in negation. Paine was not to be held longer, and although Laskell could now surely be by himself, he could not bear the thought of staying in the city without her. There was nothing else for him to do—he accepted the invitation with the advice to himself to stop behaving at his age like a sulky child.

Paine received the news with pleasure and a change of manner. Here was our Mr. Laskell now, a gentleman ready to go on his travels. It was a thing she understood and she was pleasant as she helped him get his "kit" ready. He was a splendid fellow once again. Now that they were to separate, she regarded him as one ready to take his place, to stand in the battle of life where he belonged, at Khyber Pass or wherever it was that she localized that notable engagement.

But Laskell did not respond to her cheer. He was not in the least interested in putting up a good show. He was, after all, not a splendid fellow. That was one of the delusions of his sickbed. He was much rather, if Paine but knew it, a French poet of a man, sourly regarding his wasted, vanished youth, slack, with a body that felt gray and heavy, bitter over his fallen hair. *"J'ai perdu ma force et ma vie."*

Paine had been teasing him about the length and untidiness of his hair and a few days before he left he sent Paine out for a barber. Paine said that he ought to go to the barber shop, that he ought to walk around in the street before making his trip, but he insisted on having the barber in. During the first days of his illness, before he could shave himself, Paine had shaved him two or three times, very efficiently, and the day he had first dressed she had clipped his hair around his ears. As the barber worked, she stood by with an amateur's interest in a professional's methods. "He needs a shearing, doesn't he?" she said to the barber, and the barber said to Laskell, "Yes, sir, you certainly did need a haircut this time." But he resisted cutting the hair as short as Laskell wanted it, even after Laskell had explained that he was going to the country and his doctor had suggested that he expose his scalp to the sun. The barber supposed it impossible for a customer to have his hair cut without seeing the process in a mirror and, with Paine's help, had brought in the hanging mirror from the vestibule and had stood it up on a table against the wall. Laskell looked at himself in the glass, saw himself flanked by Paine and the barber, both in white, saw his face in all its unsatisfactoriness isolated above the big white sheet, found nothing in the face to give him comfort about himself. "Admiring himself, is he?" said Paine. "Well, you do have nice ears. There's a good deal to be learned about character from ears."

Rummaging among Laskell's things, Paine emerged from a closet with his fishing rod in its case. "You'll want this, I have no doubt," she said. She was pleased by her find. Her pleasure would have been unspeakable had she also found an express-rifle and a boar spear.

"I guess not," Laskell said.

"Not? Are there no streams where you're going?"

"Yes, I suppose there are." He knew there were. The Crooms had talked of streams when they bought their house, making a point of the fishing they could offer him.

"Well, then!" said Paine. "You'll want your fishing gear with you."

"No," said Laskell.

He did not refuse only in order to spite Paine. He simply could not imagine himself on a stream doing and thinking all the small, pleasant, necessary things. He was not a deeply devoted fisherman, nor a particularly skillful one.

"No?" said Paine sharply. "Then what will you do with yourself all day? Most certainly you will take it." And she flounced back into the closet and came out with his waders. She set them down on the floor with the air of standing no nonsense.

"Those mean another bag to carry," Laskell grumbled. But he was mollified and he himself found his fly book and his leader-case, his old hat and his knife, and all the odds and ends of equipment that used to give him pleasure. Paine discovered the creel and got a rag to dust it.

"No," Laskell said. "Now *that* I will not take. It's too big to fit into the suitcase with the other stuff."

"No need for it to fit," said Paine and held it up by its strap. "You'll hang it on your shoulder, as is meant."

And she continued to dangle the willow basket by its strap, as if tempting him. Laskell had always admired his creel, so finely shaped and so closely woven. But he was not tempted.

"You've already made me take an extra bag and the rod," he said. "The creel isn't necessary."

For answer, Paine simply and decisively put the creel down by the open suitcases and the rod. "You can make up your mind when you're leaving tomorrow," she said. She had the air of not deigning to argue further.

"Paine, I won't take it! I just won't!" he said fiercely. And he might have succeeded in forcing the squabble on Paine if at that moment the bell had not rung from downstairs.

Paine went to push the button. She stood at the door, waiting for the caller to climb the two flights and she admitted Gifford Maxim with his huge body and scarred face, with his ironic, revolutionary eyebrow and the ready, almost maternal, look of solicitude with which he habitually gazed upon human suffering, called forth now by his friend Laskell attended by a trained nurse.

Laskell did not know whether he was very glad or very sorry to have Gifford Maxim's visit. If what he wanted was to have his connection with life renewed, Maxim was the man to do it. For that he was in some ways even better equipped than the Crooms. And Laskell did want to be taught again what it meant to be affirmative and full of hope. Yet it seemed to him that he could not now sustain the enormous moral pressure that Maxim exerted. Maxim stood there in his tight suit and damp shirt, huge and strong, straining his clothes, big and untidy with what he contained, the great events to come, the bloody and apocalyptic and moral future.

But when the visit was over Laskell knew that he was wholly sorry for it. There was no more moral pressure from Maxim by the time they had finished talking. There was no more morality in Maxim to exert the pressure. His connection with the moral future was gone forever.

It was not merely that Maxim had broken with the Party. That would have been disturbing but bearable. People did break with the Party and Laskell had met a few who had. They had seemed decent enough and they often took pains to indicate that they were not reactionary, yet Laskell had always had to check a feeling of revulsion. He told himself that it was not fair to have such a feeling. There was a large element of theory in such matters. He himself was not involved in theory, but those who were involved were bound to have differences and to act on them. But it was always difficult not to feel that a personal treachery had been committed. And perhaps if Maxim had dealt with theory, Laskell would have been sorry and deprived, but he would not have felt the disgust he did feel. But Maxim scarcely touched on theory. By the time the visit was over, Laskell's disgust was touched with pity, but that made the interview even more painful.

Maxim sat there smoking Laskell's cigarettes. He was a frightened man, but not so frightened that he did not conduct the whole business in his high, dramatic way. When the purpose of the visit had become apparent, Laskell saw that not a single detail of it lacked its purpose. He had been a little surprised that Maxim had made a point of introducing himself to Paine and by his own name, even going so far as to impress it on her by making a joke about it to cap Paine's joke about her name. And then Maxim had involved Paine in that long debate on whether today was the twelfth of July or the thirteenth. All this was part of the method of Maxim's madness, for it was exactly his identity that he wanted to establish, the fact of his existence on a certain day. It had slowly appeared that what he had come for was to enlist Laskell's influence with Kermit Simpson to get a job on Kermit's rather foolish magazine. Any job was what he wanted, any job that would put his name on the masthead of *The New Era*. And the mad, the disgusting, reason for this was his belief that he was not safe unless he acquired what he kept calling an existence by becoming a public fact. He had vanished as a person, and now he could easily be done away with. The idea was so extravagant that Laskell received from it his first intimation of the break in Maxim's reason; he had tried to reassure him that things had not yet gone so far that a radical was in danger of being murdered by the police. It was then that Maxim had given evidence of his insanity by his quiet explanation that he did not fear the police but the very Party he had once lived for. No incredulity could shake him, no argument could move him. And in weariness and pity Laskell had telephoned Kermit Simpson at Westport and had used the influence he knew he had with Kermit.

It had made an inappropriate ending to the period of Laskell's illness. It had made a distressing ending too, for when Maxim had learned that Laskell was leaving for Connecticut the next morning, he had insisted that they travel together. There was no missing his fear of going alone, his certainty that Laskell's company would be a protection.

3

Mrs. Folger looked up bright and capable as Laskell came
into the kitchen.

"Well!" she said, and stared at him as if he were a surprising
though not unwelcome phenomenon. "And how did he sleep? And
now I suppose he wants his breakfast?"

"He slept fine and he certainly does want his breakfast."

It was very successful. The naughty boy that Mrs. Folger had
called him when they had first met was now Laskell's role at all
mealtimes, especially at breakfast. A chief element of his naughtiness was the ravenous hunger he was supposed to have.

The side door opened and old Mr. Folger came in, very slowly.
In one hand he carried four eggs. "Good morning," Laskell said,
very loud. The old man nodded two or three times and mumbled
into his mustache. He went very slowly and carefully about the
business of placing the eggs in a bowl. Laskell's fear that he would
have to eat his meals with the old man had proved groundless. The
Folgers ate in the kitchen by themselves at a different hour, and
Laskell's meals were served by Mrs. Folger at a little table near the
window in the dining-room. But now, after a week with the family,
it would not have troubled Laskell to eat with old Mr. Folger. He
was even gratified by the old man's presence in the family on, as it
were, equal terms. Old Mr. Folger was so on the edge of life that
he was scarcely a person any longer, yet he was kept a person by his
inclusion here, by the little duties he performed such as this one of
fetching the eggs. It was impossible to believe that he had stood at
Gettysburg, but he had indeed.

"Would you like an egg *this* morning?" Mrs. Folger asked.

"No, thank you."

64

"Go along then and I'll have your coffee ready before you can say Jack Robinson."

"Jack Robinson," Laskell said.

She shooed this audacity out of the kitchen. He went and sat on the porch to wait for breakfast. The three hounds were lying on the grass and they rose lazily to see if they could get some affection. Laskell sat on the edge of the porch and pulled their long ears for them.

There was no doubt about Laskell's getting well. Twice a day he tested his urine as Dr. Graf had ordered, using the test tube that Dr. Graf had given him, heating it over a lamp and dropping in the acetic acid when it boiled. Each time the urine was clear and not cloudy, free of albumin. He went on fairly long walks without getting tired. His pallor was giving way to tan.

The mornings were chilly, and when Laskell woke he would lie in bed with the illusion that it was winter or autumn or early spring, not those seasons as he knew them now but as he had known them as a boy. He remembered the seasonal procession as it had been celebrated at school, the marking of the vernal equinox, Arbor Day, Halloween, Thanksgiving, and Christmas. He remembered the ritual objects cut out of paper with which the schoolrooms were hung, and the appropriate poems. As he lay snug under the many thin blankets and patchwork quilts, dropping off to sleep and waking again, he would recall certain days with a peculiar intensity. There were emotions connected with the suburban field of snow over which a glittering crust had formed. The sky that day was absolutely blue. He had felt that it was making a conscious effort to be as blue as that, that it was alive and trying. And as he had walked across the field he had repeated over and over again part of a poem he had been made to memorize at school.

> Blue, blue, as if the sky let fall
> A flower from its cerulean wall.

It was always of his childhood that Laskell thought as he lay in bed in the morning. He was surprised to discover that he had a fondness for himself as a boy. He forgave, as it were, the boy he had been. He exempted the young John Laskell from blame for all the dirty and embarrassing things that that child had done. He remembered quite nice things about him, such as his reciting the poem about the fringed gentian; or how, on one autumn morning that was robust and russet just as the books said autumn was, his mother had given him as the day's clothes a khaki shirt and pants which seemed so precisely the outfit in which to meet life heroically that he had cried "Hurray!" and had kissed the shirt in affection and had been rebuked for excessive and eccentric feeling; or how large and metaphysical had been his sense of freedom when for the first time each year he was allowed to go out without his overcoat, with just a sweater beneath his jacket.

It was true that here, at the Folgers', as the exhilaration of the morning faded and before the evening closed comfortably in, there were certain hours, from noon on, when the sun was hot and high, in which Laskell lacked energy, or perhaps will. But the bad early afternoon hours were unimportant compared to the clear, beautiful morning hours. The way he felt in the morning seemed, somehow, to prevent him from being ashamed of his weak attachment to his illness or his foolish attachment to Paine. Now and then he had a vague personal sorrow for Gifford Maxim, but no more than that. He was neither angry at Maxim nor disgusted with him. That was in part because it was unreasonable to feel such things toward a man so little responsible as Maxim now was. But chiefly it was because in this simple life of sun, food, sleep, and trees the ideas that Maxim had once stood for and now had deserted did not seem as real as they once had. There was perhaps a kind of truth in the belief held by some people that the politics of the city and of the country must necessarily be different. Maxim—the old Maxim—had once explained why this was a shallow view of things, but Maxim was refuted by the happy blankness of Laskell's mind.

Mrs. Folger stood at the screen door and said, "Well, do you want your breakfast to get cold after I've been to all the trouble?"

There were three prunes, a large bowl of oatmeal, a pitcher of milk, some cool toast, and a large pot of hot weak coffee. Except for the quality of the coffee, it was not a bad breakfast. Nor, on the other hand, was it a very good one. Like the rest of Mrs. Folger's meals, it was plentiful but dim. Nancy's estimate of Mrs. Folger's cooking had been borne out only by Mrs. Folger's cakes, which, to be sure, were good and frequent. But Laskell was not particular about his meals. He had been forbidden albuminous foods and this made a bond between him and Mrs. Folger, a fine relaxation about eggs. At his first breakfast, Mrs. Folger had approached him to open negotiations in the matter of eggs—her anxiety suggested a business no less large than that. When Laskell was able to say what was no more than the truth, that he was permitted to eat no eggs at all, Mrs. Folger twinkled at him with a deep appreciation of his moral fineness. He was better able to understand this when he learned that the money from the sale of eggs went into Mrs. Folger's own particular fund. It was a large consideration to her that he was not going to sequester and consume a dozen eggs a week. She offered Laskell eggs every morning and every morning Laskell affirmed his moral stature by refusing.

On the whole, Laskell liked Mrs. Folger very well. She was a gossip and a snob and she had a quick mind. She set a high value on intellectual prestige, having once in her girlhood taught school. Her relation to Laskell's intellectual life was continuous and strange. She often asked him about his work and his training for it, and once she asked him if he owned many books, but always in any such conversation she would interrupt in the midst of his reply and vanish with some remark about a household duty; and Laskell, who always entered these conversations with pleasure, happy to see how small, really, were the separations between the educated and the uneducated, had the impression that she was gratified by her ability to be heedless of this educated man. He disliked himself for having this idea. If he turned on the radio, she was pretty sure to say with sympathy and approval, "You do enjoy that good music, don't you?" and then with a casual word of apology she would turn the dial "to get the weather report," listening on the way to bits and snatches of other programs.

Within her question, "You do enjoy that good music, don't you?" there was concealed another question: "Do you really?" Laskell, who never had anything to say to Mrs. Folger when she turned the dial, had the less to say when it occurred to him that Mrs. Folger, all unknown to herself, resented his absorption in "that good music." He did not know whether she was jealous of the music or of him—whether her self-esteem was injured by the absorption that drew his attention so far from her, or whether she

resented his ability to be interested in something to which she
was indifferent. He found it painful to reflect that in our day intellect and sensibility, thought and art, had been made to confer
status and to generate snobbery.

There was no way for Laskell to express the irritation he had begun to feel at Mrs. Folger's interference when he listened to the
radio. But one day the situation was strangely cleared between
them. Laskell had made a stab at a station he could not usually get
and by some luck of atmospheric condition he broke into the re-
corded Glyndebourne performance of *The Marriage of Figaro*. It
was in full flight and nearing its end in the magical last scene
where farce moves to regions higher than tragedy can reach. He
saw the cloaked figures searching with lanterns in the dark shrub-
bery, the plots and disguises of the garden, everyone deceiving, no
one being the person he or she is taken for, and then all the dis-
coveries—

"Il paggio!
"Mia figlia!
"Mia madre!
"Madama!"

the recognitions coming with burlesque excess. The Countess
knelt to the Count to win pardon for all the miscreants and then
the Count understood that it was he who must ask pardon of her,
and asked it in the unimaginable gravity and grace of the aria
Contessa perdona, and then was seconded in his plea by the swell-
ing cathedral chorus of all the raffish, disguised characters, in
which supplication was made the lovelier by the certainty of its
acceptance. Laskell was listening to this, waiting for the chorus to
rise to the height from which the Countess would begin her reply,
she soaring higher still, almost beyond reach, to say that she was
too fond to do anything else than say yes; the Countess had just
begun her reply, raining down influence, when Mrs. Folger, who
had been standing in the doorway, went to the radio and turned
the dial.

There was a squawk and without thought Laskell cried, *"Mrs.
Folger! Leave it alone!"* His voice was so fierce that Mrs. Folger
quite started. She turned back the dial, but she missed the exact
point, and Laskell had to make the adjustment. By then the Count-

ess had finished her great flight, and the orchestra and the chorus were launched on the carnival march which winds up with a bang the whole absurd business of the opera, brushing aside all questions of guilt, rushing off to heedless life now that forgiveness had come.

Mrs. Folger was looking at him strangely, entirely without resentment of his burst of temper.

"I'm sorry I snapped that way," he said. "It's just that I'm particularly fond of that piece of music."

"Oh, that's all right. No offense whatever," said Mrs. Folger. Her eyes seemed mild and satisfied. "If you like something, you don't want anybody to interfere with it."

She seemed content and Laskell dated from this moment of sudden thoughtless anger a new ease in his relation to Mrs. Folger. She seemed much more pleased with him and trusted him more.

The question of intellectual standing interested Mrs. Folger very much, and more than once she turned the talk to Arthur Croom. Laskell found in the Folger parlor a copy of Arthur's book on business cycles with a warm inscription to the Folgers on the flyleaf, and Mrs. Folger moved about and about the question of whether or not it was a good book. She wanted to know what an Assistant Professor was. Did Arthur Croom, as an Assistant Professor, the status the title page announced, assist some "big" professor in his work? She was interested in the rewards of the intellectual life. Did Assistant Professors earn much money or little?— she had heard two accounts of the matter. She wanted to know if Nancy was an educated woman and if she worked or had ever worked. She made infinitely subtle appraisals of Laskell's feelings about the Crooms, probing with softest pressure of gentlest fingers for where the weak spot in the connection might be.

She could be forthright too, and she flounced and bridled and was charmingly animated when she gave him information about Emily Caldwell, whom he had seen on the road before the Crooms' but whom he had not yet met. Emily Caldwell's intellectual pretensions were the first matter of comment and then, what seemed connected, her manner of dress. Close upon these came Emily's self-indulgence, a certain affair of strawberry jam bought with relief money. It was an indiscretion made more culpable by Emily's remark when the question had come up. Emily had said, "Man cannot live by bread alone," a statement which seemed to claim scriptural authority for strawberry jam.

And all this was made the worse by other elements of Emily's questionable conduct. There was her openly expressed belief, for instance, that little boys and girls would do well to run around together with no clothes on at all. And then there was the statement she had made a few years back to Scott Tilden when he was still a boy in high school. She had said, and in front of listeners, "You have a beautiful body, Scott." And Scott had never been able to live that down. It was still a good way of getting him angry to remind him of it.

Mrs. Folger said she was willing to grant, as many people did, that Duck Caldwell was not all he might be, yet she wondered what he would have been like if he had had a different kind of wife to steady him up.

Laskell at first liked Mr. Folger rather less well than his wife, but then he knew Mr. Folger less well. There was a good deal of the bore about Mr. Folger, but he was an interesting bore. He had much eccentric dignity and a high manner. He carried irony very far, so far that he almost never communicated directly. When he talked, he sent his voice in some other direction than toward his listener, as if he intended it to reach its destination by ricochet. He liked to talk about the injustice that prevailed in the world. He read an odd little paper got out by an isolated socialist group in Hartford. When Laskell read the paper, he saw in his mind's eye pictures not of "workers" but of "workingmen." They wore square paper caps and aprons and carried hammers—honest workingmen they were. He had a kind of admiration and affection for the little group with its insistence on the honesty of the workingman and its flavor of William Morris and of meetings held on Sunday afternoons, its appearance of having discovered socialism for the first time and its implied refusal to mix itself up with extravagant foreigners, the red-revolutionaries of Paris and the Second International. He wondered in how many little communities throughout the state solitary men entrenched themselves in its doctrine and felt that they were holding the outworks.

Mr. Folger liked to talk against the interests, the gas and electric and water companies, which he thought should be owned by the public. When Laskell responded with the situation in housing, Mr. Folger seemed to prefer not to listen.

Although Mr. Folger put some of his time into a small truck patch and drove his three cows to pasture and milked them, his chief work was in connection with the big black limousine in which he drove Miss Walker, the elderly lady from Boston. Often Laskell overheard Mr. Folger talking to Miss Walker on the telephone and his attention was much engaged by the mixture of subservience and dominance that he heard in the voice of this big grave man. The irony was then all withdrawn, or perhaps it was operating at some deeper remove. Mrs. Folger showed Laskell the plans for the house that Miss Walker was to erect for the Folgers on her property, a modern, ugly, disguised house, with plumbing and all the kitchen conveniences. It was to bring Mr. Folger within easier reach, permitting him to look after Miss Walker's little estate.

When Nancy Croom said of the Folgers, "Aren't they wonderful?" Laskell could say yes. But his Folgers were not precisely the Folgers of Nancy's representation, and when he tried to suggest that there was a difference in their agreement, by inquiring about the relation to Miss Walker, Nancy drew back a little.

"Miss Walker is an old terror," she said. "A tyrannical old terror, and she exploits Mr. Folger dreadfully. He's at her beck and call. But they do need the money. They're not young any more. And for people like that to put a son through Harvard—"

It was the first Laskell had heard of that educational venture or indeed of that member of the Folger family. He could not help wondering what reticence had operated in so much talk of education.

And the exigencies of advancing age or the son at Harvard did not wholly explain the tone that Laskell heard, the quiet masculine voice of Mr. Folger talking to Miss Walker on the phone, the brilliantly subtle compound of humility and command, spiced with what was surely the special irony of the absence of Mr. Folger's characteristic irony. And when Mr. Folger turned from the phone after giving Miss Walker his advice about how to deal with a remiss contractor, his face would have the high, dignified impassivity of a great minister of state who gives to an aged queen not only his counsel and support but a supply of energy, even a touch of danger in her isolate life.

And in the supplying of Miss Walker with whatever it was that was supplied, Mrs. Folger had her own part. Her tone on the telephone made the offer of Mr. Folger to Miss Walker and yet kept the gift valuable by never relinquishing her hold upon it or diminishing its worth by any relaxation of admiration. Few husbands of Mr. Folger's age could have had the satisfaction of so much wifely regard as could be heard in the tone Mrs. Folger used when it was she who answered Miss Walker's call, the tenderness for his effort when she said that he was out in the barn but would call back presently, the adoration of certainty with which she could say, "Oh, yes, Miss Walker, he'll know just what to do about that." And the tender valuation was the same whether Mr. Folger was really out of the house or sitting there listening to the conversation.

It was not a duchy that was to be their reward, but they moved as gracefully and precisely as if it were. After all, in the proportion of the matter, something very like a duchy was at stake—there was the new house with its ugly saddle roof, its veranda and all modern conveniences, that Miss Walker was to build. Mrs. Folger spent much time choosing among the low-cost ingenuities suggested by the Department of Agriculture pamphlet. She and her husband preferred not to recognize that Laskell had any special knowledge about the planning of houses. The house was the crown of their life, the haven of their approaching old age. It was peculiarly theirs, its shape chosen by themselves from the offerings of an architectural catalogue, and they glazed over in polite inattention whenever Laskell, before he understood their feelings, made any comments save those of approval. The house, after all, was indeed their duchy, a thing of fairy tale, plucked from the unlikely chances of life. And the liveliness of their sense of the reward, their innocent, gentle skill in the affairs of court, made for Laskell a warm and interesting surrounding. The Folgers, he was always glad to say in answer to Nancy's question, were wonderful indeed.

But the Crooms were wonderful too. Any lingering tension, any repudiated vestige of reserve that Laskell may have felt after the episode at the station, quite vanished just before their first dinner together when Nancy asked him to step out of the cosmos. She was showing him her flower beds in the deepening twilight and suddenly she said, "I'll thank you, John, to step out of the cosmos." Unaware, he had put his foot into the bed of feathery cosmos shoots and had crushed several of them. Nancy stood bewildered while Arthur and John roared with laughter. This was just like Nancy. She was seldom consciously amusing but she was often amusing as an accident, so to speak, of her intense earnestness; and then, when the joke was greeted with laughter, she would look so bewildered, even a little apologetic. It was a manner that Laskell found very endearing. "I'll thank you to step out of the cosmos" became a communal joke, their family witticism, the formula when any two of them met coming opposite ways through the kitchen door, or when there was any disagreement in discussion.

Laskell had never before fully known how much pleasure and confidence his affection for Nancy and Arthur could give him. Now, as they went about their daily vacation lives, the mere sight and sound of them was salutary to him. The certainty of their relation to each other was a tangible thing. When they differed about some trifle and got a little hot at each other, the sputter of their disagreement was but the underscoring of their connection. They lost their tempers but never their love. And Laskell, seeing them in their passion and their reason, felt that his two friends were really a justification of human existence. He could think of them in terms quite as large as that.

His sense of what they meant came to Laskell from small things. It might be suggested by Arthur leaving his writing to come down to work about the house or the lawn, moving with complete simplicity from the intellectual to the physical, from the theoretical to the most tangible practicality. Or it might be made clear by Nancy caring for Micky so firmly and simply, or directing Eunice in her tending of the child, ignoring so well the difference in education between herself and the girl, and this in the face of a certain reserve on Eunice's part, or by Nancy sitting with her marketing list, muttering to herself in housewifely perplexity. This was the same girl who so passionately had at heart the injustices of the world, who spoke so spiritedly of oppression—of the Negroes and Jews at home, of the colonial peoples, of the imprisoned and tortured libertarians abroad.

Laskell, watching Nancy absorbed, say, in the planning of a meal, her pencil in her mouth to help her think, was inclined to believe that the middle class, for all its failures, so many and so apparent, could yet produce the models for the human virtue of the future. He even approached a theory of this, not taking it too seriously yet finding a kind of dialectical confirmation in it, that from a decaying class or culture would come the seeds of the future. Certainly he could want nothing better for the world than what the Crooms suggested. He could want nothing better than this much sturdiness and this much grace, this much passion and this much reason, this much personal concern and this much involvement in large affairs. Perhaps anything that attempted to be better than this would cease to be truly human.

The Crooms took Laskell in and cherished him. At times they no more noticed him than they noticed each other. They had their bursts of irritation before him and their casual matter-of-fact reconciliations. They took him shopping and gave him lists to fill to lighten their work. It was a matter of course that he should set the table when he came to dinner and that he would help with the dishes afterward. Once the thought came to him that an unmarried man in such a relation to married friends was in danger of becoming neuter and dull, a *Hausfreund*. But it was not possible to hold for long so conventional and damaging an idea, not under the liveliness of the Crooms' interest and the constant excitement of their unremitting talk.

The three of them talked endlessly. They talked university matters and housing matters and the situation in Washington, they talked child-rearing and usually from there they went on to exchange anecdotes of their own childhoods, trying to explain how they had become the people they were today. Again and again they returned to politics, not so much its theory as its gossip. Yet often as they talked of their friends, Laskell did not tell the story of Gifford Maxim's visit, which was surely a very special piece of political gossip. Several times Nancy referred to something that Maxim had said to her, speaking of him with the respect that Maxim was

almost always given. Laskell could feel his heart quickening out of
all proportion to the occasion. "Speaking of Maxim," he could have
said, or, "Since you mention Maxim." But he rejected each of these
occasions.

Sometimes he believed that he was not telling the story to the
Crooms because he wanted to spare them the pain and confusion the story was likely to give them, or that he was sparing himself the story's dark implications. But he knew that the real reason
for his not telling the story was the other thing that they did not
talk about. They did not talk about Laskell's illness or about his
having been so near death.

The Crooms were wonderful, but now and then Laskell did
find himself regarding them with curiosity, even with resentment.
He thought that he had settled with himself, the evening of his
arrival, the matter of his impulse and his right to tell them about
his illness. But he had not settled it. And as the days went by,
he wondered why it should have to be settled. There was nothing wrong in having been sick, in nearly dying. It was an experience like any other. It could be talked about. Certainly among
friends it could be talked about. But the Crooms would not talk
about it. They withdrew themselves in a polite, intelligent, concerted way whenever Laskell mentioned it, as if they were the
parents of a little boy and were following the line of giving no
heed to the obscenities their son had picked up on the street and
insisted on bringing to the dinner table. They did not scold, for
that would have been to confirm him in his naughtiness, in what
was presumably an effort to get attention. They simply, in a sensible
modern way, paid no attention at all.

They might all three be walking in the dusk and Nancy might
comment on the quiet of the countryside and Laskell would then
speak of his sense of the quiet of the city at night as he had lain
in bed. At that the whole subject of quiet would come to an end.
At another time he tried to tell them something about Paine.
They liked Paine—they said they had made a point of calling his
apartment in the evening because Paine was so much more satisfactory to talk to than that other nurse, that Miss Debry. But
it was Paine they insisted on having in mind, not what Laskell
had felt about Paine. Toward this they maintained the attitude

that it was but a sick fancy of their friend, which, for his own sake, they preferred not to hear about. Or the matter of dogs once came up, whether or not Micky should have a dog in a year or two, and Laskell asked about Dr. Graf's bulldog, which had so surprised him. In a precise way the Crooms gave what information they could about the bulldog and hurried on to keep Dr. Graf himself from becoming the subject of conversation.

As the days went on and this became unmistakably a settled policy of the Crooms, Laskell felt a clear and distinct annoyance.

It did not change all his other feelings toward the Crooms, and he did not cherish or nurse it, but whenever one of their stubborn disciplinary silences occurred he had a little flicker of anger. He was angry because they were forcing him to tell himself that there really had been nothing wrong in his having been sick and nearly dying. The Crooms, when the situation was present and critical, had taken care of everything. They had provided him with Dr. Graf and the two nurses, with sufficient sheets and pajamas and oranges. They had seen to every practical detail of his illness. But now, when he wanted to tell them just what it was that they had helped him go through and what it was that they had helped him escape, they did not want to hear. Nancy had handed him over like a sick boy to Mrs. Folger to take care of, to keep from being a nuisance. And there, she insisted, her relationship to his illness ended.

Laskell had to recognize that his not telling about Maxim had in it an element of sulky revenge—if he might not tell about what he wanted to tell, he would not tell about what the Crooms would want to hear. But more decisive than this was his determination that the only way he could tell the story of Maxim was to make it part of the story of his illness. Without the account of what he had felt during those weeks in bed, the story of Maxim would lack the particular force it had in his mind.

But, after all, the Crooms' strange refusal to listen to what he wanted to say modified very little Laskell's sense of the Crooms' wonderfulness. His feeling about it was isolated, encysted from the rest of his feelings, and he even came to regard it with what he thought was amusement. He was very happy in his long peaceful country days with his friends.

Early one evening, about a week after his arrival, Laskell was sitting on the lawn with the Crooms and he saw the same sight that had so enchanted him the day of his arrival. Emily Caldwell and her daughter came up the road for water. Emily stopped, seeing them on the lawn. She set the empty pails on the stone wall and leaned over them as if to achieve some intimacy. She said, "I'll return the book tonight, if I may."

She spoke the word "book" as though it were a secret and a bond between herself and the Crooms. Her voice was cultivated and even perhaps a little affected, with a rather pleasant hoarse note.

"Oh Lord!" Nancy said under her breath. And she said in a whisper to Laskell, "That's so she can meet you."

Arthur, with a warning glance to Nancy, said aloud, "Did you like it?"

"Simply wonderful!" Emily Caldwell said. "Just wonderful." Then she went on her way up the hill with her daughter.

"That's Emily Caldwell," Arthur explained. "Duck's wife."

"He knows," Nancy said.

"Yes," said Laskell. "Nancy told me."

"Our Little Emily," said Nancy. "Our Emily Dickinson Caldwell. Our Emily Brontë Caldwell. Above all our Emily Bovary Caldwell."

"Isn't it Emma Bovary, not Emily?" Arthur asked.

"Yes, dear—Emma, not Emily," said Nancy with an irony appropriate to such dull literalness in a husband. "She's such a bore."

"She's good-looking, isn't she?" Laskell said. For some reason he felt sorry and deprived. The woman no longer had the mythological glow she had had when, in the confusion of his arrival, he had first seen her. But she still had the charm of a woman seen at a distance. "Where does she go for her water?" he said.

"Up the road to the Polish family, the Korzinskis," Nancy said.

"For heaven's sake, why doesn't she get her water here?"

"Habit," Nancy replied tersely.

Arthur laughed. "And not a habit our Nancy is going to help her break." He looked at his wife affectionately. Then he said to Laskell in a reasonable voice, "Actually she's quite sweet. Emily, I mean. She's a little silly and pretentious—"

But Nancy was in a most absolute mood. "A little!" she said. "She's so unreal. She's as unreal—as—as—" But there was no measure that Nancy could find for Emily Caldwell's unreality, not until she said, "She's as unreal as Duck is real."

"Granting that Duck is worth six Emilys," said Arthur.

"Six!" said Nancy, astonished at Arthur's conservative estimate.

Laskell wanted to say that Duck might be very real, but that in point of fact he had not materialized when he had been most wanted. Now he could say it humorously. But Nancy was continuing and the moment for the remark passed.

"She's cheap Village, cheap Provincetown, quaint tearoom. She did run a tearoom once, as a matter of fact."

"It's not exactly a penitentiary offense, Nan." But Arthur liked to see his wife pitched high and angry.

"Yes, it is! At least she ought to be penitent. I suppose I'm silly, but sometimes it does get me mad, in a world like this, to see that foolish display of temperament. I suppose she'd call it individualism. She was born in 1912—spiritually I mean—and she died in 1930, and she doesn't know it yet."

"That's true," said Arthur with the cheerful dogged resistance of one who knows the world and understands that it cannot be just as one would like. "That's all true. But then why can't you think of her as I do?—as an historical monument, like a castle overgrown by time? Going on about her the way you do is like getting into a passion against feudalism."

"I suppose so," Nancy said. She sat there, gloomily considering her lack of historical perspective. Then she declared a feminine independence of such high considerations. "But I can't help it. She affronts something in me. Don't you feel the same way, John?"

"You'd better, John," said Arthur. "Or else you'll just have to step out of the cosmos. Nancy will have no two ways about this matter." He rumpled his wife's hair. "Will you, Nan?"

"You'll agree when you meet her," Nancy said and took her head from under Arthur's hand.

And Nancy was right. By the time Emily Caldwell had ended her visit that evening Laskell was permitted to step back into the cosmos. Emily came with the book—that precious book—and Laskell saw her with a simple and objective eye, as Nancy saw her. In that view she was not so handsome as she had first seemed in the golden dust of the road, nor did she have anything like the significance that distance and confusion had lent her. And there was no doubt that she was, as Nancy had said, affected and foolish.

Emily Caldwell took the cigarette Arthur politely offered her and awkwardly accepted a light. She held the cigarette with a certain conscious delicacy, as if she attached importance to smoking but was not used to it. She was not at ease, yet she seemed glad to be here. She held the borrowed book on her lap, the explanation and talisman of her visit. It was one of the two volumes of Spengler's *Decline of the West*. The evening was cool and there was a fire in the new fireplace. For a moment she watched it with a critical gaze, protecting her shyness by an act of intelligence.

"I'm so glad you decided to have a fireplace," she said. "It finishes the room so well. There really isn't anything like a good fire!"

She caught herself, for even before the phrase was fully out she was making a quick satirical flourish with her hand, as if to put quotation marks around her sad, worn cliché. But the gesture was too late and the self-protection was so transparent that Laskell felt embarrassed for her.

Between the remark and the gesture there lay a whole cultural generation, that is, a full decade. Emily Caldwell had come to her freedom and maturity when that remark about fires was good current coin. Laskell could see her in shabby Greenwich Village rooms which were made desirable by nothing save their cheapness and a fireplace. He could hear her saying, just before a new lover took her hand preparatory to kissing her, "There really isn't anything like a good fire!" The absurd little sentence would be assurance, the sign of a kindred spirit, an invitation to comradeship. And the fire itself would be a symbol of revolt and of purification, of comfort and asceticism, to those who watched it and warmed themselves by it, not the less because it meant escape from the life of steam-heat and from the shape of cast-iron radiators.

Emily Caldwell then said in a brisk, practical way, "It does draw well, doesn't it? I think Duck did a very nice job on it." She cocked her head and looked at the fireplace severely.

Nancy and Arthur hastened to agree with her. "It's a grand job," Arthur said. "There's nothing harder to build than a good flue."

"Oh, Duck does a good job with everything," Emily said. Her voice had pride in it, yet it was judicious. Her statement limited itself precisely. It did not go an inch beyond approval of Duck's craftsmanship. Yet there was no vulgar hint of an intended disapproval of her husband. There might even have been a depreciation in it that came from great pride. But perhaps that was not it, for she said to Laskell, "I'm sorry Duck missed you when he was supposed to call for you."

Laskell had the sense of Nancy's tightened attention. He said, "Not at all, it was nothing."

Arthur said, "The station man told Duck that the train would be half an hour late."

"Oh, *Duck!*" said Emily Caldwell. She moved her hand in tolerant dismissal. "Duck can get himself told anything he wants to be told."

The sentence was difficult to deal with. They could not say, "Duck can*not* get himself told anything he wants to be told." So Arthur contented himself with saying with some stubbornness, "Duck's all right." And so as not to seem contentious, he smiled at her to show that he knew that that was her opinion too.

But Emily Caldwell was no longer interested in her husband. She had taken out of her large raffia bag a painted wooden bowl which she held out to Nancy. "Do you like this?" she asked. "I'm making several for the Bazaar."

Nancy held the bowl at arm's length and examined it with appropriate gravity and for a sufficient time. It was a chopping bowl, small and sturdy, and on its inner surface had been painted a bold "unconventional" design in strong red and blue. "It's very nice," Nancy said. "What's it supposed to be for?"

"Oh—walnuts. Or fruit. Anything you want. Decoration mostly." Mrs. Caldwell waved aside the question of function with an airy indifference. "It's just a *bowl*," she said, as though she had just this moment discovered its principle. "I'm doing three of these small ones and one large one." She said to Laskell, "You must come to the Bazaar, Mr. Laskell. It's our summer Church Bazaar." Her tone was that of a person offering a visitor an interesting and significant sight, an opportunity to observe the local habits.

Nancy was still trying to be pleasant about the bowl. She was studying it as though searching out the true quality of its design. Actually the design, for all its boldness, was a dull one, and whatever aesthetic value it had came from the memory of the time when the designs of Leon Bakst were startling. Laskell knew that Nancy was comparing the painted bowl with what it had looked like before Emily Caldwell had got to work on it, seeing the plain wood before the sticky color had been applied, remembering the bowl when it had existed only for its function and not as a mere ornament or as the ground for the display of Emily Caldwell's creativity, as doubtless she called it.

"It's been years since I've done any work like that," Emily said. "It's nice to get back. What do you think I ought to charge? I thought fifty cents for the small ones and a dollar for the big one."

"Well," said Nancy judiciously, "if you think people can pay that much." And she added, as if Mrs. Caldwell were the summer visitor, "You know, cash is scarce in a farming community."

"Oh, for hand work!" Mrs. Caldwell said.

And with that she rose to go. "Good night, Mr. Laskell," she said. "I hope our air does you good." The manner was good "social" manner and quite of the city. Then she said, "Good night, all," and was again wholly of the country. She turned to go and was almost at the door when she cried, "Oh, the *book!*" and was back in the circle. "Isn't that just like me?" she said. "I *came* to return the book and here I am going off with it in my hand." And she reached out to Arthur the great black volume.

"Thank you so much," she said. "It's a wonderful thing. It's so much there." She seemed to attach an importance to the adverb. "Are you acquainted with it, Mr. Laskell?"

"Yes, I am."

"Don't you think it's wonderful?"

How could he explain that for this book a vocabulary of discussion had existed a few years ago and had then died? For all intelligent people of good will, this book, once seductive in its vision of tragedy, now existed only as a curiosity or a bad example, the early symptom of a disease which was now a terrible reality. There had been a time when it had been attractive because it expressed the modern alienation in the largest possible way, but now it was known to be entirely reactionary because it cut off all hope of the future.

Amused, the Crooms watched Laskell groping for an answer. Now he knew what it was like to have to deal with Emily Caldwell. Laskell's first impulse was to dismiss the matter with irony, but he checked that. The *Untergang des Abendlandes*—the down-going of the evening-land. He remembered all the political sins that Spengler had committed in his book, and then his later political declaration, ambiguous but sufficiently bad. And yet, he thought, perhaps we hate the book because it has so hideous a possibility of being true, and we hate the man who wrote it as in our hearts we would blame the physician who told us of our unknown but suspected disease.

But while he was searching for the language in which to explain to Emily Caldwell the error of her admiration, she said, "Doom! A vision of doom!" She made the great syllable vibrate. And neither he nor anybody else could have anything to answer to that. She went on, " 'My name is Ozymandias, King of Kings. Look on my works, ye Mighty, and despair.' 'The Lion and the Lizard keep the courts where Jamshyd gloried and drank deep.' If ever there was a lesson to live your life, to snatch the moment, because the cycles just keep on and on, and in the end what does anyone ever have except just perhaps a little fleeting moment of happiness? How does it go?—'A little light in all this darkness, a little warmth in all this cold.' Spring, Summer, Autumn, Winter—we are in the Autumn cycle. And Megalopolis—the great grim city, how well do I know *that!*"

There was nothing to say to her. She held them silent with her tags of poetry and her scraps from Spengler's wicked book from which she had taken only what suited her small purpose. For a moment Laskell remembered how, at his first glimpse of her, she had appeared in a character which made it not inappropriate that she should speak of the cycles of the seasons, the seasons of decay and barrenness as well as the seasons of hope and fullness. And he thought of winter as he used to think of it when he was a boy and as he had been recalling it as he lay in bed in the morning at the Folgers'—with its meaning of adventure and courage and more and more awareness of the charms of safety and warmth than any other season, and, really, a surer though more brooding sense of himself.

It was Arthur Croom, with his pedagogic tact, who came to their rescue. He looked at Emily Caldwell seriously, as he would at some eager but mistaken student who must be set right without hurt feelings. "Do you really, Emily, do you really believe with Spengler that man is nothing but a puppet of the cycles of culture? That man can never make his own fate and that he is passive to the will of forces which he can see but not control, and that his civilization rises only to reach decay?"

He was so serious as he thrust forward his ugly face for his answer, and really so kind in his assumption of his professional role, that Emily Caldwell was not wholly confused by the extent of his challenge.

"Well!" she said vigorously.

It meant nothing more than her wish to indicate that she was still intellectually present and intended to cope with the question. She stood there, and Laskell could see her intellect struggling among emotions that were so much stronger than itself, trying to arrange them for an answer.

"Well!" she said again. And then the recollection of an old trick of argument came to her help. "Just what," she said craftily, "just what do you mean by 'passive'?"

So far as she herself was concerned, the trick worked—at any rate, no one answered her. She followed up her success with magnanimity. "Oh, why should I argue with you, Mr. Croom?—you're so learned and all. I just say what I feel."

Nancy should not have interfered. It was not an intellectual situation, only a social one, and it seemed to have been settled. "When actually," Nancy said, "history shows that man is dialectically developing and improving himself all the time. There is no limit to his potentialities."

Emily Caldwell did what always lends at least some dignity to a face—she lowered her eyes. She stood there for a moment with her eyes down and her face quiet. "But not for the individual person, Mrs. Croom. For mankind in general, I suppose you're right. But for the individual— No, there I disagree with you. There it is dark. And any light and joy—"

"But don't you think," said Nancy, and did not see Arthur's frown to her, "but don't you think, Mrs. Caldwell, that we should learn to think in terms of mankind in general?"

"I suppose so," Emily Caldwell said. Nancy's proposition was so large that Emily's indifference to it was monumental. "I suppose so. But my motto is, 'Carpe diem.'" Having produced this new tag, she expounded it to them. "'Snatch the day,'" she said, "'and put very little trust in tomorrow.'" And then she said, "'Carpe diem: quam minimum credula postera.'" It astonished them all, Emily Caldwell herself as much as the others, for she clapped her hand over her mouth as if she had uttered some small impropriety. "Goodness!" she said. "Latin! I used to love it when I was a girl. What a crazy thing I was! And here I am talking when I have so many things to do!"

Then her eyes shone with mischief and she said, "'Dum loquimur, fugerit invida aetas—even while we stand here talking, envious time is speeding on.'"

She took up her raffia bag. "Good night, all," she said again, prettily and rurally, and was gone.

"Goodness!" said Nancy.

She made a gesture of despair, turning up her open hands. "Now you see what I mean, John."

"It's sort of touching." And Laskell had been curiously touched. But he saw what Nancy meant. The woman was a fool. Certainly she was not what she had appeared on the road that first afternoon.

"Touching? Oh, maybe. All that dated, foolish hedonism. It's really awful."

Nancy got up and with her elbow on the low mantle stood looking down into the fire, glowing with a kind of moral passion, even with a political passion. The set of her strong young body, the clear line of her chin, the intense energy of her head were to Laskell at that moment full of promise for the world. He was glad to be at one with Nancy, young and hard and realistic.

"With her scraps of Latin. And then when I think of her condescending to Duck, who's so real—" And Nancy shook her head in exasperation and gave up the subject.

Laskell wished that she had given it up a moment before. Her point had been entirely made without the mention of Duck to muddy the clear sense of futurity he had. But Duck or no Duck, the point had been sufficiently made.

So that one morning, a few days later, when Laskell was walking from the Folgers' to the Crooms' and was greeted by Emily Caldwell and invited in to inspect her odd little house, he accepted because there was no way of refusing, but he accepted with the sense of somehow going back on a pledge to Nancy.

Emily Caldwell had been crouching down at a flower bed in the dry soil. She stood up smiling, trowel in hand, her feet apart, and she looked strong and firmly rooted, yet her legs were slim. Laskell was struck again, quite against his will, by the illusion of dignity created by her coronet of copious braids. Her good morning was bright, with a rising, conscious inflection. "Did you sleep well?" she asked. "Can I give you a cup of coffee? I'd like you to see my house." It was impossible to say no.

The Caldwell house was a tiny thing, strangely shaped, apparently two sheds brought together. It was painted a rich thick green except for the window sashes and the door, which were a bright red. The color scheme did indeed suggest that Emily Caldwell had once had a connection with a tearoom. Yet Laskell had to admit that it was very gay.

Emily held the screen door open for Laskell and he entered a little room. It narrowed to an alcove just large enough to hold a crude sink and a small stove. He had never seen so compact a place. There was something about the room that was very taking. It had the charm of a snug nest or hide-out, such living-nooks as Dickens describes, or a Pullman compartment.

"I'm so proud of the house, I must show it to you. This was an old tool house, you know. Of course it had no windows except that one." Emily pointed to a tiny window over the stove.

"I had all the windows put high—like that." And she made him look at the front wall. Laskell saw then what gave the room its strange distinction. The windows had been cut high, in a long narrow rank. They went across the top of the little wall with authority and elegance.

"In that way," she said. "I saved all the wall-space underneath for cupboards." The cupboards rose to half the height of the wall and made a shelf on which were vases of flowers, a few books, a sewing basket, and three wooden bowls of the sort that Emily Caldwell had brought to the Crooms on her visit.

"And beyond is the bedroom." She darted through the little cooking space and opened a tiny box of a room. "And here is Susan's room," she said. "And now you've seen all my little castle."

"It's charming," Laskell said. And it was.

"Do you like the windows? The windows are a scandal."

"Why, they're not, they're very well designed."

"So *you* think, and so *I* think." Emily Caldwell was delighted. "So *we* think. But the neighbors don't think so. Oh, dear, no. Who ever heard of windows put there? Windows were made to go up and down, like a guillotine, and they're supposed to be low. I haven't yet heard the end of it. The people around here are dear good people, but oh, they are so *sot* in their ways."

Laskell felt that an appeal was being made to him for some kind of partisanship. And he did not want to give it—the more because at that moment Emily Caldwell felt a strand of hair upon her cheek and put it back in place, using both hands and raising her arms in a full graceful movement which made Laskell suddenly aware of her physical and feminine existence.

"Take for example," she was saying, still at work on the strand of hair, "the whole business of diet. The oranges, for example. I brought up the matter in the Ladies' Auxiliary. Well, of course, in a sense, I was the last person to bring up the matter of oranges, with us taking relief. I said that oranges for children were necessary and that I for one always saw to it that my Susan got one orange a day."

Laskell found that he was noting this example of sensible, practical, and communal activity and was referring it to Nancy on Emily Caldwell's behalf.

"The remarks," she went on. "The remarks that were made about oranges! And strawberry jam!" Laskell knew something about the strawberry jam.

"You see," she explained, "I once bought myself a jar of strawberry jam and they've never gotten over it. It was an impulse."

And she looked at him with so much confidence that he would feel the whole explanatory force of this word that her face seemed suddenly full of innocence.

"An impulse," she repeated. "I suddenly *wanted* strawberry jam. What would life be like if you didn't act on impulse now and then? Of course, if you're on relief— Well, they made out that oranges and strawberry jam were on the same level and that it was pretty cheeky of me to go preaching to them about luxuries. I told them that man cannot live on bread alone. They thought I meant that you had to have strawberry jam on your bread. But you can't imagine how much farinaceous food they eat with no vitamins. Potatoes and rice *and* spaghetti, all at the same meal."

From his stay with Mrs. Folger, Laskell knew that this could be true.

Emily Caldwell, before she dropped the subject, said, "And the way they cook the spaghetti!"

She was remembering the ritualistic spaghetti of her past. It came after the antipasto and soup and before the veal scallopine at some Guido's or Neapolitan Gardens, all thick and rich with to-mato sauce, the whole cheap, decent Italian dinner that main-tained the life of art.

The door was suddenly thrown open and his hostess's daughter stood on the threshold. She surveyed the visitor with calm surprise. Emily Caldwell's eyes brightened. She reached out a hand to the child and said, "Susan dear, this is Mr. Laskell."

Susan paused for a moment, put her hand in her mother's, and, moving a step forward, laid the other in Laskell's. The movement was like that of a dancer in a chain-figure. She looked straight into Laskell's eyes and searched them and said, "How do you do, Mr. Laskell."

Her thin face was tan and lightly freckled and she held her head high on her long neck. If there was a kind of shyness in her manner, it was the shyness of an animal, impersonal. It had noth-ing to do with anything she thought either about herself or about Laskell. And the shyness played but a small part in her deport-ment, for Laskell was suddenly aware of a happy feeling, and, look-ing for its cause, he saw that Susan was regarding him not merely with curiosity but with pleasure. He was confused, for the child's regard was very direct and he did not know how to respond to it. The force of the grave eyes was more than he could sustain with grace, and he acted falsely. He said, "How do you do, Susan?"

with a kind of teasing severity which somehow made her own poised air a little ridiculous.

"I promised Mr. Laskell a cup of coffee, Susan," said Emily. "Go get it for him, there's a dear."

Laskell, caught for a longer visit, sat down. Susan went back into the little galley and returned with a great cup of black coffee on a tin tray with a bowl of sugar and a can of evaporated milk.

"Do you mind evaporated milk? We have no cream," Emily said.

"I take it black," Laskell said, and helped himself to sugar.

"I might have known!" Emily Caldwell cried. "Just like me. Coffee is my nectar and ambrosia, my great dissipation. I drink cups and cups. And black, black."

It was a bore to have the coffee made into another symbol of the free life, but it was strong and fragrant coffee. Laskell took out his cigarettes and offered them to Mrs. Caldwell. Now that he was here, he might as well make the best of it. A look passed between the mother and the daughter as Emily Caldwell took a cigarette. Susan's eyes shone with excitement. Emily tapped the cigarette with determination on the arm of her wicker chair. Susan was ready with a match and her mother drew a deep inhalation and let it out slowly while the daughter watched each movement with pleasure and suspense. She said, "Oh, you do it wonderfully, mother."

Emily Caldwell was pleased and flustered by her daughter's praise. She looked young and Laskell saw that she was quite young —certainly far younger than she was made to seem by her addiction to the outworn attitudes and symbols of her youth, now so thoroughly passed by in the march of events.

Suddenly Susan said to Laskell, "Are you a writer?"

Laskell checked the adult facetiousness that was about to color his answer. He also checked any modification that might confuse the young questioner. He said, simply and casually, "Yes, I am."

"Do you starve?"

The question came as a surprise, but Laskell quickly understood. "Do you think all writers starve?" he asked. For it was apparent that the child did think something like that. "No, I'm afraid I eat with great regularity."

Susan looked dashed and puzzled. "Mother says that all the best writers starve. It's good for them, then they can never become satisfied."

She turned her head to take in her mother's face, and Emily Caldwell looked guilty. But Laskell came to her support. "There's a good deal in what your mother says," he said seriously. "Very often it's true. But I'm lucky, you see. I inherited some money, and then I make money from the other work I do. You see, I'm not only a writer. I don't really think of myself as entirely a writer."

"Are you satisfied?"

"Do you mean, so that I don't try to do better? No, I think not."

The answer seemed to give Susan reassurance. She said expansively, "And then you can help the others. The poor ones who don't have any money or a job, like you."

"Oh," said Laskell. "Of course." At the moment he could wish that a little of the money that had gone to committees and leagues had gone to some individual Marcel, to some Rudolph for his ailing Mimi with cold hands.

"Then you don't have so much money left and that keeps you from losing your—inspiration?" Susan directed the question to her mother to see if she had used the right word.

"Of course, it doesn't make so much difference with me whether or not I have money," Laskell said to get himself out of his false position. "Perhaps it's more important for poets and other creative writers. But you see, when I do write, I'm just a critic of other people's work."

This, he thought, would perhaps save both the fact and the myth, but there was Susan staring at him with frightened, almost horrified eyes.

"Susan thinks she'd like to be a writer," Emily Caldwell said.

"Or maybe a painter," Susan said, modifying almost mechanically, for she was not thinking about her future. And with a great effort, steeling herself, she confronted Laskell. "Are you really a critic? Mother says critics make life miserable for people."

Laskell saw what he had done and how far the myth had gone. He saw the old romantic regimen of the artistic life, the starvation in the garret, the pawned overcoat, the pure flame of the ideal which, everlastingly tended, kept the poet somehow warm, the gay loves and generous comradeships, the shared stews and the simple wine of the people, the grim implacable critic whose word was law and fame and fortune, that word spoken for some lucky and deserving few, the unselfish joy of friends and then the danger, the terrible danger of success, of satisfaction, of loss of inspiration, and then the question: who were the truly fortunate ones, the truly successful ones—those who had reached fortune, or those who had been kept in the old, deprived life?

It was a touching and generous dream, and it occurred to Laskell how much of the desire to be an "artist" was not so much the wish to do a particular kind of thing, but rather the desire to be a particular kind of person, to live a life of sentience and morality. It was one of the disciplines of virtue, like chivalry or courtly love or religion.

But he had to make haste to set himself right with Susan. "I'm not that kind of critic, Susan," he said. "Mostly I write about technical books. And when I write about art it's about the art of people who are dead."

This seemed to Susan a sufficiently benign function and she relented.

Emily Caldwell said, "Yes, Susan wants to be a writer. But first she's going to college. Aren't you, Susan?"

"Yes, to Vassar or to Smith's."

"Smith, dear."

"Smith."

"If she can get a scholarship. Some day I must speak to Mr. Croom—Professor Croom, I suppose I should say."

"I think maybe I'll be a dancer," Susan said.

"Indeed? Isn't that a new idea?"

"Yes. But I think I would like to be one—a dancer."

"Well, perhaps," said Emily. She said it with a kind of stiffness and a shadow passed over her face. Laskell wondered why dancing —or the dance, as she would no doubt call it—should seem to Emily Caldwell so much less noble than the other arts.

"Professor Croom is quite an influential man, I suppose," Emily Caldwell said.

But her voice was not simple and frank, it had plans in it, and Laskell said coolly, "Oh, more or less."

The subject was not pursued. Laskell rose to go.

"May I walk with you?" Susan said. "Just part of the way?" And having asked the question of Laskell, she looked doubtfully at her mother.

Emily Caldwell neither gave permission nor withheld it. Laskell could not keep down the absurd pride at having his company claimed by a child, one who, as it appeared, expected him to walk with her hand in hand, for she put her hand in his.

They were nearly at the road when Susan's mother caught up with them. "Please be careful not to walk too fast—the hill is very steep."

It presumed on a very short and not wholly satisfactory acquaintance and Laskell said brusquely, "I'm really quite well now."

"Oh!" said Emily Caldwell. "Oh, yes!" She was much confused, and Laskell was sorry for the sharp way he had answered. For, after all, her caution could only have been friendly.

4

Mrs. Folger took the fourth cup-and-saucer from the china-closet and placed it carefully on the table before Laskell, having first turned over the cup to look at its bottom. No collector who haunted the little shops for Meissen or Royal Dresden could have handled the cup with more awareness of its charm. It was English and of the eighteenth century, as were all the other three. It was the most beautiful of the four and therefore kept for the last. Of a fine, soft white with a floral pattern of intense green, it was wide and low-slung, quite perfect in its shape.

"I suppose they had sets of them and used them for everyday," Mrs. Folger said. "Imagine! And all I have left is one of each. And this plate."

She reached into the closet for the plate. Because Laskell was still admiring the cups she did not intrude it on his notice but sat down and kept it out of sight until he should have done.

All the cups were now before them on the table and they looked at them together in a community of respect.

"This one is cute, without any handle at all," Mrs. Folger said, and she touched the rim of a very small cup, octagonal in shape and made without a handle in imitation of a Chinese cup.

"That's the way the Chinese made their cups—without a handle at all," Laskell said.

Mrs. Folger did not particularly notice this piece of information.

The cups sat there with their air of having temperaments and minds of their own, each one not merely with its own shape but even with its own expression. They were not at all passive but looked back at their observers.

"Yes, that one is very nice, but I think I like this one even better," Laskell said, and pointed to the last of the cups.

They sat for a few moments in admiration. It was true that Mrs. Folger wanted an ugly new house and that she interrupted him ruthlessly when he listened to music. But over the teacups they were quite at one. How much, Laskell thought, I am involved these days with women and their housekeeping prides!

"They are the only old things I have, that have come down to me," Mrs. Folger said modestly, "except this," and she put the plate down before Laskell.

It was a scalloped plate, with a small gray vignette islanded in a sea of dimmed white, a heavyish ware, not delicate. The vignette was of a solitary man musing in a rural scene. It was clear that he was musing—one knew from the position of his walking stick, which he held behind him. There was an elm and a church, and there was a stream with a small bridge. The man was short and stocky, and he was plainly dressed, with a broad hat, as befits one who pauses to muse. He was no doubt a Solitary Traveller who had come home to his native place, and the representation of him was pleasantly funny, he was so solemn and self-conscious, yet he was so much part of the time in which he had been conceived and executed that he had all the elegiac dignity that his artist could ever have wished for. Time had given the work what the artist himself could not. The little man on the plate, standing there with his thoughts, his musings, his meditations—they were surely meditations on the Transitoriness of Human Life or on the Ruins of Empire or some such admired subject of his period—was a very solid little figure of a man, his small personality both compact and free.

"It's very nice," said Laskell.

"But I think the cups are nicer," said Mrs. Folger.

Laskell looked again at the cups. Sitting with Mrs. Folger over her precious pieces of china, taking pleasure in the objects and seeing life in them, Laskell was happy in the mild relationship with this worn, elderly woman who was so far removed from his usual existence. As he sat in the dim, damp dining-room he had a strong emotion about the life in objects, the shapes that people make and admire, the life in the pauses in activity in which nothing is said but in which the commonplace speaks out with a mild, reassuring force.

There was now nothing more to say about the cups and the plate. He said, "What sort of man is Duck Caldwell?"

It was only after he had spoken that he realized that the eighteenth century had worked upon him precisely the effect it had chosen as its own—he was trying to turn reason and common sense upon the one thing now in his mind that was extravagant and merely personal. Nancy and Arthur saw Duck Caldwell as a high manifestation of ordinary life and as such he gave them a moral pleasure, much as the teacups and plate gave Laskell pleasure. But Laskell saw Duck as not at all part of the daily normality and took not the slightest pleasure in him. It was absurd that he should have any opinion of Duck, for he had never spoken to the man. Yet he not only had an opinion, but a very intense one—try though he did to invalidate it. He believed that he had subtracted all feeling against Duck for not having met the train. What had happened on the Crannock station platform was not really Duck's fault. All that Duck could be held responsible for was the fretful impatience that another guest of the Crooms might have had if he had been left to stand on the platform when he expected to be met, or that Laskell himself might have had at some other time. Duck could be blamed only for having caused inconvenience; Laskell alone was responsible for the terror. And as, with the passing of time, the memory of that meaningless terror became less and less sharp, became nothing more than a rather abstract recollection of pain and the judgment that it was the worst experience he or any man could have, Laskell could more easily suppose that in his opinion of Duck the incident at the station had no part at all. Yet he not only disliked Duck but feared him.

He had not yet met Duck face to face, and had had only glimpses of him at work at the Crooms' or leaving his work and coming now and then to borrow the Crooms' car. Possibly he was responding not to the person himself but only to the amount the Crooms talked about him. Sometimes it seemed to Laskell that Duck was an almost obsessive subject of conversation at his friends'. As he listened to what the Crooms said about Caldwell, he would come to think that his own quick contrary feelings, really based on no knowledge of the man, must be some last vestige of his illness. The Crooms talked about Duck incessantly. Laskell, on this score, even asked himself if he was jealous. After all, the Crooms who talked so happily about Duck were the same Crooms who so firmly refused to talk about a certain matter which he had several times offered them. It was not unnatural that Laskell should wonder if an opposition were not being set up between Duck and himself. It seemed the more likely when Laskell understood that Nancy and Arthur talked about Duck as if he were not so much a man as a symbol. He was a symbol of something good, of something that deserved to be talked about endlessly; and if that were so, then Laskell might suppose that he himself, whenever the Crooms had jibbed at talking about his illness and closeness to death, was to them a representation of something bad.

What Laskell saw in Duck, or conceived of him, was so at variance with what Nancy and Arthur saw that sometimes the difference angered and alienated him. The Crooms admired in Duck a quality which they referred to in various ways, but most often as the thing they called Duck's reality. Duck's skill with his hands, which was undoubted, the depths of his roots in the district, a gift of racy speech he was said to have, his poverty, his resistance to the claims of domesticity, his outspokenness about these claims and his rejection of his wife's vague gentilities—all these traits seemed, in the eyes of the Crooms, to contribute to Duck's quality of reality. Even when the Crooms themselves were put to inconvenience by Duck's dislike of work and of keeping engagements most solemnly made, even when the progress of their beloved house was delayed by Duck's failure to show up, they were ready to set aside their disappointment in deference to Duck's independence. "He has," Arthur said, "his own way of doing things and he can't be hurried." It was a characteristic which Duck shared with reality itself.

And yet, Laskell could not help reflecting, the Crooms wanted to hurry other manifestations of reality. If they laid claim to having any work in the world, they would have said it was exactly the expediting of reality. They were not quite so committed to haste as Maxim once had been, but they were committed enough. They would have liked to hurry the reality of class into understanding and the reality of the better future into being. Why, Laskell wondered, was the reality of Duck exempt from the general hurry? Why should he alone, of all things, be allowed to move at his own pace? Was it because Duck represented to the Crooms some final goal toward which all realities were driving? There was something in their voices as they spoke of Duck that made this conceivable, but it was of course a foolish speculation. For the final reality that the Crooms wanted was one of application and hard work and responsibility. And all they reported of Duck, apart from his manual skill, suggested only anarchy and evasion.

One thing about his own extreme opinion of Duck disturbed Laskell especially. He did not like its extravagance—for it was far too extravagant to think of Duck as wicked and even "evil." Nor did he like its putting him at odds with the Crooms. But most of all he did not like a connection he somehow made between his disapproval of Duck and his visit from Gifford Maxim. He could not have put into words the reason why Maxim's lies about the Party should so have conditioned his attitude toward a man who had never knowingly done him harm and who clearly had nothing to do with politics and parties. As much as anything else, it was to drive the effect of Maxim's story out of his mental system that he had asked Mrs. Folger for her view of Duck. Her view was bound to be normal; it would supply a simple corrective to his own extravagance.

"His grandfather, now," said Mrs. Folger. "I remember his grandfather very well from when I was a little girl, driving around in his buggy. The family's been in these parts since Lord-knows-when. And the grandfather, old Senator Caldwell, he was in the legislature, a lawyer. He lived on the fat of the land, the old Senator did. Yes indeed, the fat of the land. He had that big place that's now Miss Walker's. But the father, now, he speculated, and Duck, he drinks, not that he drinks much, but a little of the strong stuff goes a long way with him. . . ."

So round and round went the wheels. Duck, said Mrs. Folger, was bad enough, shiftless and pretty lazy, often drunk, a good deal of a liar—but even as she spoke the words of moral judgment, her tone and indeed her whole manner created a large aura of exemption around him. She viewed Duck's lapses from absolute grace, it occurred to Laskell, much as Paine would have viewed the *real* Maxim, had Laskell told her about *him*. Certainly it was clear that Mrs. Folger thought Duck the more interesting because of his notable ancestry, and his fall, or his father's fall, from a high place.

There was relief for Laskell in this opinion. Mrs. Folger lived so fully in the life of the world—with Miss Walker and the little duchy in view it was almost the life of the court—that her opinion came to Laskell with authority. The Crooms might be misled by their generous idealism. But not Mrs. Folger. She saw the world and the way it went, she knew about vanity and about love, she knew something of their price. This was clear from the conversations with Miss Walker that Laskell overheard. Mrs. Folger was not, like Nancy, involved with ideals, and to Mrs. Folger Duck was not what he was to Nancy, the victim of a general injustice, the embodiment of a reality that one might not ignore. Nor was Duck to Mrs. Folger what he had, up to now, seemed to Laskell— the agent of some undefined evil. In the normality of Mrs. Folger's view, he was simply a man, with a man's errors and virtues, and a man—what was more—of a rather engaging, if not entirely admirable, sort.

Mr. Folger came in while Mrs. Folger was talking about Duck. He stood silent, listening. He seemed, without saying anything, not to concur in his wife's opinion. But then he was possibly only registering a masculine protest against Mrs. Folger's ever-so-vague appreciation of some special sexual gift of Duck's. Perhaps unknown to herself, Mrs. Folger saw Duck as having a saving touch of the satyr.

Between Mrs. Folger and her husband an attitude came down the ages, fresh and pure from the distance it had blown, almost fragrant with its simplicity and its long history. Montaigne's neighbors had talked so; Pascal had overheard such views in the salons of Paris. And back beyond, in Rome and before that in Sumer, men and women had judged each other as the Folgers judged Duck Caldwell. They had their little gossip and went about their business.

Mr. Folger said, "I'm driving to town."

He looked at a point on the wall about ten degrees to the right of Laskell's head. That angle of indirection, as Laskell now knew, meant that Mr. Folger was addressing him. He understood that this declarative sentence was by way of being an invitation.

He hesitated, not knowing whether he ought to accept the invitation at this stage or wait to see if it developed further. Mr. Folger turned his large impassive head and let his eyes rest on the wall, this time about ten degrees to the left of Laskell's head. There was a look of patience on his face. His eyebrows were ever so slightly lifted. Laskell knew that the invitation was now fully offered. "I'd be glad to go if you could take me with you," he said.

Mr. Folger got up, having received his answer. "Sitting all day in the same place never did any man any good," he said, as if he were giving himself and Laskell a reason why one should not think Laskell's statement unreasonable. He frowned reflectively at the spot on the wall.

They drove in the big old car which, as Laskell had learned, was not Miss Walker's but had been bought by Miss Walker for Mr. Folger. Driving, Mr. Folger did not have to find new places from which to ricochet his communications. He simply kept his eyes hard on the road.

"Big tract over there cleared of tent-caterpillar by those CCC boys. They fed with us while they were in the district," he said, lifting his head high to inspect the road.

They passed an orchard that was sad and scant. Mr. Folger said, "Gypsy moth," and raised his shoulders to see what might have happened to the asphalt ahead of them.

"I suppose you know the story of how the gypsy moth first came to this country," Laskell said. It was Laskell's one fact in entomology and he was pleased to be able to impart it. Mr. Folger looked at the road as if it might suddenly be developing hidden dangers that could wreck the car. "It isn't native to America, you know. A French naturalist was trying to improve American silkworms, he thought he could breed them with a certain European moth, so he imported some eggs and he reared the caterpillars in an enclosure to keep them from escaping. But a storm came up. It broke his screens and some of the caterpillars got away. I guess it took about ten years for anything to happen. That was back in the eighties. But the caterpillars appeared. The insects had just been getting used to the country. It took them nearly twenty years to spread, and even now they're thickest in Massachusetts."

Whether or not Mr. Folger found this interesting was not clear. He gave no other response than to take the car with an increased care through the cruel reefs that lay ahead. It was his way of receiving Laskell's story, not exactly an enthusiastic reception, yet Laskell did not feel that his offering had been entirely snubbed.

The town of Crannock was very small. Its residences were chiefly outlying, but it was truly a town if only because it had a little common, rather scrawny but not without charm, and even not without continuing use, for at one end was a bandstand. There were large trees on the common, and a small school stood at one side.

Mr. Folger's business was with a carpenter, and while he went about it Laskell stopped in at the drugstore, not because he needed the toothpaste and soap he bought but to occupy the time. The drugstore was dark as he remembered drugstores of his childhood, and it smelled twenty years back of drugs and of soap-perfumes that were long outmoded. The man who waited on him was not a clerk but a druggist, a scholarly looking man. And as Laskell went out with his purchase, even the striking force of the sunlight reminded him of the sudden light he had always experienced, in his childhood, on emerging from the special darkness of a drugstore.

He strolled about. waiting for Mr. Folger, feeling oddly contented and happy, as if he were in a foreign town. In a side street—but it was scarcely a street at all, just a different direction in which the boxlike structure of three stores faced—he saw what was called a tavern, a long narrow room, even darker than the drugstore. From it came a smell of beer. He was about to go in and then he decided to wait for Mr. Folger. His invitation would be something that Mr. Folger would have to deal with directly. He looked forward to forcing Mr. Folger's diplomatic reserve.

But Mr. Folger, when he appeared with his slow, discreet bearing, turned out to be in the tradition of socialism that looked upon the workingman's glass of beer with a doctrinal tolerance. "I don't mind if I do," he said politely and went ahead of Laskell into the tavern. If he had any reserve in the matter it was shown by his stationing himself at the near end of the long bar, where the window lighted it. Back where it was so dark that, at first entrance, one could scarcely make out the figures, there was a group of men.

There were four men, and as his eyes grew accustomed to the dimness, Laskell saw that one of them was Duck. And Duck was quite the center of their interest. When he began to speak, their heads leaned forward to catch what he was saying in a low voice, and when he finished, their heads went back in laughter. It was a rather extravagant, histrionic laughter which, with its slapping of thighs or of bar, was intended to demonstrate that the laugher was laughing. But when they laughed the three men were together among themselves, apart from Duck. They responded as he wanted them to, but they remained superior to him. It was as if he were imparting to them some wisdom and wit whose value they recognized, although they scorned him for having it.

Duck was drunk. He stood facing the bar, erect, a man whose sense of worldly ease, coming from what he has drunk and from old images of himself, can be taken from him at any moment. He continually made a little cocking gesture of his head, a small side-wise toss, and he raised his eyebrows in a quick understanding way, as one who knows the world and disdains or is indifferent to what he sees.

Mr. Folger ordered beer and Laskell had the same. Mr. Folger raised his glass and bowed over it before drinking. There was a large stag's head over the back of the bar and Mr. Folger's bow seemed to offer courtesy to the stag, but Laskell returned it. He liked Mr. Folger very much.

One of the men at the other end of the bar leaned over Duck's shoulder to disturb the conscious isolation in which he stood. The man said something in an inaudible voice and gave Duck a poke. Duck looked modest and even shy. But at last, with a shrug, he consented. The three men drew around him. He must have been telling his story well, for the men drew nearer and nearer to catch his words. When they were as close as he wanted them to be, his voice became more distinct. This made it seem rather foolish of them to be crowding up to a man who spoke to them in a loud clear voice.

Laskell heard the words, "And her maybe three months gone, maybe more . . ." Then he heard, ". . . lays one hand on her belly . . ." At this point Duck stopped his narrative and made a demonstration. He protruded his belly and laid one hand hard upon it. He went on, "And then he lays one hand on her tit." And Duck clapped himself avidly on the breast. He held both hands in place, acting both the man and the woman. He stood there in demonstration, lifting each hand and clapping it down again on himself to show how it had been done.

"Wahoo!" cried one of his listeners in conventional but intense enthusiasm.

"Yowee!" said another.

Duck surveyed his effect calmly. "And then . . ." Duck said and his voice dropped again, the heads were bent to him. Then his voice lifted in a calfish bellow of passion, " 'Nancy darling,' " he said. He answered himself in a falsetto bleat. " 'Oh, Arthur, please!' " He surveyed his success and said, "And then, what do you think he does?" His voice dropped again and when he finished there was the extreme explicit laughter.

But as the men laughed they had an understanding among themselves from which the performer was excluded. The information about life which they had received was interesting and valuable to them, but they looked down on the man who had such information to impart.

Mr. Folger was not looking at the group, nor was he looking at Laskell. He looked into his glass of beer, criticizing it. He was uncomfortable that Laskell's friends were being discussed.

Duck snapped his fingers three times in the direction of the man in charge of the bar, who drew four glasses of beer and took them down to the group.

Mr. Folger did all that could be done at the moment. At least he did all that could be done by the method of diplomacy. He directed his gaze and voice to the shabby head of the stag. "There is a kind of man," he said to the stag, "there is a kind of man, even his own wife isn't sacred to him. Even his own wife."

It tactfully opened such depths of Duck that the present incident could almost be lost in them.

Just then Duck turned, as if to take cognizance of the possibility that there might be someone else at the bar. But it was not Mr. Folger and Laskell that his eyes rested on. His wife had come in.

Emily Caldwell had paused for a moment just over the threshold. It was the only place in the long narrow room which the sunlight reached and she seemed very conspicuous with her yellow print dress and her bright coronet of braids. Duck stood and lowered at her, waiting for her to come closer. She did not hurry. Nor did she ignore Mr. Folger and Laskell. "How do you do, Mr. Folger, Mr. Laskell," she said, giving them for an instant all her attention. She walked the length of the bar, and the men watched her approaching, knowing what she had come for.

It was a bad situation for any woman to be in, a wife coming to take a man away from his companions for his own good. Emily nodded to Duck's friends, casually and pleasantly. And as they nodded back, their nods carried them into a subtle shift of position that made their group stand separate from Duck.

Emily said, "Come, dear, we must go."

"In a minute, in a minute," Duck said. He made the point of dignity by not looking at her. He turned elaborately to the glass of beer on the bar. "I have a drink to finish."

But she was too quick for him, for she reached out and took up the glass of beer before his slowly moving hand could encompass it. "That's easy," she said. "If you don't mind." And she raised the glass and drank half of it. "I was so thirsty," she said to her husband and his friends. And "See, I've drunk it all, such a pig," she said when she had drained the glass very competently.

She held up the glass for them all to see. She had compounded whatever sin the three companions thought they were committing, she was not judging them or her husband. She said to Duck, "We must go or we'll be late."

What appointment she and her husband could be presumed to have and what force punctuality could have in their casual country life did not seem to matter to her. Business or social engagements called them away, so sorry to have to run off—her manner insisted that this was the case. She involved the whole situation in this social manner; it was foolish but it hid from sight the wife snatching her husband from a bar under the very eyes of his friends. The men might snicker at her when she left but they could not regard her with cold hostility any more. Yet nothing she could do saved her husband from his raging shame. He glared at her, his face swollen with anger. At last he brought himself to speak. "Go ahead," he said, looking at her intently, with a kind of scientific curiosity, holding his gaze upon her, his mouth pulled back tight at the corners to show that he regarded her with a disgusted objectivity.

She turned and went. As she passed Mr. Folger and Laskell she nodded good-by. She did not look defeated. And she had no reason to, for Duck, when he had picked up his glass, looked at its emptiness with profound irony, drained the few drops of foam left in it, and carefully set it on the bar, followed Emily out of the tavern without a word to his friends.

Mr. Folger addressed himself to the stag. "Not an easy life," he said. "I wouldn't say she had an easy life at all."

Laskell liked Mr. Folger so much that he ventured a suggestion. "Do you think we ought to give them a lift?"

One of the tines of the stag's antlers was broken off and Mr. Folger seemed to be commenting adversely on this defect as he said, "I guess not."

And Laskell liked him well enough to believe that Mr. Folger was not only expressing a disinclination from implicating himself, and the car consecrated to Miss Walker, with the Caldwells, but also, perhaps, a kind of delicacy, a feeling that the Caldwells had best now be alone. On the drive home they passed the Croom car driven very slowly by Emily Caldwell with Duck asleep in the seat beside her.

If the incident made any changes in Laskell's view of things, it was not in his view of Duck—his opinion of Duck could only remain what it had been before—but in the way he saw Nancy. He sat with her the next morning as she knelt before the flower border at the north side of the house. She was pulling weeds and loosening the earth around the asters. Her pregnancy seemed more apparent today. Perhaps that was because it had been so notably referred to in the tavern yesterday. Or it may have been because Nancy seemed suddenly so very young to be a mother—so young to be so very much involved in life. She was involved up to her ears, with a child here and a child to come, with husband and house, with her own trimness and efficiency, and then with her full, generous hope that all she had and all she was could be what the world had—she was too modest to hope that the world could be as she was, but Laskell could hope it for her. And what she did hope for she was passionately sure would come, for she knew that most people had her own clarity of spirit. It was a very large faith, a very large involvement with life.

But now Laskell saw her as he had never seen her before—in an aura of self-deception. It was that which made her so very girlish today, for after all she was twenty-six. She was like some thoughtful adolescent who utters a starry sentiment that she has learned at home or at school, from a good but mistaken parent or teacher; she sets her chin sternly against any knowledge of the world in which she will have to make her sentiment prevail, and the sternness of her self-deceiving pose of maturity makes her seem even younger than she really is. For the desire to refuse knowledge of the evil and hardness of the world can often shine in a face like a glow of youth.

What Nancy talked about quite confirmed Laskell's new sense of her. She put down her hand rake, pushed back her hair, and turned on her knees to him.

"John," she said seriously, "I want to ask you something."

Her youthfulness appeared here in her intense seriousness and he could not help teasing her. "Please feel, Mrs. Croom, that you can speak freely to me."

"No," she said quietly. "I'm serious. John, tell me—do you think we could have a rock-garden next year? Would it look silly?"

"You have one already," Laskell said. For there was a pile of the large stones that Nancy had collected from her flower beds.

"Seriously, John. Would it look silly?"

"No more silly than any other kind of garden."

"You know," said Nancy, "there are certain kinds of rock flowers that I like better than any other flowers in the world. But I don't know. Maybe it *would* look silly."

"What *are* you talking about?" said Laskell. "Silly in what way? If you like them."

"I mean inappropriate. I've always associated rock-gardens with suburban homes, even estates. And this is such a simple community. It might look funny. You know—affected." She was quite shy about it.

"Oh, for Pete's sake, Nancy!"

But Nancy seemed scarcely to notice the interruption. "I'd like to think of this as really our home—our *place*. I love the people here, but naturally they have their own ideas about things. And even small things that one does can make them uncomfortable." Then she added, "As it were," as if there would have been a disloyalty in her meaning it too literally.

"In that case," Laskell said, "I should think you'd have to give up thinking of this as really your home."

"I won't!" she said. The quick refusal, the stubbornly outthrust chin, made Laskell smile. She really was like an independent child. But he thought of the scene in the tavern and Nancy's opinion of Duck and knew that an independent child was not enough to be, not as the world was.

"Did you ever have a rock-garden?" he said.

"When I was a little girl we had one. My mother was mad about it, spent hours on it."

The memory of that seemed to reassure her, as if it told her that she was not asserting a whim but affirming a tradition. She sat silent, presumably thinking of rock-gardens.

Laskell said, "I drove to town with Mr. Folger yesterday afternoon."

"Did you? Isn't he the finest person?"

"I like him very much. We stopped and had a glass of beer together. I saw your Duck there."

"*My* Duck? Yes, he borrowed the car yesterday."

"He was drunk."

Nancy sighed elaborately. "He just can't drink," she said. Her tone was elegiac, and like any elegy it mourned the hard fact, accepted it, and was reconciled to it in the end. Laskell, who suspected that he had already said too much, would not have gone on if Nancy had not explained, "It's his weakness, but there's something wonderful about him, a quality of life, a kind of unexpressed affirmation."

He stared at her. "You really think so?"

And she, catching the real question in his tone, stared back at him hostilely. "You know, John," she said in a considered way, "I begin to think you have a prejudice against Duck." She held up a hand to stop any disclaimer he might make. "Yes, I think you have. You've never talked to him and yet whenever his name comes up, it seems to me that there is a kind of antagonism in you. I know you well enough, John, to know what you're feeling, even when you don't say anything." It was likely to be true. Still, it was surprising to him that she should have been able to read his feelings about Duck.

"He's a very important *kind* of person," Nancy continued, "even if you don't consider him just personally. It's not like you to judge a person without knowing him."

There was nothing he could say. He could scarcely mention the single concrete fact he might use in evidence against Duck—he could not tell Nancy about Duck in the tavern. And because the evidence could not be used, it lost some of its value. Perhaps one could not judge a man by an incident, however distasteful it seemed. Best to surrender his stand, and maybe, indeed, there was no need for a stand at all. All he said was, "Perhaps you're right."

"I know I'm right, John," Nancy said gently. She was willing to let the subject drop.

For a while Nancy gardened in silence. Then she asked, "Are you fond of flowers, John?"

It was one of those things that one friend can say to another only under such country circumstances—while one of them worked and the other idled, in the open air, with plenty of time ahead, with no particular concentration on each other, not wanting any special answer or any answer at all. It came like a greeting and suggested how valuable life could be without struggle, or ideas, or commitments. A hundred, a thousand other questions could be asked that would have the effect of making two people as simple and without strain as Laskell suddenly felt that he and Nancy were. It seemed to him that such conversations could go on forever. "Are you fond of flowers?" "Do you like dogs?" "Do you like whisky?" "Do you like to read poetry?" And there were untold numbers of answers. "Yes, I am quite fond of flowers and my favorites are peonies but I also have a great feeling for delphinium." "Yes, I like dogs. If I had one, I would have an Irish terrier. I've also thought of dachshunds. Schnauzers I don't like, nor boxers, nor Scotch terriers. But I'd only have a dog if I lived in the country." It could go on forever.

It would have been better if, lying there on the ground, with his hands clasped under his head, he had just stayed with one of those imbecile answers to Nancy's question, one of those responses that gently said no more than that he was alive and she was alive and that they were aware of this fact about each other. But instead he said, "It's funny you ask. Because I never gave it a thought until I got sick. But while I was sick I seem to have got myself enormously involved with a flower. It was a rose."

"Oh, roses!" said Nancy, wrinkling her nose. "Queen of the flowers."

"I could look at it for hours. I never knew what it meant when people talked about contemplation. But that's what I did with that rose—I contemplated it. My nurse Paine said—"

"I liked that Paine. Not the other nurse, not at all. But Paine I liked a great deal."

"She liked you too. She had a great admiration for both of you, you and Arthur. After I had been looking at that flower for days, she said, 'You seem to be having quite a love affair with that flower.' And I suppose she was right. It was a clever thing to say."

"You were quite a Ferdinand," Nancy said.

His eyes had been closed against the sun. Now he opened them and looked straight up into the sky. It was very blue, and the longer he looked the higher it became. He remembered that in Latin there was only one word for high and for deep. The Romans spoke of the heights of the sea and the depths of the sky. He tried to let this oddly remembered fact fill the whole of his mind.

But it would not fill the whole of his mind. It would not displace the strange, contracting pain he experienced at Nancy's calling him by the name of the hero of that children's book so popular with adults, about a young bull who liked to look at flowers and did not charge around like other bulls. When Ferdinand was sent to the bull-ring in Madrid, instead of resisting the matador and being hurt and killed, he sat down in the middle of the ring and enjoyed the flowers in the hair of the ladies who had come to see him fight. In consequence he was disgraced but safe, and he was sent back to the ranch where he spent the rest of his life looking at flowers. A good many political feelings became attached to the story and people chuckled over it as if it were a piece of folk-wisdom.

Laskell said, "Why do people like that story so much?" He was still looking deep into the sky.

"I do. I can't wait for Micky to get old enough so I can read it to him."

"Why do people like it? Why do you like it?"

"For its moral, I suppose."

"They seem to like the idea of a bull going against the nature of bulls."

"Oh, no, that's not it. The moral is that if people just refused to fight there would be no more wars. I suppose Ferdinand is just simple human reason, the reason of simple human people refusing to cooperate in their own exploitation and slaughter. After all, Ferdinand wasn't killed, the way all the other bulls were. He lived to enjoy himself."

"Is that something?"

"Well, isn't it?"

"If the Loyalists were to act like Ferdinand?"

"That's different. They're fighting for something."

When Laskell spoke again, he spoke carefully. "When you said just now that I was quite a Ferdinand, you were teasing me, weren't you, not praising me?"

"Why, John!" Nancy said. "Why, John Laskell!"

"No, I'm not being sensitive. But really, it's serious. You say you admire Ferdinand. But when you want to make fun of me, you say I am quite a Ferdinand. That puzzles me. It's like the people who give parties for Spain—they're the same people who admire the sissy bull."

Nancy was ruffling. "We have to make a distinction between immediate necessity and ultimate hope, don't we? We have to hope that eventually we will be able to change man's nature."

"I'm not so sure." But the conversation was becoming very heavily charged and Laskell felt tired. "I suppose," he said, "the bull who smells flowers and doesn't charge when he's attacked is the modern version of the lion who lies down with the lamb." Nancy made a gesture to show that she didn't quite accept the parallel. He had not yet been able to look at Nancy, he was still looking deep into the sky. "I think the old version was nicer. The lion was still a lion and whenever he lay down with the lamb it was a fresh surprise. I don't think we really admire Ferdinand, Nancy. I think we really despise him. What bothers me is that we praise something we really despise." And then he said, "I wonder if we're not developing a strange ambivalent kind of culture, people like us. I wonder if we don't rather like the idea of safety by loss of bullhood. A kind of Kingdom-come by emasculation."

He had successfully carried it away from himself. And the sudden pain he had felt when Nancy called him Ferdinand had sunk almost to nothing. He had talked very fast and he had headed, as the occasion seemed to require, toward generalities. He had talked with half his mind, loosely, and he was rather startled by the place he had come to. He had never before generalized in this adverse way about the people he lived with, the decent people, the people of good will. It frightened him a little. He wondered what Nancy would say.

Nancy had picked up her hand rake and was thoughtfully scratching the grass with it. For the life of him Laskell could not think of anything to say that would carry their conversation in a new direction. He felt that he had said something for which Nancy might not easily forgive him.

But Nancy chose not to deal with his generalization at all. She said, "I didn't mean anything when I said that about Ferdinand. It was just a way of speaking. Anybody would have said it to a person who spoke about being devoted to a flower. Really, John, I wasn't making fun of you!" And then she said with the rights of their friendship, "And since when, John Laskell, have you got so sensitive? Just you stop it. You're acting spoiled—your illness has made you sensitive and spoiled. I won't have it from you."

She had justice on her side, and the right to command him. He sat up, grateful for the opportunity she gave him to accept defeat —and defeat on the basis of friendship. And then briskly looking for something to talk about, he thought to take out his wallet and he dug with his fingers into one of its pockets. Nancy was watching him with interest. There was really a good deal of the child about her and he had diverted her by making her curious about what he had to show. He drew out the snapshot that Maxim had given him in one of the absurd tactical moves of that mad visit. Maxim had laid it on the table between them with the explanation that he had come across it while destroying some papers.

"Who is it?" said Nancy as she reached out to take what she saw was a snapshot. She looked at it. "John, have you gone and—" Then understanding broke upon her, perhaps from the fashion of the dress in the photograph, and she said, "This is— Is this—?"

"Yes," Laskell said. "It's Elizabeth. I don't think you've ever seen a picture of her."

"No, never. I never have."

She was examining the photograph carefully. She looked at it longer than she need have, even for a thorough examination. Then she seemed able to speak. She turned her gaze to Laskell. Her eyes were very wide and her face had paled beneath her tan. She was struggling with some emotion, she was trying to find the thing to say. Her face told him what he had done. He was horrified at himself. When Maxim had given him the photograph Laskell had understood the part it played in Maxim's plan of manipulation. He had known that it had been intended by Maxim to flood his mind with emotions that would make him the more accessible to Maxim's request for help. Specifically it was intended to remind him that people really did die. Elizabeth Fuess died, Maxim was saying, in the midst of our safe life—if you doubt that I too can die, let this picture remind you of her and convince you about me.

To show a snapshot of Elizabeth to Nancy at any time would be momentous. But to show it at this instant, with disagreement, and that particular disagreement, just behind them—no, his mind had not been innocent when he had done that. Had he not, in some way, wanted to tell her just what Maxim had wanted to tell him, that people really do die? And if he had, without thought, quite unconsciously, undertaken to give her that cruel lesson, what deep alienation had sprung up between them?

"She is— She was—" Nancy struggled with the tense. "There is something very attractive— Gifford Maxim once told me about her. He said she was very attractive—very pretty."

"Never pretty."

Nancy looked at him to see what the denial meant. "Beautiful?"

"Sometimes. Not always. Seldom, really."

"Giff seemed to admire her a good deal. But when I tried to get him to say why, he said he couldn't explain. And the things he said about her didn't seem to be the kind of things that would make him admire a woman. He said she never worked."

"He liked her very much."

"Did she like him?"

"Moderately."

"Only moderately?"

"She never quite liked his relation to his ideas. It wasn't the ideas themselves so much, but his relation to them, she used to say."

"Oh?" said Nancy. "I don't quite know what that means." She said it without much inflection, not quarrelsomely, but it put her in opposition to Elizabeth's expressed opinion. Laskell felt that there was no reason to come to the defense of Elizabeth's opinion. It had been all too well confirmed by the facts. Elizabeth had been remarkably right about Maxim. Laskell remembered the indifferent interest with which she had listened that time to his own enthusiastic description of Maxim's powers, the little shrug of her shoulders to depreciate not his estimate but hers as she said, "I somehow don't quite like his relation to his ideas."

Nancy gave back the snapshot. "You know," she said, "when you showed me the picture, I first thought it was a girl you had met and got interested in. John, would you let me say something? It's something I thought of while you were ill. I thought of you lying there with no one to take care of you except nurses, and I thought, 'Oh, why doesn't John get married?' And now when I think of you living in the past— Somehow I never realized how much you must do that. I mean, like carrying that picture in your wallet. It isn't like you, John. It's not like you to be so morbid. Life makes demands on us— We have responsibilities, to others and ourselves. I'm younger than you, but maybe I have the right to remind you of that. You're young and attractive and comfortable. John, do you mind my talking like this to you?"

He was putting the picture back into the wallet and the wallet back into his hip-pocket. He buttoned the pocket. "How could I mind?" he said.

"Are you sure? Do you think I'm right?"

He did not mind—he had no mind to mind with. He wished that Nancy were not looking into his face to see how he was taking it. He wished he had the sky to look into and lose himself in as when Nancy had said he was quite a Ferdinand.

"Are you sure you don't mind? Do you think I'm right?" Nancy said again.

She surely could not have meant anything—was it not what at some time every married woman says to every unmarried young man she is fond of?—but she was terribly worried that her ordinary little sermon had hurt him, she was rather miserably looking into his face for evidences of hurt. And then he knew that he had hurt Nancy and that she had in some way meant to hurt him. Ferdinand and marriage were her answers to his mention of illness and death.

"Nancy," he said with sudden clarity. "Nancy, why are you so scared of it?"

"Of what?" she said as if she would just like to hear him name the thing she was scared of.

"Of death. Why are you so scared of the word being said?"

He had no need to argue the point. She had gone white. "I have only to say the word and you turn the subject. I have not been able to say anything to you about my being ill—you and Arthur did everything for me while I was actually sick, but you jib like a pair of colts whenever I try to speak about it. You won't have me say a word about it—either of you. I have only to show you a picture of Elizabeth and because she died you are thrown into confusion." He did not go on to say, "And you respond by attacking as subtly and cruelly as possible." But he did say, "You talk about morbidity and living in the past—as if you thought that death was politically reactionary."

It was a great comfort to him to have said it at last. And it was some comfort to Nancy that he had uttered so many words, some of which she could reply to. She looked very stricken at his outburst and not quite comprehending. Her eyes filled with tears. She was a generous girl, for her voice as she spoke had clearly the intention of defending not herself but their friendship. "John," she said, "you misunderstood. I wasn't criticizing you. I didn't mean to make you angry."

The appeal was not to be resisted and Laskell put out his hand and rumpled her bright, sunburned hair. He was enormously grateful that at that moment Micky charged toward them over the lawn, followed by the watchful Eunice. Micky saw Laskell and stopped. He looked at Laskell with challenge in his eyes, and when Laskell, as slowly as possible and with large exaggerated movements, began to get into motion, showing that he accepted the challenge, Micky veered off and ran. They had developed a kind of tag in which, if Laskell ran slowly enough and Micky ran fast enough, the chase could go on for quite a way. At last the pursuit ended and Laskell brought Micky back on his shoulder.

Eunice said to Nancy, "He got himself all dirty."

Laskell took the child from his shoulder and held him up for inspection. "Filthy!" He grinned.

Nancy said to Eunice very kindly, "A little boy has a right to get dirty. Don't you think so, Eunice?" Eunice acknowledged the rule but did not answer the question.

Laskell put the boy down. The run had given Nancy a chance to recover herself and her face was almost cleared of its unhappiness.

"I'm going to lunch now, Nancy," he said. "I'll be coming in after dinner this evening. I have some news for you. It's about Gifford Maxim. I should have told you before but at least I want to tell you now."

"News? About Gifford Maxim? Tell me now—tell me now, John," Nancy said.

"No, not now. I want Arthur to hear it too."

"But I'll tell Arthur if it's interesting."

"It's interesting enough. More interesting than you might guess. And more important. And more disturbing. It's a long story, I'll tell you tonight."

She looked at him, surprised by the gravity of his tone. She did not protest the postponement. She said, "Is it something bad?"

"I'll tell you tonight."

5

ALKING back to the Folgers' for lunch, Laskell felt the great relief of having made up his mind to tell the Crooms about Gifford Maxim. In the natural course of things he should long ago have told them. But he had not been following the natural course of things. He had been trying to punish the Crooms. He had to see that and he felt the better for seeing it.

It was hot and still on the road. The light, dry dust rose with each step he took. There was not a breath stirring and the unmoving leaves of the trees were dusty. At a rise in the hill he stopped to look around him. He could see a fairish distance in two directions and, standing there with the hot, pictorial landscape before him, the quiet farms in the foreground, the little hills behind, he found it very difficult to remember his apartment and what had gone on in it the day before he had left to come here. Those city emotions seemed so far off in time, so uncertain in texture. But Laskell forced his mind to reconstitute the event detail by detail, for his account to the Crooms must be clear and circumstantial.

He remembered that he and Paine had been engaged in that pointless squabble about his fishing things when Maxim rang. And he remembered how Maxim, when he entered, was taken aback by the sight of Paine, although she must have explained her presence and function when he had telephoned. But it was Maxim's business not to be dull about the unexpected. It was also his business to know how to deal with misfortune of every kind. He was, as it were, a technician in human suffering. His tone was full of accurate, firm sympathy. He said, "I'm sorry you've been so ill, John."

The presence of Paine in her white uniform was a help to Laskell. It made it easier to bear the brunt of that great moral authority of Maxim's.

Certain things were clear between Laskell and Maxim. It was established that Laskell accepted Maxim's extreme commitment to the future. It was understood between them that Laskell did not accept all of Maxim's ideas. At the same time, Laskell did not oppose Maxim's ideas. One could not oppose them without being illiberal, even reactionary. One would have to have something better to offer and Laskell had nothing better. He could not even imagine what the better ideas would be. He sometimes regretted this but, after all, although he was an intelligent man, he could scarcely set up as an original thinker. He was left very much exposed, not to Maxim's arguments, for Maxim seldom argued, but to Maxim's inner authority. This Laskell did not regret. Maxim never formulated an accusation in words, yet he did make an accusation. He made it by being what he was. This accusation was unlike any other—it was benign. It brought the guilt into the open, the guilt of being what one was, the guilt one shared with others of one's comfortable class. There was a kind of relief in admitting the guilt to this huge dedicated man.

After the first surprise, the first shying away from Maxim's great moral force, Laskell was not at all sorry to see his friend. In fact he was glad. He felt ready to greet the approach of life in its grimy tangibility and high hope.

Maxim looked at the packed bags and said, "And now you're going to the country. That's good. It will do you good, you need it."

His voice was full of the direct sympathy he knew how to give. It was conscious but not insincere. Laskell had seen Maxim give his sympathy to overworked waiters or soda-clerks. Some of them responded happily to this gentling of their strained nerves. But some became restive under it. They were no doubt confused by this tone coming from this big man with the scarred face and the shabby clothes and the voice that was of another class than theirs.

"When are you leaving?—right now?" It seemed to Laskell that there was a shadow of apprehension on Maxim's face.

"No, I leave tomorrow morning."

And there was no doubt that with this answer the shadow passed.

Laskell remembered that Maxim, on his last visit, had asked him to dismiss the Negro cleaning-woman. Now perhaps something should be done about Paine. For Maxim surely had another request to make. And all Laskell's unhappiness at that refusal of his came back to him now and with it the hope that this time Maxim would ask something of him to which he would not have to say no. He did not know how to get rid of Paine so that Maxim could make his request. And he ought to introduce Maxim to Paine, but he did not know by what name to introduce him. He was helped out of this difficulty by Maxim himself, who turned to Paine and said, "My name is Maxim—Gifford Maxim," and put out his large hand.

"How do you do, Mr. Maxwell," said Paine. "My name is Paine. Isn't that a dreadful name for a nurse?"

"Not Maxwell—Maxim, like the silencer," Maxim said. "Yes, it's a dreadful name for a nurse and I bet you live up to it too."

This was wonderfully in Paine's line and she grinned back at Maxim. She saw, as her remarks to Laskell later showed, right beyond the shabby clothes, the dirty shirt and the heavy scarred face, to the pride of family that lay so incongruously beneath them, saw the courage and the violence, the lack of regard for ordinary notions, and she said to Laskell that evening, "That friend of yours, that Mr. Maxim, is a real gentleman." Laskell snapped, "Oh, yes— a *proper gentleman*," furious at them both. But she missed the point of that and she was not really of the class that would say "a proper gentleman." "Yes, he is indeed," she said and brooded with pleasure on her intuition of Maxim's aristocracy. But Laskell by then had had his fill of Maxim and rather more than his fill, and would not discuss him with Paine.

If Maxim was using his real name and even insisting that Paine get it right, perhaps there was no need to get rid of the nurse. Yet to be safe, Laskell said, "Paine, do you think we could all have some ice cream? You'll have some, Giff?"

"Yes, thanks, I'd like it," Maxim said. "But why don't I go for it? It's terribly hot."

"Just as hot for you as for me!" Paine said, peppery and friendly. "You stay here and talk to your friend." And she added darkly, "He needs talking to." She had the tone of a nursemaid who punishes her charge by turning her regard to the visiting little boy, the good little boy who really knows how to behave.

"It's terribly hot," said Maxim. "Probably the hottest July thirteenth on record. It is·the thirteenth, isn't it?"

"No, the twelfth," said Laskell.

Maxim said to Paine, "Is it?" His manner with her was very bold and gentle. He was "establishing contact" as Laskell had seen him do. He was succeeding very well with Paine.

"I rather think you're right," said Paine. "The thirteenth."

Laskell bitterly remembered how often the date had been mentioned between Paine and himself, for he was to leave tomorrow, the thirteenth.

"Have you a calendar or a newspaper?" Maxim said.

"It's the twelfth," said Laskell irritably.

Paine found a newspaper in the wastepaper basket. "It's the twelfth," she said, granting the point in a sporting way.

"I could have sworn it was the thirteenth as sure as my name is Gifford Maxim."

But Paine faced up manfully to the error they had shared. "No, the twelfth," she said.

Laskell felt a wave of boredom sweep over him as the date was settled and this dry little flirtation came to an end. Maxim had the look of a man who has accomplished something.

Paine went out for the ice cream. Laskell was left alone with Maxim, who took off his jacket. His shirt was nearly transparent with sweat. He sat down in the armchair opposite Laskell's. He took a cigarette from the box on the low table between them, lit it and drew in the smoke deeply, as far as smoke would go. Then slowly, carefully, analytically, he let it out. Laskell laid his head back on his chair. He was suddenly very tired. The pressure from Maxim was enormous. He wished that Maxim would make his request without further preliminaries. He admitted that the indictment was a true bill. The benign accusation was made by what Maxim was and also, perhaps, by what he kept secret. What Maxim was, was centered in that great dreadful scar on his cheek, down from the cheekbone to the chin. It was said to have been made by a glancing blow from the steel shoe of a policeman's horse, rearing in a crowd as such horses are taught to do.

Maxim looked mildly and patiently at Laskell. Then he looked over Laskell's heâd and beyond it and asked his question. "Are you still a friend of Kermit Simpson?" he said. And not until the question had been asked did he let his patient gaze come to rest again on Laskell's face.

It was strange—in these infrequent meetings between Laskell and Maxim there was always a period of questioning. Maxim seemed to be investigating certain lines of communication. Usually the questions were about people he no longer saw. He seemed to want to understand the connections that existed between them. He seemed, too, to want to learn something about Laskell's life and state of being.

When Maxim asked his questions, he used a slow, gentle, but very direct manner. He might have been conducting an inquiry of a high official sort. Laskell never felt that he was a criminal in the inquiry, but a respectable and important person consenting to give information, although there was indeed the chance that one of his answers might strip him of respectability and importance, much to Maxim's regret.

Laskell found that he answered Maxim's questions as briefly as possible. He acknowledged the authority of the interrogation by guarding himself against it. At the same time, he tried to be very direct and truthful and was conscious of his directness and truthfulness, as if he were contending with the impulse to lie to Maxim.

"Are you close to Simpson?"

"What do you mean by close?"

Maxim looked tolerantly at Laskell, acknowledging Laskell's privilege to attempt evasion. He said patiently, "Do you have any influence over him?"

"Influence? Why should I have influence over him?"

Kermit Simpson was one of the few really rich men Laskell knew well. And although he had answered, "Why should I have influence over him?" uttering the word *influence* with irony, he knew, now that he was in Maxim's orbit, that it was a natural question to ask about someone's relation to a very rich man: Do you have influence over him? It was especially the question to be asked if the rich man was, like Kermit Simpson, politically idealistic and the owner and editor of a rather sad liberal monthly.

"You see him, don't you?" Maxim asked, still most patient. "On the whole, you see a good deal of him?" He was making a new start, back of the question Laskell preferred not to understand.

"Yes," said Laskell in a neutral voice, yielding the point but not giving much weight to it. And then the impulse to be entirely honest when Maxim questioned him made him say, "I spend week ends with him now and then and we've gone fishing together."

Maxim received this statement with a look of kind approval. He turned his head to see the creel and rod which lay together near the suitcases. His manner was more relaxed, was very relaxed, as he drew his conclusion. "Then you're going up to stay with him?"

"No," said Laskell. "I'm going up to Arthur Croom's place." And he decided to ask a question himself. "Have you seen the Crooms lately?" Maxim gave no sign of having heard.

"Could you get Kermit to take someone on?" Maxim said. "On *The New Era*, I mean." *The New Era* was the monthly magazine that Kermit Simpson ran on what he called Jeffersonian principles.

"What do you mean, take someone on?"

"Give him a job."

"It wouldn't be a very good job."

Maxim ignored this and Laskell felt foolish for having said it. "Could you do that?" Maxim said.

"I don't know. I've sent him friends who wanted to write—review books and that sort of thing. But of course an actual job is different."

Maxim nodded understandingly. In these questionings there was always a moment when Laskell felt that he was hedging and knew that Maxim was aware of it. Maxim never accused him of hedging. He seemed to expect reservations and always let them be made, never fighting them. He really had no need to fight, because Laskell always felt how shameful the reservations were. For to Laskell, Maxim was never quite alone. Laskell saw him flanked by two great watching figures. They were abstracted and motionless, having the air that figures in a mural have, of being justified in the exclusive contemplation of their own existence and what they stand for. On one side of Maxim stood the figure of the huge, sad, stern morality of all the suffering and exploited men in the world, all of them, without distinction of color or creed. On the other side of Maxim stood the figure of power, noble, fierce, indomitable. Both figures appeared to Laskell's mind as male but sexless. The face of the one was old and tragic, the face of the other was young and proud. Yet both had that brooding blind look that is given by men to the abstractions they admire, in the belief that a lack of personal being is the mark of all great and admirable things. Behind Maxim and his two great flanking figures were the infinite dim vistas of History, which was not the past but the future. The vistas were corridors, and every answer made by Laskell, every evasion or reservation he might attempt, was listened to not only by Maxim himself, whose great scar made its sardonic comment on everything that was false, but was listened to also by the two great figures of suffering and power, and every answer reechoed down the everlasting corridors of History, identified as the answer of the one poor meaningless unit, John Laskell, who was so concerned with his own being, his own poor little unit of will. Reservation and evasion were impossible.

"Then," Maxim said, summing up conclusively, "Kermit has listened to your advice before."

As Maxim put it this way, so minimally, Laskell knew that Maxim understood how much influence he really did have over Kermit Simpson. Kermit was a man of sudden attachments and enthusiasms, and more than one person had reported to Laskell the admiration for his good sense that Kermit had expressed. Like many rich men, Kermit Simpson was always looking for a wise friend, a perfectly disinterested adviser. This year Laskell was the friend. Maxim, with his gift for picking up information, surely knew this.

"Good," Maxim said. "That's what I wanted to be sure of. If I asked you to recommend someone for a job, would you do it? And even put a little pressure on Kermit to get him to say yes?"

Here, then, was Maxim's request. It was of course political, and if it was political, it was important.

The two great figures bent their gaze on Laskell, and the corridors of History were ready to reverberate with his answer—for they have great acoustical properties, these corridors, and echo every word, no matter how softly spoken. For some reason Maxim wished to place one of his people on Kermit Simpson's *Era. The*

New Era was a chucklehead of a magazine and the only thing that might give it any value at all, any place in the long historical vista, was for it to be used by Maxim.

Yet Laskell had always had a kind of affection for *The New Era*, exactly because it was so chuckleheaded, so simple and gentle in its liberal and humanitarian faith. If Maxim wanted to place one of his people on *The New Era*, it could be only with the idea of influencing the policy of the magazine, perhaps of getting control of it. Once that happened, it would of course no longer be really *The New Era* at all. But this did not seem to matter so very much—under Maxim's eye, *The New Era* shrank in importance for Laskell. It appeared to him only as the means of a small favor that he could do for Maxim.

"You mean," Laskell said, "that you want a job on *The New Era* for one of your people?" And then, because he had made up his mind to try to do what Maxim wanted, he felt that he had the right to ask, "What do you want that for?"

Maxim made a strange answer. "I have no *people*," he said.

There was sternness in his voice and his eyes narrowed. But it was a foolish evasion and it weakened him with Laskell. To a frank and open Maxim much could be given easily, *The New Era* among other things. But an evasive Maxim was very different. It was often necessary to hide one's Party affiliation, but Maxim's had always been open and known. It was one of the important things about him. He did have "people"—he both gave orders and took them.

And now he said again, "I have no people." And before Laskell could challenge the false statement, Maxim said, "And you are jumping to conclusions. Would you recommend me for a job?"

"You!"

Slowly Maxim took another cigarette from the box and lit it. He inhaled the smoke as if searching out with it depths of his being that could be reached in no other way. He shook out the match and then blew the smoke out of his lungs in a long desperáte exhalation.

"Yes," he said. "Me."

He got up slowly and went over to the luggage. He picked up the creel by its strap and looked at it curiously as it dangled. He turned to regard Laskell with a still, hooded, waiting amusement.

Laskell understood this tactic of pacing the conversation slowly, all the pauses dictated by Maxim. It put things in Maxim's hands. It was intended to give Laskell time to doubt and question himself. And Laskell had always submitted to this device, feeling obscurely that a man who had so much to do with the tempo of events had the right to dictate the tempo of conversation. But now he did not submit to it. It even made him a little angry. Maxim was standing there with his hooded gaze so full of the knowledge of motive. But for Laskell at this moment some of his great authority had diminished.

"Will you please tell me what you're up to?" Laskell said. "Why do you want this job?"

Maxim said, "A man must live."

It was no answer. Not only was it no answer but it was exactly the kind of thing Maxim could not say, not even if he said it in irony, as no doubt he had. It was another evasion. Maxim did not have to think about making a living, though of course his salary from the Party was ascetically small. Laskell sat tight, saying nothing, as able as Maxim to say nothing and to dictate the pauses.

And he won. He was frightened by his victory as Maxim said in a rush, "Look here. You've *got* to do this"—in those two phrases there was a personal, a merely personal, urgency. There was even, as Maxim threw out his big hand in a kind of appeal, a throwing away of all political and moral superiority, a dismissal of the two great mural figures that went about with him, a shutting up of the corridors of History.

"I want you to call Kermit Simpson. I want you to call him now." Maxim pointed to the telephone beside Laskell's chair. "I want you to remind him of my existence after all these years and tell him I'm all right. I want you to get him to publish an article, not a political article, a literary article. Here—I have it here."

Maxim picked up his jacket and took from its inner pocket a folded manuscript, holding it out to Laskell as if it were proof of something. "I want him to publish it right away, in his next issue. And I want a job on his staff. I don't care what the job is or what it pays. But this must be done right away."

Laskell's question came very quietly after the intensity of Maxim's demand. "And what name will you sign?" he said.

"My own—my own name. That's the point."

Something is wrong here, Laskell thought. This was a strange Maxim, with a look in his eye and a note in his voice that he had never before thought possible. It was a personal look and a personal note. Maxim wanted something for himself. And as Laskell looked at him, he knew that what Maxim wanted was help, was safety.

"Look here," Laskell said, "what are you up to?" He spoke sharply because he felt in himself something very like fear at this new aspect of Maxim that could want personal assistance.

"I've told you what I'm up to," Maxim said reasonably. "A man must live. I'm trying to live."

His voice was sardonic but his eyes were not. He did not mean making a living. He meant not dying.

"In order to live," Maxim said, "I have to exist. You've got to help me exist. Because I don't exist now."

It was like facing a man suddenly stripped, and it was more terrible than it should have been. It was Laskell himself who had always had to guard against what he might disclose to Maxim of the narrowness, the merely private character of his own motives, and now, for some reason, the roles were reversed—Maxim was the one charged with the personal motive. At no time could that reversal have been anything but disturbing, yet Laskell, in the midst of his unreasonable fear, knew that his disturbance was too great.

But although Maxim might have lost authority, he had not lost his skill. In his pacing back and forth he had come on the photograph of the Crooms that stood on one of the bookcases. He picked it up and said, "I hear there's a good chance that Arthur Croom will go to Washington. This is a good picture of them." He set the photograph back on the bookcase. "By the way," he said, "speaking of photographs reminds me—"

He went to his jacket and felt in the inside pocket again. And Laskell went cold with anger as he knew what Maxim was going to produce.

"I was going through some old papers to destroy them and I

came across this." And Maxim held out the snapshot. Laskell's heart hardened against Maxim as his premonition was shown to be foreknowledge. He did not take the photograph. Maxim put it on the low table.

Laskell remembered the occasion when Maxim had come into possession of the picture. He had come in one evening, unannounced, as his habit was. Elizabeth was there and she and Laskell were going over a batch of snapshots taken during a recent week end. Maxim had asked to see the photographs and had gone through them very intently and Laskell had felt that it was a stern yet benign inspection of their private life. And then, when Maxim had looked at all the pictures once, he had started through the little sheaf again and then held one up and said, "I want this one." And when the demand had been met with confusion and the natural question, "Why?" he had answered with that disconcerting directness, perhaps intended to disconcert, and that long deep look of his, "Because you're good." It was really a very alarming thing to say and Elizabeth had frowned as if she were angry, as if it were not at all a compliment. But there had been nothing else for her to do except let the picture go.

Laskell did not look at the snapshot where Maxim had laid it on the table. He said, "What do you mean, you don't exist?" His mind was cold and clear, very firm now. He was very angry. Maxim wanted to confuse him with this recollection of the past. He wanted him to realize sharply, at closest quarters, that people really did die. It was a cheap, manipulating trick.

Maxim mashed out his cigarette in the ash tray. He did it slowly, thoughtfully. He said, "It's been a year since you last saw me, isn't that so, John?" He did not wait for an answer. "In that time no one has seen me. No one, that is, who could *say* he saw me. Or *would* say, if he could. There's no record of a person called Gifford Maxim. No one could say that on a certain date I came to dinner. No one could even say that in a certain month he met me and stopped to have a drink with me. I could vanish like that"— and he made a gesture—"and no one would know that I'd been missing. I've been working underground, as they say."

"As *they* say?"

"I vanished," Maxim went on, not heeding the interruption.

"And very skillfully. I ceased to exist. That was necessary for the job I was doing. And now I must exist again. Or I may vanish for good."

But surely he looked existent enough as he sat there, a more than usually substantial man. His scar looked very real, a unique identification. He did not look like a man who could either cease to "exist" at will or vanish very easily. "A man who does not exist can be got rid of easily," Maxim said.

"What do you mean, *got rid of?*"

"I mean," Maxim said brutally, "killed."

Laskell had known what he meant but he had to have the word. And now that he had it, he naturally did not believe it. Or rather, he believed it and did not believe it. In the same way he believed and did not believe that it was the police that threatened Maxim's existence. It was the courage with which Maxim faced the danger of his work that gave him so much of his power. He staked his safety on his ideas. The scar was a token of how ready he was to do that. But he staked nothing now. He was frightened. He was not merely professionally aware of danger in the line of his duty—he was shaken and afraid. To Laskell it was quite terrible to see this, as if something solid were vaporizing before his eyes. He sought for common sense. He said, "You really mean the police would—"

"I don't mean the police." Maxim's voice was level with what he did mean.

"Then what *do* you mean?" Laskell said fiercely. But he knew what Maxim meant, or almost knew. He had really known that Maxim did not mean the police. Maxim just looked at him, waiting for him to formulate the answer to his own question. There was a sly, an almost malicious smile on Maxim's face.

"Who then?" Laskell said in bitter exasperation. "Who then? Tell me what you do mean."

And Maxim answered him as he knew Maxim would answer. "Look," Maxim said wearily. "I'm through with the whole business. Finished. Washed up. *Kaput.* I've broken. Now do you understand?"

Although the answer, when it came, was not unexpected, still the meaning of what Maxim had just said broke slowly over Laskell because it brought with it the hideous intention of Maxim's earlier statements. *"You!"* Laskell said almost inaudibly. *"You!"* And as he said the pronoun twice, he heard how great was his incredulity and how much more than incredulity there was in his voice.

Maxim looked back at him, impassive under the surprise, the contempt, the revulsion. It was revulsion that Laskell was feeling, a deep physical disgust.

Laskell said curtly, "All right then—you're through. But why all the melodrama?"

Maxim looked at Laskell a long time and then said, "Melodrama," repeating the word neutrally and curiously, a new word he was learning in a foreign language. "Melodrama," he said again. Then he said very politely, "My work was very special, you know. And secret. Special and secret. I'm supposed to go back to talk things over. The point is that I'm not going back. I've wanted perverse things in my time, but I still haven't developed a yearning for the ocean bottom or for a pistol behind my ear."

The room was suddenly very quiet. But from the street came the hot summer noise of children at play, passionate and irritable from the heat. They were the same children whom Laskell had heard calling to each other in his illness, their voices gay and far off, speaking tenderly of life, the background to his mood of rest and peace. Now the voices were ugly and protesting. They were all crying to someone to throw the ball here—"Throw it here. Here y'are. Hey! Here y'are!" And then there was a long concerted shout of disgust, and one voice cried in harsh, distinct denunciation, "You dumb cluck!" There was an enormous empty place in the world where Maxim and his ideas had once been.

He said, "Do you mean to say you believe that if you went back—?" He was surprised at how much force Maxim still had, for Maxim had already made him accept the idea of *back,* although it was one of the beliefs of decency that, for people of Maxim's Party, or former Party, there was really no such geographical or political direction as *back.* People of liberal mind understood that the belief in Moscow's domination of the Party in America had been created by the reactionary press, and they laughed at it. Yet Maxim spoke as if *back* were a simple fact and had made Laskell accept it.

At Laskell's unfinished question, Maxim turned from the window. On his face was an expression of ultimate pity. It was the pity of a man who knows the worst for the man who hopes for the best. But Laskell met Maxim's look with a pity as great—it was one thing for a man to abandon his loyalty to the cause he had lived for; it was quite another thing, and far sadder, for him to spread foul and melodramatic stories about it, such terrible stories as were contained in Maxim's silent stare, in his talk of ocean bottoms and pistols behind the ear.

Then Maxim said with the air of saying his very last word, "John, get this into your head. Just let your mind take it in. I know it's hard, but you're a liberal—you're supposed to keep your mind open to new ideas. What I've been working at has nothing to do with strikes or unions, nothing to do with voting or with relief funds or with publications. I'm not going to say what it was, but use your head. I was *special*."

"Giff, you're crazy!"

It was the kind of thing one friend says to another in the extremity of exasperation and it had friendliness in it. But having said it, Laskell found himself flushing, because it was so close to the literal truth. Gifford Maxim could not be insane—he who had been almost the embodiment of Reason in action. Yet he was not in his right mind. Otherwise he could not sit there so unmoved, talking about such things as if there were no possible doubt of them, as if there were nothing morally wrong with them, only something to be personally avoided, attributing these things to the very forces that made for the great future. It was a form of paranoia, the persecution-mania.

Yet Laskell, although he clung to this formulation, knew that it was only a formulation, not a belief. Or it was one of those things he believed and at the same time did not believe. So far as he believed in Maxim's insanity, it expressed his full sense of the tragic bitterness of the world, the deep confusion of our times, that had distorted a life and a mind so fine as Maxim's, despite all the great protection of Maxim's ideas. So far as he believed Maxim was insane, he could pity Maxim and not condemn him. He held hard to his belief and felt it establish itself within him.

"When did you get your new view of things?" he asked.

"You mean what led me to the break?"

"Well, yes—" But that was not what Laskell had had in mind. He was ashamed that it was not. His first question should have been about doctrine and line. A truly political man would have asked just such a question, at this point or earlier. At my age, he said to himself, I should be politically mature enough. But what he had meant was, when had Maxim got the new conception of things that led him to assume this violence, to believe that he would be in danger of his life if he went, as he said, back, and even if he did not go back? In the large, mature, practical view of things, the question about doctrine and line was the first one to be asked. But it was the other question that Laskell pressed. "When did you come to believe such things as that you'd be in danger—there?"

"And here," said Maxim. "And here too. I've always known it." His simplicity was unexpected. It threw into a very strange light the certainty and skill of the answers he had made to Laskell when Laskell had asked him to explain the Moscow trials and the rumors about the actions of the Party in Spain. Maxim shrugged. "I've always known it. It's just that now I'm in it—me—myself."

"You've *always known* it?" Laskell was not sure which word he wished to emphasize.

Maxim nodded. "Yes," he said flatly. Then he said in modification, "Of course, not *always,* but ever since I've been in a position to really know things. And that's been a long time."

"Long enough so that you can now say that the things you told me were lies?"

"I wasn't lying—I was defending a position."

"It never made any difference to you before? It's only when you yourself are in danger—or consider yourself in danger?"

"I was a professional," said Maxim in a cold voice. "What mattered to me were results. I always knew what the means were. They are not delicate or charming. They are even brutal. Please understand that I never had any of the liberal illusions about that. I was not, as you are, interested in *ideals.* I was interested in results. As a revolutionary I was wholly professional. But now the results do not please me. The present results and the inevitable later results. It's not what I bargained for."

His voice became explanatorily simple, as if it were Laskell who was in trouble, not very serious trouble, just some intellectual perplexity. "It's not a sudden view, it's been forcing itself on me for some time. I've kept quiet—if you take the professional attitude about revolution, you don't permit yourself the luxury of ideas. You give them up with a certain pleasure. Up to a point. But I reached that point. And passed it. And since I know the means, I don't want any such means applied to me. As I said, I've wanted perverse things in my time, but not—"

Laskell broke in, "I can understand a change of heart or mind. But I can't believe you when you talk of terrorism. I've known several people who have broken with the Party for one reason or another, and you know them too—"

"It isn't only that I've changed my mind. I was special. I told you I was special. I am still special."

"Yes, you've told me. 'Special and secret.' But I don't know what that means. Do you want to tell me what it means?"

Maxim seemed to consider. "No," he said at last.

"Was that business with the letters when you were last here—was that part of it?"

"Yes," said Maxim casually. "Didn't you know that then? Wasn't that why you refused?"

"No. I don't know why I refused."

Maxim raised his expressive eyebrow. "You don't? I think you're wrong. You knew. Though perhaps you didn't know that you knew."

"No, I didn't know." But Maxim might be right. Perhaps there had been in Maxim's manner some indication, unobserved but responded to, that suggested that this matter went beyond what Laskell was ready for, beyond what Maxim scornfully called ideals.

"I think you knew then," said Maxim. "And that's in part why I'm here."

Maxim seemed to see the mistake he had made and sat perfectly still, a little pale. Laskell said, "You actually think that because I refused to receive those letters I have declared myself ready to help you now—now that you've turned? You're fantastic!"

Maxim's best tactic was not to say anything at all. He knew it and sat silent. Then Laskell said, "What made you come to *me* about those letters? If your business was so special and secret?"

"I had to ask someone. Someone in your position. If you said yes, well and good. If you said yes, I would have known I could trust you."

"Thank you."

Maxim was silent again, looking as if there were nothing more for him to say.

"Granting there is danger if you go back—though I do not grant it—what danger is there if you don't go?"

"I've told you. I don't exist. I was important. I knew a great deal. I still know it. Too much. And I don't exist. Not as a—citizen." He smiled at the idea of his being a citizen. "And if I don't exist, something can happen to me. No one would know it, no one would report it. Someone must know of my existence. You know. And that nurse of yours, Paine, she knows now."

So that was the point of that pointless conversation with Paine! It was not likely that Paine would forget that she had seen and talked with a Mr. Maxim on the twelfth of July.

"But that isn't enough. I must have a continuous existence, an office I go to every day, so that it is perfectly clear that if one day I don't appear, questions will be asked. I must be on record to be safe. I want my existence established on, say, the masthead of *The New Era*. The more I exist and the more I exist publicly, the safer I am. Now do you understand?"

Laskell said, "For God's sake, Giff, put your mind to this. I know the people you're talking about. You've introduced me to some of them yourself. I don't accept all their ideas, but they're ordinary people, some of them really just middle-class citizens with decent social ideas. Gentle people. They couldn't do such a thing."

"Those people wouldn't do it," Maxim said.

"They couldn't even order it done." It was astonishing how he could pick up Maxim's malign implications. "They couldn't —it's not in them."

"They wouldn't have to. They would never know about it, the ones you know."

"Who would then?"

"It would be done. There's reason for its being done and it can still be done safely. *Can be*—until I get myself an existence."

Maxim said it as if this time he had really said his last word.

And it was the last word that he uttered, the word *existence* that he kept repeating, that decided Laskell to believe that Maxim was not in his right mind. He felt ashamed of himself for not having acted on his first perception of this, for allowing himself to be drawn into political argument with a demented man, for harassing a mentally ill man with the quibbles of reason. He smiled to Maxim and reached for the telephone.

"What are you *doing?*" Maxim cried, leaping from the chair and seizing Laskell's wrist.

If anything was needed to show Laskell how deeply that powerful mind was enmeshed in its wild corrupt fantasy, it was this sudden start from the chair, the iron hold on his wrist, the suspicion that some treachery was about to be committed. Laskell said, "I'm calling Kermit Simpson."

Maxim slowly sank back into his chair, looking ashamed of his fright.

There was no reason why Simpson should not be called into service. It was no longer a matter of politics, no longer a matter of making political use of Simpson's dim little magazine. Kermit had a good heart. He liked to say that he was non-partisan in his liberalism. If Kermit knew the facts, he would be willing to help.

And then, with the phone in his hand, Laskell wondered what he meant by "help"—had he been caught in the net of Maxim's fantasy? Did Maxim really need the help he demanded? Was Maxim actually in the danger he spoke of so wildly? But then Laskell understood what he was doing. He was quieting Maxim's strange panic by finding for him some kind of anchor or base, something to hold on to. But he had never thought the day would come when he would take command of a situation that was beyond Maxim's control.

There was no one in *The New Era* office except a secretary and Laskell could hear in her voice the lonely isolation of the secretary who keeps the office in summer during that profound lull when the poorest of intellectuals seems able to leave the city to its wide and echoing emptiness. And Laskell thought of his poor crazed Maxim, trying vainly to establish contact with his old friends in this empty city, thought of what Maxim must have felt when he came in to find the bags packed for yet another departure.

"Kermit is up at his place near Westport," he said when he had this information from the desolate secretary. "I'll try him there."

Maxim sat there with his reason all about him, except for the single rift that delusion made. It was perhaps but temporary, the result of some terrible emotional crisis. Kermit Simpson had a large soft heart and Maxim could surely be left in it.

He reached Kermit in Westport. Kermit was full of congratulations for Laskell's recovery and all reminiscent pleasure at the mention of Maxim's name. But at the proposal that he give Maxim a job on *The New Era* he checked and pulled up short. He had the idealistic rich man's first response, the fear of being used. "There's no money in the budget for the job," he said. "You know I run *The New Era* on a budget." He was very proud of that budget. "And besides," he said, "he's a pretty political character." But it did not occur to Simpson to ask why so political a character should want a job on his magazine. He was a very innocent man.

"No," said Laskell and glanced at Maxim, who sat unmoving, and then permitted himself a cruelty. "No, I wouldn't say he's a political character any more. Not in the way you mean."

Maxim did not give even a flicker of response and Laskell's heart smote him for having taken so easy an advantage of a corrupted man, a weakened mind. And that led him to say with great intensity of persuasion, "Kermit, I want you to see him, I want it very much."

Simpson said, "All right. Can he come up to see me tomorrow at noon?" Laskell could hear in his voice the division between the desire to do good and the fear of being taken advantage of.

"Can you go up to Westport tomorrow?" Laskell asked Maxim. Maxim nodded.

"About noon?"

Maxim nodded again.

"He'll be there, Kermit."

And somehow all of Maxim's loss of moral glory was in that sentence that made him a disposable object—"he," the poor sad patient whom the well-dressed doctors were trying to help.

Paine came in with the ice cream and Maxim went to the kitchenette to help her serve it out. He made no comment on the arrangement, offered no gratitude. He seemed quite to accept the role of patient. But when they were all three eating the ice cream, he said, "Where do the Crooms live?"

"In Connecticut, a little place called Crannock. I go to Hartford and take the local train from there."

"Tomorrow? On what train?"

"The ten-twelve."

"I'll call for you and we can take the train together." It was not a suggestion but a statement.

"No!"

The idea of the trip alone had been frightening to Laskell—it was astonishing how he had lost his nerve about so ordinary a thing. It was impossible to contemplate taking the trip with this man in whom one could almost *hear* the dim, slow sound of disintegration.

"No!" he said again.

"Why, what an excellent idea!"

It was the sure voice of Paine, the voice of nannies and nurseries, of coal fires and bad drains, of bread-and-butter and cambric tea, and an egg to tea, of rooks in the elms and the Christmas pantomime, of not whimpering and of keeping your chin up, of all the comfortable certainties of his childhood reading in English books.

"You're very rude," said Paine. "An excellent idea. And Mr. Maxim can help you with the luggage. You have to be careful lifting things, you know, after such a long fever. The muscles are weakened, particularly of the feet, and many people get fallen arches as a result of insufficient caution. But Mr. Maxim looks strong enough for two."

Betrayed and trapped, Laskell sat there with nothing to say and nothing to do except to fight down as best he could a rising fluttering in his stomach.

He woke weary the next morning, drained and dry behind the eyes. He had remembered in the night the claim that Maxim had upon him—Maxim's quiet company evening after evening in the days after Elizabeth had died. Now Maxim, in his loss, had come to Laskell. Beyond his use of the photograph, Maxim had not uttered the claim, and Laskell, now, was glad that he had not, that Maxim had got what help he had without any bargaining. He was also glad that, since the claim did exist, he had given Maxim what help he could. He found it strange that not until he was alone and sleepless that night had he remembered there was any claim at all. And when he did remember it, he remembered the stern and hollow feeling of those days. And he more than remembered it, he suffered it again, experienced the negation and hopelessness just as if three years had not passed.

It did not make the coming trip a happier adventure for Laskell that Maxim presented himself at eight o'clock, dirty, dark-eyed, unshaven, and asking for breakfast and a bath.

"Well, *you've* been on the tiles, my good man," said Paine happily and went to draw the bath.

"She speaks truer than she knows," Maxim said. "Except that your roof is tin."

He had spent the night on the roof. Laskell had to put the fact from his mind, it was too awful even to contemplate.

He had saved until the moment before the farewell the gift he had ordered for Paine. There had been no trouble in choosing it. He had had merely to order what he had decided would make just the right gift; he had found it easily enough one morning when Paine was out marketing, by making a single telephone call to the likeliest store. It was a handbag of heavy pigskin, as plain as if designed to army specifications and stitched to endure forever and to descend to Paine's grandnieces. Paine received it with the air of protest and surprise that is learned by people who receive presents in the way of business.

Paine said, "Oh, Mr. Laskell, too good of you, really. What a lovely handbag," very genteel and not looking at him. She held out to him a dry hand. Dressed now in her street clothes, she looked shabbier than ever. "You've been a nice patient," she said. She meant it, but there was a kind of forgiveness in her voice, as though she knew she had been imposed on all along and had decided not to mind. "Now I want you to be a good boy and take care of yourself."

It was only nurses' talk—there was no longer any connection between them, nor did she have any remembrance of a connection. She had bathed him and shaved him, she had been with him when his life was in question and she had first heard his voice in the obscurities of delirium. So long as her function lasted she had thrown her protection around him, and to him it had appeared in the form of love. Now her function was at an end. Laskell thought of the gift he was to have given her every year at Christmas, the dull quiet evenings he had planned to spend taking his old nurse to dinner and theater. Now he knew he would probably never see her again and this first gift of his was the last. The gray and peaceful illusion was over.

Maxim, mad or not, corrupted or not, could help with the chores of closing the apartment, could pick up all the bags, Paine's as well as Laskell's, leaving Laskell only the rod and creel, could carry them down the stairs, turning his head to say to Laskell, "Take it easy now," and could go to the corner to find a taxi.

"I took the creel, Paine," Laskell said as they stood on the sidewalk with nothing to say, and he pointed to it in proof.

"Oh—sound idea. Good boy." He had asked for her approval and she gave it. But she was not much interested.

Paine got into the taxi with Maxim and Laskell. She was to be let off at Fifth Avenue and Twenty-eighth Street. Why just at that place she did not say. At Twenty-sixth Street she again held out her hand in farewell. "Be a good boy," she said. She nodded briskly and cordially to Maxim. "Good-by, Mr. Maxim. See to it that he behaves."

With that her tie to him ended and there she was, standing on the sidewalk, alone and indistinguishable, looking for a way to cross the avenue, rather inept, her competence hidden. It was the last he would ever see of her.

Alone with Maxim, Laskell wanted to say something about Paine that would refer to his own large feelings and yet suit those still larger social considerations which he had often discussed with Maxim, the nature of modern society, the individual and his relation to the social whole, the breaking of the communal bonds. But any remark that would reflect his own isolation would be lacking in tact to this man who was really so much more alone. The remark itself would not actually "hurt" Maxim, but the deficiency in tact would be offensive to him, for Maxim always insisted on the code of delicacy and politeness, bourgeois though it was.

What Laskell said was, "By the way, do you have any money?"

"Enough for a while."

Laskell took out his wallet and drew three ten-dollar bills from it. "Will thirty be enough?" he said, and then he felt himself flush at the number he had chosen. Had something in his mind wished to offer the traitor Maxim thirty pieces of silver?

But Maxim had not noticed the number, or gave no sign of noticing. "Thanks, John. Can you spare it?"

"Yes, I can get more if I need it." And Laskell thought that there was this notable difference between them, that Maxim meant money while he had meant cash.

In the station, under the great blue dome with its faint gold constellations, Laskell felt how weak and inadequate his legs were.

"Don't hurry," Maxim said. "Plenty of time. You're still a little shaky, aren't you?"

It was so. Even Maxim was a comfort here among all the people so brutally intent upon making trains or appointments. And Maxim chose a double seat on what, when they emerged into the light, would be the shady side of the car, and heaved the bags up on the rack—it was a great relief. Laskell could forget the disgust with which he had regarded Maxim's moral defection, if it was that, or the pity with which he had regarded Maxim's madness, if it was that.

But he did not miss observing that Maxim had chosen the last car of the train. He could at first suppose that this was to save a long walk down the platform. But when Maxim chose a seat at the very rear of this last car, Laskell was sure there was strategy in it. Their position had been chosen to lessen the chances of anybody approaching from the rear. And Maxim then substantiated Laskell's conclusion by saying, "I guess this is the best place for me."

It was terribly sad, this absurd precaution, but it was the only sign of delusion that Maxim gave. For the rest he was an almost pleasant companion. He asked about all kinds of people they had known together in the days before Maxim had given the whole of his life to the Party and had cut himself off from so many things. He was as social as anyone traveling in the direction of Westport.

6

TELLING the story of Maxim's visit to the Crooms was even more difficult than Laskell had anticipated. How difficult he expected it to be he understood when, walking to the Crooms' house that evening, he had to acknowledge that his heart was quickening its beat. The sensation was not entirely unpleasant. It had something of the normal anxiousness he might have felt if he were just about to make a public speech on a difficult matter, though with every reason to suppose that he would in the end do credit to himself. But it was odd that he should have felt even this much excitement at the prospect of telling the story. After all, it was nothing more than a piece of news to be imparted to Arthur and Nancy. Yet he had eaten his supper that evening with an enforced calm and had even been at pains to make himself neat for the occasion, going to his room to change his shirt, though it was quite fresh, and to brush his hair. While he was in his room he recalled that he had not made the test of his urine that day—lately he was beginning to forget to do this—and he heated the test tube over the lamp he had lit on his dresser and dropped in the acetic acid when it boiled, noting with satisfaction that the liquid did not turn cloudy.

It was a warm night, though damp, and there was a mild, drifting mist. The days were noticeably drawing in and Laskell needed a flashlight for the road. The segment of mist that was lit by the conic beam of the flashlight was turbulent, but he had only to look outside the cone of light to see that its main movement was large, slow, and drifting. The air was filled with the perpetual sound of crickets, the sound of summer that speaks of summer's end. It spoke of this now to Laskell, as it always had, ever since boyhood, with its pleasant melancholy of things ending, a conscious and noble melancholy leading to hope and the promise of things to come, of things beginning, all the liveliness of autumn, of new starts, the renewed expectation that, this year, one's personal character would learn the perfect simplicity one wished it to have.

The Crooms had finished dinner and were sitting in that unfinished but already charming living-room of theirs when Laskell arrived. He naturally did not knock when he entered, the sound of his steps on the path being enough, and they greeted him as casually as if he had not arrived at all but had merely come back after having stepped out for a look at the weather.

Arthur said, "Hi, feller!" and went on whittling the block of wood that was to be a boat for Micky. There was newspaper spread out at his feet to catch the shavings. Nancy was wearing a long house-coat of light blue and her sunny hair was turned up and bound with a ribbon. She sat under a lamp and her only greeting to Laskell was to say aloud what she had been murmuring to herself, "Forty-seven, forty-eight, forty-nine, fifty, fifty-one," warning him that he must not speak to her nor she to him until she had finished the count of her knitting stitches.

Seventy-four was the number of stitches she was counting and when she reached it she said, "Hello, John." But while the counting continued, John Laskell had a perception. The sound of the crickets filled the Crooms' room and to Laskell it suddenly seemed that the sound no longer spoke with the sweet melancholy of the end of summer. It seemed to him that it was the sound made by the passing of time, a very different thing. It was not like an elegy heard with pleasure in its sadness, but like the inexorable ticking away of life itself. The Crooms in their house together had shut themselves off from it as snugly as they would have shut themselves off against a storm. They had made everything tight, seen to all the windows, looked in on their child to see that he was undisturbed, and now were the happier for what was going on outside. But Laskell could not share the shelter which they had together. He felt suddenly exposed to the whole force of the movement that was indicated by that ceaseless noise of time rushing away. He had a desire, not for shelter—he could not hope for that much—but for something he could hang on to as standing against the movement of time he now heard around him. Summer spoke of its end but did not go on to speak of new beginnings. It spoke only of the end of all other summers. Laskell, standing there while Nancy counted, had the sense—and he wondered if it came eventually to every man and if it always came so early in life—that there was really no future.

He did not mean that *he* had no future. He meant that the future and the present were one—that the present could no longer contrive and manufacture the future by throwing forward, in the form of expectation and hope, the desires of the present moment. It was not that he had "lost hope," but only that he did not make a distinction between what he now had and was and what he expected to have and be. The well-loved child of the middle class is taught about the future by means of the promises made to him—the birthday gifts will come and the Christmas gifts will come, and the performance at the Hippodrome, and camp and college and the trip to Europe. And all the promises and their fulfillment are symbolic of the great promise, made to him by everyone, that he will grow and change. This great promise he takes into himself in the form of a pledge—made to himself and to everyone—that he will grow and change for the better. He takes it into himself too in the particular form of his vision of time, in which the future is always brighter and more spacious than the present. How the mind of the fortunate young man of the middle class is presided over by the future! It is his mark, his Muse—for it is feminine in its seductiveness—and sets him apart from the young men of the truly lower class and from the young men of the truly upper class.

What happened to Laskell, all at once, was that he realized that you couldn't live the life of promises without yourself remaining a child. The promise of the future might have its uses as a way of seducing the child to maturity, but maturity itself meant that the future and the present were brought together, that you lived your life *now* instead of preparing and committing yourself to some better day to come.

His new perception of the nature of time struck him with very great force. Yet it was not especially startling. The only thing that was startling about it was that it came so suddenly, in this moment of differentiation between the Crooms and himself. It was not painful—or no more painful than the change that had taken place when, at a certain age, the special and mysterious expectation of Christmas and birthdays was no longer appropriate and his parents began to give him his gifts quite as a matter of course, most affectionately still, but without their eyes shining in the excitement of seeing their son's wonder and impatience being now satisfied and even exceeded by reality; or just as going to the theater was no longer a matter of waiting for that blessed Saturday on which would be revealed Annette Kellerman in the tank or Charlotte on the ice but became a simple transaction, a call to the ticket-agency, with no interval, if one didn't want an interval, between the decision to go to the theater and the going.

It was not a gay feeling, this change in the character of the relation between present and future, but it was certainly not an unhappy one. The well-loved child of the middle class had always done everything with an exemption granted, for the future was made not only of promises but also of opportunities for forgiveness, and redemptions, and second or third chances. As Laskell looked back on this evening with the Crooms, he found that his odd idea about the future and the present being one brought its own heroism. It had a kind of firm excitement or excited firmness that was connected with his feeling that at this very moment he had the full measure of existence—now, at this very moment, now or never, not at some other and better time that lay ahead. If at this moment he did not have the simplicity of character he wanted, he would never have it; if he was not now answerable for himself, he would never answer.

"Sixty-nine, seventy, seventy-one, seventy-two, seventy-three, seventy-four." Nancy finished counting and said, "Hello, John."

Arthur, released from the necessity of silence, said, "Nancy tells me that you have news from Gifford Maxim." He was still whittling at the boat.

"Why no," Laskell began. Nancy made a surprised and questioning sound and Laskell said, "Not news from him but news about him." And although he had planned to lead up to it, for the sake of verisimilitude, he now thought it best to let them have it all at once. "Maxim has broken," he said.

They looked at him both in amazement and in lack of understanding. But if they were amazed, they must understand, and if they did not understand, how could they be amazed?

"Broken?" said Arthur. "What do you mean, broken?"

But Arthur of course knew what it meant and Laskell found himself not answering. He looked at Arthur, waiting until Arthur should consent to understand. Then it occurred to him that this was a trick of Maxim's and he said, "Broken with the Communist Party, of course."

"*No!*" said Arthur. Then he said, "For Pete's sake!" Then he said, "Giff *Maxim?*" And not until he had expressed his amazement in three separate utterances did he feel that he was beginning to come into possession of the astonishing fact.

Nancy's incredulity was more coherent. "I don't believe it," she announced. But there was nothing else for her to do except believe it. "I *can't* believe it," she said, meaning that although her mind gave a formal assent to the truth of the statement, she had no emotions with which to accommodate it, and no real desire for such emotions.

Laskell did not try to deal with their incredulity. He simply sat and waited for it to pass. The story had yet to be told and its difficulty pressed upon him.

Arthur put aside childish things, laying the pocket-knife and the block of wood on the sofa beside him. He had the set, strong, and chastened look of a man who has just had information of the highest importance which does not at that very moment affect his personal life, although, as he well knows, it must eventually touch him adversely in some personal way. Yet the event is so great, so dramatic, that he cannot but feel a pleasure in his excitement, which he tries to suppress. Arthur Croom had probably looked not much different at the moment he had learned of the Reichstag fire. He and Nancy for a moment had nothing to say. If Gifford Maxim had been susceptible to compliment—but that was impossible— nothing could have flattered him more than the silence in which they sat.

In retrospect Laskell knew that the Crooms were not at all pleased with him for being the bearer of such news. And even as he told the story—or rather, as the Crooms put their questions to him afterward—he had to resist the feeling that he was telling a story on himself rather than about Maxim. But he did resist it. A particular tone came into his voice as he answered their questions, a note of strictness and even of irony. It was this note in his own voice that made him aware that his sense of time, his feeling about the future, had really changed. The Crooms seemed to be asking their questions with the assumption that if everything was not right and clear about Gifford Maxim, neither was everything right and clear about John Laskell. And ordinarily he would have let them rest in this assumption until it should pass of itself, as of course it would have done. He would have been sympathetic to their need to blame someone, to hold someone accountable immediately, a need so pressing that they were even willing temporarily to hold Laskell accountable. He would have been willing to let them impute some guilt to himself of which he could be sure the future would clear him. But tonight he resisted this impulse to feel guilty, and he repelled the Crooms' imputations—unconscious imputations, of course—at the very moment they were uttered, not waiting for the future to set them right.

Thus, when he told them about the trip with Maxim, he explained about Maxim's choosing the last car and the last seat in the last car and said, "He did that so that no one could come at him from behind."

At this Nancy said, "Did he say that was why he did it?"

Laskell answered, "No, not in so many words. All he said was, 'This is the place for me.'"

Nancy said, "And you thought that that meant he would be attacked? Why should you think such a thing?"

Laskell said, "I didn't think he would be attacked. I thought that he thought he would be attacked." And his voice was clear and firm. It required Nancy to understand the truth now, at this very moment; it refused to allow her to indulge even for a short time the relief she might find in supposing him in the wrong.

The question of Maxim's belief in the possibility of attack led the Crooms to the question of Maxim's sanity, for when Laskell explained very precisely that the idea of the attack was not his but Maxim's; Nancy said, "Oh—he's mad. I mean *really*—he's insane."

She had expressed that view before. She had listened in silence

to Laskell's account of the visit up through its climax, heard in
horror Maxim's belief that he did not exist, that in order to be safe
he needed a public certification such as Kermit Simpson's magazine would give him. She had barely been able to take it in. She
had been incredulous when she had heard that Maxim had broken
with the Party. She had sat silent, looking puzzled and annoyed
when Laskell told of what and of whom Maxim was afraid, much
as if she were listening to some new conception of the universe so
abstract that it was hopeless for her to put her mind to it. She had
said nothing until Laskell came to the detail of Maxim's having
slept on the roof. Then she had said, "Why did he do that?"

And Laskell had answered, "Presumably for safety."

At this she had cried out, "Why, the man's insane! He is, isn't
he, John?"

Laskell had said, "It certainly occurred to me to think so."

Nancy had then used the word not quite literally, meaning perhaps no more by it than that Maxim was mistaken in the extreme.
But now she was quite literal, entirely clinical. She said in a very
literal voice, "He is insane, isn't he, John?"

"Well—" Laskell paused to consider.

"Don't you think so? You said you thought so."

"Yes, at the time the idea did come to me, in a way."

"In a way? At the time? Don't you think so now?"

"I don't know."

"You don't know? But you said so. You were with him. You
heard him say those things. You yourself heard him say he was in
danger. You said he slept on the roof and that he was afraid of being attacked from the rear. He's obviously insane."

Arthur said, "I doubt if you'll get very far in politics, Nan, with
the language of individual psychopathology."

"I'm not talking about politics," Nancy said irritably. "I'm talking about Gifford Maxim. If insanity isn't the opposite of reason,
what is it?"

Arthur said as gently as possible, "But think how many people
talk about the German developments as if they are to be understood in terms of individual psychopathology."

"And so they are! That and the weakness and vacillation of the

Social Democrats." She said to Laskell, "What is he, if he isn't insane?"

Laskell had not thought of the alternatives before, but he considered them now. "He might be mistaken," he said slowly. "Or he might be deliberately lying." And then, merely in the way of the next step in a series of possibilities, "Or he might be right," he said.

"You think he might be right?" Nancy said. "My God, John!"

And Arthur said very gravely, even a little sternly, "Do you really, John?"

It was, of course, a very important question. He did not answer quickly. "I didn't say so. I was only stating all the possibilities. I'm simply not sure that we can finish it off by saying that he's insane."

"No, I agree with you," Arthur said. "But if he's not insane, what is the matter with him? What could have led him to this?"

Again Laskell hesitated. "You must remember that he's a professional—that he *was* a professional," he corrected himself with a smile. "Lenin said that for effective revolutionary action there must be a small group of professionals. Giff knew a great deal and was very deeply committed. That's why he seemed so important to us, isn't it? After all, we've been nothing but liberals and perhaps that's all we'll ever be. That's all right, but it means that we pretty much limit ourselves to ideas—and ideals. When we act, if we can call it action, it's only in a peripheral way. We do have sympathies with the Party, and even, in a way, with its revolutionary aims. But maybe, sympathetic as we are, we prefer not to think about what the realities of such a party are."

Arthur said in a very quiet voice, "Then you're saying in effect that Maxim was telling the truth. And apparently you're basing your belief on the assumption of a conspiratorial party. But surely you wouldn't say that that assumption stands up? You don't actually think he was telling the truth, do you?"

"No," said Laskell. "I didn't say I did."

A silence fell now, one of the many silences of that evening. It was no longer possible for Laskell to evade the fact that, in the Crooms' eyes, he was touched with Maxim's guilt. Not that they were precisely blaming him for anything, but they felt that he had been led into error somehow. And waiting out the silence as he suddenly could, Laskell thought how much of life was being conducted as a transaction between guilt and innocence. Even among people who were devoted only to ideas of progress and social equality and not at all to action, there had grown an unusual desire to discover who was innocent and who was guilty, who could be trusted and who needed to be watched. This was strange when one reflected on how much the idea of personal responsibility had been shaken by modern social science. Educated people more and more accounted for human action by the influence of environment and the necessities and habits imposed by society. Yet innocence and guilt were more earnestly spoken of than ever before.

Laskell remembered the strange confessions of the great Commissars, the former heroes of the Revolution of 1917, which were so difficult to understand, not because it was inconceivable that the men should be guilty—their guilt, after some doubt, had become quite clear to Laskell—but because the spiritual quality of what they said was so little in accord with an age of reason, because the defendants were so deeply involved, as their speeches of confession showed, with the idea of personal guilt. It was an apparent contradiction in Marx's *Capital,* that would some day be worth putting his mind to, that in the great chapters on the working day the industrial middle class was denounced on moral grounds, although in a preface the writer had explicitly exempted individual industrialists from moral censure, saying with an almost gracious reassurance that it was not they but the historical process that must be blamed. And the events in Germany would seem to show that even among those terrible people there was the preoccupation with guilt and innocence—so many words to explain the wrongs done to them, for the wronged and the weak are the innocent; so much cruelty to separate themselves from the guilty, for those who are punished are guilty and those who punish are innocent; so much adoration of strength, for the strong who once were weak are never guilty.

Arthur broke the silence. "John, I'd like to ask one question," he said in a frank voice. "Why did you wait until now to tell us this?"

And Nancy said, "Yes, John. Why did you?"

It was the question that Laskell had of course been waiting for, and in a way it was a relief to have it asked, to have the charge made.

He decided to lie. "I don't know why I did. It was pretty unpleasant, after all. I just didn't want to talk about it."

They accepted the explanation generously. Arthur nodded in understanding. Nancy said, "I can see that. It's a horror, no matter how you look at it. But you should have told us."

But of course he had not yet told them anything. He had told them only that Maxim had come to him with the information that he had broken with the Party, that he feared for his life and wished to establish an existence, that he had slept on the roof and taken the train with Laskell, choosing the last car of the train and the last seat in the car because he feared an attack from the rear. And the true story was so much more than this. The true whole story was so much more than the mere record of the facts of Maxim's defection. It was that Laskell had been sick and that he had been deeply involved with himself and two nurses, that he had been inexplicably interested in questions of being, in questions of his own existence, and that he had become well and bickered endlessly with Paine; it was that he had thought of Arthur Croom and Maxim as contradictory but complementary parts of political life; it was that Maxim had come in when he and Paine were quarreling about his taking his fishing gear, when Paine had been encouraging him to this assertion of health. Then they ought to know certain things about his feelings in connection with Maxim, such as his sense of submitting to a *procès-verbal* when Maxim talked to him, and his absurd notion of the great mural figures that went around with Maxim. Then there was Maxim's trick of bringing out the photograph, and Maxim's claim upon him, that very special claim which he had not realized until after Maxim had gone. And there was the farewell to Paine.

These things, under almost any circumstances, were not easy to talk about, yet he had been in the habit of talking with the Crooms about difficult matters, though not usually difficult personal matters. But the point was that this was the story they had all along not wished to hear—the story of his illness which was so much a part of the Maxim story. Of the *true* story he had so far given them only a little official version.

"I think," he said, "that I was even more disturbed than you might guess, and for reasons you wouldn't know. It was, as a personal experience, very shaking."

"It must have been," Nancy said softly. "You looked dreadful when you got here. I was frightened by the way you looked. And you weren't yourself. You were very strange. I said so to Arthur—I said you seemed not like yourself at all. And now I scarcely wonder, traveling with that—" Unable to name Maxim, she was even unable to characterize him. "Yes, I can understand your not talking about it."

So Nancy forgave him for not talking about it on his arrival? Laskell smiled. "It's more than that, Nancy. You see, I've known Maxim longer than you have, and I've known him in a different way. You think of him politically. I suppose I've thought of him that way too for quite a while now. But I've known him in a different way. I suppose it's important in the way I felt. I suppose it's important in the way I felt that Maxim suddenly produced an old snapshot of Elizabeth that he said he wanted to return to me." Laskell lit a cigarette. "It was the picture I showed you this morning, Nancy."

He saw Nancy's face set. He had expected it would. Her voice was very precise as she said, "Yes. But why?"

"You mean, why did he show me Elizabeth's picture? I don't know, really. But I can guess several reasons. He may have wanted to confuse my emotions. If I could give you an idea of his manner that afternoon, you would understand what I mean. It seemed as if every smallest thing he did or said had an intention. Or perhaps he wanted to remind me of the past—to make me emotional so that I wouldn't have my wits about me. Or—" Laskell paused; he realized his hands were trembling. "Or perhaps he only wanted to make it real to me."

Nancy said, "Make it real to you? Make what real?"

"That people do actually die."

Arthur said briskly, "Aren't you being a little hypersubtle? A little too psychological?"

Laskell shrugged. "Maybe so. But we aren't exactly in a context of simplicities, are we?" Laskell waited just a fraction of a moment, then he said, "It may be, of course, that his motive was much simpler. He may have wanted to remind me of a claim he had on me for my help."

Nancy had put down her knitting some time back. She was sitting with her feet neatly together and her knees neatly together and her hands tightly clasped on her knees, her head bent over her hands. She had been looking at her clasped hands. Now she looked up sharply.

"A claim on you? What kind of claim could he have on you?" Her voice was cold and even. "I should think that after what he told you, all claims would be at an end. At an end immediately."

"It was a personal claim—he was very good to me after Elizabeth died."

"Oh." Nancy picked up her knitting.

Well, it had been done. The "claim" and Elizabeth's death had been brought together. They had been spoken in one sentence. Never before in his life had Laskell said anything to anybody in order to see if it would produce a particular response. He was stricken and ashamed that he should have done it first with Nancy. He had introduced the mention of the snapshot to test her. She had not passed the test. He had introduced the claim Maxim had on him, again to try her response. She had responded badly. She had disclosed herself as he had maneuvered her to—she had disclosed her deficiency of emotion, her fear of talking about the dead Elizabeth.

But his own intention had been mean and coarse, and Laskell would now have given much to be out of the system of innocence and guilt to which he too consented by testing his friends. How had he allowed Nancy to move so far out of his system of love, how had he put her into this system of accusation? But now accuse her he must. "Claims" were of the past, the dead were of the past. They had no place in Nancy's bright, shining future, and he, Laskell, by giving them place in his thought, had committed what amounted to an obscenity. It was what he had been suspecting ever since his arrival in the country and now he had his proof. When it came to acquiring significant information for the dossier, he was a perfect little Maxim of an interrogator. A great weight settled on his spirit.

It was Nancy who resumed the conversation. She said, "John,

you said that you hadn't seen Maxim for a year and that you thought he was angry at you because you had refused to do something he had asked you to do. What was it you refused to do? Why did you refuse?" Her voice was soft and rather tired.

Arthur said reasonably, "John had no commitment, Nan. He's helped with particular things, just as we've done, when our views have happened to coincide with the Party's—specific issues, like free speech or relief for political prisoners, things like that."

"Yes. Of course," said Nancy quietly. "I wasn't blaming John. I just wanted to know what and why."

"I'll tell you what I refused," Laskell said. "But I'm not sure I can tell you why. Gifford asked me if I would receive certain letters addressed to me and addressed in a particular way that would distinguish them from the rest of my mail, and then turn them over to him, or to someone he would send, without opening them."

Arthur said, "Oh, that! Yes—he asked us the same thing. We refused too. I have no doubt the thing was perfectly all right, but the element of secrecy put me off. So we said no."

How enviable it was, the easy, guiltless way Arthur spoke of his refusal. His naturally political temperament permitted him to grant or refuse requests according to nothing but reason.

"What do you suppose all the secrecy was about?" Laskell asked.

Arthur shrugged. "That was Maxim's business. I don't know and I didn't ask."

"He said that his work was special and secret. Those were the words he used, 'special and secret.' He made a point of saying that it had nothing to do with organizations or strikes. But when I asked him what it did have to do with, he wouldn't say. He just repeated that it was special and secret. But he did admit that the letters had something to do with whatever was 'special and secret.' What do you suppose it was?"

"I don't know," Arthur said, and his intelligent ugly face showed no curiosity. And then he gave Laskell the benefit of his guiltless political nature by saying casually, "It's just as well that you refused too."

It was at that moment that Laskell had the sensation about Nancy. For it was a sensation and not a perception—it was as simple and direct as if it were a sound or a smell. It was as if he could feel her existing in a circumambient reservation, as if she were not in the same relation to himself and Arthur that he was in to Arthur or Arthur to him. She was in a relation to something else, to herself, or to some special knowledge she had. But it was not until he was back at the Folgers' and in his brass bed that Laskell understood what the sensation meant. Then it came to him with perfect certainty: Nancy had not said no to Maxim's request. Arthur had said no for both the Crooms. Nancy had allowed him to think that the answer stood. But Nancy had not said no, she had said yes. She had separated herself from Arthur and had sought out Maxim and had privately said yes. It was surely the first separation of herself from Arthur that Nancy had ever made. It was very puzzling and rather frightening. But he did not know whether he was frightened for Nancy or by her.

He lay a long time in the dark that night, listening to the very faint movement of the tree outside his window. Once more he turned over in his mind just what it meant to feel that the future was no longer real, or that, if it was real at all, it was coexistent with the present. And once more he thought of the future as a characteristic concept of the well-loved young man of the middle class, brought up on promises.

And what has changed? he asked himself. Was it that he was not well loved? Or not of the middle class?

Oh, surely of the middle class. Perhaps not so well loved as he once had been. And surely no longer young.

He lay there, excited by that recognition, not depressed by it. He could not sleep, but he did not mind that. There was a kind of gratification in the grave and not very happy thoughts he had. He was not able to identify this gratification.

There was much to think about in connection with the conversation he had been having. There were certain questions that occurred to him. For example, he found himself asking why Arthur, who was so political, had accepted the fact of Maxim's break with the Party without inquiring into its reasons. He himself had avoided that inquiry, although Maxim had expressly given him the chance to make it. He had been ashamed that he had not gone into the theoretical grounds for Maxim's action. But why had Arthur not done so? For Arthur was really political. Arthur's agreement with the Party began where theory left off and where morals and will began. He had many differences with the Party and was sometimes even inclined to smile at the economic statements of the Party's theorists. He thought the Party ought to exist for its moral influence in politics, but he went no further than that. Yet he had not asked for an explanation of why Maxim had broken.

He had not, it was true, gone quite the whole way with Nancy in giving insanity as the reason. Still, he had not thought of explaining the break by attributing it to political disagreement. "What could be the matter with him?" was the only line of questioning Arthur took. He was quite willing, it seemed, to leave the Party as a fixed point from which all deviation implied something wrong with the person deviating. Not ever being at one with the Party was all right; but deviation, after having been at one with the Party, was wrong. Arthur was a political man, but even for him the Party was not really political, and a break with it was not an action in politics—in practical politics, as people said, wishing to make a distinction between that unfortunate kind of politics and some other, better kind—but rather an action in morals.

And then: why had Arthur so severely questioned him when he had mentioned Lenin's view of the need for small groups of professional revolutionaries, asking him if he really thought that the Party was conspiratorial? Yet Arthur had said that the affair of the secret letters had been Maxim's business and therefore not to be inquired into. Then to confuse the matter further, why had Arthur felt that because of the secrecy it was as well that the Crooms and Laskell had refused to be involved?

But Nancy was involved. Of that Laskell was sure. Why had she said yes? Was it because she, like him, had been reared as a well-loved child of the middle class, brought up on promises which had to be fulfilled? If at first Laskell had been ambiguously frightened by his knowledge of what she had done, now, as he thought of her in the light of their common past, thought of her as the spirited girl in the genteel suburb to whom so much was promised and so much given, he had a kind of tenderness for her action. It had a directness and innocence about it, a fresh, young immediacy.

John Laskell had never looked at the Crooms from so much distance before. But he found the distance by no means at final odds with his great affection for them. Quite the contrary, as the excitement of thought began to wane and sleep began to come, he thought of the Crooms with a new affection. They did not have the secret of life, of the perfectly simple character, but that only endeared them the more. Not until he saw that they did not have it was he aware that he had ever believed that they had had it.

After this evening, Laskell and the Crooms did not of their own will revert to the story of Maxim. And perhaps, though that was doubtful, it would never have been mentioned again had it not forced itself upon them. It did so three days later. Laskell was at the Crooms in the afternoon and Nancy gave him his mail. She said as she handed it to him, "There's a card from your friend."

"My friend?" said Laskell. He knew whom she meant, but he said, "Have I only the one?"

"Your Maxim," Nancy said dryly.

"*My* Maxim? Surely as much yours as mine. Or as little mine as yours."

"I saw the card, John. Really, Kermit Simpson is not a responsible person. And you must be held to blame too, you really must."

For the postcard bore the printed name of *The New Era* and on it Maxim had typed a brief message: "I greet you from my existence." He had both typed his name and signed it. There was an asterisk at the end of the single sentence of the message, and it referred to a footnote below. "A man," the footnote read, "is the cause of existence but not the cause of essence of another man (for the latter is an eternal truth): and so they can certainly agree in essence, but in existence they must differ, and on that account if the existence of one of them perish, that of the other does not consequently perish; but if the essence of one of them could be destroyed or made false, the essence of the other must also be destroyed. Spin. Eth. Bk. I, Prop. XVII, note."

"Have you read it?" Laskell said.

"No. Of course I haven't read your mail."

"I'm sure he meant you to read it. At any rate, you've read enough for his purpose. You read his name and *The New Era*. You know, as he wanted you to know, that on a certain day in August Gifford Maxim wrote from the office of *The New Era*. I'm sure he's sending out as many postcards as he can. Here, read it."

She took it as if it were dangerous or befouled. "What does it mean?" she said when she had read it through.

"Did we ever really know what Maxim meant by anything? The quotation is from Spinoza's *Ethics*—I don't know what he means to say by it."

This was not wholly true. But he spoke bitterly. He was angry with Maxim for this trick. He did not want to hear from Maxim on this presumption of friendship. He did not want the presumption of friendship to be the pretext for the further establishment of Maxim's monomaniac existence. So he would not let his mind rest on whatever meaning the card had. But he did not tear it up. He put it in his pocket.

And then a few days later they had forced on them yet another evidence of Maxim's existence and of his redoubtable efforts to establish it. The August issue of *The New Era* arrived for the Crooms and Gifford Maxim's name was on the masthead. He appeared as an assistant editor. There was no announcement of his having joined the staff, simply the addition of his name to the names of the two young men who were also assistant editors. But on the cover was the announcement of an article: "Spirit and Law. . . . Gifford Maxim." This, no doubt, was the article, "the literary article," that Maxim had waved at Laskell the day of his visit. Perhaps its inclusion in the issue was the reason for the issue's being so late. And when the Crooms handed him *The New Era* in wry silence, Laskell felt enough connection with the article to admit that if they wanted to hold him to account for its publication, they had some justification.

The New Era was a long, double-columned, rough-stock publication, similar in appearance to the American and English liberal weeklies, although Kermit Simpson made a point of saying that it had been modeled in format as in policy on the old *Freeman*. Maxim's article ran to two pages, an unusual length for *The New Era's* literary section.

"Have you read it?" Laskell said.

"Not yet," said Arthur.

"No," said Nancy.

Laskell took it out to the lawn to read. It was an essay in the form of a review of a new edition of Melville's *Billy Budd, Fore-*

topman, a limited and costly edition. "It is now twelve years since the discovery and first publication of the masterpiece of Herman Melville's old age. Yet even now *Billy Budd* is not generally known to American readers." It began so, and Laskell thought that Maxim had established a new existence indeed: he wrote quite in the Anglican manner of Matthew Arnold and T. S. Eliot. But the older Maxim appeared in the next sentence: "The Porpentine Press has just brought out this great work in an edition scarcely calculated to give it wider currency. Five hundred copies on hand-made, woven rag-paper at fifteen dollars a copy, the type hand-set and prim and self-conscious, and then distributed so as to insure the scarcity-value and snob-value of each of the numbered copies— thus does 'culture' ape the values of the market-place." It was not until much later that Laskell learned that all this was Maxim's joke. There was no such edition of *Billy Budd,* there was not even such a press as the Porpentine.

Maxim gave a few more sentences to the sins of the Porpentine Press and spoke sharply of the line-drawings which illustrated the book in, as he said, "a bad imitation of the worst manner of Rockwell Kent." Then he launched into his subject. As Laskell read, he was filled with astonishment. He had never speculated on what views Maxim might come to hold and now that he had the opportunity to see what they were, it was almost unbelievable. Not unbelievable that anyone should have them, but that Maxim should have them, and presumably not all of a sudden but developing them at a time when everyone believed him to be holding views exactly opposite.

Because, as Maxim said, the story of Billy Budd was not well known, he undertook to tell it briefly. He established the great triangle of Billy Budd, Claggart, and Captain Vere—Billy Budd, The Handsome Sailor, the youth of so great a natural goodness that everyone loved him, and physically perfect except for the one flaw, his stammering inability to speak when under great emotional stress; and Claggart, the master-at-arms of the English frigate, a fallen gentleman, the man of evil, who is drawn to goodness but envies and hates it; and Captain Vere of the frigate *Indomitable,* "Starry" Vere, as he is called, the man of passionate but reasonable virtue, of intellect and duty, a captain potentially as great as Nelson. Maxim quickly told the story of Claggart's perverse persecution of Budd, his denouncing Budd to the Captain for mutinous schemes, the Captain's dislike of Claggart and his intuitive trust of Budd, the confrontation of Budd and Claggart in the Captain's cabin, the accusation made, Budd's confusion and anger rendering him incapable of speech, so that his answer had to be his blow on Claggart's temple, Claggart's falling dead and the Captain's cry, "Struck dead by an angel of God. Yet the angel must hang." Such is the goodness of the young sailor that even the small minds of the ship's officers are moved to be merciful. But they are swayed by "Starry" Vere's speech to them, in which, though torn by his paternal love for the young man, Vere argues for the necessity under law of condemning him to death. Maxim quoted the scene of the hanging at dawn, so that his readers might have the full force of it, Billy's utterance, as the noose was around his neck, of his only words, "God bless Captain Vere!" the words "delivered in the clear melody of a singing bird on the point of launching from the twig," the massed ship's-company echoing the cry without volition and almost against its will, the Captain on the quarter-deck momentarily paralyzed by the cry: and then the going aloft of Billy, which is made to appear as an ascension rather than a hanging, the sudden light in the sky and the hanged figure miraculously not twitching in its death-throes.

"The modern mind," Maxim wrote, "is not really capable of understanding this story. I mean the modern mind in its most vocal part, in its radical or liberal intellectual part. For such people, Billy Budd will be nothing more than an oppressed worker, and a very foolish one, an insufficiently activated one, nothing more than a 'company man,' weakly acquiescent to the boss. And Captain Vere will seem as at best but a conscience-ridden bourgeois, sympathetic to a man of the lower orders but committed to carrying out the behests of the established regime.

"Melville, of course, intended no such understanding of the matter. The story is a political parable, but on a higher level than we are used to taking our political parables. It is the tragedy of Spirit in the world of Necessity. And more, it is the tragedy of Law in the world of Necessity, the tragedy that Law faces whenever it confronts its child, Spirit. For Billy is nothing less than pure

Spirit, and Captain Vere nothing less than Law in the world of Necessity. We have, of course, a story of God the Father, of Christ and of the Devil, but this we must not interpret in too traditional a way.

"I have said that Billy is pure Spirit, but that is not quite accurate. He is not wholly pure. He has a flaw, symbolized by his impediment of speech. And he sins, despite the fact that the man against whom he directs his anger is Evil itself. His blow is given out of an impotence.

"Yet, as Spirit, Billy is pure enough to make the tragedy of Captain Vere. Vere must rule the world of Necessity because Claggart —Evil—exists. The belief of the modern progressive is that Spirit should find its complete expression at once. Everything that falls short of the immediate expression of Spirit is believed to be an ignominious moral inadequacy. To such minds, Captain Vere is culpable because he does not acquit Billy in defiance of all Law. To them, Vere's suffering at being unable to do so is a mere sentimentality. It is even an hypocrisy. The modern progressive believes that he will not palter with anything less than perfection. He considers this the mark of his virtue. But perhaps it is rather the mark of his lack of belief in the truth and reality of Spirit. He cannot believe in Spirit unless it is established in institutions. He cannot believe that he really exists as Spirit unless he sees himself matched exactly in external forms. It is not the *strength* of the inner life that makes this demand. Rather it is the *weakness* of the inner life that will not tolerate any discrepancy between what Spirit can conceive and what Necessity can tolerate. Melville's perception is that Spirit and the Law that is established in the world of Necessity are kin, yet discontinuous. It is not merely that Vere understands that Billy is his son, the Isaac to his Abraham; it is that Billy understands that Vere is his father and blesses him in his last words. Spirit blesses Law, even when Law has put the noose around his neck, for Spirit understands the true kinship.

"As long as Evil exists in the world, Law must exist, and it—not Spirit—must have the rule. And Vere's is the suffering, his is the tragic choice of God the Father, who must condemn his own son to death. But not as in the familiar transaction of Christian theology, as a sacrifice and an atonement, but for the sake of the Son himself, for the sake of Spirit in humanity. For Billy Budd is not only Christ, he is Christ in Adam, and is therefore imperfect, subject to excess. But we cannot understand Vere's suffering choice because we do not understand tragedy. And we do not understand tragedy because we do not understand love."

The essay did not stop there, but went on to speak at length of tragedy and love.

It was as well that it did, for Laskell had found that he had been a little caught by Maxim's words. One sentence in particular, in which Maxim spoke of the reign of Spirit being in the everlasting future, while modern men thought that they could establish it now, suited what Laskell had been thinking about the future. But as Maxim went on to speak of tragedy and love, using the words over and over again, the odor of corruption came to Laskell and freed him from any enchantment with Maxim's mind. Tragedy and love, love and tragedy, tragedy depending on love, love depending on tragedy: Maxim wove a crooning litany of the two words until Laskell felt an intellectual nausea and thought that there were two words that decency could not utter, however real were the things they represented. Perhaps only because Maxim spoke them, and spoke them so often, Laskell felt that never again could anyone say the words tragedy and love.

He sat in the canvas deck chair and wondered how it was possible for a man who had once so loved freedom and the future to make so impassioned a plea, in the name of tragedy and love, for the *status quo*, the accepted thing, the rule of force. Maxim was no disaffected revolutionary. He was the blackest of reactionaries. He was not a man who had no party for his progressive but divergent ideas. He had moved so far as to be on the other side.

"What do you make of it?" Arthur said when Laskell brought *The New Era* back into the house.

Laskell shrugged in impatience. "I don't know. Read it yourself and see." He felt at that moment a disgust for the whole world of ideas that allowed such shifts as Maxim's to be made so easily. He wanted to be off by himself.

The Crooms brought themselves to read the essay and their response to it surprised him. He himself could not understand it save as proof that Maxim had thrown over all his aims and hopes.

Maxim took pleasure in explaining that Spirit—as he called it—was not yet ready to establish its rule on earth. He meant that it would never establish its rule. Perhaps Maxim did not really believe in his own elaborate obfuscation, his vague religiosity that demanded an understanding of tragedy and the exercise of love and required events to stand still while "Spirit" perfected itself, which, of course, it would never do. Laskell did not know which was the more repulsive, a Maxim who really believed this or a Maxim who pretended to believe it because he thought he would be the safer if he made clear and absolute his difference with the Party.

But the Crooms, oddly enough, did not feel as he did about the article. They certainly did not like it. "There's an awful lot of sheer garbage in it," Arthur said. "I never thought Giff would go off on that quasi-religious line. I thought he'd organize a splinter group or go over to the Trotskyites." And Nancy said, "That mystical nonsense, it's disgusting." But they did not quite see eye to eye with Laskell when he spoke of the piece as reactionary.

"If you think about it," said Nancy, "you see that it is really quite applicable to the Moscow trials. Even if those men were subjectively innocent—I mean even if they had good motives for what they did, like Budd—I don't believe that's so, but even if it were so —they may have had to be executed for the sake of what he calls Law in the world of Necessity. And you remember how they all concurred in their punishment and seemed almost to *want* it. Certainly before they died they had a proper appreciation of Law. They realized that the dictatorship of the proletariat represented Law. Of course, God wasn't mentioned, but it was the same thing in effect and they said that their punishment was necessary. No, I think you're wrong, John, in the way you've read the article. Don't misunderstand me—I'm sure he's insane, but that makes it all the more surprising how much insight he still has."

And Nancy's voice had now a touch of sorrow, a touch of pity for Maxim that she had not been able to muster before.

Arthur said, "Yes, there's a certain amount of real insight in it. I don't mean that business about God or all that talk about tragedy and love. But if you read the article without letting that come to the fore, it makes some real sense. You find a good many people these days who think things can be made perfect overnight, that a revolution insures a Utopia in an instant, without difficulty and trouble, without compromise and without the use of force. Mind you, I haven't any sympathy with the article, but it does have a core of realism. The great danger to the progressive movement these days, as I see it, is that liberals are going to confuse their dreams and ideals with the possible realities. You see that happening already—people become disappointed and disaffected because everything isn't the way they would like to have it. They see economic democracy developing over there and that doesn't satisfy them—they begin shouting for immediate political democracy, forgetting the realities of the historical situation. Yes, Maxim in this respect has more sense in him than I thought he would have. People who break usually don't have that much sense."

Laskell thought that perhaps, some time, he would read the piece again. He did not defend his own reading of it. "Perhaps you're right," he said. He thought too that some time he would consider why Arthur had looked at him with a special, personal intensity as he made that rather long speech of his and a certain stubbornness that Arthur's whole body seemed to be expressing.

7

> " 'And did those feet in ancient time
>   Walk upon England's mountains green?' "

When she mentioned feet Susan Caldwell's hand swept down to indicate her feet. When she referred to mountains, it swept upward and suggested a mountain.

" 'And was the holy Lamb of God' "—and now with cradling arms and downward gazing eyes she indicated a lamb and its tender care—" 'On England's pleasant pastures seen?' " Her widely separating hands suggested both the extent of the pastures and the breadth of the question.

Laskell, holding the book, was appalled.

But he had already questioned her twice and did not like to do it again. He had been writing in his room that afternoon and had seen her drifting vaguely up and down the Folgers' lawn, looking at the upper windows, carrying in her arms—in much the same way she was to "carry" the Lamb—the big book. He came down to her, thinking that she might possibly want him, and it turned out that she had come on a visit to him. The visit was not wholly social. Or at least she did not present it as wholly social. She wanted Laskell to "hear" the poem she was to recite at the Bazaar. But her intention to make use of him did not diminish and even increased the odd little flattery of the visit. They sat down on the lawn together and Laskell addressed himself very seriously to the duty she had imposed upon him.

She handed him the book. It was a big college anthology of English literature. She opened to the place marked by a slip of paper and gave him the volume at a double page of Blake's songs. "Which one is it?" he said.

She stood over him and pointed to one of the poems on the page. It was not a Song of Innocence or a Song of Experience, but the four stanzas that Blake had prefixed to *Milton.*

"Why are you reciting this one?" Laskell asked.

"Is it wrong?" said Susan, her eyes wide.

"Wrong? Oh, no. I just wanted to know why."

She explained. "For the entertainment we can each do anything we want. It's a very informal entertainment. One of the girls is going to play the piano and render the 'Parade of the Wooden Soldiers.' Did you ever hear that piece?"

"Yes, I have," Laskell said.

"And one is going to sing. And I'm going to recite this poem. Mother read me a lot of poems and I liked this one. She said I could choose one I liked. I liked this one. So I chose it." The logic could not have been clearer. She went beyond logic to explain. "It's an easy poem to recite because of the gestures. It has a lot of gestures."

"Gestures?" But Laskell was not so young that he could pretend to ignorance of the tradition of recitation with expression and gestures. He said, "Oh, I see."

And now Susan took her stance. But first she shook herself from the shoulders, her wrists loose. She agitated them violently and very seriously, as if she were giving herself over to the uncontrollable spasms of a dreadful neurological disorder.

"Goodness, Susan!" said Laskell. "Why are you doing that?"

"It's so my arms will hang loose and naturally by my sides. Mother taught me to do it."

"But you won't do it in public, when you recite?"

"Of course not," said Susan, mildly surprised by his stupidity. "I'm just practicing."

She thrust her left foot forward and put her weight on it. She tried her arms for looseness and naturalness and seemed satisfied with their condition.

When she had finished the first stanza, she said, "Was that right?"

"Yes," said Laskell. "Perfect." He meant that she was word-perfect. He was not referring to the larger aesthetic question.

She undertook the second stanza on the same system of gesture.

> " 'And did the Countenance Divine
> Shine forth upon our clouded hills?
> And was Jerusalem builded here
> Among these dark Satanic Mills?' "

She made a graceful reference to her own face to suggest the
Countenance Divine. Her hands came forth in a wide delta to
indicate the Countenance in the act of shining forth upon the
clouded hills. There was a complex upward movement of two
hands to show Jerusalem being builded here. And then there was
an even more complex flutter to indicate not only the Mills but
also her revulsion from their dark Satanic quality. This time she
did not interrupt herself at the end of the stanza, but, having
paused weightily, went on.

> " 'Bring me my Bow of Burning gold:
> Bring me my Arrows of desire:
> Bring me my Spear: O clouds unfold!
> Bring me my Chariot of fire.' "

With each "Bring" she reached out like a stage magician, snatching things from the air to astonish her audience. She grasped the
bow and arrows appropriately, and in the very act of grasping them,
fitted at least one arrow to the bow. She seized the spear and, still
holding it in her right hand, well out from her body in warlike
fashion, she seized the reins of the chariot of fire in her left hand
and leaned forward to meet the wind of the chariot's speed. She
was now fully equipped to utter her declaration of war. She came
out of the crouch that was necessary for the control of the speeding
chariot and stood upright.

" 'I will *not* cease from Mental Fight' "— And she stamped her
foot in a passion of refusal.

"Hold it!" said Laskell.

She stopped and looked at him. "Did I get it wrong?"

"Why do you stamp your foot?"

"To show I mean it."

"I don't think you ought to do that."

"Why not?" she said in reasonable surprise.

"Because it's as if you were a child being stubborn. And I don't think you ought to say, 'I will *not* cease'—you ought to say, '*I will not cease*,' all on a level: '*I will not cease*.'"

She fully considered the criticism and also the really great compliment that was bound up with it. Then she said, "But I am a child, really."

It was certainly a point. Laskell thought about it. "Yes," he said. "But you haven't said any other part of the poem as if you were a child, and then suddenly, just at the end, when the poem gets so determined, you change the character of the speaker."

She took it in very thoughtfully and was on the point of coming to agreement. But Laskell was now sorry he had raised any objection at all. The manner she had devised—or more likely, been taught—was of course absurd, but he had no right to correct it. Elocution with expression would scarcely be under the same reprobation at this country function that it might have been in other circumstances. And yet Susan was so simple and so alight with intelligence that he did not want her to diminish herself by this absurd manner.

"I'm sorry, Susan," Laskell said. "I shouldn't have interfered. You go on and do it your own way."

"No," said Susan. "If it isn't right, it isn't right."

"No, really. It's all right. Just go ahead and say it the way you always do."

"No," said Susan with a final firmness. "Let me try." She took her public stance again, her left foot forward, her knee slightly bent, her weight on the left leg. "'I will *not* cease.' No. Wrong! '*I will not cease. I will not cease.*' There! '*I will not cease* from Mental Fight.' Is that right?"

"Yes. Fine."

"'*I will not cease* from Mental Fight.'" She smiled at him and he smiled back.

"Good," he said with an odd little satisfaction. "Now go on."

"'*I will not cease* from Mental Fight.'" A little frown appeared on her forehead. "'And'"—she began and cast about for the next line.

"'Nor,'" Laskell prompted. "'Nor shall my Sword'"—

She looked blank for a moment. "Oh, yes. 'Nor shall my Sword sleep in my hand.'" She held her hand forward and to the side, clutching the unsleeping sword. Then she raised it before her, reaching it high.

> " 'Till we have built Jerusalem
> In England's green and pleasant Land.' "

And she brought the dedicated sword down in conclusion.

She looked to Laskell for his word. "Very good," he said. "Very good indeed."

"You really think so?" she said with the artist's everlasting dubiety which, when voiced, is half real and half insincere.

"Oh, beautiful," he said. His sincerity came not from his admiration of the "rendition" of the poem but from the amusement he felt at her puckered and hesitant face as she canvassed the true value of her performance.

"*Beautiful!*" she said with the childish scorn that expresses childish embarrassment at a really big word of praise.

"Truly," he said.

"Oh pooh!" was her answer, with an awkward movement of her shoulders to fight off the voluptuous sensations of sudden praise. "*Beautiful—pooh!*" And she sat down.

He lightly tapped her twice on the head with the big book. "Don't you make fun of me," he said.

"Don't you make fun of *me*," she said and giggled freely. She had come for a particular purpose, to have him hear her rehearse, but now that her purpose was accomplished, she did not go.

"What poems do *you* know?" she said. She simply assumed that if she knew poems by heart, he must know poems by heart. And, as it happened, she was not wrong. He had once been made to memorize ten sonnets in a course in college. He was perfectly willing to recite them for her. He recited "Let me not to the marriage of true minds admit impediments," and "When to the sessions of sweet silent thought," finding them in the book so that she could check on his accuracy. He recited "Since there's no help, come let us kiss and part," and "When I consider how my light is spent," and "The world is too much with us," and "Earth has not anything to show more fair." She followed each of them carefully and corrected him gravely when he slipped.

"Why, you know everything," she said when he stopped.

"Well, not so much as *that*," he said with a modesty that was wholly fatuous. He said, "Aren't you going swimming today?" He had often seen Susan and Emily coming up the road on clear afternoons with towels and wet hair.

"No," she said, a little bitterly. "Mother decided not to."

"Where is your mother?" The question was really a rude one, but Susan and her mother were almost always seen together, like a foal and a mare. The question of where Susan's mother was was not quite so important as where her father was, for Duck Caldwell had vanished for the past three days. This was not so unusual as to cause concern, but it made some trouble for the Crooms, for Duck had left a job of plastering half done.

"Mother's getting water at the Korzinskis'," Susan said.

"You usually go with her," Laskell said.

"Yes, but today she said I shouldn't. She said I should come and have you hear my poem."

It took something from the pleasure of Susan's visit that she had not thought of it herself, but it did not take as much from it as Laskell might have expected.

"I can speak some Polish. The Korzinskis taught me." She spoke some Polish. "Good-by, thank you very much for your kindness."

"Good-by, Susan. You're very welcome."

"No—that's what it means, that's what the Polish means. Then they say to me, 'Panyenka'—that means young lady—" She said a sentence in Polish. "And that means 'You're welcome.'"

"Is it far to the Korzinskis'?"

"Not very. Mr. Croom asked us to get the water at his house, but Mother says it would hurt the Korzinskis' feelings. Anyway, Mother says that she and Mrs. Croom are unsympathetic." She said it as if being unsympathetic were a cozy relationship possible only to adults.

After this first visit with its particular purpose, Susan paid Laskell several visits with no purpose at all. He would look out of his window when he was working on the planned cities of antiquity and see her on the Folgers' lawn, walking slowly up and down, or sitting with her legs tucked under her. He understood, recollecting it from his boyhood, that she was in that terrible state of children—she "had nothing to do"—and he would come down to talk to her. When the friendship had progressed a little, she ventured beyond waiting to be noticed and took to calling up to his window, "Mr. Laskell, are you busy?"

They played a good deal of mumblety-peg. The three hounds, with their impulse to sociability, always came to sit close to them during Susan's visits and had to be safeguarded from any mischance of the knife. Laskell and Susan thought it unfriendly to chase the hounds and before they began a game, Susan would seize one after another by the scruff of his neck and urge and drag him to a safe distance. They used Laskell's old stag-handled pocket-knife. Susan knew the first passages of the game and was fairly good at them—the knife thrown from its cradled position in the clenched fist, the knife tossed up from the open palm. She knew the finger-flips but she did not know over-the-fence. Laskell taught it to her and she became quite good at it. From there on it became pretty much Laskell's game. Susan conceived a great admiration for his skill, and she herself acquired a growing adeptness. She read a good deal. For all her devotion to the life of art and her choice of the Blake poem, she read chiefly comic books. She said that her mother did not approve of her reading them. She could not have been given as many dimes as she had books, but despite the scarcity of children in the neighborhood and Susan's rather unhappy distance from the few who were within reach, she seemed to be a member of some invisible circle of the young which saw to it that these documents were circulated and fell into the right hands. She herself had no great respect for these books but she had an addiction.

The growing friendship with Susan naturally developed the acquaintanceship with Susan's mother. He often met the two on the road or before their house, and since now he had to stop to chat with Susan, he had also to chat with Emily Caldwell. These more frequent meetings dimmed his recollection of how she had first appeared to him, as well as his sense of her foolishness that evening at the Crooms'. She began to take her place in the commonplace, the quite pleasant commonplace, as the mother of a little girl he was fond of. And through Susan, as it were, the same thing happened to her father. Laskell met Duck face to face one day after one of the visits had come to an end and he was walking to the Crooms'. Susan was walking with him to her own house. Duck came toward them. Laskell felt strange, even a little guilty, walking with the man's own child, but it made a condition of friendliness that had to be recognized and he said, "Hello!" and Duck answered, "Hi!"

"Susan has just been paying me a visit," Laskell said.

"What do you want to bother people for?" Duck said to Susan.

It was much what most fathers would have said under the circumstances. There was no exception to be taken to it.

"She hasn't bothered me, I enjoyed it."

"Well," said Duck dubiously.

If Laskell did not quite like a too-long, too-objective stare that Duck gave his daughter and a certain constriction of Susan's recently expansive being, that was probably only imagination. It was enough of a meeting to make a country acquaintanceship, even though an acquaintanceship in dislike, and thereafter when Laskell was at the Crooms' he called a greeting to Duck and they even talked about the problems of the reconstruction of the house.

This made enough of a relationship between Laskell and Duck to confirm the truce that had been established between Laskell and the Crooms since the evening he had told the story of Maxim. That evening had been the first expressed tension between them. But tensions are elements of friendship and on the whole they were as gay with each other as they had ever been. Nevertheless the tension was there, and Laskell, for his part, pulled on his end of the rope. He pulled firmly but all his feeling went into the pull itself—he was not annoyed with the Crooms and he made no reservations in his relationship with them. He knew that there was a difference between them and he felt better when he kept himself aware of it. It was now no longer his intention, for example, to hide his dislike of Duck. If Nancy were now to have said to him as she once had, "I think you have a prejudice against Duck," he would have answered with a cheerful grimness, "I certainly have." Now, when they talked about Duck, he put in his protest; and when they depreciated Emily in Duck's favor, as they often did, he also put in a protest. He did not admire Emily Caldwell but her good looks pleased him, he liked her cleanly sturdy quality and found that if he had to think, which he did not really like to do, of the juxtaposition of Emily and her husband, there was a certain rightness in standing up for Emily. The Crooms looked at him oddly for this open declaration of Caldwell partisanship. They may have thought that it had something to do with their judgment of Laskell on the Maxim evening, as of course it had. After a while the Crooms gave up talking about the Caldwells almost entirely. That lessened the strain considerably and things went on gaily until Nancy's picnic.

Nancy and Arthur had agreed on a picnic, but they had had some difficulty coming to an agreement on what kind of picnic it should be. Arthur had the modern idea of a picnic and it was essentially masculine in nature. What he wanted was a thick steak and roasted corn and coffee, all made on the spot. But Nancy would have none of that. She wanted what she called an old-fashioned picnic. She wanted exactly what Arthur said he wished to avoid—dozens of well-made sandwiches wrapped in wax paper, hard-boiled eggs, tomatoes, and perhaps a jar of little pickles, a big cake. As for coffee, that might be made on the spot, although she would actually prefer to take it in the big thermos bottle.

It was Nancy's kind of picnic that they were to have. It became clear to Arthur as well as to Laskell that the picnic had a special meaning to Nancy. Perhaps she had an image of her mother sitting on a steamer rug, the basket by her side, urging sandwiches on the family around her. Arthur groaned and spoke of ants and spiders, but he gave way and Nancy boiled her chicken and chilled it and stripped it and made it into her sandwiches which she neatly wrapped in wax paper. They had the pickles and the tomatoes, and the coffee in the big thermos. Nancy took the picnic very seriously and had arranged with Mrs. Folger to be called for by Arthur so that she could supervise the baking of a large cocoanut layer cake.

They were to leave at eleven to drive the short distance to a place the Crooms knew of. There the river widened out handsomely and there was a bit of sandy beach for Micky to play on. They had a good day, bright and cool, and Laskell, as he came up, saw that the expedition was already organized. There was a pile of rugs and blankets on the porch, the thermos jug with Micky's lunch, the pair of thermos bottles in their case, Arthur's large camera and the big wicker hamper. Nancy must have had the picnic long in mind to have brought this hamper from the city with so much else. It was an imposing old hamper. From the look of it, it was fitted inside with plates and forks and knives, and it spoke, somehow, of a rich, vanished day when a large hamper was part of the equipment of a family in easy circumstances. It had belonged, surely, not to Nancy's parents but to her grandparents.

There was no one on the lawn save Susan Caldwell and Micky Croom. Susan had made a handkerchief doll and she talked to it with animation and made it answer back with an agitated wagging of its head and a dancing of its loose cotton legs. Micky was following with great interest what the pair of them were saying. It gave Laskell pleasure to know that Susan was going with them.

At last everything was ready. Eunice came out and picked up Micky and held him in her arms over her shoulder so as to have him ready to get into the car when the moment came. He did not want to leave the fascinating dialogue between Susan and the handkerchief doll. So Susan tried to continue the game while he squirmed in Eunice's arms and looked over Eunice's shoulder.

" 'I will *not* cease from Mental Strife,' " she made the doll say in a high thin voice, waving its cotton arm.

" '*I will not cease,*' " she said in a deeper voice in her own character.

" 'I will *not* cease,' " " '*I will not cease,*' " " 'I will *not* cease,' " " '*I will not cease.*' " Back and forth waged the war of emphasis and Micky began to kick with pleasure. She was a complicated child, for she was doing three things at once and each of them wholeheartedly. She was amusing Micky and flirting with Laskell and mocking Eunice. Eunice certainly did not like what was going on behind her back for she turned and faced Micky in another direction, casually and as if without purpose. Susan circled so as to come face to face with him again and continued her game. She went too far, for Eunice, after she had turned the child twice more with silent forbearance, swung about and said to Susan, "Oh, for God's sake! Cut it out, will you?" Susan stopped short in her game, looking rather chilled and scared.

Nancy and Arthur came out looking very spruce, as if they had every intention of honoring this picnic to the utmost. Arthur brought the car around and Eunice at once got in with Micky.

Arthur and Laskell stored all the paraphernalia in the trunk. Nancy took her place in front. When everything was quite ready and the rest of them were about to get into the car, Nancy said with the air of calamity which picnics generate, "Oh, Lord, Micky's sweater! I left it on the table." And leaning out of the window, she said to Susan, "Would you get it for me, Susan, like a dear? It's a red sweater."

"Yes, I will," said Susan and dashed toward the house. She came out with the little red sweater and Nancy said, "Thank you, Susan."

It was not the tone that is used to a member of the expedition, a sharer of the adventure. Arthur slipped into his seat at the wheel, Laskell got in beside Eunice. It was Laskell's task to close the door of the car, making the final gesture, the definitive slam, of Susan's exclusion.

"Have a nice time," Susan said to them all, and did not have a sufficient impulse of self-protection to run off before the car started, on business of her own, but stood and waited for them to leave her.

"We should have taken her," Laskell said.

"It would have been nice," said Nancy turning in her seat. "Mais la jeune fille ici—la bonne—n'aime pas la petite. Ce serait une occasion très désagréable si nous avions les deux ensemble."

The drive was a short one. They parked the car by the side of the road and went across a field, Arthur carrying Micky seated on his shoulder, Laskell carrying the hamper and the thermos jug, Eunice carrying the thermos-bottle case, Nancy carrying the rugs. The spot they came to was quite perfect for a picnic. They spread the heavy steamer rug under a tree on soft, feathery grass. The bank fell away sharply to the little beach, which was dry enough for Micky to play on, and they set him there with Eunice and his big dump-truck which he did not yet quite know how to control and a kitchen spatula for a shovel. The river took a wide curve here and the sun was full on it. No place could better have established the picnic mood, which is a thing of art and ritual in which we celebrate our conquest of the fears of nature and pay our respects to the old life now that it no longer holds any terror for us. Arthur, who had campaigned against Nancy's idea of a picnic, mocking and teasing it, now led them in the mood. When once Micky was established with Eunice on the sand and the rugs were spread, he opened the hamper and took out a flask of whisky. It was a flask suited to the hamper and must have come from the same owners, for it was of heavy glass with its bottom sheathed in pewter; this pewter sheath was removable and could be used as a cup; the top was cased in leather and sealed with a heavy metal screw. Laskell jumped down to the river and filled two enamel cups with water and they sat and drank whisky and water. And shortly their appetites were so high that the hamper had to be opened. Micky was brought up from the little beach and established among them with Eunice to oversee his eating. She herself, with an ungenial tolerance, ate what was urged on her.

They were drinking coffee and smoking when Duck appeared. He came along the bank through the brush that bordered it and in his hand he carried a string of fish. His appearance startled them, but he had seen them from a distance and his face reflected the knowledge of their presence.

Arthur said, "Hello, Duck. Where in the name of the Lord have you been?"

"Yes, where have you been?" said Nancy. "We were worried."

"Oh, just been," said Duck. "Hello, Eunie," he said and he made a pass at her face with the fish so that they almost grazed her cheek. She jerked back her head and expressed a settled disgust.

Laskell, to have something to say, said, "You caught a lot of trout."

Duck held them up for his own inspection. "These?" he said, as if a little surprised that he should have them. He looked at them coldly, without approval.

"Will you have some cake and coffee, Duck?" Nancy said.

"Don't mind," Duck answered. He sat down with them, laying the fish on the grass. He ate his cake and drank his coffee while Nancy watched him with satisfaction. But after only half the cake was eaten, he put it aside. With his coffee cup poised on the way to his mouth, he said to Laskell, "You a fisherman, Mr. Laskell? That rod and creel they got at their house, Mrs. Croom says is yours." And he took a swallow of coffee.

"Not much of a fisherman—not a very good one." Laskell said it as innocently as he could. He had heard a latent intention in Duck's voice that had put him on guard.

Nancy said, "You haven't fished at all yet, John. Duck will have to take you to show you the good places."

"You a fly man maybe?" Duck said.

Here was the intention. Laskell knew exactly how Duck wanted this conversation to go. He knew it with the insight of his dislike of Duck. Step by slow step Duck would disclose his opinion of the sport of taking trout on a fly. It was an old American joke—the expensively equipped fisherman with the empty creel meets the barefoot boy with the old fish-pole and a heavy string of fish. Laskell's friends shared the joke whenever they knew he was going fishing. Somehow the joke was pointed in the direction of democratic simplicity. Often it went with an admiration of folk-art and a dislike of trained singing. It suddenly occurred to Laskell that Duck did not have even a fish-pole with him.

He said neutrally, "Yes, I use flies. Do you?"

Duck thrust his head forward and made several little movements with it, quite openly comical, suggesting but not uttering the quizzical answer of, "You might say yes, you might say no." He was not telling, he had his secret.

"Duck doesn't make a religion of his fishing," Nancy explained. "If he wants fish, he gets fish."

"I used to use flies now and then," Duck said judiciously. "But like Mrs. Croom says, if I want fish, I get fish. Sometimes a worm gets them best, and then sometimes you spear them, and then sometimes you seine them. Those little bought flies cost more than a fish is worth to a man in my position, not to mention all the trouble." He was looking at Laskell with wide, innocent eyes. "Of course, if you want to get yourself a really big mess of fish in a hurry, you take a stick of dynamite."

Laskell looked at Duck and saw all the strange subtlety in his face. Duck was conscious of what he was doing. He knew that to certain ears his description of the way he fished would be like explaining his way of raping virgins. He was assuming that Laskell was a loftily dedicated fisherman. But Laskell was a very simple fisherman. He knew about the elaborations of the elegant business of taking trout on a fly, but he had always been indifferent to them. Now, however, something more than the art of angling was in question. The Crooms must have caught the note of challenge in Duck's voice, for they had suddenly become alert.

Nancy said, "You must remember that not everyone is in the favored position of choosing ways and means—there are people who need the fish for food."

Her words were as pedantic as his were to be. They sounded like learned counsel on opposing sides.

"Yes," he said, "but some of the poorest people I've known have been the best fishermen. That was when I was in the Smokies. They had respect for the fish and they found pleasure in the sport and liked to give the fish a fighting chance."

He should have known the effect this would have on Nancy. Perhaps he had known it and was pushing things as far as they would go.

"Now *that*," said Nancy, "is sheer snobbery—the fanciest kind of snobbery. I suppose that the fish really likes the whole business and finds it very sporting too."

"No. We can't assume that."

With her eyebrows and a quirk of her head, Nancy made a gesture of large ironic surprise at his admitting so much. It was such a schoolgirl gesture of intellectual triumph that Laskell could not suppose it unfriendly. He met it with a smile, but he received no smile in answer. It struck him that the conversation about Ferdinand the bull and the showing of Elizabeth's picture, his telling them the story of Maxim—all these incidents bore belated fruit in that gesture. He forced himself to say very quietly, "No, we can't assume that the fish likes it. But the sport at least limits itself. The line is light, the leader is tapered very thin, the hooks are small, and some fishermen even use hooks without barbs to make the risk of losing the fish even greater. You set limitations, and if you overstep them, the pleasure is gone."

"How very romantic!"

"No," he said heavily. Suddenly he did not feel clever enough to handle the situation he had created and he wished he had never started. "Not romantic. It's a tendency that human life has—"

But he stopped. He was embarrassed by having used the word

life. He finished his sentence lamely. "—to make certain demands on itself beyond its obvious needs."

Nancy said, "I don't know what that means."

"It makes requirements and sets limits to itself," said Laskell.

"*What* does?"

It was dreadful to have to say the word again, all by itself. "Life," he said. "It sets limits and it insists on acting within them."

He passionately wished he knew what he was talking about— that is, knew it to explain, not just to feel. He reached out blindly and said, "It's like making sonnets."

That really seemed to help and he went on. "You set the pattern, a difficult pattern, and the effect comes from conforming to it. And when you conform to it successfully, you overcome it and it serves your purpose."

All his effort had produced nothing more than this old, worn paradox!

"*Conforming* to it, indeed!" There was a full contempt in Nancy's emphasis. She said, "You sound positively feudal." And then she said, "Sonnets!"

She had no special dislike of that verse form, and it was not sonnets she was holding in such contempt but the very idea of conforming. It was a little confusing, for he remembered at that moment her interpretation of Gifford Maxim's article and the relative leniency with which she had spoken about the Commissars who had confessed and, at the end, had cried "God bless Captain Vere!" And yet that confusion strangely enlightened him—that confusion in which Nancy both admired conformity and despised it. For he saw that Nancy's feeling was not about conforming or not conforming, not about freedom or submission. It was a feeling about human nature, a profound dissatisfaction with the way human beings had ever been, some leap of her imagination toward some way she hoped they would be. He could not understand why Nancy, who had been so fortunate at the hands of human nature, who had been so much cherished and so much admired, should have this dissatisfaction at the root of her political feelings. And he could not understand why Duck should be, as Laskell guessed he was, the model of the human nature that would be achieved by truly progressive action.

Nancy, having once said "Sonnets!" now said it again, as if she had not put enough feeling into the word the first time. "Sonnets!" she said, and she let her gaze fall on Duck Caldwell, as if, after having for too long listened to fantasy, she were now consulting reality. And in her gaze there was, together with her reassurance of herself, the pity she felt for Duck. The dispute had long since passed out of Duck's hands. Nancy said, "At this point in the world's history!"

She said no more, but Armageddon was in her voice.

Arthur saw that his wife and his friend were in crisis. He said, "I think that what Nancy means, John—" but he had begun his explanation after Laskell had begun to speak. What Laskell said was, " 'Since there's no help, come let us kiss and part.' "

Nancy's eyes went wide and her face went white. Laskell heard but did not understand the gasp of her suddenly intaken breath.

" 'Nay, I have done, you get no more of me,' " he was going on. It was one of the sonnets he had recited for Susan.

And then all at once he saw what was happening, that Nancy had supposed that the first line of Michael Drayton's poem was John Laskell's own declaration. Her wide eyes, her sudden paleness, her sharply indrawn breath showed that she thought he had announced the end of their friendship.

Laskell spoke the rest of the poem as fast as possible. He rather rattled out the lines, exaggerated his manner, made it unmistakably clear that he was speaking from someone else's impulse, not from his own, that he meant only to cite an example. But even as he was hurrying through the poem, he understood not only that Nancy had taken it to be himself speaking, but also that he had chosen this poem of parting from among all the sonnets he knew by heart because he and she were so opposed to each other.

He reached the last couplet with its offer of the last saving chance for Love gasping on its deathbed—

" 'Now, if thou wouldst, when all have given him over,
From death to life thou might'st him yet recover.' "

He added in an effort of self-burlesque, "Orthodox sonnet of the Shakespearean type." But his voice was tired and even now he could not exclude all earnestness from it as he said, "And I hope that explains the principle of fishing for trout to the young lady in the back row, and if it doesn't, she can see me after class."

He was trying to throw the whole matter away, as far from them as he could. He received as reward Nancy's rather bleak smile of recognition.

And certainly their mood returning from the picnic was not as gay as their mood in setting out. That was of course to be expected of any picnic, more to be expected of a picnic than of any other social event. As ritual, a picnic has too much actuality in it to be satisfying for very long after its beginning, and not enough awareness of its ritualistic intention to transform the actuality. But Laskell could not set down to the inevitable last mood of picnics the feeling that existed among them as they collected the trash of their meal and folded the rugs and made their way over the field back to the car. Nancy and he had compounded their quarrel for the moment. But they had not yet said what they were quarreling about. Therefore they could not compound their quarrel fully.

On the Croom lawn the next day Arthur was surrounded by cans of paint, of oil, of turpentine. Laskell watched him as he poured white paint into a bucket, added linseed oil, stirred it deeply, and let the mixture drip from the stirring-stick. He dipped a brush, pressed out the excess paint against the side of the bucket, and lightly brushed over a clapboard of the house. The new white streak glistened in the sunlight against the suddenly gray-white of the old paint. Arthur looked critically at the streak and then called, "Oh, Duck!"

There was no answer. A strong steady hammering began inside the house. Arthur waited until it stopped and then he called again, "Oh, Duck!" There was no answer and the hammering took up again. Then it stopped and a voice said, "Yes, what is it?"

Arthur said, "Come out here a minute, Duck, and look at this, will you?"

The hammering began again. Arthur stood over the paint bucket and waited.

Duck Caldwell came out with his hammer in his hand, dark and compact, with a little lurch in his walk, like an engaging boy swaggering off a piece of mischief. Arthur said, "Duck, will you tell me if this paint is all right?"

Duck looked into the paint pot. He contemplated it a long time. The two other men said nothing while he peered into the white depths. Duck took the stick, stirred the paint about, and let it drip from the lifted stick. Then he took the brush, dipped it, and laid a streak on the clapboard above Arthur's streak. "Little more oil," he said.

Arthur poured a little more oil, stirred again, and held up the stick for Duck to see the rate of drip. Duck nodded. "Plenty," he said with judicious finality.

He started back into the house with his hammer, but at the door he turned and said, "Going to paint out the green cornerboards, Mr. Croom?" His voice had suddenly a note of respectfulness, even of deference. But there was a double meaning in his smile.

Arthur looked up from stirring the paint. "No," he said in a very cool voice.

Laskell caught something in the interchange and wondered what it meant. He sat down in a canvas chair and watched his friend at work. Arthur handled the brush well, covering a section of the clapboard quickly, working the paint into the overhang of each clapboard, picking up the surplus, smoothing out with light swift strokes. After working for a while in silence, Arthur turned and said, "Funny how this sort of thing gives me satisfaction."

"Yes," Laskell said. It gave him satisfaction to see his friend working, and he was glad of their friendship.

"Would you like to try?" Arthur said. "I have another brush."

"Tom Sawyer stuff," Laskell jeered. But he was drawn to it. "Yes, I'd like to try," he said.

Arthur went and got the other brush and poured off a quantity of the mixed paint into a small pot. They worked side by side for a while. After a polite interval, Arthur stopped and looked at Laskell painting. He watched for a moment and said, "You do it very well." And then he said, "Here, take this brush and give me yours. You'll like it better."

"This one is all right," Laskell said. It was not a very good brush, it was stubby and stiff, but it got the paint on.

"No—that's just an old brush I found around the place and cleaned up. This is a good one. You'll have more fun with it."

Laskell took the brush and Arthur waited while he tried it. It was almost uncanny the difference the new brush made. It seemed to have mind in it—to know what it was for and to want to fulfill its purpose. It was like having a living thing in his hand as he felt the bristles against the clapboard. He turned to Arthur and acknowledged the great difference. "It's a wonderful brush," he said.

"God-damned expensive," said Arthur proudly.

It was an oddly gratifying kind of work and it took more skill and attention than one would suppose. But beneath the attention he had to give, Laskell felt a glow of relationship to Arthur. They did not talk but now and then they made curt comments to each other on the progress or the problems of the job. They fell into the same rhythm of painting and occasionally paused to inspect each other's work with the eyes of indulgent criticism.

After a while Arthur said, "Did you get that crack of Duck's?"

Laskell said, "What crack?"

"About painting out the cornerboards. He was ribbing me. He's a shrewd article. He knew that Nancy and I had a disagreement. I wanted to paint the cornerboards white but she wants them left green. It's crazy, it spoils the shape of the house but Nancy wants it that way. All the houses in this part of the country have green cornerboards."

The Croom house was very small and very simple, a box of a house, but with a very happy proportion between length and height. The green cornerboards, by outlining the white walls, made the house smaller and needlessly emphatic and less elegant than if they had continued the white of the walls.

"Look better all white," said Laskell. This elliptical form of his own speech surprised him and he sought in his mind for its reason. He found it in the manner that boys use when they are imitating in their play the simple manly manner of workmen or technicians. He remembered the flow of male affection that used to be expressed in such play, the warmth that was hidden and expressed by the brisk, masculine language of cooperation. He spoke so again. "Look a good deal better all white."

"Of course," said Arthur. "Nancy admits it. But she says we can't be different from the rest. She says it would make us just summer people if we brought in our own notions of how things should be done."

"But you are summer people, after all."

"We are now. But suppose I lose my job? We could come up here and make out. At least as long as Nancy's little income lasts."

"Lose your job?" Laskell said in alarm. "Has something happened?"

Arthur's university career had been rapid and rewarding as such careers go, and Laskell had always supposed that now it could only improve. But in addition to alarm, he felt an excitement as his mind rapidly calculated what sum he could make liquid to offer the Crooms as a loan.

"No, nothing's happened," Arthur said dubiously. "But the way things are going. I've been mixed up in a few things and it isn't doing me much good with the university administration."

Laskell was relieved but a little disappointed. As the warmth of his impulse to help the Crooms was taken from him, he felt a little annoyed that he had responded so quickly to the Crooms' fantasy of danger. He remembered the esteem in which Arthur was held and the talk about the Washington appointment. He should not have said as lightly as he did say, "Your only danger is that they'll decide to make you a dean or something."

Arthur looked remote and hurt and then angry, and Laskell realized he had done wrong in refusing him his place at the center of the drama of these troubled times. But as a matter of fact what had been increasingly interesting Laskell about his friend was how remarkably Arthur flourished in these new dangerous circumstances. Until things got a good deal worse, Arthur Croom was wonderfully suited to the world. He was not a man of the ultimate future, though he borrowed a little from the ultimate future; Arthur was a man of the immediate future, one of the men who might effectually make a go of things for a while. Yet Laskell knew that he could not advance this view of Arthur against the Crooms' own view of themselves living an enforced life of subsistence in their pretty house.

Arthur did not have a chance to argue the possibility, for Nancy came out and stood behind the two men and said, "Danger: Intellectuals at work! A very gratifying spectacle, I must say. You do it well too, John."

"Oh, I do, do I?"

Nancy took a chair and sat down in an extreme attitude of luxurious leisure. "Let me see what it feels like to just sit while you men work. What have you been talking about?"

Arthur said over his shoulder as he went on painting, "John has just been telling me that I'm likely to be made dean. I'm in such favor with the administration."

"There's as much chance of that as that you'll lose your job," Laskell said.

"I don't know about that." Arthur spoke as if he had some secret knowledge.

"You're wrong, John," Nancy said simply. "Arthur is on every committee of protest and the students are always coming to him to sign things and speak at their meetings. He's by no means safe." There was so little question of it in Nancy's mind that there was nothing more to say. She looked at her husband with admiration. She wanted a life of danger and morality and she loved Arthur for his help in supplying it.

The connection between Arthur and Laskell was broken. But it would have been broken by Nancy's having come out to join them. Or it would have been broken by their having finished painting the stretch they were working on. Arthur went to fetch a ladder. He set the ladder against the roof and was about to go up to hook on the paint pot when Susan Caldwell came up the path to them. In her hand she had a little bundle of letters. Emily Caldwell called from the road, "We met the mailman and brought you your mail."

Susan went to Arthur with the mail and he put down the pot of paint and took the letters from her. "Thank you, Susan," he said.

There was a letter for Nancy and he gave it to her, reaching it out to her absently as he read a postcard for himself. "Well," he said, "here's a business!"

Nancy opened her letter. "What's a business?" she said.

"This is from Kermit Simpson. He's driving up and wants to stop over with us."

"That's nice," said Nancy absently, reading her letter.

Laskell could see from Arthur's face that it was not as nice as Nancy thought.

"He has Gifford Maxim with him," Arthur said.

Nancy did not put aside her letter at once. But when she did put it aside, she put it aside very thoroughly, folding it and laying it with its envelope on the grass. Then she said, "You're joking."

"No, I'm not joking. They're coming in a trailer."

"What?"

"In a trailer. In Kermit's trailer."

"When?" said Nancy. Her voice was level. "When are they coming?"

Arthur consulted the card. "He doesn't say. All he says is, 'Making leisurely trip with Giff Maxim. We plan to drop in on you in about a week for a day or two. We won't be a nuisance; we are self-sustaining. All we need is a piece of level ground for the trailer. Much to talk to you about. Greetings to you both and to John.'" And Arthur nodded toward Laskell to convey the message directly.

Nancy said very simply, "Arthur, you must stop them."

"I'm afraid it's too late. They've left already." He consulted the other side of the card. "I can't make out the postmark, but it's not from Westport. Kermit must have mailed it on the way."

"They can't come," Nancy said. "I won't let them stay. You won't let them stay, will you?"

"I don't quite know how to tell them to go away, Nan," Arthur said reasonably.

"'How'?" Nancy repeated after him indignantly. "You just tell them. Just tell them they can't stay. I don't want to hurt Kermit's feelings but if he puts himself in that position it will just have to be said to him. And what does he mean—'much to talk about'? Talk about Maxim and his lies? That's what he must mean. He's so weak and impressionable. He's been taken in and corrupted."

Susan had been looking from one to the other with wide eyes, and at the word "corrupted" she blinked intelligently. She, of course, knew about corrupted. There had been the conversation with Laskell about artists. From the road her mother called her. "Come along, Susan," Emily Caldwell said. But Susan did not hear.

"Susan, your mother's calling you," said Nancy. With an effort the child tore herself away. But she walked so slowly in her desire to learn about the life of moral danger that her mother had to call her again. And so Susan hastened her steps and did not learn how intense the life of moral danger could be. She did not hear the passion with which Nancy said, "I simply won't have him near me."

Arthur said, "None of us wants him, Nancy."

But Laskell knew how inadequate that would be for Nancy. She had more reason than either Arthur or Laskell for not wanting Maxim. He said, "Look, Nancy—I don't blame you for not wanting him around. But don't exaggerate things. He hasn't turned into a devil, he doesn't have horns. You yourself found things to admire in that crazy essay of his. And I want to tell you—maybe I should have mentioned it before—that I was struck by a kind of honorableness he still had, even though he did desert the Party. For example, he wouldn't tell me what his secret and special work was. I asked him if he wanted to tell me and he made a point of saying no."

It was the best he could do to give Nancy the reassurance he knew she needed that Maxim would not come in shouting references to letters addressed in a certain way.

Perhaps she took some comfort from what he said, for her voice when she spoke was much gentler. She said, "I'm not exaggerating, John. You and I don't feel alike on these things. No, not really. That's natural. You live for yourself, you don't know how real certain things can be to other people. It's simply that your mind is turned in a different direction. I never realized it, I suppose. But the way you love the past, for instance—" her voice was now infinitely kind, so kind that it destroyed him. "I do think you care more about the past than you do about the future, John. And that's your right, it's understandable, I do understand it." She frowned with her concentration of friendly understanding. "But it makes you tolerant of things I can't be tolerant of. I don't *think* about them, I just feel them. I just feel them here." And she laid her hand upon herself and upon the developing child that was her guarantee.

So full a statement seemed to have discharged her feelings wholly, for she broke off and said, "I'm sorry I made a fuss." She turned to Arthur. "It was foolish of me, dear. And I won't make a scene when they come. If we possibly can, we'll get Kermit to take him away. Or maybe we can say that we're just going off on a little visit ourselves. We'll work it out somehow."

She had closed the subject. There was nothing more to be said. Not that Laskell could have said anything. He did not dare speak for the destruction that was going on within him. It was a soft destruction, almost voluptuous.

Duck came out and said, "Mr. Croom, come in and look at this for a minute." Arthur went and Laskell was left alone with Nancy. She was sitting in a chair and he was sitting on the grass facing her, in a quite ordinary summer attitude, his knees drawn up and his hands clasped around them. It was an absurdly incongruous position for what was going on inside him.

As Laskell looked back on that moment, he was appalled to think what might have followed if he had said nothing. It was not merely that his friendship with Nancy would have ended, and thus his friendship with Arthur. More than that: his friendship to himself, such as it was, would have ended too; he himself would have ended. Nancy's gentle definition of him was at work, making a deep voluptuous emptiness in him. It frightened him, but it also drew him. Something within him was cooperating with Nancy's definition to dismiss him from the world of men. If self-preservation is a virtue, he deserved from himself more credit than he knew in doing what he now did.

He said, "You did receive those letters for Maxim, didn't you? Arthur refused, but you said yes. Isn't that so?"

His voice was strange and dead. His only conscious impulse when he spoke was to assert a dominance which should out-top Nancy's cool, kind, killing knowledge of him, to meet knowledge with knowledge. At the moment when, as it were, his manhood hung in the balance, he reached for the crudest impulse he had. But suddenly her two hands went to her cheeks, which were white, and she looked at him with scared eyes. He was reminded of what he had forgotten, that she was a woman and one for whom he had love and that she was in guilt and trouble.

"He told you! He told you!" Nancy cried. And then she said bit terly, "Of course, how like him."

"No," he said. "He did not tell me. He was very careful to tell me nothing."

"Then who told you? How do you know?"

He could recognize that she was a woman for whom he had love, but he felt no affection for her. He said, "I saw it the evening I told you about him."

"You saw it? What do you mean, you *saw* it?"

He said irritably, "*Saw* it—something in your manner. It just came to me. I don't know how I knew. I just knew."

She made a puzzled impatient gesture such as a child makes to whom something is incomprehensible, letting her lack of comprehension stand as a comment on the foolishness of the thing. "Intuition," she said with a slighting dryness.

"Call it intuition. It doesn't matter how I knew, does it?"

The impatience in her face again changed to fear. But Laskell continued, "Why did you do it? And what did you think you were doing?"

"Why did I do it? Because nobody else did it. I suppose I did it because you can ask that question." Fear did not make her timid. It never would.

"Or because Arthur said no?"

He did not quite know why he had asked that question.

"Don't be ridiculous," Nancy said. "What do you think I am?" But then her face cleared and she said in a frank, puzzled way, "Maybe. Maybe because Arthur didn't."

"What did you think you were doing? What made the great secrecy, all the mysterious flummery?"

She did not answer.

Laskell said, "Then you do know? Maxim refused to let me ask any questions. He refused to let Arthur ask any questions. Did he let you ask questions? How do you know?"

"I didn't say I knew."

"But you know."

"Is this the intuition again?"

"Did Maxim tell you?"

"Oh," she said, "I don't really know. I only know in a general way. I know more or less why they were important."

"But you won't say?"

"No, I won't say."

There was so much of a note of tragic, conscious heroism in the way she said it, that there jumped to Laskell's mind the possibility that it was to be accounted for by a love affair with Gifford Maxim. But then another clandestine possibility came to his mind—something clandestine must account for the high intensity of her dedication—and it was this second possibility that he chose, rejecting the first. "Nancy," he said, "are you a Party member?"

"It's not exactly a crime, you know. There's no law against it that you should ask in that tone of voice."

"Then you are?"

"No!" she cried desperately. "No, I'm not. But is it such a horror to contemplate? No, I'm not exactly a Party member."

"Not exactly! What does that mean? Do you have a card or don't you?"

"No. Of course I don't!" After all she had said, it was not clear on what ground she was repelling the imputation as if it were a slur upon her. "Of course I haven't got a card. But I'm considering it, I'm so tired of all this liberal shilly-shallying talk. I want to do something real. I'm so damned tired of the Kermit Simpsons with their civil liberties and their Jeffersonian democracies."

"And the John Laskells?" He said it gently and in joke, but his voice was weary. He had an image of the world's misery, of what was to be faced, and he did not know who was strong enough to resist it.

But Nancy's voice was wearier than his. "Oh, John—no," she said. "It's just that in all this world, with things so terrible and moving so fast, it's just that some action, something positive—" And she made a sad little gesture of helplessness. "I don't know. It's so frightening. I want to do what I can."

"Yes," he said.

"Maybe I'm wrong. Maybe I did something foolish. You think I'm wrong?"

"Somehow, yes."

She said nothing for a moment. Then she said, "He really didn't tell you about the letters? You really knew without his telling you?"

"No, he didn't tell me."

"I'm glad you know," she said. "Somehow, I'm glad you know."
She looked at him ruefully, but he could see that she was really
glad. Her face looked tired, but it had a freshness of genuine relief
in it. "Probably Arthur should know too," she said. And then she
looked at him with great appeal and said, "What's the matter?"

"Matter? Nothing's the matter."

"You looked so— Are we not friends?"

She had seen the look on his face from his fresh full knowledge
of what he had to escape in Nancy, of what this charming and
moral woman friend of his could do to him, and was willing to do,
until he asserted his own will consciously against her intention of
which she had no awareness.

Laskell, looking at the hand she stretched out to him tentatively,
for she was not sure it would be taken, could say, as he took the
hand and held it between his, "Yes. We are very good friends." He
could say it firmly and surely. But he could not tell her how sad he
was for his friend, and not only for his friend but for the world.
And yet it was a calm sadness, and they were truly friends, and to
show her that this was so, when Duck came out with Arthur, Laskell said to Duck, "I wonder if you could show me the stream
some morning. The fish don't rise much this time of summer, but
I'd like to try anyway."

8

IT WAS four days later that Duck Caldwell and John Laskell went to the stream together. They walked on a little way beyond the Korzinskis' house and then turned off and cut across a stubble field.

It was a misty morning and the mist made ten o'clock seem early and even adventurous. Laskell had two sandwiches in the khaki tackle-bag on his shoulder. The sandwiches and all the paraphernalia of fishing made the occasion yet more adventurous, and so, in a way, did his feeling about Duck. He could not say that he liked Duck any better than he ever had but he felt reconciled to him, and he thought how weak the human imagination is because it so dully represents peace and brotherhood. A careful, shabby Hindu student and a skinny Methodist student shake hands and agree that there are no real differences between people that cannot be overcome by mutual understanding and education and the cider and doughnuts they will presently be offered by the religious director. The world's imagination of strife was surely much more attractive. It allowed men their force and their selfhood as well as their evil. Yet in actual fact, Laskell thought, the true emotion of reconciliation is an heroic one. Hamlet never appears in fuller virility than when he offers Laertes his hand, and nothing he says rings with a sweeter and graver note of masculinity than his "Give me your pardon, sir. I have done you wrong."

They were crossing the field and Duck was walking a little ahead of Laskell. The lurch and swagger of his walk were to be seen and disliked. But Laskell knew that he did not have to like Duck in any usual way to feel the warm pleasure of reconciliation. A true image of peace, like the world's false image of strife, also allowed a man his force and selfhood, and if force and selfhood involved a little malice, the true image of peace allowed that too. Duck had his little malice, but it was not always easy to maintain the self in its force without the help of a little malice. This was the heroism of true peace, that it was not frightened by what force and self might involve.

Yet how precarious peace was. How difficult it was for men to keep in comradeship. Duck turned around to say, "This walk being too hard for you, Mr. Laskell? You got to remember you been sick."

Laskell said, "I'm fine," very sharp in his answer because it seemed to him that Duck took pleasure in reminding him of his illness.

"Sure. Sure you are," Duck said soothingly. "But you got to be careful after you been sick."

"I've been careful long enough," Laskell said dryly.

"Sure. Maybe so," Duck said.

Laskell felt ashamed. It was not Duck who had broken the peace but he himself with his quick defensive response to the malice he had heard in Duck's tone. But then Laskell put aside the impulse to blame himself. If malice is to be permitted, he thought, it must be met, and he had met it with his sharp answer. They could be at peace again. Perhaps peace between men is a series of reconciled conflicts between equals. And suddenly Laskell felt how truly Duck was his equal. As they walked together, Laskell saw the pattern of the other man's life and understood that it was by that pattern that Duck was to be judged, that it was the pattern that was Duck's true personality, much rather than the things Duck said out of some false notion of how to represent his self and his force to the world. Judged by that pattern, Duck was perhaps not only Laskell's equal but even his superior. He had refused the usual claims of society, the whole absurd contest that modern life invited him to. It was no mere laziness that kept him in the little house that he had made of two sheds, doing odd jobs when he chose or needed to; it was rather a response to something he saw in life that he did not want for himself. Perhaps it was something he had seen at first hand in the career of his grandfather, the Senator, with his fine horse and buggy and his living on the rural fat of the land, or something he had seen in the career of his father, who speculated. At any rate, by his own pattern, he had done well, he had done better by a good bit than John Laskell.

And he had more. If one were to judge Duck Caldwell, there was his daughter Susan to take into account. Duck's quick and subtle intelligence showed itself not only in his malicious perceptions of human weakness, but also in his child. In any estimate of Duck, it had to be taken into account that he was Susan's father. And, really, it had also to be taken into account that he was Emily's husband. It was perhaps no small thing to be, Laskell suddenly saw, as he thought of Emily, not as she was in her mind with its rather foolish, dated ideas, but as she was in her body.

Laskell had sometimes thought that people in their imposed functions were rather better than the same people when they stepped outside their functions. The girls in the office who were notable for the simplicity and directness in their characters, for the pleasure they took and gave in being efficient, might, at the Christmas party, when they were talked to only in a social way and about things in general, become rather petulant and self-pitying people with no firmness of character at all. The colleague whose sense of performance organized him so well when he was being professional, became, when you had cocktails with him, in the effort to get to "know" him, as soggy as a soul could be. And now that Laskell had lately begun to see Emily Caldwell as a mother and even as a wife he had to modify the not very high opinion of her that he had originally made. As Susan and he had become more and more friendly it seemed more and more natural that he should stop to talk with Susan's mother. They did not talk about very much, such things as gardening and Susan and Susan's education and the Bazaar. Once his first mythological view of Emily Caldwell had been dispelled, Laskell had not found her very interesting either as an intellectual or as a rebel. She really did not have the gift for being either. But in her function as Susan's mother with her worry about Susan's education, in her function as housekeeper with her little prides in the midst of poverty, in her not at all striking talk about ordinary things, Laskell had found her more and more impressive. She had a womanly dignity that did not depend on intellect—a kind of biological intelligence. Laskell did not like to admit it, but he had to admit it—Duck Caldwell had chosen a woman who was,

if you got to know her, at least of full size. Mrs. Folger had seen in
Duck what there was for a woman to see, and probaby Emily had
responded to that when she had chosen Duck. It was much the
same thing Nancy had seen when she had made her remark about
Duck's resemblance to the gamekeeper in *Lady Chatterley*. Laskell
had heard their female judgment with irony—naturally enough,
any man would. But now didn't he have to admit that their female
judgment was right?

From the field they had struck into woods. It was very hot and
damp in the woods and Laskell found that he was breathing hard
in the steamy air. He had put on his waders on Duck's assurance
that the stream was not far off. They made his legs and thighs feel
sweaty and pneumatic. Laskell had snapped at Duck for suggesting that the illness had had a continuing effect on him, but the
fact was that he was not in very good shape. He heard the sound
of water with relief.

"Is that the stream?" he asked.

"Yes. But you wouldn't want to fish it here."

"Why not?"

Duck shook his head. "You'll see," he said.

What Laskell saw, when they came to it, was a deep gorge. The
walls were very steep and the little river came fast into the dark
pool. It came in noisily over a bed of large stones, breaking on
the boulders at the mouth of the gorge. The black surface of the
pool was laced with long streamers of white foam. The air here
was cool, almost chill. The pool looked very promising.

"This looks very good," Laskell said.

"Not bad," said Duck. "But if you fish them dry flies upstream,
you better start further up." He looked at Laskell and then at the
water. "You'd have a hard time working up from here."

Laskell saw that Duck was right. The stretch of rocky footing
would be rather too much for him today. He had fished water as
difficult as this, but when he had been in better shape. On his first
day out it would be better to start farther up. And on the whole
he was glad that it was not here that he would part with Duck.
There was something frightening about the gorge.

They stood looking into the chasm together. Duck said, "I call
this Cherry Gorge."

"Is that its name?" said Laskell.

"No. It hasn't got a name. But my name for it is Cherry Gorge. This is where all the girls around here lose it. The boys take them for a ride and the road comes in close by the other side. *He* says, 'Would you like to look at the gorge, Mamie?' And *she* says, 'Why that would be just *lovely*.'" In the voice of Mickey and Minnie Mouse, Duck acted out the false casualness of the boy and the false innocence of the girl. "'Why that would be just too sweet,' she says, and down they go and lucky if they don't break their necks over some couple that's got there first. Maybe the noise makes the girls scared and shivery and they're willing for you to get close. Anyway, they don't come up like they went down."

It was the old freebooting sexual camaraderie of men, and the embarrassment it precipitated in Laskell made him angry at himself for being so cut off from simplicity and directness. Duck looked down, spat out into the gorge, and prepared to leave. "I'd like to get me that Eunie Folger down here some night and see how she's made. I wish I had your chances, sleeping right near her every night."

There must be something to answer. Laskell hated his stiff inability to respond in the same tone as Duck's. But he could find nothing to say. And Duck knew it.

"I guess," said Duck, and looked at Laskell with his clever eyes, "I guess you think I've got a dirty mind, kind of low. But the way I figure is that we got just about enough hypocrisy. I work it out like this, a man's made a certain way, a woman's made a certain way, the natural result is they got a need for each other. A woman's got just as much need for a man as a man's got for a woman. I don't care what they tell us different, it's so. That Eunie Folger, for instance, I bet she's not so cold if you could just once put your hand where it would do the most good. The women make believe it's not so, but it is. They carry their heads high and they carry their tails proud, but it's so. Am I right?"

"Oh, sure," said Laskell.

"Sure!" Duck nodded firmly. "Let me tell you—we got cat-houses for men, if we had cat-houses for women, they'd do just as good business. Just as good. And then comes in religion and a bunch of hypocrites and it's no business of theirs but they make it their business and they interfere. It's none of their god-damned business. It's just nature. Am I right? And if it's just nature and just a personal matter, who are they to interfere? Let me tell you a thing. If you got yourself up one night and had an inspiration and went into Eunie's room and give her a couple of pokes, you'd be doing her a favor. I don't care how tight she goes around looking. You're a man got a good education. *You* tell *me*—am I wrong?"

"No of course you're not wrong," said Laskell. "I mean, I don't know about Eunice—"

"So there you are, just like I said. And mark my words, the day will come when people going to get some sense. That's my way of thinking about it."

Duck turned full to Laskell and said, "And I want to tell you another thing, Mr. Laskell." He paused to arouse curiosity about the other thing he was going to tell. He stood with his mouth poised to speak. Then he said, "You may think I got a low mind. But I ain't talking like a young kid that wants his first piece and can't wait till he gets it. I mean to say: there's just so many apples on a tree. A man's got just so much in him and no more. And believe me, I didn't spare none of mine. Maybe you know how that is. Guess maybe I'm older than you but maybe you live the same way, not sparing yourself, and maybe now you're pretty pooped out. What you got you got, and what you lose you don't get back." And Duck opened his mouth and pointed to the gap in his upper teeth. "Even if I got me some store teeth, they might look good, but they wouldn't be my teeth. What's gone is gone. Well. Anyway. What I was saying, what you lose, you lose, so I'm talking from my head." Duck covered his brow with the palm of his hand. "It comes from here," he said, "and not from you-know-where." And Duck clutched you-know-where. "So it ain't a crazy hot idea," he concluded. Then he added, "Yet still," and he grinned, "yet still I'd like to have me a poke at that Eunie Folger."

They left the gorge and cut a wide circle and came to the stream again. It was strong and rapid even now in August, but it ran more tamely here between soft banks. "You can follow up from here easy enough," Duck said. "And when you want to find your way back, you'll see where it cuts in close to the road and that's only a mile on the road from the Folgers' house."

And he stood there while Laskell jointed his rod, fixed on the reel, threaded the line through the guides, and tied on the leader. The fly that Laskell chose was a Coachman. It was not a rational choice, but he could not, under Duck's eye, stop to study the stream as Kermit Simpson had taught him to do. When he was ready, Duck said, "Well, good luck." Then he said, "You one of those fishermen takes a flask with him?"

"I'm sorry, I didn't bring one."

"I just thought," Duck said.

He went away. But he left his void behind him, left it with Laskell and in him. His mind was not dirty or low as he had said Laskell might think it. It was simply void. It was nothing, the pure will of nothingness. Or it was the nothingness of, pure will. It was not wickedness. It was emptiness masking itself as mind and desire. Laskell thought of the wan white Eunice Folger of Duck's speculations, and of Emily, Duck's wife, whose relation with this man he, Laskell, had but a few minutes before made to count for so much to his credit. And he thought of Mrs. Folger and Nancy, and of their poor misplaced confidence in Duck's "manliness," and of his own misplaced confidence in their female judgment. It was perhaps funny that he had no sooner decided to accept their estimate of Duck's masculinity than Duck himself had been to such pains to set him straight. But Laskell felt no impulse to laugh.

Lack of practice made him awkward with his casting. He dutifully reminded himself of all the things he must think about—arm close to the body, wrist loose, the fly to touch the water before the leader. He did not believe that it made any difference. He did not really believe that there were fish in the stream, or that he could catch them, or that fish had ever been caught by this method. You equipped yourself expensively, you learned the technique, you did everything the way you had been taught, and even, for the deceptive pleasure of it, you debated the theory of flies with other fishermen, arguing about just what it was that the fish saw when the fly floated over its head. But nothing really happened, or whatever happened happened for quite other reasons and not because you did what you did.

He moved slowly upstream, unsure of his footing. His thighs were tired and he moved more carefully than the current required.

He did not like the way he moved. He was not being wary but nervous.

But the stream began to do some of its work on Laskell. The morning mist cleared away and the air freshened. The sun came through the overhang of the trees. He saw a muskrat standing by its hole and then vanish into it. A kingfisher worked the stream ahead of him for a few minutes. It was as blue and direct as lightning.

His blood began to pick up a little with the exercise. Some sense of possibility returned to him. He began to like being alone. He forgot about Duck, forgot about Mrs. Folger's estimate of Duck, and Nancy's, and his own, and how they had just been contradicted by Duck's own statement. He forgot about everything except himself, and then he forgot about himself. He began to note the likely places to drop his fly and to feel that they might yield something. After an hour he could do as well with the rod as he had ever done.

By noon the sun was out full and the sky was clear. He settled on a broad shelving rock to eat his sandwiches. He ate slowly, then he lit a cigarette. He was enjoying himself enormously.

But perhaps he sat too long. Suddenly he felt too much alone, and he began to think what he was alone in. His awareness of the life of the stream and of the banks became intense. He did not think of the trout he was presumably fishing for but of the blind and primeval things, the things of slime and darkness, the slugs and hellgrammites and leeches that must inhabit the stream. He thought of the eels that lived here, whose flesh made as fine eating, in its own way, as the trout. He remembered that it was said that the eels of every stream, all over the world, eventually made their way to the Sargasso Sea to die, moving from tributary stream to stream, in their necessity sometimes crossing the land to come at last to the sea, where, in the interlaced company of millions of their kind, they gave up the eel ghost.

He got up to enter the stream again and he saw, just behind where he had been sitting, the corpse of a huge white moth, of a staring and powdery white, with a body like a ship and a spread of wings like sails. Its big chrysalis lay near it, so perhaps it had never flown even once since it had emerged, but had been attacked while

it waited for the first impulse and knowledge of flight to come to
its wings. It lay there wrecked and dead, and insects worked their
careful way in trains into the hull of its body. Seeing it, so white
and wholly dead, Laskell shuddered.

The woods thinned out as he made his way up the stream. The
banks were broader here, and there was a heavy bordering brush
of laurel. The sun was now very strong on the surface of the water
and it hurt his eyes.

They were standing there in the full light of the sun and
seemed to emerge from the glare of the water, and their heads were
piled with white soapsuds, so that, what with one circumstance
and another, they at first seemed an illusion of brightness.

They stood with arms upraised, shampooing vigorously. The
water came to Susan's waist and Emily's thighs. They were facing each other and laughing and Emily reached out and rubbed
the suds into Susan's hair. She stooped so that Susan could do the
same for her. Then Susan pushed her mother backwards into
the water and when Emily emerged her long hair was washed of
the suds and hung dark and heavy on both sides of her face. She
shoved it behind her ears and then, in retaliation, she pushed
Susan down, but with a kind of slow care, holding the child's
hand.

She examined Susan's hair to see that all the soap was gone from
it. It seemed not to be, for at a word from her mother, Susan
ducked down again, disappearing under the water with a single
movement, as though she were curtsying. Emily too ducked under
the surface again, and for a moment her hair floated out on the
surface. She stood up with her head bent to one side and wrung
out the hair as if it were a cloth or a hank of yarn. Susan's gestures
were as large as her mother's as she wrung out her own smaller
crop. Then they trudged out of the stream and were lost to Laskell's sight. And yet by a strange ocular confusion, he was not
wholly certain that they had left the stream—they had seemed so
dissolved in sunlight that he had thought they might still be there
but not clearly seen. Then he heard their chatter and laughter on
the bank.

Laskell stayed where he was. His body felt extraordinarily alert,
poised for movement, but he was willing not to move. They had

not seen him and for all Emily Caldwell's reputed principles about nakedness, he did not want them to know that he had seen them. He did not move—the sight seemed to be still there even after Emily and Susan had actually left the stream.

The pair dawdled a good while on the bank, and Laskell waited carefully. The memory of the sight suffused him with light or reason, or both. His line drifted downstream behind him. When he no longer heard their voices on the bank, he knew they were gone. He slowly reeled in his line and took off the Coachman, which had not brought him a single strike. He put on a Quill Gordon, which, he thought, might be better for the glare of the stream. Fastening the knot, he thought of Emily and Susan walking home in the sun with towels over their shoulders and their hair spread out on the towels to catch the sun.

There was no point in casting over their bathing place. What fish were there would now have been hopelessly disturbed, but he did cast over it anyway. Her voice was so unexpected—"Any luck?" was of course what she said—that he turned in the very act of the cast, and it may have been that a stone beneath his foot moved with his shift of weight, or it may have been that the cause of the accident was beneath another surface than that of the stream, but his ankle twisted and he felt his balance going with that slow, conscious deliberateness with which balance always goes, the illusion that at any moment it can be saved, and then he was down and under. His awareness, once the self-protective jump of his heart had passed, was of humor and relief and of the light on the bottom.

Emily Caldwell was standing there beside him when he got up, making gestures toward helping him. She could scarcely have thought there was any danger—still, when someone falls into the water one naturally goes to his help, and she was there to rescue him if there were need. But there was actually nothing to rescue except Laskell's hat. It had begun to float placidly downstream. She snatched for it with a kind of indignation at its waywardness.

"It's my fault, all my fault," she said. "I startled you. I'm sorry."

But Laskell was laughing. The waders were filled and were holding the water. He was encased in water and he stood holding the rod out from him as if he feared getting it wet.

"It's my fault," she insisted.

He felt ridiculous and happy. She handed him the hat and he put it on his head so that its wet and drooping brim would complete his comic ruin. She looked at him and burst out laughing.

With his heavy weight of water, Laskell walked to the bank. "What *are* you going to do?" Emily said. Her own skirt had got wet halfway up; and she wore no shoes.

"I'm going to sit here and dry out," Laskell said.

He unlaced his wading boots and drew them off with difficulty. His ankle was sore from the twist, but it was not sprained. He took off the big woolen socks. He unfastened the shoulder straps of the waders but he could not get the heel of the waders down over his own heel.

She saw this and said, "Would you like me to pull?"

"Please," he said.

It was never easy to get them off and now it was harder because they were wet inside. But she was strong and persistent and they came off at last. He wrung out the cuffs of his trousers. The shirt that he took off she laid neatly on a rock to dry. There was nothing else to do, so she sat down beside him. She fluffed out her hair in the sun.

He smiled at her. "Where's Susan?" he said.

"Oh, Susan's gone to pick berries." And she blushed, for anyone could hear in her tone the certainty that Susan would not be coming back.

She said, "How do you know that Susan was here? Could you hear us?"

"Yes, I could hear you. And I saw you—saw you washing your hair."

"Did you?" she said quite comfortably. She was clearly a woman of some vanity. He thought she had good reason to be.

He looked at her frankly and curiously. She could not but be aware of what their situation might hold, what with her assurance to him that her daughter would not be coming back. Yet she met his look with a kind of sadness, not at all pained or fearful, only submissive. It was not in the least to him that she was submitting and that was what, to Laskell, made that look of hers so wonderful. It illuminated for him the presence that had been in his voice, unbidden, when he had said, "I saw you washing your hair." She was submitting to the quite impersonal presence that had made his voice ring so simply and wonderingly as he said that. His heart began to quicken with excitement.

But he made no move, and she, not abashed by whatever he might have seen in her face, not put out because he did not immediately act upon what he saw, said to him, "They tell me you have been very ill. Are you all right now?"

"Oh, yes!" he said, as if there had never been any question of that. "Never felt better."

"But you were very ill? Was it dangerous?"

"Well," he said, and thought about it. "Yes, I suppose it was in a way."

"In a way?"

"I mean the doctor told me afterward that there had been some danger. But I never knew about it until after."

"Danger is danger," she said firmly. "Who took care of you?"

"I had two nurses," Laskell announced. He grinned reminiscently.

"Two?" She was much impressed.

"Yes, two. Day and night. As different as day and night. Miss Debry and Miss Paine."

It was funny that he should tell her about Miss Debry first, about her starch and her cap and her talkativeness and her beauty. Emily Caldwell listened quietly with her large, mild look turned to him. She did not interrupt or ask questions until he reached the point where he had told Dr. Graf that he would prefer to keep Miss Paine, letting Miss Debry go.

"Oh!" said Emily.

"I know," said Laskell, "I must have been sicker than I thought. Yes, I must have been very sick—in my mind too. I could lie there for hours on end just looking at a flower. It was a particular flower, a rose."

And, strangely enough, here he was telling Emily Caldwell what he had not been able to tell Nancy or Arthur or anyone else, about the complex emotions he had had about the flower. It was difficult to tell. But not because he was embarrassed or because she was unreceptive, but because he was no longer very much interested in it and found it hard to remember the details. And yet he wanted to tell it, so that it would be no longer part of him, so that it would be an object in the world, existing outside himself.

"Paine said to me, 'You seem to be having quite a love affair with that flower.' And she was right."

"Ah well," Emily said, "so long as you were in love with something!"

It was too easy an escape and he refused to accept it. He presented her with the worst of his conclusions about that affair. "I think it was death I was in love with."

She looked at him very hard. "What makes you say that?" she asked brusquely.

He shrugged. "It's an idea I had," he said. And then he gave her the reasons he had worked out. He told her about the "satisfaction" that Dr. Graf had heard in his voice when he had asked the question about nearly dying. He told her of Paine's arch remark, "I think he doesn't want to get well." And as best he could he told her of his perception that his sense of perfect rest, of an existence without any of the conditions of existence, his feeling of identification with the perfection of the flower, was but a disguised desire for non-existence. And as he told it, almost querulously insisting on his point, he became aware of the area of weariness that he had within himself, the spot of fatigue around which all his energies, when he had them, were organized. Yes, he insisted, he had been in love with death.

"And if?" said Emily.

"What?" he said.

"And supposing?" she said. "And supposing you were?"

He was puzzled and annoyed. "What do you mean?" he said.

"I'm not sure you were. When Susan was a baby I used to do the same thing—I mean just look and look and look. It became like a trance. I felt she was so complete and I was so complete. It wasn't that I was admiring her. It was— Well, I don't know what it was. But it wasn't what you say it was."

He was not ready to admit the similarity of the two experiences. Nor did she press it, but returned to his. "And supposing you were?" she said again.

"Were what?"

"In love with death a little. It was only a little. Supposing you were. You have a right. Are you supposed to hate it?"

He did not then know from what authority she spoke, but he heard authority in her voice, enough to make him stare at her and not answer.

"Are you?" she insisted, a little passionately.

"No," he had to admit.

"Well then!" she said, bridling with pleasure and tossing her head at having won the argument.

He could not have reconstructed the dialectic by which she had reached her victory and he did not try. He was quite satisfied that she had won. He felt the legs of his trousers. They were still very wet. He stood up to shake them from his legs to which they were clinging. He went to the rock on which she had laid his shirt and felt the shirt. It was dryer than his trousers but still pretty damp. She, as if in politeness, as if to join him in this interest in damp clothes, squeezed out the hem of her skirt and spread it out over her knees. She lifted her arms and fluffed out her long hair and tossed it about in the sun. He came and stood beside her and looked down at her. She did not stop tossing her heavy hair until he knelt down beside her, and even then she did not take her hands from it—she met his look with motionless gravity, her arms still raised. She did not take her hands from her hair until he first touched her.

It was only later, when they were lying precisely side by side, their clasped hands hidden from sight between them, that Laskell felt that he understood not so much the logic as the basis in fact of her argument. His mind, submerged deeper and deeper beneath the dark and unoppressive somnolence of his body, held a last awareness of its willing extinction, the price of the passion it had been unable to stop and scarcely able to observe. It made a last effort at its autonomy—it concurred in its evanescence, and as it faded into the doze, it drew the expense of spirit that had just been made into a conjunction with all the expenditures of spirit of any kind, this sexual kind, or the exhaustion and stillness at the end of a work, or of a life fully and finally expended; and it even, before Laskell closed his eyes on it, flaunted the recollection that men had used the word "die" for the last destroying agony of love, which they sought.

It all seemed very clear to Laskell at the point of his falling asleep, but when he awoke it made no sense at all, but was only one of those revelations that come from the influence of sleep or drugs in which the sensation of understanding is so great that one has the certainty that one has understood *something*. It seemed that he opened his eyes almost immediately after closing them. And he opened them on a world of difficulty. He saw that he was in a "situation," he wondered if he were "involved."

The words that carried the meaning of his fear were so vulgar that he shook his head to drive them away. His body was grateful, but his mind, as if in revenge for its defeat and submergence, raised the ugly and vulgar question. He felt more truly himself than he could remember having felt for a long time. The carping remnants of his illness seemed finally to have gone, and not until they were gone did he know how much they had been there. For this, he saw, he must be grateful to Emily Caldwell. Yet how much more grateful to Emily Caldwell he would now be if she would vanish, at this very moment, having made this strange beneficent visitation of hers. That would be the right and proper way for the event to shape itself, the economical way. What she had done, what she had made known of herself, these were of this very instant, of this time and place. It could never happen again by so complete and fortunate a chance—and he would spoil what had happened by trying to reproduce it. In order to see her again he would undertake to circumvent all the circumstances that surrounded her. There were her husband and her child and her poverty, and Nancy's hostile eye, and Mrs. Folger's. Above all, he thought, there was the barrier of her own mind. He did not know by what great chance she had today said just the right things which had had so strange and relieving an effect upon him, not when he remembered the many affected and pretentious things she had said in the past. He wished that the astonishing truth of her few chance words and the astonishing truth of her body would never have to give way to the foolish articulations of her intellect. He feared the moment when she would speak. She would say something about "freedom" or "paganism." He wished that now, at this moment, she would vanish in the golden cloud in which she had come.

But she gave no sign of vanishing. She lay there beside him, very much in the ordinary flesh that does not easily vanish, her hand still in his, her ankles lightly crossed and her skirt neatly over her legs where he had disposed it for her. No sign at all of vanishing, but only of being about to speak. She turned her head and smiled at him. She seemed to begin with difficulty, and apparently to make it easier for herself she sat up. In what she said there was nothing silly or affected or in the fashion of what another decade had been in the habit of saying after its love-making. When their conversation was over, the cloud had appeared in which she was to vanish. She quite brought to an end all question of there being a "situation" for Laskell, of his being in any way "involved." The cloud she conjured up for herself was, however, not exactly a golden one.

Her beginning was not promising. She said, "It shouldn't have happened. Should it have?"

To this he could not consent. "Of course it should."

She was docile and modified her opinion at once. "Then it must not happen again."

To this he must refuse to agree. "Why not?" he said huffily.

She really had no tenacity about her views. She sat with her legs drawn up, her skirt wrapped neatly around them, and she looked over her knees at the stream. "Then it mustn't happen this way. I don't mean— What I mean is—" She was very miserable. "If we ever do meet again—I mean like this—would you— That is, if you ever do want again—" She had not been well trained in the frankness on which her culture prided itself. "I mustn't take any chances. Do you mind? But if I were to become pregnant—"

It was the practical discussion that all lovers have to have. She had now turned a little toward him and her weight was on one hand while with the other she poked intensely at the ground, as if to distract his attention from what she was saying. She was blushing and looking down at her finger's work.

"You see," she said, and looked up at him in full apology. "It's because of Susan."

"Susan?"

"I mean if I were to become pregnant."

It was not her husband that she spoke of in connection with this contingency. As Laskell looked at her face, he saw no slightest sign of guilt in it. And he felt none himself. Still, he thought, guilt or no guilt, it would be no light thing that he would be implicated in. No light thing at all, considering it apart from morality, considering it only practically, poverty being what it was. But that was the colder of the two ideas that were in his mind. The warmer one was the contingency itself, the idea of a pregnant Emily.

"You see," she said, "Susan is so ill."

"Ill?" And he heard that his voice was rough and suspicious. "She doesn't look ill."

"She doesn't, does she? And she doesn't know—doesn't really know. But ever since she was little. It's her—it's the heart." She seemed to prefer to say "the heart" rather than "her heart," as if it made the weakness less immediate.

He did not believe it. But he remembered the evidences that showed that the child's mother was determined to act as if she believed it. There was the time when she had called after him when he was walking away with Susan, cautioning him against walking too fast up the hill—it was not him she was concerned for but Susan. He remembered how cool she had been to Susan's declaration of her ambition to become a dancer. He understood why it was that Susan could violently tumble Emily into the water with only the gentlest retaliation from her mother. There would have to be retaliation, Susan would have to be ducked in revenge, but only, as it were, in token form. And yet Laskell did not really believe what Emily Caldwell was telling him.

"I try to make a life just as if nothing were the matter with her. And I want her to have every pleasure now."

He remembered her *carpe diem*, the swift passage of envious time. Yet still somehow Laskell did not believe her. As she spoke of the threat to her daughter, she had the air of one of those young women—Laskell had known several—who make up elaborate and romantic lies about their lives, transparent lies, which give them significance or excuse their actions, either their sexual fear or their sexual excess. They invent tragic events in the past and speak with certain knowledge of tragic events to come, early betrayals by men or fate, or family "tendencies," illnesses of mind or body that are yet to appear, either in themselves or in some member of the family to whom they will have to devote themselves, or insisting that some sad incident in the lives of their mothers must inevitably recur in their own lives. It is for this reason, they say, that they will never marry, for they can only bring sorrow to the men they marry, or it is for this reason that they are so prodigal in their sexuality. In such lies and fantasies of fate, there is always the dignity of necessity, no matter how easily the lies can be seen through—they are needed and therefore one listens to them with a kind of awe.

For the moment, he was convinced she was lying. But whether she was lying or not, the extremity of her statement—of her truth, if it was the truth; of her lie, if it was a lie—quite drove from Laskell's mind any thoughts about being caught in a "situation." It was not only because she was saying, whether it was a lie or not, that she had her own large and particular fate in which he had no part. It was also because her speaking of her daughter standing on the edge of mortality made irrelevant everything that a critical mind might hold against her—her having been a schoolteacher or librarian with ideals, her being the wife of Duck Caldwell, her having run a tearoom, if it was true she had done that, her sad artistic slang, her foolish reading of Spengler, her foolish painted bowls. All these things that had stood as a barrier between them, now, as she spoke of mortality, whether in truth or in falsehood, became quite beside the point.

He said quietly, "Are you sure about that? Was it only the local doctor who told you?" For he had the city man's lack of faith in country doctors.

"Yes, it's sure." And she looked at him with something like an apology, as if she were very sorry to have to force the inescapable truth upon him, as if she were sorry that she could not let him prove his doubts. "Yes, I've had her to two Hartford doctors, very good men."

Then suddenly she said in a panicky way, "Oh, I shouldn't have told you. I *shouldn't* have. She doesn't know—nobody knows. You won't speak of it to anyone, will you? Not even to Mr. and Mrs. Croom. Especially not to Mrs. Folger. Even her father doesn't know."

He did not even bother to give his promise of secrecy. "Her father doesn't know! How could you not have told him?"

Emily looked puzzled. "I don't know," she said. "He wouldn't respect her."

"Wouldn't respect her? What do you mean?"

It was the only thing she had ever said that could be construed as a criticism of her husband, and when he asked her what she meant by it, she could not explain.

After a moment of silence, she said passionately, as much to reassure him as herself, "But of course it's just a *condition*. Nothing *has* to happen."

And then she said, referring back to the consideration which had led her into an account of these circumstances, "So you see!"

"Yes, I see," Laskell said.

He had to believe it now, he did believe it, and yet somehow he saw it as a fantasy, a thing that he could believe only for its own kind of truth. If it was a fact at all, it was not so much a fact in life as a fact in a poem.

So here it was, the cloud in which Emily Caldwell would vanish after her visitation. Here was the circumstance that would keep Laskell from being involved in a situation, that would make it possible for him to go his way when the few weeks of summer that were left should have passed. It set her apart and marked her off— she was committed elsewhere. It therefore put the term to his commitments and his necessities of feeling. And at the same time it gave great dignity to Emily Caldwell and to the eventual separation from her.

What Laskell did not know then was that, for their relationship, whatever that was, it was fortunate that almost immediately it had to take a third person into account. Whatever that relationship was: Laskell did not know what it was, neither now nor later. It was apparently not love, not in any sense in which Laskell would have used the word. There was no promise in it, no exchange of things undertaken, no futurity or desire of futurity. They were to say little to each other and find out little about each other. Laskell was able to see Emily in the light of the simple sexual dignity she had, her quiet gravity, and he saw her in the cloud of mortality in which she walked, whether he thought of this as invention or as fact. But he felt none of the pride or possessiveness he might have expected. He was grateful, but gratitude did not make the bond that connected him with her. Laskell never was able to understand what their connection was, what it might have become or what name it ought to have; but he did come to understand that what made it so really strong, so wholly inexpressible, was its being limited and hedged, its being conditioned and defined, and not only by time and circumstances, and not merely by their own wills or by their own capacities for feeling, but by the existence, the perhaps precarious existence, of a third person, who moved all unconscious of what was between them, and all unconscious of the precariousness of her own existence.

9

I T WAS generally admitted among Kermit Simpson's intellectual friends that you could not possibly dislike Kermit. It was natural, as things go, that the attempt should have been made. Kermit had a great fortune, from New York real estate on his mother's side, from Western chemicals on his father's. He was very handsome, a big, rangy man who was good at field sports, court games, and boating, and it was said that he still took an interest in such things. He had a wife who was expected to be impossible because of her prettiness, her social position, and her name, which was Sheila, but who was really a modest and rather intelligent girl with a very solemn sense of duty. Kermit had two children who charmed everyone and a country house so simple in its beauty that even the poorest and most socially maladroit of Kermit's friends were not ill at ease in it. All this endowment of his life—or, indeed, the mere fact that he had once played polo and still owned horses —should have closed him out from the sympathy of the people who were his friends, and that it did not was a great tribute to his character and intentions.

But Simpson was not really a fortunate man. The ease and luck of his life made demands on him that he could not meet. At this time the way was beginning to open for men like Simpson to have a career in government, just as it was opening for men like Croom. But Kermit had been well-born just a little too late to think of government as a career. He needed an American Revolution to match a fate to his fortune, needed to fight at Yorktown and to have pledged himself to the Continental Congress. Failing that, he should have been English and in the Foreign Office. His sense of social responsibility had been formed at a time when senses of social responsibility were likely to be in conflict with government.

He declared that his magazine was devoted to Jeffersonian ideas, but that only made an irony—as one heard him say "Jeffersonian" in his beautiful Westport house, one might be tempted to think of Monticello and to understand how far apart the two houses were; and one might think of Mount Vernon too when Kermit stood at his full Washingtonian height and his streak of stubbornness appeared, as it did now and then. But he had never lived in danger, he would never put his ideas or his life or his fortune or his sacred honor to the test of establishing them at Yorktown, he would never face responsibility or defeat or disgrace.

Kermit was all too bland. There was no roughness in him. He never followed passion where it led, nor did necessity ever constrain him to resistance. The blandness was fatal to his character. Yet as soon as this was seen, one had to see the queer grace he had. He was really an innocent man and he wanted everyone to have what he had. Only now and then did he show the rich man's sense of vulnerability, the awareness that he could bleed and be bled more copiously than most men. At that time people were quoting an exchange between two American novelists on the subject of the very rich. "The very rich are different from us," one novelist had said, and the other had replied, "Yes, they have more money." It was generally felt that the second novelist had disposed of the first, who had shown himself to be a snob, but Kermit Simpson suggested that the very rich are indeed different, that they move at a different tempo, have a different density and intensity, that they have different nerves and, when they are innocent, as Kermit was, a different kind of innocence.

Another man showing off his new trailer would have been silly, but Arthur and Nancy and Laskell were now crowded into the trailer and gravely followed Kermit's demonstration with scarcely a teasing word. Kermit showed them how the beds came down; he showed them the washstand that folded away, the gas stove with its fierce blue flame, the concealed lights and the unexpected lockers.

"It's a special feeling," Kermit said, "to have a complete home on the move. I must have Scythian blood. You know, the ancient Scythians went around with little wicker houses and they must

have felt the way I do. Do you remember D. H. Lawrence's book
of poems about the tortoises? I know why they interested him so
much, the snugness and privacy, you travel with your home on
your back."

But the documentation and the justification by means of the
ancient Scythians and D. H. Lawrence's observation of the tortoises were not quite enough and Kermit went on. "You know,
don't you, that Sheila and I are going to make a tour of the country? She's never been around in the United States and she and I
want to see things at first hand, really on the road, no hotels." The
day of seeing the United States from the road was really about
over, but Kermit was usually a little late with things, though none-
theless sincere, and nothing could have better justified the sleek
aluminum magnificence of the trailer than a tour to inspect the
condition of life in America.

"What about refrigeration?" Arthur asked.

It was Arthur who was asking the questions. The trailer was
sanctuary, and while they were in it, asking questions and getting
explanations, they were safe from the confrontation of Nancy and
Maxim. In the general exchange of greetings it was not particularly to be observed that Nancy and Maxim did not approach each
other. Maxim had the manner which was not very different from
the manner he used to have at meetings of "sympathizers." He was
detached from what was going on, his manner said, these people
had to make their own decisions in their own way, yet at the same
time he was enormously alert and ready to speak, quietly and
mildly, if things should by any possibility go wrong. He was outside the trailer as the inspection proceeded, and Laskell, looking
through the window, could see him sitting quietly on a rock. He
was wearing an open shirt and light flannel slacks. They were
Kermit's and too tight and too long for Maxim. In their failure to
be negligible they were ignoble. Maxim was no longer bulging
with the future. And though his scar was visible, it no longer had
its old meaning. He looked, as he sat on the rock, lonely and lost.

"Refrigeration?" said Kermit, and in mild triumph he disclosed
the little refrigerator, all gleaming white and purring gently. "How
is that for refrigeration? And here," he said, and took out a huge

steak and held it up for them to see, "and here is your dinner. You three are having dinner with us tonight. I think I'd better leave the steak out now."

"No!" said Nancy.

"I don't think steaks should be let get too cold," Kermit explained.

"No, we can't do that, Kermit. We can't have dinner with you."

"Of course you can. You didn't know just when we were coming so you couldn't ask us, so I'm all prepared to ask you. If you want to be formal, you can invite us tomorrow."

"Kermit—I can't eat with Gifford Maxim," Nancy said, as precisely as possible to clear away Kermit's misunderstanding.

And some part of that undeveloped gift of Kermit Simpson's appeared, for in answer, quite without surprise, Kermit put his arm around Nancy's shoulder and said, "Ah, you just can't imagine how easy it is. I know what you mean, but he's not the man you think."

His arm was so simple in its friendliness and there was so warm an overtone of faith and promise in his voice that Nancy had nothing to say in reply. She did not consent to come but she did not insist on the refusal.

The place they found for the beautiful trailer was a patch of ground just off the road opposite the house. Kermit backed the car and trailer onto it and swung around so that the trailer's door faced the road. They were shaded by a clump of trees. When they were established on the site, Nancy and Arthur left them but Laskell stayed behind.

Simpson and Maxim brought out a folding table and folding chairs of light metal and then glasses and whisky and ice. Laskell saw in what a practiced way and with how few words they made camp. The intimacy between them seemed very sure. It had been there to be heard in Kermit's voice when he had said to Nancy that Maxim was not the man she thought he was. He spoke as if he understood Maxim deeply. Laskell was no longer Kermit's wise friend. That place was now held by Maxim.

Maxim opened the whisky bottle and poured drinks for them all. He did it with the same quiet significance with which he would have poured his own whisky. He was careless about the amount he poured, he had not the scientist's interest in quantity, but each time he held the bottle over the glass it was as if he were making a subtle decision that involved universal considerations.

He was still giving the whole of his attention to the drinks and he did not look at Laskell when he said, "How are you feeling, John? Did you make the trip all right? I was worried about you."

"Worried? Why were you worried?"

Maxim went on with what he was doing. Then he looked at Laskell with all his irony. Only the impossibility of Maxim's knowing what had happened on the trip kept Laskell from believing that Maxim knew all about it.

"You were on the verge," Maxim said, as if it were pretty dull that he had to make any explanation.

If Laskell were to press for the meaning, if he were to say, "On the verge of what?" he would get no other answer than that look of irony again. Maxim had the trick of really good fortune-tellers and palmists, of putting things so generally and so dramatically that what was said had to have some sort of relevant meaning, and then if you asked them what they meant, they looked at you with mockery and annoyance, as if you were being willfully stupid, you with all your intelligence and sensitivity.

But in Maxim's mockery there was now a new element, a kind of weariness. He still pretended to his knowledge of hidden motive, but the hidden things he pretended now to see were different from the hidden things he had pretended to see before. He looked at Laskell as if he were saying that there was now a virtue in what he saw. He smiled, as if in this obtuse and stubborn Laskell he saw things that made him very tender and forgiving. But he would not explain and he said very little during Laskell's short visit that afternoon. While Kermit conscientiously reported his observations of New England—for he did not want it to be thought that his trip had been wholly for pleasure—Maxim sat squinting in the sun smoking cigarettes and drinking whisky.

Nancy came to dinner. Whatever she felt toward Maxim, she came with at least some good will to the occasion, for she had piled her hair high on her head to display her ears in an almost ceremonious nakedness and she looked very pretty. But she kept herself remote, as if she had made an agreement with Arthur about her behavior and was living up to it as gallantly as she could. She said nothing to Maxim and did not look at him.

Kermit had a fire going and the table set. His salad was ready for the dressing, the potatoes were nearly done. For cocktails he had brought champagne of a modest vintage, for he planned this as a festive occasion, and the two bottles were icing in a bucket. Kermit was a good practical cook, silent and without any of the sense of *cachet* that men so often cultivate about cookery. He had learned from guides and fellow hunters, not from chefs or books.

When their glasses were filled, they all made that queer little abortive gesture of modern people when they drink wine, an embarrassed directing of the glass at the company—they cannot completely carry out so archaic a ritual as drinking *to* anyone, yet they cannot quite let the custom die.

But Kermit said in his mild voice, from his great height, making the occasion specific, "We must drink to the new assistant editor of *The New Era*." He said it in just the right voice to make it gracious but not solemn, and raised his glass toward Maxim. Maxim dropped his eyes. They drank to Maxim, all except Nancy, who twirled her glass and looked at the bubbles with curiosity. In the still air they could hear the snapping of Kermit's fire as it burned down to the coals he wanted. Arthur and Laskell looked thoughtful.

Arthur said, "John told us about your—your break, Giff. What are you going to do now?"

Since it was clear that so far as work went, Maxim was employed by *The New Era*, Arthur must have meant that he wanted to know what Maxim was going to do about his political life. Arthur had asked the question in full good nature. He did not expect the answer he received and perhaps did not deserve it.

"I'm going to secure my safety, Arthur," Maxim said courteously.

Arthur's face darkened. He did not reply at once but seemed to wait for the first flush of his anger to subside. Then he said, "Do you mean that?"

Maxim said with the same soft courtesy, "Yes, I mean it."

"It's a hell of a thing to say—and mean." Arthur spoke with the direct intention of insulting Maxim. But then he seemed to have heard the calculated note of contempt in his voice and he said earnestly, almost pleadingly, "Giff, I'm *sure* you're mistaken."

"If you choose to think so, Arthur, you may of course think so. You asked me and I told you."

"But it's so unlike you—it's such a reactionary thing to say!"

Perhaps it was an impulse of kindness in Arthur that made his voice so boyish, made it seem as if he were not appealing to Maxim's better nature against his reactionariness but against his being unsportsmanlike, or even, going back a few decades, caddish.

Maxim said, "That depends upon what you mean by revolutionary. Or perhaps, whatever you do mean by revolutionary, I really am what you say—perhaps I am reactionary."

But Kermit would have none of that. "Cut it out, Giff, we've been through that. I don't know that I agree with all your ideas, but you're not reactionary."

Maxim shrugged, refusing argument.

Kermit said, "I agree with you in certain respects that things in the Soviet Union are not what we ought to admire. I think it ought to be said that we don't, and I'm a little ashamed of myself for not having said it openly enough in *The New Era*. After all, we are a libertarian paper, and if a revolutionary experiment curtails freedom even temporarily, we ought to say so. And say it openly. After all, that's the only way we are going to bring about any change: by saying things openly. And we have the right to say them, especially if we have a full realization that it is an experiment and that every social experiment, no matter how liberal its ultimate aims, is bound to generate certain contradictions and difficulties of a temporary sort. But it's absurd to call that position reactionary."

"That is not my position," said Maxim.

But at the same moment Nancy said, "And you are going to say that kind of thing in *The New Era*, Kermit?"

Kermit preferred to answer Nancy's question rather than Maxim's denial. "Yes," Kermit said. "I've had it troubling my conscience in a vague sort of way for some time. You know how those things can be. In the back of your mind you have a vague feeling of illogicality, but it doesn't come to the fore until something brings it there. After all, civil liberties are civil liberties, no matter

where and no matter what the underlying philosophy of the particular state that negates them." He turned to Maxim again and
repeated what he had concluded before. "But Giff, it's just perverse
to call such a view reactionary."

Maxim shrugged again. "Call it what you like," he said rather
brutally. He helped himself to champagne, drank it off, and filled
his glass again. "Call it what you like. It's your position, not mine,
so call it what you like. Names don't bother me as much as they
bother you. They don't bother me at all. I've tried to tell you, Simpson, I've tried to tell you for weeks now what I think and you won't
understand. I can't make you understand. I don't think I'll ever
make you understand—it's not in your nature, it's not in your
good-nature, to know what I'm talking about. But I want you to
be sure that I tried. I'm taking a job with you simply because—"

"Yes, I know," Kermit said, smiling. His smile showed that he
was hurt by Maxim's tone, but was trying not to be. "I know.
You're simply 'using' me. You've told me that. All right. But I'm
using you too. Don't forget that—I'm using you just as much as
you're using me. There's an area where we don't agree. I grant
that. I grant that I don't understand that area. There are some
things about you that I suppose I never will understand. Your
bitterness and hopelessness and the way you overstate things. But
I've made plenty of use of you. I've learned a lot from you and I
think I'll learn more still."

It was irresistibly disarming, even for Maxim. And Maxim admitted that he was disarmed. He was looking at Kermit with a sour
irony, a kind of bitterly grudging admiration of Kermit's method
of argument. Kermit had disarmed him with his boyish earnestness
and Maxim seemed to be admitting that this, after all, was an
effective technique, as effective as one of his own. Laskell thought
that it came very naturally to both Arthur and Kermit to be boyish
when they were earnest. Maxim said with a final fatigue, as if
there were no arguing with Kermit, "O.K." But then he revived
and said, "But get it straight, Simpson. You don't understand.
That's right, you don't. But you don't even know what it is you
don't understand."

Kermit made a little gesture with his head and mouth and eyebrows, as if to say that that might well be but that he had his own

opinion. Laskell saw that he had been bullied by Maxim all the time they had been together. Kermit had learned how to take the bullying gracefully, with a little gesture to indicate an opinion held in reserve.

For a moment they sat silent, waiting to see if Kermit would reply beyond his gesture. But Kermit did not say anything.

Nancy said, "No, he doesn't understand." She said it very quietly. She meant that she understood but that a person of Kermit's innocence would naturally not understand the depravity to which Maxim was confessing. She said in the same quiet voice, "Why did you come here, Maxim?"

Her addressing him by his last name carried the question out of the present moment and immediate scene into a clear abstract realm of morality where perhaps the matter belonged. It was very striking. Laskell had been calling him Giff, and even Arthur, when he was most contemptuous, had called him Giff.

Maxim looked down into his empty glass on the table. He took the stem between two fingers and twirled it slowly. It was an oddly elegant gesture for his bulk. He was smoking a cigarette and it had burned down to as small a butt as possible. He took one more pull at it, slowly, shutting one eye as the smoke curled up and stung it. He looked at Nancy and dryly said, "For purposes of corruption, I suppose you'd say." He dropped the cigarette and ground it carefully into the earth with his toe.

"That is exactly what I do say. You did your best to draw us in and now you'd like to undo your work. By every lie and insinuation you can utter."

She had risen and was standing with her clenched fist pressing down hard upon the table for support. But she was very quiet. It was impossible to interfere. They were both so quiet and kept the matter so precisely between them that none of the three men was able to enter the conflict to turn it.

"Draw you in?" Maxim said with surprise. And his voice was filled with the politeness of centuries of humanistic culture, with the bows and curtsies, the fauteuils and carpets of many civilizations, as he returned the shot that Nancy had fired with such effect a moment before. "You are mistaken, Croom," he said softly.

It was more terrible than Nancy's "Maxim" and Nancy flinched under it. They all flinched under it. They all saw what Maxim wanted them to see. They saw it even though it was a travesty that Maxim had conjured up—the committee-room in which politics was brought to the ultimate issue, in which, since the issues were final and lives were staked on them, the antagonists stripped themselves as much as possible of their ordinary human conditions, and of their names kept only what was essential for identification, Nancy giving up anything so charged with the irrelevant condition of femininity as Nancy or Mrs. Croom.

For a moment Maxim let them take it in and then he said, "You are quite mistaken. I didn't draw you in. The dialectic of the situation"—his voice permitted itself a note of intellectual bitterness which swelled as he went on—"mind you, *the dialectic of the situation* detached certain disaffected portions of the middle class from their natural class interests and connections, and attached them to the interests of the oppressed classes."

There was insult in his language. But his tone was politely explanatory. "You happened to be part of that disaffected portion of the middle class. It was not that you consciously responded to external necessities but rather that you expressed certain internal conflicts which reflected contradictions in the world outside."

As he went on it became clear that he was not insulting Nancy but rather the language that he was using. The force of his attention was not on Nancy now, but on his own words.

He said, and closed his eyes and changed his cadence to show that he was quoting, " 'I should be the last to hold the individual responsible for conditions whose creature he himself is, socially considered, however much he may raise himself above them subjectively.' I think that is verbatim. And in the logic of the situation —it is called the *inexorable* logic of the situation—you were drawn only to the ideational aspects of the movement, to the emotional superstructure of the movement, not to its base in reality. So much so, that when I made one single attempt to—as you say— draw you in, to involve you in the more practical aspects of the movement, I had no success whatever. I asked three of you—John Laskell and Arthur and yourself—to *do* a certain thing, to receive certain letters of great importance. You all three, every one of you, refused. And when I thought that perhaps I ought not take Arthur's refusal as valid for his wife, too, and asked you again, when you were alone, whether you would give me this help, you refused again."

With his eyes on Nancy's face, Laskell saw that Maxim's odd point of honor had been communicated. He saw the puzzled, stopped look that Nancy wore as she understood what Maxim was saying to her, that he was telling her he would not even now betray her secret. She had opened her mouth to reply. She had been on the point of replying to this man she so hated. But he had stopped her, if only for this moment.

But Arthur said, "Maxim! Do you mean to say that after we both refused together, you went and asked Nancy by herself?"

"Yes. But she refused."

"That was a fine, son-of-a-bitch thing to do," said Arthur.

"It was," said Maxim. Then he explained demurely, "But you see, I was a member of the Party then."

Arthur had nothing to answer and Maxim went on with his lecture to Nancy. "So you see, I have very little hope of drawing you one way or another. You will go the way of the dialectic, whatever way that happens to be for you, and so, no doubt, will I. You can be sure that the thesis is now being prepared with reference to me and my kind: 'Certain disaffected portions of the professional revolutionary class will be infected by the virus of the rotting bourgeois culture from which they originally sprang on the impulse to make the revolution serve their individualistic aspirations for romantic action and utopian morality and will betray their revolutionary commitments to wallow in the slime of idealism from which they came.' In a short time I will be known as Maxim & Co. Perhaps you yourself can see the froth of the counter-revolutionary mad-dog on my mouth. As for you, you will, I hope, go a nobler way."

They were all silent, deeply embarrassed. Even Kermit felt that Maxim had gone too far. He got up and laid the steak on the grill. Laskell had been complexly moved by the outburst, for he had only once before seen Maxim yield so completely to merely personal feeling. Yet at the same time that he felt an obscure pity, he felt a kind of disgust. Maxim might be right in all he said about the movement, but Laskell was sure he would never again be able to look at him without disgust. However good the reasons, he thought, that make a man desert his cause, he will always be unpleasant to see, his moral equilibrium will never restore itself. Better, perhaps, to stay in the self-hatred of an enforced conformity than to enter the self-suspicion of even reasoned and justifiable treachery.

The spectacle of Maxim was shocking enough to carry Arthur past his anger. It was as if one could not be angry with a Maxim in this condition. Arthur said, "Giff!" using again that boyish note of straightforward appeal that was so winning. He tried to recall Maxim to his former and better self. "Giff! What brought you to this point?"

It was clear that Maxim could not be given a single opening, for now he lifted his head and looked at Arthur, his lower lip caught reflectively between his teeth, and said very gravely, "There was a fly in it."

It took them all a moment to recall the dirty joke with whose tag Maxim had answered Arthur. They all hated him for the brutal levity of the answer.

But Arthur was not to be drawn into anger again. He said, as if Maxim had given him a perfectly satisfactory reply, "What's your position then?"

"Position?"

"Yes, position," Arthur said, his mouth now set and his jaw out.

Maxim gave way. "I have no position, Arthur," he said kindly. "At the moment I am *hors de combat*. Simpson has given me a job on his magazine at—what is it?—forty dollars a week. I'll work for Simpson for a while, at least until I am sufficiently *established*, and then I'll see. I've lost, you know, the work of nearly half my life."

It was true—nearly half a life. This they knew, this even Nancy knew, but she was evidently not willing to let herself be touched by it. She said, "But meanwhile, all the suffering people all over the world— You'll sit and consider while they die in their misery?"

For a moment Maxim did not answer. Then, "Is it not strange," he said, "do you not find it strange that as we become more sensitive to the sufferings of mankind, we become more and more cruel? The more we think of the human body and the human mind as being able to suffer, and the sorrier we feel for that, and the more we plan to prevent suffering, the more we are drawn to inflict suffering. The more tortures we think up. The more people we believe deserve to be tortured. The more we think that people can be ruled by fear of suffering. We have become our brother's keeper—and we will keep him in fear, we will keep him in concentration camps, we will keep him in straitjackets, we will keep him in the grave."

He was speaking in a quiet, a too quiet, voice. They could see the sweat breaking out on his forehead. He rose and poured himself a glass of champagne. He saw that the other glasses were empty. He stood there with the bottle in his hand and then gave it to Laskell to fill the glasses. He may have believed that the others would not accept wine from him.

"And never has there been so much talk of liberty while the chains are being forged. *Democracy* and *freedom*. And in the most secret heart of every intellectual, where he scarcely knows of it himself, there lies hidden the *real* hope that these words hide. It is the hope of power, the desire to bring his ideas to reality by imposing them on his fellow man. We are all of us, all of us, the little children of the Grand Inquisitor. The more we talk of welfare, the crueller we become. How can we possibly be guilty when we have in mind the welfare of others, and of *so many* others?"

"*We?*" It was Nancy who asked the question.

He sat there gloomily, not answering.

"Why do you say 'we'? I should think that very distinct differences could be made. Do you mean that we can think of the Nazis, that we can think of the cruelties of the Falangists in Spain—and still say 'we'? I should think that very sharp distinctions could be drawn between such people and the decent people."

He said nothing.

"Don't you?" she said to awaken him from his silence.

"No."

They were all relaxed by this. It was now clear that they were not dealing with an opinion but with a condition. They could take it more lightly, or with more pity.

"You really don't?" said Nancy with an air of having reached the end of the argument.

"The heart—" Maxim said, and for a quick strange moment Laskell vividly saw Emily at his side on the river-bank and heard her, as she spoke of Susan's illness, refer so to the child's infirmity. "My heart—" Maxim said, his voice taking on a lyric or elegiac quality, and they were all conscious that the twilight had deepened, that the tops of the trees were being stirred by a breeze that did not move the leaves of the lower branches, so that the trees murmured in a far-off way. The image, or rather the idea, of Emily Caldwell was intensely present to Laskell, and he suddenly felt that it carried him outside the circle of his friends, beyond their dispute and the reasons for it, making strangers of all of them, Nancy and Arthur, Kermit and Maxim. "My own heart," said Maxim, "is full of hatred and pity. Sometimes I cannot tell one from the other. When I feel the hatred I know it is generated by pity. And when I feel the pity I know it is generated by hatred. And when I do not feel either one or the other, then it is only emptiness, only emptiness. But whenever I feel anything at all, it is for all. All. We are all members one of another. Not in our suffering only, but in our cruelty as well. I have been in Spain, and I have seen Kermit Simpson shot and worse, and Nancy Croom shot and worse, and John Laskell and Arthur Croom. And myself. And I have helped. I have done it. You have helped. And even if I had not been there to see, I would know that I was involved. I am involved in the cruelties I have never seen and never will see. On both sides. You think only of what the other side must do to gain its ends and you feel separated from everything that is foul in them. But I know what 'our' side must do, and not merely do; the doing would not be so terrible if we did not have to be what we do, and I know what we must be."

The voice ceased its lilting, for Maxim had been speaking in a kind of sing-song. They all sat silent. None of them had ever heard anything like this before, this much devastation of spirit.

Laskell wanted to say something quickly. He said, "It seems to me, Giff, that you have lost your sense of community with men in their suffering and goodness and found it only in their cruelty and evil."

Maxim dropped his eyes as if to consider what Laskell had said, and then raised them and looked at Laskell with his face all exposed. He said simply and conclusively, "Yes."

It seemed as complete as an admission could be and it made him entirely the object of their hushed regard. It cut him off from them except for their awareness of his self-torture. They could not argue with him. And his aberration was so great and so open that it could not contaminate them. It was as if he had said that he was soon to die of a disease that could not possibly be contagious.

Kermit got up and went to the fire. He put the steak on its wooden board and held it out for them to see. "Ready!" he called. "Sit down."

"But perhaps," Maxim went on, paying no attention to Kermit's call and disregarding the fact that the others had risen to take their places at the table, "but perhaps that will mislead you about the nature of my community. My community with men is that we are children of God."

At this they all paused in their movement and looked at Maxim, who had not yet stirred. There had been nothing to say to Maxim's reply to Laskell's question and there was nothing to say now to his further statement. It came as an anticlimax, which was perhaps what Maxim wanted it to be, a remark to be heard and ignored on the way to dinner. They seated themselves at the table, but Maxim stayed where he was, silent, until Kermit called, "Come and partake, Giff, come and partake." He said to the others, "Now you know what it is I don't understand."

Maxim got up and brought his chair to the table and took his place at the end opposite Kermit and between Arthur and Laskell. His words had produced a certain solemnity and from it he himself was not excluded—it seemed that he was nearer to them now that he had shown how very far away he was.

Kermit carved, of course, with great skill, slicing the steak diagonally into inch-thick slabs, and the others did what best suited the situation, they talked about the steak. They praised Kermit for the perfect gradation of its color from black char through brown and pink to red and they went on to talk learnedly of the various theories of broiling steak. It was mooted whether a steak should first be coated with olive oil as some people advocated, and questions were raised about whether the prevailing method of quickly searing the steak was as good as it was said to be. Maxim stayed in the isolation of his announced belief and drank the red wine that Kermit had opened. Once he got up and looked to the coffee that was being prepared in the galley of the trailer and came back and took his place silently and went on eating and drinking. The disagreement had gone beyond the possibility of any further discussion and all of them were able to chat quite easily among themselves.

Yet they were all a little relieved when they heard footsteps and Duck Caldwell appeared in the deepening twilight.

"Don't want to disturb you folks at dinner," Duck said.

Kermit had risen and stood in a host's attitude. The paper napkin in his hand had almost the appearance of damask, so gracious was his stance. Duck looked at Kermit with his mocking self-possession and said, "Don't disturb. I heard about the trailer and I thought maybe I could get a look for myself."

Nancy said, "Kermit Simpson, Duck Caldwell," and made a little gesture with her two hands to bring them together.

Kermit, looking awkward in his size beside Duck, put out his hand and said, "Happy to meet you, Mr. Caldwell. You're not disturbing us at all."

For a moment Nancy hesitated and then she said, "Mr. Maxim, Mr. Caldwell." Maxim remained seated, and if anything was needed to revive Nancy's antagonism, it was the curt nod that Maxim gave Duck and the almost baleful look from lowered eyes. Kermit was quick, almost too quick, to escort Duck into the trailer, to turn on the lights and then to leave him to his own and the trailer's devices.

They were silent as Duck inspected the trailer, as if waiting for some verdict for which he had withdrawn. He came out at last and said to Kermit, "Mighty fine thing you have. But that's no job for a poor man now, is it? That's no factory job—looks to me custom-built."

"Well yes, yes it is. Yes, you're right—it was made to order." Kermit spoke in admiration of Duck's cleverness in seeing that it was custom-built. He was feeling the weight of his wealth and privilege and the cleverer he could make Duck the less guilty he would have to be. His discomfort made him as explicit as possible. "I worked over the plans with the people at the factory. I worked with a man named Norton, very intelligent man." He seemed to cling to Norton, for like many wealthy people Kermit liked to conjure up the personality of the artisans who had made the things they owned, speaking of their tailors and cabinet makers in all the odd quirks of their little, ordinary humanity, with the result that the things they owned, their suits and their furniture, seemed to cost nothing at all and derived what little value they had only from the human quality of the men who had made them. "But some of the ready-made jobs are first-rate. They really are, very well designed, very comfortable. There was one I seriously considered for a time and almost took it."

"But you didn't," said Duck with great clarity.

"No. That's right, I bought this one."

"Well," said Duck, not much inclined to press his advantage, "if you ever get tired of it, let me tell you where you can apply—right here." And he poked his chest with his forefinger. "That's living, a thing like that. If I had a car and a set-up like you got here, I could get me out to California the right way."

"Oh," said Kermit, relieved that Duck had his own freedom and plans for pleasure. "Are you thinking of going to California?"

"I'm thinking," said Duck. "But that's all I'm doing."

He was so apart from them all. He stood there small and resistant and envious. Things were going on inside his head and at this moment he was not justifying himself to anyone. He was not making a connection with any of them, and not trying. He did not even, just now, have a connection with Arthur and Nancy. They all sat before him, except Kermit, who stood. Their good will was not enough to overcome their superiority. Kermit, who defended Duck's liberty to say what he pleased; Arthur, who, if the talk was true, might be one of Duck's servants in Washington; Nancy, who conceived for Duck the saving myth of his oppression, honesty, and inner strength—none of them could make the connection. Maxim, who had once had a gift for "making contact" with the underprivileged, just sat and glared at this slight, tight, excluded figure. Why Maxim seemed so hostile Laskell could not guess, but he knew that the others were being held at bay by the accusation

Duck was subtly making, which had reference to the steak and the wine and the salad bowl and the trailer. Perhaps of them all it was John Laskell who came closest to Duck at that moment.

Nancy made an effort but she did not do very well. In fact, she went quite off her usual line. She said, "Who knows? Maybe with luck, some day—" It was like a mother carelessly trying to pacify a child with the offer of a hope she knows is vain, and it made the moment worse.

"No, not the way things are, Mrs. Croom. There have to be big changes before I get anything like that."

Well, he had a kind of courage—he looked straight at Kermit Simpson, looked at him meaningfully, out of his isolation and bitterness. He had the courage to know in his subtle way that these people were ashamed before him, especially Kermit. So he stood and looked at Kermit. There was no theory in the look, just a personal measuring, and Kermit standing with his napkin must have had the sense that he was a great deal too tall as well as a great deal too wealthy.

They heard Emily Caldwell's voice saying, "Good evening!" She came with Susan in her wake. Nancy seemed almost glad to see her, glad perhaps for Duck to have someone close to him here. She said most cordially, "Oh, good evening, Mrs. Caldwell." She made the introductions and Kermit offered Emily his chair. Emily said that she must not disturb them, that she had come only because Susan wanted to see the trailer, but Laskell saw how her glance went to the wine bottles and the glasses and he knew that she had her own reasons for coming. She had been afraid that they would start Duck drinking.

This time it was Maxim who rose to demonstrate the trailer. He had responded to this introduction very differently, had smiled with great openness to Emily, and had said to Susan in a very direct way that he was glad to meet her. He put his arm around Susan's shoulder and put out his hand to help Emily up the steps.

"Won't you join us in a glass of wine, Mr. Caldwell?" said Kermit.

And Duck screwed his head about and considered and said, "Don't mind if I do."

But when Kermit came back from the trailer with the two

glasses he went to fetch, Emily Caldwell was with him. Emily firmly took the glasses from him and put them on the table.

"Thank you, it's friendly of you but we can't stay," she said. And she called, "Susan!" She said, "We'd love to stay but we can't. But I hope we'll be seeing all of you at our Church Bazaar tomorrow. You gentlemen will be here that long I hope. Do come. Oh, not that it will be anything—it's nothing really—but you might like to see it." And she called again, "Susan dear!"

Duck stood with the sour look of a man whose rational pleasures are being interfered with. Susan put her head out of the door of the trailer and said, "Yes, Mother?" and Emily went to her and drew her down the steps though the child was protesting that she had not yet seen everything.

"Oh, let her stay, Mrs. Caldwell!" Kermit pleaded warmly for Susan. "And you and your husband stay and have a glass of wine with us."

"Yes, Mother, *please*," said Susan.

"No, really—" said Emily.

Laskell saw her deep apprehension, saw Duck standing there smiling and grim. She was not now the woman he had known on the bank of the little river, she was confused and distracted. Yet she was that woman and he stood up and went to Susan. "You can come back tomorrow, Susan, and work all the gadgets. Mr. Simpson and Mr. Maxim will be glad to have you. I'll come too and you can make tea for us on the stove if you'd like. Would you like that?"

"Yes, I would," Susan said decisively.

So it was settled and Emily Caldwell was able to sweep her family together and away from the dinner party. She was fussy and nervous and her "Good night—good night all," rang without gratification in Laskell's ears. And he got no pleasure from her air of social authority as she said to Nancy, "Mrs. Croom, you will bring all your friends to the Bazaar, won't you?"

When they had gone, a fresh heaviness descended on the failure of the dinner party.

"Are they natives here? Are they farming people?" Kermit said.

"He is native, but she's not," Nancy said. "She comes from Hartford."

"Are they farming people?"

"Not exactly." Nancy said it defensively. "He works at odd jobs. He's a very good carpenter."

"The little girl is sweet," said Kermit.

"The husband is a very remarkable person. But the wife—" And Nancy shrugged.

Maxim spoke. "Remarkable, yes. I know the type—the criminal personality with the strong, narrow streak of intellect." He spoke with a remote objectivity, as if from notes. "It's a modern type and extremely useful in making revolutions. It has to be liquidated eventually, either by changing its character or by—or in other ways. Some examples of it can be converted into small bureaucrats. But others like their revolutionary role too much. You see something of the same sort of thing in the middle class too. But in the middle class the deep, narrow envy runs more to intellect, to the envy of ideas and of personalities."

"Oh, Giff, come off it," said Kermit.

Maxim shrugged.

Nancy spoke from such depths of revulsion that her voice was scarcely agitated. And what she said almost seemed to be spoken in friendliness. "Oh, something terrible has happened to you," she said. "It has—something terrible. You have only to hear someone speak with a sense of his class and you hate him and traduce him. What kind of change has taken place in you? What do you think men are? Only a few months ago you would have been interested in that man," and she pointed in the direction Duck had gone, "and you would have admired him and tried to politicalize him. Now you call him a criminal type—exactly because you see the determined quality in him. If he had your class advantages, or any of ours, he would be something positive, a leader. Of that I'm sure. He's wasted here, I admit that—he never had a chance and his wife is a fool. But to you he's nothing but a *criminal type.*"

"Look here—" Laskell had broken in. It was impossible for him to hear Emily spoken of so disparagingly.

"Nevertheless—" said Maxim stolidly.

But Laskell was not heard and Nancy was not to be stopped. "When John told me what had happened to you, I could scarcely believe it, I was horrified. Then, when I read that article of yours,

I thought, 'John did not get things quite straight.' I thought that the man who wrote that might be wrong in many respects, or confused, but such a man could not be actually counter-revolutionary. He knows that things cannot be judged by absolutes, that a great social experiment must be judged by new standards, that it has to be considered realistically."

Maxim's face seemed to have lightened and he leaned forward as if now for the first time he did not have to deal with something that was old and stale. His leaning forward was not the preface to an interruption but an invitation to Nancy to go on.

"You seemed to be admitting that certain things could not be judged by mere liberal standards. A ship, a state that is surrounded by enemies, cannot afford the liberal notions of justice. And I thought, 'Maxim isn't one of those weak souls who has got all upset by the trials—and—and things like that.' But now I see I was wrong. You're worse than I thought."

"Nevertheless," Maxim said, "your man is a criminal type." He stopped just long enough to drive home his point. "At least to the extent that he's gone off with a pint of Kermit's whisky."

"What are you talking about?"

"Not that it is important, I'm sure Kermit will agree. But there were five pint bottles of bourbon in the locker and now there are only four. As I saw when I showed the trailer to the little girl."

With the irony of misery and desperation Nancy said, "I scarcely think a pint of whisky will ruin Kermit."

"Oh, scarcely," said Maxim in hearty agreement.

"I don't care in the least," Kermit said. "And I think what we ought to do is open one of the four bottles and have a drink." He looked around at his friends hoping for cooperation toward sociability. "And I'll get a lamp," he said. For it was nearly dark.

"No," said Arthur. "We must go now, Kermit. Nancy has to get to bed early."

They left after brief farewells. Kermit went into the trailer to get the whisky, turning as he went to say to Laskell, "You'll stay and have a drink, John?"

"Yes, I'll stay a while." He felt an odd, dry balance of mind. He felt he would be equally alone whether he went or stayed and he liked the feeling.

When he and Maxim were alone, Maxim said, "You read my essay, John?"

"Yes, I did."

"And you didn't interpret it the same way, I gather?"

"No."

"What did you take it to mean?"

"It seemed very explicit." Here was Maxim asking questions again. But Laskell had no worry about his answers. "You said that this world was the field of Law and Necessity not of Justice and Freedom. You denied in effect the possibility of the ultimate social aims of revolution. It seemed when I read it that you spoke from a religious point of view and that, as I gathered tonight, was correct." He said it in a dry indifferent voice. Maxim had asked for the interpretation and he had given it. He was not interested.

"Yes," Maxim said. "That's right, of course. And that view"— here Maxim's voice became tentative, almost humble—"that view of things, does it interest you at all?"

"No."

Laskell recognized Maxim's recoil of disappointment. It was so out of the nature of things to have Maxim only disappointed that he almost added some words of explanation to blur his answer. Then he decided to say nothing more.

For a moment they sat without speaking. Then Maxim said, "You're having an affair with Caldwell's wife, aren't you?"

Laskell's apprehension and anger rose simultaneously. Then he thought that Maxim was very clever and that what he saw would not necessarily be seen by anyone else, and he thought that Maxim needed to show how much power of cleverness he had. He said, "That's none of your business, Maxim."

"I knew it from the way you spoke to the child."

Laskell did not answer.

"I'm glad you are, John," Maxim said with a touch of his old, almost maternal tenderness. "She looks like a real woman."

There still seemed to Laskell no reason to answer.

Maxim said, "What's the matter, John? Have you decided to hate me?"

"No," Laskell said.

"Just entirely finished with me? Is that it?"

"Yes."

"And with a lot of other things too?"

"That's none of your business either."

Kermit came out with three highballs in his hand. He had things to say about the unfortunateness of political disputes when unity among people of good will was so necessary. He spoke about Nancy's overwrought state—"Though I confess," he said, "that I never thought she had that good a mind"—and he chided Maxim gently for having let himself be provoked by Nancy and provoking her in return. But he soon discovered that he was speaking in monologue and fell silent with the others.

Laskell drank half his drink and rose to go. "I'll see you tomorrow," he said.

Maxim said, "Don't forget you asked Susan to come for tea."

"So I did. I'll pick her up and bring her about three."

He had not gone far on the road to the Folgers' when he heard a whistle and saw the butt of a beam of light on the trees on the road. He turned, holding his own flashlight to mark his place, and waited for Kermit Simpson to come up the road.

"I'll walk you to your place," said Kermit. "Is it far? I need the exercise."

"Not very far. What's the matter?"

"Nothing's the matter. I told Giff I wanted to ask you about fishing. But it's pretty late in the season. What I wanted to ask you about is Giff. Don't tell him, though."

"What about Giff?"

"John, do you believe what he says?"

"About God?"

"No, that's just his way of talking. He doesn't mean it. No—about the Party. Do you think he's telling the truth about his danger?"

"Don't you?"

"I don't know. He seems to be. But I just can't believe such things. Think of the people we know. Do you believe it? You sent him to me, you must believe it."

Laskell walked on a way without saying anything. Then he said, "You took him on, you must believe it."

"I took him on because he was in trouble, or said he was. I didn't

make up my mind one way or the other. I've always admired Giff—
his courage and his intelligence. And his commitment. He's a terribly committed man. You haven't said whether you believe it or
not—you keep putting me off. Why can't you give me a direct
answer?"

For a while Laskell gave him no answer at all. They passed the
Caldwell house, which was all dark. Laskell did not let himself
think of Duck and Emily. He did not know whether or not he believed Maxim's story of his danger. Ever since Maxim had told it,
he had suspended his answer and turned off the question. It did
not seem a question for him. But now he supposed he had to answer. He had a certain responsibility to Kermit Simpson, for he
had brought Kermit and Maxim together.

He said, "Suppose it were true, Kermit? What then?"

And Kermit's answer came immediately and solemnly. "It would
be terrible to contemplate. We would have lost one of our guide-
posts, one of our guiding principles. The alternatives we face now
would not be the same. In fact, John, I'd go so far as to say that it
would make political thought as we now know it impossible."

Kermit's flashlight was huge and its beam was so wide and white
that Laskell had put out his own. In the intense white beam all
the stones on the road stood clear and distinct and the dust rose
brown and powdery up to the height of their knees.

"Would it really?" Laskell asked.

"Oh—impossible!" said Kermit.

Laskell had asked his question, "Would it really?" with a certain
irony. It was directed toward Kermit's almost boyish innocence.
He thought of himself at that moment as wise and scarred by experience. He became, as it were, the Maxim to Kermit's Laskell,
taking an instant's cruel pleasure in his power to throw this good
man beyond his habitual alternatives. But irony and cruelty passed.
They yielded to the knowledge of Kermit's wish to be a good man
and to do his duty as he saw it. Kermit already knew the truth
about Maxim, yet when Laskell would put it into words, Kermit
would be pained by it. Laskell could anticipate no superiority in
inflicting this pain—if he had learned nothing else this summer,
surely he had learned a respect for the innocent heart. He said
softly, "Kermit, I believe Maxim is telling the truth."

"You do? You really do?" And Kermit swung around, flashlight and all, so that the beam was directed at Laskell's belly and lit up their faces and bodies grotesquely. "Oh—sorry." Kermit turned away the light as Laskell's hand went up to protect his eyes from the glare. "Sorry," said Kermit again. "Then you really believe he's telling the truth." Laskell heard the heavy, sorry tone in Kermit's voice.

"Yes, I do."

"But *what* makes you believe it? After all, we only have Giff's word for it."

"Look here, Kermit," Laskell said. "If you think Maxim is lying, tell him to get the hell off your staff. You don't owe him anything. If you thought he was lying, why did you take him on your magazine?"

Kermit said ruefully, reluctantly, "Yes. That's so, isn't it? But he seemed to be in trouble, so I helped him."

"He was in a particular kind of trouble and you gave him a particular kind of help. If you didn't believe him, you could have helped him some other way—given him money maybe." And then, because Kermit seemed to emanate a childlike bewilderment, Laskell said, "Look, Kermit. Belief is difficult and complicated. You believe this, but you don't want to believe it."

"Can you blame me?" Kermit cried. "Do *you* want to believe it?" His voice was agonized.

"Shush—you'll wake the people."

"Sorry," Kermit whispered. "Can you blame me?" he whispered. And in a whisper he said, "Not that I've ever considered myself a Communist, or even a fellow-traveler. Everybody knows that. But still, you know how one feels. I have to talk to you about this. Nothing has ever needed more thought."

"Perhaps not. But not now, Kermit."

"There are some things," Kermit whispered, "some ideas that we can't abandon. We will have to select very carefully."

"Very carefully," said Laskell. "But we will make the selection tomorrow."

"Don't joke about it, John," said Kermit hoarsely.

"It's just that I'm sleepy."

"Sorry—I shouldn't keep you."

"We'll talk about it, Kermit. Don't let it throw you." There was now no teasing in his voice.

"No. Well, good night."

Laskell watched the progress of his deprived friend as Kermit went off up the road, his bright light cutting the darkness ahead of him.

10

HAD Kermit asked him what ground he had for believing Maxim, Laskell could not have given him the true answer. For he could not say, "I believe that Maxim is telling the truth because of what I have learned about the Crooms." He could not tell Kermit that the summer had shown him a kind of passion in Nancy Croom—in his Nancy, whom he had so much admired—the ultimate consequence of which might logically be just such an act of destruction as Maxim feared for himself. When Maxim had first reported the danger in which he lived, it had seemed the fantasy of a corrupted intelligence or the contrivance of a malign one. But Laskell had come to Crannock and strange things had happened. Abysses of feeling had opened between him and his friends. He had seen in Nancy a passion of the mind and will so pure that, as it swept through her, she could not believe that anything that opposed it required consideration. When one had a reference as large as Nancy's, when it was something as big as the future or reality to which one conceived oneself dedicated, nothing could possibly have the right to call it to account. Arthur's dedication was not so absolute, yet even Arthur's instinctive knowledge of the way of the world, his firm respect for fact and the paradoxes of power, which Laskell had always thought of as the armor of Arthur's idealism, now presented themselves in a different light. Arthur did not flare into shining affirmations as Nancy did; he even mocked them in Nancy and spoke out to moderate their extravagance. Yet he needed Nancy's absolute intransigence. He might tease his wife for the fierceness of her spirit, but he was charmed and excited by the feminine boldness with which she was ready to challenge the world. And he needed her extravagance and ardor as support to his own cooler idealism: it was as if his concern with fact and practicality was then a correction of her excess rather than a limitation of his own moral vision. Nancy made the affirmations —Arthur did not have to make them but only to be husband to the passion from which they came. It was thus that he assured both the masculinity and impersonality of his own more muted political attitude.

Laskell had not thought of the Crooms when he gave Kermit his answer. The answer had come merely as the proper reply to the question. But when Kermit had gone off up the road with that excessive flashlight of his and Laskell was alone in his room, he had to ask himself why he had answered Kermit with so much certitude. And only then did the reason formulate itself clearly. What surprised him was that he had no unhappy emotions about this discovery, although it was not a very pleasant one. Nor did he have any unhappy emotions about his avowal to Kermit, although it was of the greatest importance. As soon as he made it, he was aware of a large vacancy in his thought—it was the place where the Party and the Movement had been. It was also the place where Nancy and Arthur had been. The Party represented what he would reach if he ever really developed in intelligence, virtue, and courage, and the Crooms had pointed out the way he must travel to reach this high estate. He had often thought that he would never reach it by following the path of his natural growth; he had sometimes conjectured, in his moral and political daydreams, that he might be the sort of man who needed street-fighting and barricades—the open crisis of political deterioration—in order to come to full political maturity. But now, where there had for so long been this strength of moral ambition, there was simply a vacancy. He did not feel the vacancy as a loss, only as a space through which the breezes of his mind blew very freely. He thought, "I am getting middle-aged, I am beginning not to care." The accusation carried no conviction. He did not think it true and this in itself was surprising.

He had no emotion about the loss of the Party, to which, of course, he had never been "committed," and he had no emotion about the Crooms, to whom, of course, he was very much committed. He could scarcely believe that he had lost the Crooms so far as affection went, but certainly he had lost them in their function. They no longer showed him the right direction of moral and political development. There was nothing to blame them for in this. Directions are chosen by the traveler himself and signposts merely point them out once they have been chosen. And Laskell, now that he no longer required the Crooms to demand something of him, also did not need to blame them. That was the remarkable thing, the thing that surprised him most and really gave him pleasure—that he could know that the Crooms no longer had their old function in his mental life, and yet not judge or banish them.

The very next morning Laskell had proof of how much free room in his cosmos he still was able to give the Crooms. He had come down to breakfast and, looking in at the kitchen door, he saw that Nancy was paying an unusually early call on Mrs. Folger. She did not hear him, nor did Mrs. Folger, and he had a moment in which to see that Nancy's face was unhappy, even stricken, and that Mrs. Folger was busying herself about her work with the air of one who insists that everything has been said and settled and that now things had better be put on a sensible basis and go on as before. Obviously Nancy had suffered a defeat of some kind. She looked puzzled as at some injustice, and Laskell, seeing her sit there, so mute in her inability to understand how anyone could be firmer than she or to remember how fierce her own firmness could be, suddenly had a strange experience: it was as if he felt intelligent all over. It was an intelligence as suffusive as love. The memory of Nancy's cold will the night before had not been erased, and he still hated it. But he did not hate the Nancy who could summon up that cold will. The sight of Nancy herself filled him with this almost erotic intelligence.

Nancy sat with him at breakfast, saying nothing of what was making her unhappy. When Laskell had finished eating she invited him to walk home with her, and he knew that she wanted to tell him the reason for her frustrated morning visit to Mrs. Folger.

She had indeed suffered an injustice. Eunice had appeared that morning with the information that she was to transfer her services to the Folgers' Miss Walker. Nancy had called on Mrs. Folger to protest, for Eunice was clearly not a free agent in the choice, and Mrs. Folger had been very polite and very sorry, but had made it clear that if Miss Walker needed more help and Eunice was the help Miss Walker needed, then Nancy had to do without. And she had gone so far as to say that it was very considerate of Miss Walker not to require Eunice immediately but to offer to wait as much as four days until Nancy could find someone else who would accommodate her.

"But there's no one else to find!" Nancy cried. "It's so unfair! And it's so unfriendly."

It was the unfriendliness that seemed to rankle deepest, though the loss of Eunice to help her with Micky put Nancy to considerable inconvenience.

"You can't think of it as a choice between two people, you and Miss Walker," Laskell said. "You know the relation the Folgers have with Miss Walker."

"That's just it. It's degrading for them. She's made them break their word to me—we agreed Eunice would work for me all summer."

When they arrived at the house Arthur was standing in the road with Kermit and Maxim, who were on their way to Crannock and had stopped to see if there were any errands they might do.

"There's no appeal," Nancy said to Arthur. "Julia Walker commands and Eunice must go." She was very bitter.

"Julia Walker!" Kermit cried, and his face lighted up. "What Julia Walker is that? Is it Theron Walker's Aunt Julia?"

Arthur said, a bit impatiently, "We've never met her. She's the local squiress."

"A bunchy little old lady, dresses in black? I'll bet it's Theron's Aunt Julia."

"We've never met her, Kermit," Nancy said.

"Oh." He was disappointed. "But you knew Theron, didn't you?"

"Who?"

"Theron Walker, the poet."

Arthur shook his head. "I don't think I've ever heard of him."

"Never heard of him? Oh, come off! Of course you've heard of him." Kermit kept up with literature very conscientiously and gave it considerable space in *The New Era,* even though he knew that it diminished his reputation for political seriousness. He was likely to think that everyone gave as much importance to literary events as he did and he looked at Arthur incredulously. But Arthur persisted in his ignorance of Theron Walker. Kermit turned to Maxim. "You know his work, don't you, Giff? Why, you must have known him personally."

"Yes," said Maxim dryly.

"Why! You knew him very well," Kermit said, suddenly remembering.

"Yes," said Maxim. "Very well."

"Of course," said Kermit, as if it were absurd to have forgotten. "It was through you he went to Spain."

"Yes," said Maxim.

"He died in Spain," Kermit explained to Arthur.

"Yes," said Maxim. "He died in Spain. And *how* he died."

Nancy looked Maxim straight in the eye. Her voice was very bright and dangerous as she said, "And how did he die?"

Laskell said quickly, "I met him once. Tall, angular fellow, wasn't he? I met him twice, as a matter of fact. Was he really a good poet?" He hoped this question might be enough to turn the line of the conversation. He did not think that this was the moment to say that he remembered talking twice to Theron Walker at some length and that he had been very engaged by the man's bright religious earnestness for ten minutes and then bored by his inner confusion the rest of the time. He had somehow never heard that Walker had died in Spain. He was sorry about it.

But Nancy was not to be checked. "How *did* he die in Spain?" she asked.

Maxim looked at her a long time without answering. She met his look unflinchingly, waiting. At last Maxim felt that he had made it dramatic enough. He said casually, "He died by stepping on a nail, a rusty nail. There was no anti-tetanus serum and he died of lockjaw. In agony."

Nancy, who had been pushing with her whole political strength, no doubt felt almost physically cheated by meeting such an insufficient counter-force. She said helplessly, "You're not telling the truth."

"You mean," said Maxim, "you expected me to say he was shot by your friends, by my former Party."

"Well," said Kermit, "I'll bet this is Theron's Aunt Julia." Nothing save the need to say something had given him reason for an increased certainty. "She was very good to Theron and gave him money when he got into trouble with the family. He wrote the Aunt Julia poems to her. You know, 'Aunt Julia on the Catarrh' and the one about her dog, 'The Pulia of Aunt Joodle.' The dog," Kermit explained, "was a poodle."

Nancy took the help this offered not only for the false step she had made with Maxim but also for what it might do for her pride in the matter of Eunice. For, naturally enough, it was one thing to be deprived of Eunice in favor of a dull local squiress and quite another to have to suffer for the benefit of the favorite aunt of a dead young American poet. An Aunt Joodle with a pet pulia was something different from an unseen Miss Walker, and she asked Kermit to tell her about the poem. "It's very witty—I can't quote any lines—but it gets quite serious. It describes the tricks the dog can do, and its daily life, and then it goes on to describe the descent of the dog from the days when it was wild and fierce and free and then became a working dog, a water-retriever, and finally the pet of an old lady. It becomes a religious poem. The idea is that the amusing, affectionate nature of the dog is Protestantism. Theron became a Catholic, you know."

Laskell had to control the impulse to burst into laughter. It was somehow too absurd. But Kermit's exegesis did quiet things down. Kermit and Maxim left to do their shopping, and Laskell went with them.

They had a sandwich in town and when the others had dropped him at the Folgers' on their way home, Laskell walked to the church. It was the not very handsome church he passed every day, but he had never been in it. The Bazaar, he knew, was to open at one o'clock. Some exaggerated estimate of things made the ladies of the Auxiliary choose this early time to set up their tables and lay out their accumulated stock. They may have dreamed that the reports of the Bazaar had traveled far and that visitors from many communities would come for the cakes and jellies and chili-sauce, the penwipers, potholders, clothespin-bags, handkerchief-cases, table-mats, and painted wooden bowls. Or perhaps it was because the ladies who had charge of preparing the chicken supper had to be here this early and the rest of the Auxiliary membership felt that they must not be outdone in diligence. At any rate, the Bazaar opened its doors at one, although the crowd would not come until four or five. They called it the crowd and spoke as if a cordon of the State constabulary would have to be thrown around the building. It was not merely their natural vanity that made them speak so but also the prospect of serving fifty or sixty chicken dinners, which indeed would make crowd enough for any Ladies' Auxiliary.

Laskell saw the children running in and out of the vestry-room doors of the church and went in. Many of the children were dressed in their good clothes and they gathered in corners to slide on the hardwood floor and to punch each other quietly. A few stayed close to their mothers, deriving status from such public importance as their mothers might have.

At one end of the hall there were seven or eight deal tables which, as Laskell later learned, were always referred to as booths. Emily Caldwell sat at one of them, her own wooden bowls before her, four small and two large. In addition to the bowls she was in charge of other merchandise, two heavily embroidered guest-towels and a small pillow of blue silk. At Emily's left sat a faded blond young woman whom Emily called Glenda and introduced as Mrs. Parks. The chief articles that Mrs. Parks had before her were small doilies tatted in intricate patterns. Laskell suddenly realized that he was on the point of becoming the possessor of one of Emily Caldwell's bowls.

"You've made six. I thought you were only going to make four," he said, and observed that Mrs. Parks withdrew some of the brightness of her smile at this indication that he had been party to Emily's creative plans.

"Yes," said Emily. She said it remotely. She assumed a look of gentle impassivity, a subtle tightening around the cheekbones intended to say that if he did show a knowledge of her plans, it was beyond her how he came by it and she did not admit it into notice. It was not a very clever maneuver against the quick eye of Glenda Parks. Then she smiled at him rather wanly and said, "I didn't think I'd have time for so many, but I did."

She was shy. And Laskell was shy as he said, "I'd like to buy one, if I may."

"Well, of course—if you—" What *if* she was going to propose, she did not go on to say. There could be no reasonable condition. But no doubt she wanted to tell him that he must not feel, merely because of what had been between them, whatever that was, that he was obliged to buy. The artist did not wish to be mistaken for the woman, but the woman was looking at him with uncertain eyes as he picked up bowl after bowl and held them out from him to study the design of each. He studied the four small and two large bowls, their designs in high red and blue, red for curves and rounds, blue for angles and sharpnesses.

"Very original, I call them," said Mrs. Parks. Loyalty to the Bazaar, and dissent from Emily, and then again some ambiguous sense of solidarity with another woman were mixed in her voice. "Very *unusual*."

Still holding a bowl out at half an arm's length, Laskell nodded gravely to Mrs. Parks. "Yes, they certainly are," he said. He spoke in the neutral, unemphatic voice of the buyer of a work of art who so truly respects the object that he must speak of it without surprise, for it is a natural and inevitable phenomenon that has always existed in the nature of things.

"So modernistic," said Mrs. Parks, secure in the established tradition of her tatting patterns.

"Yes, isn't it?" said Laskell, as if that were a recommendation.

What aspiration was contained in the unprincipled designs of these bowls he did not know. He could see the forms of Cubism as it had been picked up from the brushes of Parisians who had dropped it two decades before, picked up by men of small intellect and less passion. He could see in the angles the embodied talk about the machine age and the beauty of the functional which had always implied angles. There was arts-and-crafts and a touch of the folk and even of the peasant, the saving myth of *hand* work. There was the deep sullen modern mysticism of the abstract and nonrepresentational, here scarcely understood. Oh, it was so thoroughly not good, it was so bad and silly and derivative and yet somehow it contained so much that, though badly transmitted and ill understood, had been tried and fought for in confusion and pain and pride that it went to his heart through all the firm barriers of judgment and taste. Each of the designs was in bad taste and each, with its red and blue and its unorganized swoops of angle and curve, was deeply depressing, precisely because it denied the sunny fleshly quality of the meeting by the river. Was she at all what these darkened unhappy designs implied—as well as the woman who at first sight had suggested an ancient goddess to him, as well as the woman who had been foolish and social and pretentious at the Crooms', and as well as the woman on the river bank? And as well as the rather ordinary-seeming woman who sat here next to Mrs. Parks and not without something of Mrs. Parks' pinched, wan quality? Emily seemed troubled and uneasy, as if frightened that he might say or do something that would betray their relationship.

"I think I like this one best," he said at last. He added, "Though it's hard to choose." He tacked on the addition because he remembered the shadow he had seen pass over the faces of artists when you select one picture from all that have been shown, for by making a choice you are rejecting all the rest. "How much is it?" he said.

"Two dollars," said Emily Caldwell. She was blushing. "I—I decided that was what they were really worth."

As Laskell gave her the two dollar bills, Mrs. Folger came up in her large competent apron. "I guess you've made the first sale, Emily. Don't you think Emily's bowls are very unusual? I call them quite original. Do you think so too, Mr. Laskell? That's Mrs. Caldwell's strong point, I always say—originality. Isn't that so, Glenda?"

"Oh, yes, originality."

Mrs. Folger had a strong tie with him and it was not quite easy for him to say with all the necessary crispness, "Yes—they are extremely talented." But he said it crisply enough and the two women at once accepted this check of their subtle intention of making Emily Caldwell the object of their descriptive minds.

The bowl having been paid for, Laskell said, "Will it be all right if I leave it here until this evening? Anyway, I think your whole collection should be seen together. But be sure not to forget which is mine. Here—" and he took up a pencil and pad that were lying on the table, perhaps for purposes of accounts, and wrote "Sold" on it. He laid the slip in the big bowl.

Susan came over to them carrying in her arms her big book. "Will you hear my poem once more, Mother?" she said. Mrs. Parks smiled at the child and Mrs. Folger put her hand on her head and Laskell had the sense of how much danger Emily and Susan habitually lived in.

"Is it for the entertainment, Susan?" said Mrs. Folger kindly. "The children," she explained to Laskell, "are giving a few renditions after supper."

"Yes, it's for the entertainment," Susan said. "Do you want to hear me, Mother?"

"Later, dear," said Emily.

It was obvious to Laskell that Susan was hinting a claim on him. There was a certain lack of innocence in her face which he could interpret. It reached him at once and it moved and flattered him greatly. He said, "I'll hear your poem, Susan. Come into the corner where we won't disturb anyone."

He felt in Mrs. Parks and Mrs. Folger the quick rising of curiosity.

He led Susan to an unoccupied corner and opened the book and heard the poem. Her interpretation was much as it had been when he had first experienced it. If it had changed in any way it was to a greater elaboration of gesture. When she came to the final declaration, "I will not cease from mental strife," she emphasized the *not* and she stamped her foot in that petulant insistence which he had told her was wrong. She looked at him stricken and abashed. She was about to begin the whole poem from the beginning when Laskell said, "Look, Susan, it's not important that you do it the way I suggested. You do it your own way—it's your way and you're used to it."

For the whole method of recitation was so touchingly absurd, with its reaching and grasping of the objects mentioned in the poem, its extravagant descriptive gestures, that there was no point in putting the child under strain for this one small matter of emphasis. But now she set as much store by it as by anything else in her delivery. "If it's right, it's right," she said, "and I must get it right."

And stubbornly she went over and over the verse until she got it right.

When at last she felt secure of its impress on her memory, she said comfortably to Laskell, "Now will you take me up to the trailer?"

She had not in the least forgotten her invitation to tea and there was nothing for Laskell to do, since he had issued the invitation, except to offer to escort her. He had forgotten it, but Kermit, it turned out, had not. The tea was his reason for having bought the two boxes of chocolate Malomar biscuits, rightly guessing that any child would know that hospitality was represented by free license to destroy as many of these marshmallow mosques as she chose. Susan sat and drank cambric tea with the three men, having first made the tea. She called it, as Kermit did, cambric tea, and it made Laskell think of the strange confusion of the child's background, for no one any longer spoke of cambric tea except from the memory of a very sheltered and genteel childhood. She protested the cambric quality of the tea on which the men insisted. She herself poured for them, doing it very well, and she would have given herself an adult cup if they had not all commanded, with a superstitious fear of what undiluted tea would do to a child's nervous system, that she add the large quantity of milk. She was much interested by the arrangement of the trailer and had worked all the gadgets, but she was even more interested in her two hosts. She naturally inquired about their professions and was much gratified to be told that Kermit Simpson was an editor and Gifford Maxim a writer. She devoured more chocolate Mallomars than it seemed likely she could hold and beamed at the men.

At five o'clock the crowd back at the church was at its thickest. At six the chicken dinner was served. At six-thirty Mrs. Parks sighed and said, "Those Romans!" It quite startled Laskell, who sat across the table from her. Maxim and Kermit, Nancy and Arthur, had all arrived in time for the supper too. But Laskell, alone of them, was listening to Mrs. Parks. He looked at her expectantly, waiting for her to complete or explain her remark. But Mrs. Parks wanted a larger audience. "Those Romans," she said again, "they certainly had the right idea."

She lolled her head about in a gentle, abandoned, stupefied way. From the lolling of her head Laskell understood that she referred to the Roman conduct of a banquet. But he could not tell which of two possible Roman customs she had in mind. The bowls of sweet corn and of chicken stewed with dumplings had been eaten and removed. The great cakes had been demolished. The pitchers of milk and the pots of coffee were emptied. They had all eaten a great deal and Mrs. Parks may have wanted to say that she was so exhausted from eating that she understood the Roman habit of banqueting on couches, or she may have meant that she was so stuffed that she understood the Roman use of the vomitorium.

No one was giving her the opportunity to develop her erudition and so she said in a louder voice with a faded blond insistence, "You certainly have to hand it to the Romans—they had the right idea."

On this attempt she got the audience she wanted. She had addressed her remark to the Croom party in general. Nancy smiled vaguely but responsively. Kermit suspended a conversation he was having with Emily Caldwell over the head of Susan, who sat between them. Kermit smiled to Mrs. Parks and Arthur smiled and Laskell smiled. Maxim looked rather blankly at Mrs. Parks, for his thoughts had been engaged in what he was saying to Mr. Gurney, the minister, who sat at the head of the table.

It was Mr. Gurney who took up the remark and gave it the response that was wanted. He was closer than the others to *Quo Vadis?*, the great rural source of ancient history. "I know just how you feel," he said, and patted the stomach which he distended for the purpose. "I know just how you feel," he said again after two or three demonstrative pats which bridged the ages and, for a genial moment, made Mr. Gurney a Roman banqueter.

And Mr. Gurney was no doubt very glad to have Mrs. Parks to respond to, for Gifford Maxim had just said to him, "In short, you do not believe in God."

Maxim had not said it in an approving way, nor in a scolding way either, but quite neutrally. He had simply come to a conclusion after the facts were in.

The minister was a pleasant-looking man in his fifties. He was impressively gray-haired, in manner both scholarly and rustic. His profession had left its mark on him, for he had a practiced expres-

sion of benevolence and tolerance which gave him a look of venal-
ity. He was surely not a venal man, anything but a hypocrite, but
simply one of those people who make conscious to themselves an
aspect of their characters of which they approve and which they
try to act out. Mr. Gurney was really benevolent and tolerant but
he had made the mistake of trying to appear so. At least it was a
mistake from the point of view of the people from New York, none
of whom was favorably impressed by Mr. Gurney. And Mr. Gurney had some perception of this and was doing his best to put
himself right with these notable visitors. He quite naturally wanted
to be at one with these people of the modern world. They were
people of words and books and advanced ideas. Mrs. Folger, who
was in charge of the seating arrangements, had put him at the
head of this distinguished table. It was Kermit who had added
Susan and Emily to the group—he felt under a clear obligation to
Emily, for he had bought three of her painted wooden bowls, one
for himself, one for Nancy and Arthur, and one for Maxim, and
when Kermit bought from an artist he was always very careful to
establish a friendly relationship which would make it impossible
for the artist to feel patronized. Mrs. Folger had then brought
Glenda Parks to the table, and Glenda had just confirmed Mrs.
Folger's estimate of her intellectual right to be there by the remark
in praise of the Romans. The other five people at the table were all
simpler folk who had taken their places when Mr. Gurney, seeing
them looking for seats, had called them over and waved them
genially into the distinguished company.

Mr. Gurney had hoped that these intelligent city people would
understand him in his true character—that is, as an ordinary man
but a good one, who had the welfare of his flock at heart. In speaking to them he had not used the word *flock,* and when he spoke of
welfare he emphasized its social and material aspects. Nowadays,
he knew, advanced people identified the good with social effort,
and it was a great relief to Mr. Gurney to know this. He began by
asking Nancy, who sat on his right, if she had done much canning
this summer. He had then boasted that he himself had canned
thirty jars of tomatoes. Nancy had responded most cordially to this.
She said, "Imagine! Thirty jars!" Then Mr. Gurney talked to Arthur about farm legislation. He spoke with a comfortable unhappi-

ness about the reactionary element in the country districts. He said that the ministers of his church were considerably more liberal than the lay membership. Encouraged by Arthur's interest, he said that he was not an extremist, but that he was sympathetic to what he called The Great Experiment that was going on over One-Sixth of the Earth's Surface.

"The Research Magnificent, I call it," he said, turning to Maxim on his left. "Do you know that book by H. G. Wells?"

And when Maxim nodded economically, Mr. Gurney went on to say that in some ways religion could be said to be an effort for social justice. He said that it was significant that Jesus Christ had been a carpenter and his apostles of a similarly proletarian origin. "I looked up that word," he said. He was an honest man and he did not pretend to a classical education he did not have. "I looked it up once and it comes from a Latin word, *proles*, which means children. 'Suffer little children to come unto me!'" He looked significantly at his listeners and nodded the point home conclusively.

Everything about Mr. Gurney was clear—that he was not learned, that he was not intelligent, that he was decent. Equally clear was his desire to be approved of. All this did not make him very attractive, but Arthur and Nancy listened seriously and nodded in agreement. But the large, strange, and rather forbidding Maxim was listening even more seriously and quite without nodding. Maxim said, "In short, you do not believe in God."

It was at this appropriate moment that Mr. Gurney heard Mrs. Parks' statement about the good sense of the ancient Romans. But even after Mr. Gurney had expressed agreement with Mrs. Parks by patting his stomach, Maxim went on with his conclusion. "In short, sir," he said respectfully but sternly, "in short, you believe in society and social justice and sociology, but you do not believe in God."

Mr. Gurney was taken aback. But he recovered himself. He leaned attentively toward Maxim and smiled. "I'm sorry," he said quite urbanely, "I didn't catch the name."

"God," said Maxim with brutal simplicity.

The minister first smiled in embarrassment but then he said with sufficient dignity, "Your name, I mean."

"It's Maxim," said Maxim.

Now Mr. Gurney was wholly confused. "I beg your pardon," he said, "I'm afraid I don't follow. *What* is a maxim?"

"My name—my name is Maxim, Gifford Maxim." He said it with the real intention of being clear. "I'm sorry if I may have sounded offensive. I didn't mean to."

"No offense where none is taken," said Mr. Gurney. He then turned to the question. It must have been very confusing for him, for it had long been part of his view of the world that intelligent people were sure to be atheistic or agnostic and, if they spoke about God at all, were likely to attack even so complicated and modified a belief as Mr. Gurney himself held. This was Mr. Gurney's first encounter with an intelligent man who seemed to blame him for not believing in God. "It depends," Mr. Gurney said, "on what you mean by God, Mr. Maxim. If you mean a Being who may be understood as some divine purpose in the world, or some principle that is at bottom good—"

"Suppose we say that God is the Being to whom things are rendered that are not rendered to Caesar."

The minister looked terribly guilty, as if he had just been caught rendering something to Caesar that he should have turned over to another party, the legal owner. He no doubt looked the guiltier because he was so very poor and because he had long prided himself on the self-denial of his life. But then he said jovially, "A very good definition, Mr. Maxim. I'm very glad we agree."

"Do we agree?" said Maxim.

Laskell was startled by the far-off, stubborn expression that Maxim wore. He wondered if Maxim was really going to draw this poor, tiresome man into a theological argument. He was very glad when just then Mr. Gurney's attention seemed to be decisively claimed by something at the other end of the hall; the minister laid a hand in a confiding and friendly way on Maxim's arm. "I'd like to go on with our discussion some time. I'm sure I would have much to learn. Very stimulating." Mr. Gurney hurried away.

Mr. Folger had entered, following in the train of a lady who could be no other than Miss Walker. It was Mr. Folger's attitude that gave Miss Walker her consequence and almost her appearance, for she was only a little package of an elderly maiden lady, dowdy and graceless, but Mr. Folger's large, grave, authoritative air as he walked by her side gave her the right to be whatever she chose. Mr. Folger walked silently, a quarter-step behind her, his large face holding its irony in reserve. He looked like a minister of state in an illustration by Thackeray. He actually carried nothing, but he had the appearance of a man with a portfolio.

Mr. Gurney and Mrs. Folger converged upon the entering pair and so did the gaze of all the replete diners at all the five trestle-tables. But then, with a unanimity of quiet politeness, all eyes were turned back to the coffee cups. Miss Walker was led to a corner and comfortably bestowed there.

"That's Miss Walker," said Mrs. Parks. "She has the big place down the road. She takes a lot of interest—in the church, I mean. She had it all renovated two years ago, and painted."

They all gazed at Miss Walker sitting in her state, and Kermit got up from his chair to look. "Why, it *is* Aunt Julia, of course it is. I must go over and say hello." And he started off and then came back. "All of you come, I'd like you to meet her."

Nancy said, "Not now, Kermit. Some other time."

"No, come now. You'll like her, everyone likes Aunt Julia."

"Mother!" said Susan in excitement. "Mother!"

Emily's "Yes, dear" was intended not to encourage Susan to ask the question she was bursting with but to signal that she could consider the question both asked and answered. But Susan was not being sensitive to signals. She said, "He called her Aunt Julia. Mr. Simpson called Cousin Julia Walker Aunt Julia."

"Yes, dear."

But Kermit with his quick attention said to Susan, really addressing his question to Emily, "Are you and Miss Walker cousins? She's not my aunt, Susan, I just call her that." Then it suddenly struck him and he said, "Then you must be cousins of Theron Walker."

Emily said, "We're only distantly related to Miss Walker. Very distant."

But to Kermit the interesting thing was that they were related to Theron, just as it was the interesting thing about Miss Walker. It was interesting because Theron Walker was a poet. He said, "But then you must be related to Theron Walker, her nephew?"

"I don't know him," Emily said. "I suppose if Miss Walker's his aunt we're related. But I don't know him."

"The poet," Kermit explained. "One of our best poets. You must be cousins of some kind."

A family was a family to Kermit and he could not believe, since some relationship existed between Theron and Emily through Miss Walker, that Emily did not know of it. And a family was a family to Susan, especially, perhaps, if it could give her kinship with a poet. She shook her mother's arm to jog her memory. "Don't you remember him from when you were a little girl?"

"No," said Emily. She said to Kermit, "I only knew one nephew of Miss Walker's. His name was Ralph. He was a little boy when I knew him, about thirteen."

"That's Theron!" Kermit cried in triumph. "Ralph Theron Walker. He hated the name Ralph and dropped it."

"Oh," said Emily. She allowed the memory to come. "Ralph? And he became a poet? You see, I'm not in touch with the family. Miss Walker and I haven't been in touch for a long time. How is Ralph?"

"You don't know?" Kermit said. "He's dead. He died in Spain."

"In Spain? Fighting?"

"Well, he went to fight. But he stepped on a nail and died of lockjaw."

A shadow passed over Susan's face at this quick loss of a new poet cousin. She stood beside her mother for her mother's arm to encircle her.

And now Kermit was in one of his quandaries. For he wanted to renew his old acquaintance with Aunt Julia. But he did not like to seem to take sides in what must be a family breach by abandoning the Caldwells for Miss Walker.

"Your cousin wrote poems about Miss Walker," Kermit said to Susan. "One of them was called 'The Pulia of My Aunt Joodle.'"

"What?" said Susan in a spurt of laughter. "Oh, that's crazy."

"Yes, that's the name of it. She had a dog, a big black poodle. And he twisted the names around and called your cousin Joodle and the dog a pulia, to suggest how much they meant to each other."

"Joodle!" said Susan with great pleasure as her cousin ceased to be a dead man. "Pulia!"

"You saw that dog, Susan, when you were very little," Emily said. "Do you remember? A big black dog. He's dead now."

Susan tried hard but she could not remember.

"You played with him and he licked your face. You laughed."

Susan was struggling with the idea that a dog in a poem was an actual dog who had licked her face. Having made so lively a figure of the poet for her, Kermit now felt it was all right to leave.

"If you'll excuse me for a moment?" he asked gravely.

But only Maxim went with him, for Nancy still felt her grievance against Miss Walker, and Arthur stayed with Nancy. As for Laskell, he helped make Kermit's departure possible by turning to talk to Emily.

"It's warm here," Laskell said. "Would you like to go outside?" The supper was over. They were all rising from the table.

She shook her head as if he ought to know better than to ask. "But we could sit near the door," she said. They went and sat near the rear door. The evening was beginning to come on.

"Did it trouble you—all that talk about your family?" He knew something of the quarrel with Miss Walker which had followed the affair with Duck and the marriage.

"No," she said, "not really. Except to think of Ralph being dead. I didn't really like him as a boy. He didn't like me. He spent the vacation with Julia Walker the summer I was her companion. You know how boys are, that was the summer I met my husband. He knew what was going on. They hate things like that at a certain age. I used to climb out of my window late at night and Ralph knew it and he used to stay up and make a noise like an owl out of the window. But I suppose he changed. He must have changed to become a poet."

The tables were now all empty and were being pushed to one end of the hall while a group of men and boys set up the wooden folding chairs, ranging them in rows to face the little platform.

Susan came up to them. "Mother!" she said, "it's going to start right away. I have to get ready."

"Yes, dear. What's there to get ready?"

"I mean—it's starting soon—" and Susan pointed to the group of

five or six children who were being collected by Mr. Gurney. She
was full of impatience, any child's impatience to join the group
she belongs to. But she needed some encouragement to do what she
wanted.

"Go ahead, dear. And do nicely."

"I will," Susan said. And she turned to Laskell and said with
conspiratorial assurance, "I won't forget."

"Good—don't," he said. And for the first time he really saw that
there was a gap where one of Susan's teeth had not yet come in.
The space had always been there, ever since he had known Susan,
but he had somehow never seen it before, this always funny mark
of a child's childishness and growth. He reached out and laid his
hand on her cheek, and to his surprise she nestled the cheek into
his palm, tilting her head to do so, and then she was gone in a
bustle of importance.

"She's sweet," Laskell said.

"What is it she won't forget?"

"Oh, just a suggestion about how to say it." His answer was
brusque because he was suddenly aware that in some strange fashion he had taken a responsibility for the child. And perhaps that
was why he said, "Is her father coming?"

"If he can." She spoke as if Duck were detained by many duties
which he would hasten through to come to see his daughter per-
form. But then she said, "He probably can't." Laskell knew that
Kermit's whisky was to be held accountable.

The evening was cool and the sunlight that fell on the grass
within their view had a liquid quality, as if it were not only light-
ing the grass but moistening it as well. Emily sat quiet, looking
worn and tired. He thought that perhaps the sudden reminder of
her past had wearied her, her recollection of herself as a young
woman climbing out of her bedroom window to meet her lover
while Theron Walker hooted like an owl. Perhaps she was oppressed by the realization that enough years had passed to change
that hooting boy to a man and a poet, to someone old enough to
make the decision to go to Spain, and old enough to die there. Laskell had nothing to say to her. He knew her so little that he could
not even guess what she was feeling. So they sat there, dull and
commonplace with each other, and yet snatching together a mo-

ment of rest—she from her life of troubles, he from his life of un-certainty.

Suddenly she caught his arm. Duck was entering the hall through the other door and stood surveying the company, most of whom had found seats in the rows of folding chairs. He was dressed in a fresh white shirt. He had taken pains to prepare for the occasion, for he had shaved, and down his cheek ran a rivulet of blood where he had cut himself. It must have been quite a gash, for the blood was thick and had already dripped to stain the collar of the white shirt. Duck looked about him with elaborate dignity and chose an end seat in the second row of chairs. He walked steadily but carefully, and when he sat down he sat heavily and with a noise.

When once Emily had clutched Laskell's arm, she did nothing more, and she released her hold and seemed to regain her composure. But she did not go to sit with her husband, although there was a vacant place on his right. When it was time for them to come forward for the performance, she sat with Laskell as far back as possible, in the last row, and this was a measure of her alienation from her husband, for it was an action that would surely be marked by her neighbors.

At last everyone was seated and the performance might begin. Why it did not begin was a question that could be answered only through an understanding of the particular spirit which presides over amateur performances, a spirit with laws peculiar to itself, though not unlike the laws which govern the behavior of the spir-its that preside over nations or bureaucracies. The audience was ready, the performers were huddled together in a daze, the minis-ter walked about with apparently nothing else to do except begin, but until the spirit should be properly appeased by a full offering of whispered conferences among certain members of the commit-tee in charge, by coughs and by shufflings, the performance could not begin. At last it began.

The first number on the program, Mr. Gurney announced, was to be Columba Parks' piano rendition of "Parade of the Wooden Soldiers." Mr. Gurney had explained that the program was to be a short one and an individual one. By that, he said, he meant that it was not to be cooperative, like a pageant or a play.

"Cooperative!" said Emily Caldwell with a mild, maternal bitterness. "With all the other children getting the best parts and Susan always a maiden or a lady-in-waiting."

It was very small-minded of her, but Laskell nodded in sympathy.

Mr. Gurney went on to say that each of the children was going to make an offering of whatever he—or she—most wanted to do. If, therefore, he said, the effort was not cooperative, it was at least spontaneous. Why Mr. Gurney used language like this could be understood when he mentioned that the congregation was fortunate to have several guests whom he ventured to welcome in the name of all. And he smiled at the row of chairs which contained Arthur, Nancy, Kermit, and Maxim. And then he welcomed Miss Walker by name and said she was known to everyone here.

Columba Parks was much like her mother, appearing to have begun life at the point which her mother had reached after some years, or perhaps to have faded before she had bloomed. When she had finished her rendition of "The Parade of the Wooden Soldiers" and had been applauded in a very friendly way, she gave as an encore "The Waltz of the Roses."

"Susan was not told to have an encore," said Emily. Laskell felt the injustice of this.

"Our next little performer," said Mr. Gurney, "and I should explain that our program is arranged in order of the performers' age —our next little performer will be Susan Caldwell."

Susan rose from her seat in the front row and walked with a high head up onto the platform. Laskell felt very apprehensive. There was a spattering of applause, but above that was heard the loud measured clapping of a single pair of hands. They were Duck Caldwell's and he held them up to show.

"Susan is going to oblige us with the recitation of a little poem, a very beautiful little poem I'm sure you'll find it, by the eccentric English poet, William Blake. Susan!" And Mr. Gurney pointed a sudden finger at Susan as he said her name in a quick bark, much in the way a referee galvanizes into existence a prizefighter in his corner.

Laskell dreaded that Susan would make a curtsy, but she simply bowed graciously to the minister and was no doubt about to bow in a similar way to the audience when Mr. Gurney put his arm around her shoulder and announced, "Susan Caldwell: a poem by William Blake." The minister returned to the back of the stage and sat down.

There was applause and again the sound of Duck's hollow palms beaten together three times. Susan glanced quickly at her father, and then when the sound was not made again, bowed to her audience. She took her position of naturalness, and Laskell had to admit that it was natural enough. Her eyes sought the very back of the hall.

> " 'And did those feet in ancient time
>   Walk upon England's mountains green?
>   And was the holy Lamb of God
>   On England's pleasant pastures seen?' "

Her voice was clear and distinct and the missing tooth scarcely lessened its tranced solemnity. Laskell, glancing at Emily, saw her tense pleasure as the child was launched, saw the diminishing anxiety as Susan's down-swung hand indicated the feet, the high-swung arm indicated the mountains green, the cradling arms indicated the Lamb of God, the suppling wrist and arm pointed to the pleasantness and extent of the pastures.

Susan went on:

> " 'And did the Countenance Divine
>   Shine forth upon our clouded hills?
>   And was Jerusalem builded here
>   Among these dark Satanic Mills?' "

And now Laskell could feel Emily's lessening worry and then her relaxed pleasure as Susan began the third stanza with all its objects to be snatched from the surrounding air. As for himself, he felt himself hardening against any judgment his friends might be making upon this method of reciting. He felt very stern toward Nancy if Nancy should be feeling that there was any vulgarity in it. He looked for the back of Nancy's head to see if it showed suppressed laughter. But if he was prepared to be angry with Nancy if Nancy should laugh, he was also prepared to be angry at Emily for that part of her foolish pride in Susan's performance that went beyond proper maternal feeling.

Susan plucked boldly from the air her spear of burning gold and her arrows of desire. She expressed a certain gratified surprise that they should be brought so quickly upon her demand. She accepted her sword and commanded the clouds to unfold. Then having received the reins of the chariot of fire, she tossed them aside and was going on.

She took one step forward, as if to indicate that the mood or key was to change.

" 'I will *not* cease from Mental Fight' "— She had stamped her foot.

Dismay came over her face. But she did not make any of the gestures people make to show that they are conscious of having committed an error. Her frightened eyes moved once to the side and she began again.

" '*I will not cease* from Mental Fight' "— She said it as she had undertaken to. But she stopped and was unable to go on. Why had he interfered? Never in his life had Laskell made so foolish and desperate a mistake. He heard Emily's tight breath beside him and then her anguished desperate "Oh!" The child stood immobile, unable even to struggle against the confinement of her lapsed memory.

" 'Nor'!" said Laskell in a loud neutral voice. " 'Nor shall my Sword' "—

Every head was turned to look at him. But he was aware only of Susan starting into motion again.

" 'Nor shall my Sword sleep in my hand
Till we have built Jerusalem
In England's green and pleasant land.' "

And she dedicated the sword to sleeplessness, she built Jerusalem with a complicated upward movement of two hands, and she demonstrated the greenness and pleasantness of the land. Then she bowed and there was loud applause—not, of course, for her art, and certainly not for what she had predicted about Jerusalem and England, but for the misfortune she had suffered and sustained.

There were advantages in lack of sensibility, for Mr. Gurney came forward and put his arm around her and hugged her to him and said, "Thank you, Susan Caldwell," just as if it were the radio. "Thank you, Susan Caldwell," he said again. "That was very, *very* beautiful." And he whispered something in her ear, dragging her off balance and thus making her a child entirely.

And she was no doubt glad to be a child and not a performer, for she smiled. She walked off the stage, down the steps, and then stopped as she saw that she was being met by her father. Emily clutched Laskell's arm. Susan did not advance and neither did Duck. They stood there and looked at each other.

"Oh, God," said Emily.

Duck laid his head slowly on one side and regarded his daughter from the angle. "A fine one," he said slowly. "A fine one you are. A disgrace."

Susan only looked at him, neither advancing nor retreating. He had only to take two steps forward to reach her with his hand. The first blow, on the left cheek, was with the palm. The second, on the right cheek, was with the back of the hand.

Mr. Gurney's agonized cry of "Stop!" in an almost feminine voice came at the same time as Emily Caldwell's shriek, and when the audience recovered from the shock of these two sounds from opposite ends of the little hall, it saw that the child had fallen and it made a great rattling of chairs. It was Kermit Simpson who picked her up in his arms and laid her on the edge of the platform, while Gifford Maxim and Arthur Croom and Mr. Folger and another man stood against him with their faces to the crowd and stretched out their arms and said what on such occasions is always said, "Stand back. Give her air." Emily Caldwell had made her way forward and stood with Kermit over the child. She stood so a moment and then uttered a horrible cry, lost to all consciousness and almost to all humanity, an animal's cry, not able to call forth sympathy from anyone who heard it but only dread and repulsion.

The cry so separated the woman from everyone else, and so denied and insulted them all by its animal isolation, that someone had to interpret it. "She's dead. He killed her," someone announced.

Laskell, on the edge of the crowd, saw a figure pushing its way back against the pressure. It was Duck Caldwell, and he stood for a moment as if recovering his breath after escaping a danger. Then he ran, making for the farther door, running with his shoulders forward. He vanished through the door. Laskell ran after him.

11

THE knife, when Laskell later held it in his hand, was not much of a knife. It was only the sort of pocket-knife that any man might carry. A man who worked as a carpenter would use such a knife for scoring a plank before sawing it, or for splitting a bit of soft wood. The handle was scarcely big enough to span the palm. The blade that had been opened, although the largest of the three, was not long, not longer than the width of three or four fingers, and not at all sharp. It was the kind of blade that is rounded at the end, not pointed. It could not have stabbed easily, scarcely at all, and if Duck had intended to cut anyone's throat with it, he would have had to apply himself long and earnestly to the job.

The blade was stained and dark, anything but gleaming, and the only thing that told Laskell that Duck had a knife in his hand was the soft little round-and-round movement that Duck made, his hand held out from his body. And then Duck said, "Keep away. I got a knife."

It was not yet fully dark as Laskell ran out of the church. But it was nearly dark. Laskell looked around him but Duck was not to be seen. Behind him, in the church, he heard the beehive noise of sixty or seventy people getting a fact into their heads. It made the outdoors seem very still. And it was the stiller because of the unseen presence of Duck. For Duck must be hiding somewhere.

"Duck!" Laskell called. It was the first time he had ever addressed the man by name, that slightly ignoble nickname. "Duck!" he called again, very urgently. At any moment the loud murmur in the church would cease and the people would be coming out.

There was no answer. "Duck!" he called again. "Come out! Where are you?"

Suddenly a clump of bushes by the side of the road stirred and

257

rustled and then Duck stood out on the road. His clean white shirt was very clear in the twilight; at that distance Laskell could not see the stain of blood on it. Duck said nothing, just looked and lowered. His body swayed slightly. He was still drunk.

Laskell started to run toward him. His heart was pounding with the high excitement of what he was about to do. "I want to talk to you," he called as he ran.

Duck stood in the middle of the road. "Keep away," he said. He held up his left hand with the palm forward, like a traffic policeman. "Just keep away from me," he said with the supreme reliance on reasonableness that drunken men have.

"I want to talk to you," Laskell said.

Duck had lowered his hand but now he raised it again in the same way, palm thrust forward. He seemed to feel that there was great meaning and authority in that way of holding up his hand. "Just keep away from me," he said in a reasoning voice. It was as if he were offering a compromise. "Just don't come near me," he said. And then he began making that soft circling movement with his right hand. But as Laskell continued to approach, he said, "I got a knife. Keep away—I got a knife."

Laskell had in any case slowed down to a walk. "Listen, Duck," he said. "Don't be a fool. I want to talk to you."

"I'm warning you," said Duck. "I'm telling you. Just keep away from me."

What Laskell had to say to Duck could not be shouted. He continued to approach. He thought, and with a gleam of pride in his practicality, that once Duck knew what he was about to be told, there would not be even the appearance of danger that there was now. But he kept his eye on the gentle, continuous, circular movement that Duck was making with his right hand.

Suddenly Duck turned and ran again. Laskell ran after him. He was exasperated with the man's stubbornness and lack of comprehension. He shouted once, "Duck!" but his breath was coming hard and he made up his mind to call no more. He was not gaining on Duck but he was not losing ground. Neither of them could run very well on the rough, stone-strewed road. Then Duck stopped dead and turned and faced Laskell. When Laskell slowed down and again began to walk forward, he was nearer the man than before the absurd chase began.

Laskell said, "It's not what you think. She's dead, but it wasn't you who killed her."

It was not a very enlightening way to put it. It was like telling a riddle to a man in great danger. And Duck, his mind made up and very clear about what had happened, naturally did not hear the phrase that exempted him from guilt.

Laskell tried again, "She had a weak heart," he said.

But the statement seemed as weak as Susan's heart. It seemed ridiculous to run after a man who had killed his daughter to tell him that she had a weak heart. And if Duck heard the statement at all, it seemed to enrage him.

"God damn you!" Duck shouted in a sudden fury. His voice cracked with the fierceness of his rage. "I told you to keep away from me. Don't you God damn touch me!"

"Will you listen to me?" Laskell shouted. He was suddenly in a rage too. It swept over him, the desire to blast and blight this man who would not accept the salvation that was being offered him. And because he took another step forward, Duck rushed.

Laskell must have known in some way that Duck's threat was real, for he did not take more than the one step, and he was not wholly unprepared for the rush. And there was something inconclusive about the way Duck tried to use the knife, something merely demonstrative, as if, together with his intention of stabbing, he had also the intention of showing just how he would go about stabbing. Laskell was able to catch the wrist before the blow struck. The wrist was as strong as iron and its pressure downward was very great—greater, Laskell knew, than he could sustain for long. Suddenly Duck tried to pull his wrist free to strike again, but Laskell held on, and out of his boyhood he remembered to slip his thumb up to the tender hollow where Duck's thumb-tendon met the wrist. He remembered the excruciating pain that could be inflicted by pressure here and the legend that boys solemnly imparted to each other that "no one could stand that pain long" but was bound, upon its continuation, to drop his weapon. In spite of the impressive certainty of this statement, Duck's wrist was again pressing forward and down. Yet Laskell must have been inflicting some pain, for Duck began first to beat at his face with his left hand and then, changing tactics, to pound his biceps. This was perhaps a memory from Duck's boyhood, for the pain to Laskell was intense and he knew that he could not stand it long. He fought to catch Duck's left wrist and caught it. Then what he had learned in his boyhood turned out to be true, for suddenly Duck's hand actually opened and the knife dropped from it. But at that very moment Laskell felt Duck's balance shift and he knew that a kick was in the making and where it would be aimed and he leaped to the side, still holding the wrist. His impulse of self-protection must have been very strong indeed and very sudden, and Duck's rage and self-forgetfulness must also have been great, for Duck was lying on his side in the road.

The hand on Laskell's shoulder was Maxim's. Maxim said, "All right, John. Let him alone now."

There were six or seven other men and they stood around in embarrassment. Duck lay on the road, not moving. "Is he all right?" said one of the men.

Laskell realized that he still held Duck's wrist. He let go of it. Duck's eyes were open, but he lay perfectly still. Laskell was revolted by the sight of Duck lying there with his eyes open, and he was revolted by himself for having brought Duck to this low state. It seemed to him that there never had been anything uglier than the picture of himself and Duck as they had been through their fight and were now. They all stood there looking in embarrassment at the man lying in the dust of the road. He lay there, not moving, looking up at them. He expressed his hatred and rage in that way. Then he got up. He rose very slowly to his feet. He brushed himself off elaborately. When he had done this in his own good time, he said, "All right. Let's go."

The men did not quite know what to do about it. They had chased after Duck to take him, but now that they had him, they did not know what to do with him. He himself solved their problem for them by starting off up the road and they regrouped themselves around him loosely, so as not to make too much of a point of his being a captured man. Still, they walked close to him.

Laskell watched them go. His message was still undelivered and he had to shake off the effect of Duck lying there in the road with his eyes open, letting his supine state sink into the consciousness of the people who stood around him, letting it be a kind of insult to them. He started after them suddenly and then he felt Maxim's hand on his arm. "Hold it!" said Maxim, but Laskell shook him off impatiently. He called, "Wait a minute," and ran to catch up with them. They all stopped in the road and turned to see what he wanted and he said, "Listen, Duck—"

Duck turned very slowly and contemptuously. He looked at Laskell with a blank face and then spat at him shortly, once. The spittle did not reach Laskell, and was scarcely meant to reach, but there was such a fullness of hatred in the act that Laskell stopped dead not only in his tracks but in his being. For whether or not Duck knew it, Laskell knew that Duck had reason to hate him.

The group started on its way up the road. Laskell stood still and watched them go.

Maxim said, "Are you all right, John?" It was what he had said, Laskell remembered, that day when he had come on his visit and had seen Laskell attended by Paine. He still had his old practiced solicitude for suffering.

"I'm all right," Laskell said.

Maxim put his head close in the very dim light and looked at Laskell's face. "Your lip is cut," he said. Laskell became aware of his swollen mouth. Licking his lip, he tasted the saltiness of blood.

"Come down to the trailer and I'll put something on it. You need a drink."

Without answering, Laskell began walking toward the trailer and Maxim walked with him.

The trailer was hot and close, for the day had been very hot and had not yet cooled off, but Maxim switched on the electric fan and said, "It will be cool in a few minutes. Or would you like to sit outside?"

"No, it's all right here."

Maxim got out a bottle of whisky and said, "Have you a clean handkerchief?"

Laskell produced a handkerchief. It was clean, but Maxim inspected it before he poured the whisky on. "Here," he said, "put this to your lip a minute. It's as good a disinfectant as anything."

The whisky burned Laskell's cut lip in a therapeutic way. Maxim made Laskell a stiff drink and one for himself. As Laskell dabbed at his lip with the old strong bourbon that Kermit stocked, he remembered the smell of whisky on Duck's breath. He took a large swallow of the drink, then finished it. Maxim made him another.

Maxim sipped his own drink slowly for a few minutes. Then, as if he had just remembered something, he reached into his pocket and took out the knife. He did not look at it but laid it down in a matter-of-fact way on the settee beside Laskell. "Here's your knife," he said. "I picked it up on the road." He said it very casually, but he was looking at Laskell with a veiled curiosity.

"It's not my knife," Laskell said. Then he looked sharply at Maxim. "It's not mine. It's his. What made you think it was mine?"

It was a sizable error that Maxim had made, and Maxim seemed to think so, for he dropped his eyes and masked his face. Then he looked at Laskell and made a dry, complex gesture with his mouth and eyebrows. He seemed to mean to say, "All right, if you say so. Perhaps I'm wrong, but perhaps not so wrong as you think."

Laskell challenged the gesture. "What made you think it was my knife? That's an odd mistake."

Maxim shrugged elaborately. "After all," he said, quite as if it were an answer.

But Laskell was at the end of some patience or other. "'After all?'" he said explosively. "After all *what*? What are you trying to say?"

Maxim looked with a kind of gentle forbearance at his friend— all through the time since the trailer had arrived he had been acting as if Laskell were his friend and now he looked at Laskell with a friend's tolerance. He explained most painstakingly. "He ran and you ran after him. You were out of the door before any of us thought to move. You were very fond of the little girl. You loved her."

Whatever Maxim was intending to say was dimmed for Laskell by the sudden appearance of Susan in the past tense. For the first time he understood that the fact was not that Duck had killed

Susan but that Susan was dead. The realization came to him suddenly, and it had the effect of a blanket over his mind.

"Maybe you love the child's mother, but you loved the child too. The man ran in guilt and you ran after him in rage. It wouldn't be surprising that in the heat of the moment you wanted to kill him. So I supposed that the knife was yours. The blade was open."

Having concluded his reasoning, Maxim made a gesture of opening his hands to show how natural it was that he should have come to it. The gesture had also the effect of suggesting that the conclusion was a logical and even a right one. Laskell did not answer. He picked up the knife and opened the largest blade.

It was then that he saw how homely and harmless a thing it was, how dull and stained. It had a cheap white plastic handle. He turned it over and saw that on the other side of the handle was a picture of a naked woman. She lay at full length along the handle of the knife, long-legged, wide-hipped, notable for the size and symmetry of her breasts. Laskell could press his thumb against the dull edge of the large blade without making anything more than a ridge in his flesh. It looked as anonymously touching as a broken stone knife dug out of some ancient kitchen-midden. He held out his hand with the knife in it so that Maxim could see the picture of the naked woman. Maxim had certainly not seen it or he would not have supposed the knife was Laskell's. Maxim looked at the picture and with a small movement of his glass signed that he had indeed been in error. Laskell closed the knife and put it away in his pocket.

"What are you going to do with it?" Maxim said.

"Do with it? I don't know what I'll do with it. Give it back to him."

Maxim glanced keenly at Laskell as if to read some unexpressed motive in what Laskell had said. He said, "If you didn't run after Caldwell in rage, why did you run after him? To capture him for the law, like a good citizen?"

It was hard to tell whether or not there was irony in Maxim's voice. Laskell said, "No."

"Then why did you run after him? And what did you want to say to him after they started to take him away?"

Maxim was asking questions as if he still had the right to do so because of his commitment to the great cause of the future. He had no commitment and no right. Yet he did not seem to be asking questions idly. There was something he really wanted to find out. There was something he needed to know for some purpose of his own, though Laskell was too weary even to try to guess what that purpose was. With each moment now the fatigue grew greater.

Laskell got up and poured himself another drink of whisky. "I'd just as soon not talk about the whole business," he said. He felt that if the weariness grew at this rate he would be unable to say another word.

"All right, John," Maxim said readily. "But let me ask you this— you say you did not run after him in a rage, but are you going to give him back the knife now? I mean, are you going to do it know-ing how much worse it will be for him if it is shown in court that he pulled a knife on you?"

Laskell examined Maxim's face. It seemed impossible that even a Maxim fallen from glory could imagine the possibility of such an intention. He let his contempt come into his face as he said, "What's the matter with you, Maxim?"

Maxim paid no attention to the contempt. He said very mildly, "It's just because you said you were going to give him the knife. It obviously could only get him into worse trouble."

"I meant when they let him go—that's when I would give it to him."

"Do you expect to be in these parts when they let him go? That will be a long time from now. It's not murder, but he'll get quite a few years for manslaughter."

"No. They'll let him go," said Laskell. "The child had a weak heart. He didn't know that. But that's why the slaps killed her. They'll have to find it an accident. I doubt if it will get beyond the coroner."

"Those were no slaps," Maxim said. "Those were blows. I was sitting right there. But they'll let him go if what you say is so." And then he added craftily, "He didn't know about the heart?— but you did?"

"Yes," Laskell said. He knew he was admitting his relation to Emily. He nevertheless said it.

"That's why you ran after him? To tell him?"

"All right, Maxim. All right. You win." Laskell sat down with his drink.

It was almost amusing how skillfully Maxim had drawn the web around him to trap the information he wanted. A beautiful job—first the assumption that the knife was Laskell's, then the suggestion that Laskell intended to add to Duck's trouble by turning up with it. He was still quite the inquisitor, just as good as he had ever been.

But why should he be exercising his inquisitorial skill now? Was it simply because it was his nature to use it? No, that was not it. Maxim was asking, "Why did you care, John?" And dimly Laskell perceived that Maxim was not questioning him gratuitously, that he was after something. Shaking his head as if physically to clear his brain, he addressed himself to the question.

"Care? You mean, why did I care that he shouldn't run away, that he shouldn't try to do something foolish?" Maxim nodded to this formulation of the question. Laskell made no attempt to answer it at once. Why indeed did he care? Laskell realized he did not know the answer. He still had to work it out for himself.

He had not given the matter a thought—he had simply seen Duck start to run and had known that Duck was running because he thought he had killed the child. He had chased after him to correct the error. But why had his mind been so quick to perceive the error and why had he felt the need to correct it, a need so immediate that it had made him forget the deep visceral hatred he felt for Duck? He was not able to come to a conclusion. He was not able really to think about it, but only to "consider" it.

Even after he had been silent a while Laskell had nothing more to say than, "He's not responsible for the child's death, you see."

He said it simply, as if Maxim were a very simple person.

Maxim just sat and waited, not speaking. Laskell frowned. In some vague way he resented Maxim's pressure on him to discover his motives. Yet he would himself like to know what lay behind his "automatic" response of running after Duck. He said, "Maybe I'm just as responsible as he is."

He was surprised by the sudden gleam that lighted Maxim's eyes. Maxim at once veiled that hawklike eagerness and said softly, almost insinuatingly, "You mean—because we are all members one of the other?"

"No, that isn't what I mean. Whose language is that?" said Laskell sharply.

"Isn't it St. Paul's?" said Maxim.

"St. Paul's," Laskell repeated after him. "Yes, I suppose it is St. Paul's. No, that isn't at all what I meant. I meant that if I hadn't tried to make the child do things the right way, to do them my way, in reciting that poem, she wouldn't have fumbled and she wouldn't have forgotten the next lines. Then he wouldn't have hit her. Then she wouldn't have died." He did not add, "It was I who killed her, not Duck," but the words did not need to be spoken. "The point is," Laskell made his voice as neutral and reasonable as possible, "Susan knew that poem perfectly well the first time she said it to me, a couple of weeks ago. But I was so sensitive, so devoted to good taste that I had to start correcting the way she did it. I had sense enough to check my critical impulses, but not until I had done my damage. You were right when you said I loved the child—I guess you were right, it never occurred to me in just that way before—and I suppose that's why I didn't want her to make a fool of herself with that absurd way of reciting. I suppose, since I loved her, I didn't want her to make a fool of me. So I interfered. I had sense enough to stop, but I went far enough. Quite far enough, it turns out."

Maxim did not reply for a moment. Then he said, "That's what you meant by saying you were responsible too?"

"Yes."

"Is that all you meant?"

"Yes."

But since Maxim pressed the question, Laskell thought that he might have meant also that if he and Susan had not been so very fond of each other, if she had not come to him to "hear" her recitation, and no doubt bragged a little bit about it at home, Duck would not have been jealous—for perhaps jealousy in part accounted for the immediacy of his rage. But he did not say that to Maxim.

Maxim seemed to brood on Laskell's answer as if it frustrated him but need not frustrate him forever. Laskell, for his part, was brooding too. He was thinking about responsibility.

He thought about Emily's part of responsibility in teaching the child to recite in that absurd "expressive" way, making sure that the child would make the most of her brief moment of public appearance, and he was thinking of responsibility in general and of blame in general. He thought of the infatuation of Nancy and Arthur for Duck that had led them to lend Duck the car the day of his arrival. Had they not done that, perhaps he would not have developed his strange hatred of Duck, and then perhaps the whole sad tension with the Crooms would not have developed. And then perhaps he would never have seen Emily in the light of that odd partisanship he had felt, nor given his warmth of feeling to Emily's little daughter, nor moved on to feel whatever it was that he did feel for Emily herself. And if he had not thus strengthened his opposition to Nancy, he perhaps would never have said to Kermit Simpson that he believed Maxim was right in what he had said about the Party and thus changed the whole nature and character of his thought with which he had been so comfortable for some years now?

There was no logic in it, or perhaps there was too much logic in it. It went back, for that matter, beyond Duck—there was his illness, and Paine and Miss Debry. It probably went back even farther than that. Maybe it went back to Elizabeth's death, and even beyond Elizabeth's death—to his comfortable willingness not to be married to her, not to have *that* responsibility, which, in turn, meant that when she died there had been no way for him to realize and to express his grief, for he had not realized the relation with her, so that only Maxim had been available to him as anything like a comforter, and Maxim's company the only sign of his grief, with the result that Maxim had established his ground for that future "claim." He gave it up, it was getting too involved. When something involved so many things so tenuously, then it was ridiculous to think about it as responsibility. One could no longer *think* about it at all, one could only feel.

Maxim, after he had let Laskell sit a while, said, "Then you don't hate him?"

"Hate him? I'm sure I don't know, Maxim." Laskell's tone was dry. "I don't exactly love him."

"But you do *forgive* him?" Maxim spoke insinuatingly, as if he were trying to win some least concession from Laskell.

Laskell stared at him. "Forgive him? Who am I to forgive? What am I, God?"

"Yes, in a way." Maxim almost crooned. "In the way that if we are all members of one another, then each of us is in some part God."

"For Christ's sake, Maxim!"

Laskell rose abruptly. He did so in an impulse to get away from whatever it was that Maxim was up to. He might at that moment have walked out of the trailer. But the passion with which he had risen sufficiently discharged his irritation and disgust and he did no more than go to the ice-bucket and put some ice into his whisky. He wanted to know what Maxim was up to. He decided to ask. He said, "Giff, you're trying to say something. What is it? What are you trying to tell me? I'm tired as hell, but get it off your chest. What are you up to?"

And then, as soon as he had put the question as explicitly as that, he had the beginning of an understanding of what Maxim was up to. At any rate, Maxim seemed to suppose that Laskell knew, for he said, "What I am trying to tell you, John, you know perfectly well. What I want you can't give me."

And Laskell did know now. He knew why it was that Maxim had assumed that the open knife was his. Maxim had not, after all, pretended to that assumption. He had really made it. He had made it because he wanted to believe that Laskell had tried to kill Duck Caldwell. And he wanted to believe that for the same reason that his face had lighted up with that hawklike eagerness when Laskell had said that he was responsible for Susan's death quite as much as Duck had been. He wanted Laskell to have been guilty of the intention of killing Duck or responsible for killing Susan because he wanted company in his own guilt. Maxim had killed someone—Laskell knew it or very nearly knew it. "What I want you can't give me," Maxim had said. What Laskell couldn't give him was company in guilt.

He had refused to admit that he had tried to kill Duck. The

knife was not his. He had run after Duck not to kill him but to tell him that he had not murdered his child, only hastened her death. And when Laskell spoke of his own responsibility for Susan's death, Maxim had leaped at that, thinking that Laskell had meant that because we are all members one of the other, the whole human race was implicated in the guilt of every member. That would have given Maxim plenty of company. But Laskell had not meant that—he had meant only that if he had not interfered with Susan's way of reciting, the whole tragic business would not have taken place. That was not the kind of thing Maxim was after. It did not give him the company he wanted.

But perhaps what he wanted and what Laskell could not give him was not company but forgiveness. Was that why Maxim had asked so eagerly, "Then you forgive him?"

Laskell knew that Maxim was guilty of the death of someone, and if he did not know it fully at first, he knew it fully enough when, the next moment, Maxim held out both his great bearlike hands, the palms up. The fingers were crisped a little and held far apart from each other as if they must not touch each other, just as each hand must not touch the other or any part of Maxim. He did not look at his hands, only held them out as if they were filthy and dripping. He looked at Laskell as he said, "It won't wash off, I find. Not all the perfumes of Arabia, not all the oil of Persia can sweeten this little hand."

The facetiousness of his calling his hand little was desperate. Maxim's face was breaking up. First there was a look on it of final weariness, masklike weariness, and then the mask began to twitch. The eyes shifted from side to side, looking for a way out. It was terrible to see.

It was unbearable, this on top of all that had happened. It made all that had gone before suddenly present to Laskell as it had not yet been. The impulse to run, to put as much distance as possible between himself and this new horror, was all but irresistible, but Laskell still had the clarity and control to fight it down. For the second time in a half-hour he was face to face with a man who had killed. He was filled with revulsion. Yet he was not wholly filled with it, for there seemed to be room for pity too. Perhaps pity was not quite the word for what he felt—it was a sterner emotion than that. Certainly the revulsion was not so great as when, in his apartment, he at last had understood that Maxim had broken with the Party. He felt that he must say something to Maxim.

The only thing he could think of to say was, "Was it Theron Walker?" His purpose in saying that was to bring the dark, unknown business into connection with the known.

Maxim shook his head mutely but irritably. When he was able to speak, he said, "No." Then he said, "Of course not. I told you how Theron died. He stepped on a nail."

His voice was aggrieved. It was as though he were surprised and hurt that anyone should not believe what he said, or should suppose that he could ever, in any way, distort or qualify truth.

He said, "Can you imagine guilt only if you can name the person and know what color his eyes were? If I could give you the names and circumstances, would that make it any more immediate to your imagination? My hands are bloody because of what I was, because of what I consented to, because of my associations."

Laskell said, "You held your hands out that way simply because you were a member of the Party? Is that what you mean?"

"That is what I mean."

"That's all you mean?"

"Yes—at the moment that is all I mean."

"At the moment? And what will you mean the next moment?"

Maxim paid no attention to the hostility in Laskell's voice. He said, "At the next moment I may mean something more. Not something else, but something more, in addition. At the moment I mean because I was a member of the Party."

Laskell was very angry. "And that is your guilt? You hold out bloodstained hands only because you were a member of the Party? Is that why you are so concerned with forgiveness and why you talk so cozily about our being members each of the other? You mean members each of the other's guilt. When you yourself were a member of the Party you tried to involve us all in your virtue. Now you try to implicate the whole world in your guilt. And your guilt turns out to be nothing more than membership in the Party! You have a very fancy kind of mind, Maxim."

"If we speak of minds," said Maxim, "you seem to have changed yours since last night. Our friend Kermit told me that he went after you last night and asked you if you believed the things I said. He reported back to me that you had said you did believe them. I think, by the way, I know the reason why you believed them last night even if you had not believed them before."

This last remark Laskell ignored. He said slowly and firmly, trying to organize his mind against its weariness, "I believe what you say. But I don't like what you're trying to do. If you don't know their names, if you don't know the color of their eyes, then you're talking about some metaphysical kind of guilt that I have no interest in. I know the kind of religious manipulation that undertakes to make the whole of the human race guilty for what any member of it does, or a whole society responsible for what any one of its members does. It's a very attractive notion in some ways, but I don't care for it any more than I care for the idea that the whole human race is innocent, or would be if the social system were better, which is the line of your former party. I don't know what purpose of your mind is served by your feeling of guilt, but I do know that you are trying to implicate the whole world. You have been trying to implicate me since we came back here. You brought me here to implicate me. Well, I will not be implicated, Maxim—I don't share your guilt."

For a moment Maxim did not answer. Then he said, "An innocent man speaks!"

He looked at Laskell with an ironic curiosity. But it was not perfectly clear just how much ironic force the statement was meant to have. It must have had a good deal, but Laskell was not sure that it was wholly ironic, for Maxim was looking at him with a sort of kindness. It was exactly the ambiguity in Maxim's intention that gave his remark its power to disturb and unsettle Laskell. If Maxim had wholly meant that he was not innocent, had wholly sneered at the idea, he could have met the remark with resistance. What shook him was the possibility that Maxim in part meant that he really was innocent. It occurred to him that to be innocent or to be thought innocent was an insupportable thing.

Maxim said, "You think it is as simple as that, John? I assure you it is not. It is much more complicated."

He paused for a moment and then said, with an air of resolution, as if he were going to say something in the face of prudence, "I

said I was guilty because I was a member of the Party. You think
that is absurd. You think it is only less absurd than that I should
think myself guilty because I am a member of the human race. I
think neither of those statements is absurd. But since you have
your own ideas of guilt, and since they seem to involve a measur-
able closeness to the victim, then I will tell you that I had that
closeness. In the chain of circumstances that led up to certain acts
I was closer to the end than many people, though not so close as
some. If it pleases you to think of it so, you can think of my guilt
like Chinese boxes or Russian eggs—as a member of the human
race, as a member of the Party, and as a—because my work was—"

"'Special and secret.' Is that it?"

Maxim grinned. "Yes, John," he said. He seemed much more
composed. One would scarcely guess that he was talking about
guilt. "But I assure you," he went on, "even if I had not been special and secret, I would consider myself guilty. The immediacy of
the responsibility would be less, but I would still have the responsibility. You are right—I do think we are members of each other's
guilt. My work became special and secret because I was a member
of the Party. I became a member of the Party because I was a member of the human race and because the human race is what it is."

"And this explains your new attitude?—your religion?"

"It begins to explain it," Maxim said carelessly. Then he said,
looking in a very intent but friendly way at Laskell, "I recognize
what your interest is in resisting my effort, John—your refusal to
be, as you say, implicated in my guilt. You have been sitting there
opposite me with a little core of safety, a little center of moral certainty because of what you did this evening. You ran after Caldwell, not in rage but in charity. I've mentioned Paul once and I'll
take the chance of mentioning him again, if you don't mind too
much—do you know his text for Pharisees and revolutionaries?
'Though I bestow all my goods to feed the poor, and though I give
my body to be burned and have not charity, it profiteth me nothing.' Do you know what charity means?—*caritas*, dearness, the
sense of how costly and valuable a human life is. Even that fellow
Caldwell's—what's his name?—Duck?—even *his* life. You think
you performed an act of charity—you ran after him to tell him the

truth about his act of violence. But even that, your act of charity, was it not an act of guilt, did it not have its roots in guilt? Was it not the act of a man so fearful of his wish to destroy that he had to hide it from himself in an act of charity? I found that out about myself. My sense of guilt as a human being drove me to the Party, and my sense of guilt as a member of the Party drove me to work that was special and secret. Now I will not stay any longer in the system of Chinese boxes and Russian eggs. And I will get out of the system," and now Maxim's eyes flashed and he lifted his head very nobly. "John, I will get out of the system by admitting my guilt."

Maxim might not have had any success at all in his attack on Laskell if he had not been right about the little core of safety, the little center of moral certainty. Laskell had had it, but he had not been aware of it until Maxim spoke of it. As soon as it was spoken of, it vanished from Laskell's heart. Could no one in these days trust or know his own motives? He sat there, deprived, hating the self of a moment ago as a smug, preening prig of a self. But he hated Maxim even more than that. He hated Maxim for having pointed out that he had been cherishing his innocence, his act of charity. He said in a still, cold voice, "You're probably right. Men being what they are, you're probably right. But thank you, I will not step into your particular system of innocence and guilt. It was very thoughtful of you to invite me—but thank you, no, I can't accept." He had nothing to resist with except his anger at Maxim and his will to resist.

"You're very bitter," Maxim said.

Laskell did not answer and they sat silent, deadlocked, having no more to say until Kermit's step was heard outside and Kermit came heavily into the trailer. Kermit was full of the tragedy. It was very difficult for him to grasp the reality of certain kinds of misfortune that came to people, but he tried very hard. Over and over again he said, "That poor child, that poor child." And again and again he said, "That poor woman, that poor woman."

Kermit had brought the four painted bowls, the one that Laskell had bought early in the afternoon and the three that Kermit had bought for Maxim and the Crooms and himself. He had given what help he could in the sad confusion, and then, when there was nothing more to do, had tidily remembered to collect the bowls. They lay on the settee beside him, nested together. He looked at them and said to Laskell, "She has a strange quality, that woman. It was terrible to see her grief."

He gave it as a piece of information to Laskell. Maxim, with his genius for intrigue, had almost immediately seen the connection between Laskell and Emily. Kermit, with his impenetrable innocence, would scarcely believe it if he were told. He spoke to Laskell as if Emily were a person better known to himself than to Laskell. And perhaps she was, for Kermit had seen her in her grief. Laskell could not go to her, it was the one thing he could not do. But do something he must, and when Kermit said, "They are very poor, aren't they?" he knew what it was.

With Kermit here, Maxim would not be continuing his complex transaction with guilt. Much as Laskell did not want to talk to Maxim, or to look at him, he could not have left him alone with that business. Now he said good night and left.

When he was outside, on the road, out of earshot of the trailer, and when the idea of paying for Susan's funeral was established in his mind and, with it, the idea of Susan's death, he began to weep. He continued to walk, but every now and then he stopped and stood still in the road because he could not both walk and sob at the same time, and at last he sat down on a large stone by the side of the road and put his face in his hands and cried. Later, when he was in bed, he knew that he had cried not only for Susan, and for Emily, but for himself and his friends—for the pain of the time they all lived in and the time to come.

Laskell was not allowed to bear the whole expense of the burial of Susan Caldwell, as he would have wished to. For Kermit had been musing on the Caldwells' poverty overnight and was unable to sustain it. He said to Laskell the next morning, "I must see what I can do about helping with the costs of the funeral." Out of the habit of self-protection, he spoke as if he would first have to consult his lawyer who would then consult his trustees. And then, partly out of canniness, partly out of a sincere desire to share his generosity, he said to Laskell, "Perhaps you'd like to come in with me, John?"

Laskell checked the emotion of being forestalled. He thought that this was not the time for the exclusive possession of anything, whether ideas or funerals or generosity. In the ideal life of Bohemia which Susan had learned about from her mother, everything was shared by the generous friends, even the cost of funerals, especially the cost of funerals. He said, "Yes, I would, Kermit."

Kermit said, "Of course there's old Julia Walker. She seems to be a cousin somehow. And she has plenty of money."

"A very distant cousin, and they're not on good terms."

"Yes, I gathered they weren't. Still, she might be offended if we interfered."

"Let's take that chance," said Laskell.

So the burial was arranged quite without any vexation or strain for Emily Caldwell. The Caldwells had little enough, and of course a grave plot was not one of their possessions.

"A single plot," said the chairman of the cemetery committee. "Well now, we don't usually sell in single plots."

He was the hardware merchant in the little town of Crannock and they sat in his cubicle of an office, he in his desk chair, Kermit on a box, Laskell on the ledge of the open window, and Maxim in a corner. Through the open window Laskell could see the tiny common around which the town of Crannock was built.

"A sad business, a sad business," said the chairman. Then he said at once shyly and knowingly, "You gentlemen are arranging this business between you. On your own instance, as it were?" His shyness came from confronting an action which he believed to be generous, his knowingness came from his certainty that there was more here than met the eye. He looked from Kermit Simpson to John Laskell, but not to Gifford Maxim, for he had soon seen that Maxim was not concerned in this affair.

"Well, let's not have it talked about," said Kermit.

The chairman of the committee looked mildly offended. "It's nobody's business but your own. And her own. Of course I understand. But a single grave now, that's hard. We have them in twos and fours. Or sixes and eights. Though not so many eights these days. Smaller families."

"No threes?" said Laskell.

"Well, for three we usually sell fours. By rights, really, a four *is* a three. For four you should by rights have six. You know what I mean? You *can* get four into a four, but just about, it measures pretty close. For three I would strongly advise four."

Laskell was very glad that Kermit was there, his handsome face attentive and thoughtful, showing no sign that there was anything in the situation except ordinary business. For Laskell there was so much more, more even than when he had planned it with Kermit in the morning, for now there was in it his misery at passing by the Caldwell house, seeing through the window the tiny room crowded with female heads, and being unable to go in. And now to make him even less effective as a negotiator, he had the sense that it was mad that he should be dickering—as he was, now that a single grave seemed out of the question—for the grave not only of the dead child but also of his mistress and of her husband, a man who had tried to kill him.

Kermit said, "What do you think, John?"

Laskell was on the point of saying, "Let me do this myself." For if they did buy a plot of four graves, then Emily would come to lie in one and Duck in the other, and it became a matter for him alone.

But then he thought that the local legend had better be about two rich men from New York, the name of one of them scarcely known, rather than about a single man named John Laskell. It would be better for Emily. "Whatever you say, Kermit," he said. "I suppose four would be a good idea."

"Now I have here," the chairman said, and he spread out the map of the cemetery. "I have here a really choice spot. It's on high ground and very well drained. That's a consideration, you know. And then the view—very pretty view from here."

He spoke of the detail of the drainage with natural simplicity, but a note of insincerity came into his voice as he spoke of the view, which was a thing he supposed city people would take into consideration. Perhaps he too would take it into consideration, although he would never believe it of himself. The city people no doubt did, for this was the plot they chose.

"It's certainly a big thing you men are doing," the chairman said. "Certainly is. Now who should I make the deed out to?"

"Deed?" said Kermit.

The chairman smiled understandingly. "It's real estate, gentlemen. Just like any other acreage, no matter what you use it for."

It was the chairman's tempered joke. He looked from one to the other.

"Mrs. Caldwell. Make it to her, I guess," said Kermit. "Don't you think so, John?"

"Yes."

"Of course," said the chairman, looking intelligently from one to the other, "of course I could make it out so one of you men—or both of you—could have ownership, with provision to—"

"No," Laskell said.

"Mrs. Caldwell, then," said the chairman. "Now: care of the grave. Most families around here do it themselves. But for perpetual care, in the case of those who bury here but don't live here themselves and don't have the opportunity to come back—"

"Another time," said Laskell. "We'll talk about it another time."

"Now: setting the stone. If you want to arrange for a stone—"

"Another time."

The chairman had no more to offer. "Mr. Gurney, the minister, you talked to him?"

Kermit said, "Yes, he sent us here to you."

"Yes, sure. And Vic Harker, the undertaker. Hell of a name for an undertaker—Hark from the Tomb we call him."

It was pretty clear that nobody did call the undertaker Hark from the Tomb. That was only the chairman's own joke.

"Then I'll have the grave opened today. Funeral's tomorrow?"

"Yes, in the morning."

"Poor little thing. So bright too, I hear."

Kermit had his checkbook out and was drawing the check. He looked up and said, "How shall I make it out?"

"You make it out to Walter Burt, Treasurer. B-u-r-t. And put treasurer after it. Terrible thing to happen. And you know, the person it's worst for— Maybe you'll think this is a funny thing to say. But the person it's worst for is not the little girl. After all, what does she know now? She's out of it. I always say to my wife, it isn't the dead you should feel sorry for. They're beyond feeling sorry for."

They listened to the chairman giving voice to the solid, popular reliance on the bedrock of death, and they all saw him for the first time as a person, Walter Burt, who said such things to his wife, a thoughtful man, business-like and shrewd, with a large round face and a compact bulky body. All three of them looked at him with more attention. And as Laskell heard Walter Burt speak of death with so comfortable a belief in its finality, he thought how firmly people held that faith and how it appeared in the popular language—how the truest, surest, most reliable things were dead, dead-shot, dead-right, dead-center, dead-certainty, dead-ahead.

"The person I feel sorriest for," said Walter Burt, "maybe it will surprise you, is Duck Caldwell. I can't say much for Duck, he's pretty shiftless. But he's the one that's got to live with it. I mean, got to live with what he did. Of course, the little girl had a weak heart, so they tell me. But even so. Even so, he's the one that *did* it, if you know what I mean, and he's got to live with it. And he's the one I feel sorriest for."

Kermit Simpson and John Laskell stood in the silent consideration which men give to solemn ideas which they wish neither to agree nor disagree with. It was Gifford Maxim who spoke. "What about the mother, Mr. Burt?" he said.

"The mother, yes, I grant you. Terrible. Terrible. But even the mother—"

"You think that guilt is worse than grief, Mr. Burt?"

Mr. Burt was not used to hearing ideas put in so summary a form and he was a little startled. He looked at Maxim, taking real notice of him for the first time. Then he said, his face alight in response, "Mr.—er—"

"Maxim."

"Mr. Maxim, you put it just right. In my considered opinion, guilt is worse than grief. Much worse." He was delighted by this way of putting it.

"We must be getting on," Laskell said.

They saw the undertaker and spent two hundred and fifty dollars on his end of things. They had the impression that the undertaker did not overcharge them but merely bent all his effort to interest them in the most expensive casket, and this they did not mind. When they had finished with the undertaker they had nothing more to do.

But they had done wrong, it seemed. The news of what they had done was now general and Mrs. Folger spoke to Laskell about the mistake they had made, spoke firmly and with authority, but gently.

She was putting supper on the table for Laskell when she opened the matter. "Mrs. Bradley's here," she said.

"Who?"

"Emily Caldwell's half-sister, her sister by her father's first marriage. She's here. And I think I ought to tell you, Mr. Laskell, that she is vexed. And so is Miss Walker. They are both very vexed."

"Vexed, are they?" Laskell said and with his fork cut a piece of process cheese that lay beside a piece of cold meat on his plate. "That's quite a thing for them to be, Mrs. Folger. All things considered."

"It's you they're vexed at, Mr. Laskell," Mrs. Folger said.

They were addressing each other suddenly in a rather high stiff tone. It was not hostility, but a very stiff meeting of wills in full panoply. Something had changed in their relationship. Mrs. Folger was no longer treating him like a naughty boy. He no longer treated Mrs. Folger as if she were a piece of rural antiquity, all simplicity and virtue. They suspected each other. Laskell found that in the light of his suspicion Mrs. Folger seemed suddenly more tangible than she had ever been. He wondered if she too saw a change in the way he looked.

In the former relationship he would have helped Mrs. Folger in her next step in the conversation. But now he sat tight. He let her make her own way out of the difficulty. He did not say, "And why are they vexed with me?" He knew why they were vexed.

"It's you they're vexed at. Because of the cemetery plot and the funeral arrangements. I had a talk with them, and Mrs. Bradley and Miss Walker say that the family cannot be beholden to strangers. They were prepared to take care of everything."

Laskell looked at Mrs. Folger very openly. He said, "Is that all? Well, that can be taken care of very simply. They have only to pay back Mr. Simpson and me. They needn't be beholden—I'll send them an itemized account at once. Will you please tell them from Mr. Simpson and me that there will be no embarrassment about it?"

"Yes. I'll tell them that. If you want me to."

She had gone too far—her commission had not extended to the point of winning from Laskell a quick complete renunciation of his benevolence. She had got herself in much too deep.

"As a matter of fact," said Laskell, "I can give you the sum to tell them, it's very simple."

"No!—that wouldn't be right." There was nothing Mrs. Folger wanted less than to have to bring back an accounting. She said, "It isn't the money so much they're bothered by."

"Being beholden is what they're bothered by, you said." He felt he was pushing her almost too hard.

"Well, yes. But it's what people will say that makes them vexed."

"They need only pay the money back," Laskell said lucidly.

"They're vexed that a stranger—a young man—"

"It's nice of them, Mrs. Folger. A young man! But I'm really not so very young, you know." It was the first time he had ever denied it. To do so gave him a kind of comfort. It made him feel younger than he had been feeling for some time.

But Mrs. Folger would not accept his evasion. She said quite sternly, "You know what I mean, Mr. Laskell. A man. After all, you know Emily Caldwell—"

"Only slightly. Just remind Miss Walker and Mrs. Bradley that it was two men. Mr. Simpson and myself. Mr. Simpson arrived just three days ago. I believe that Mr. Simpson and Miss Walker know each other. If it's scandal they're worried about—"

"Oh, no—just what people will say."

"They'll say it was an act of friendship. Two men from the city just happened to be here and happened to have some money available and they took care of things to spare a woman pain and trouble. Isn't that all?"

"Yes, that's all." But Laskell heard the reluctance and resentment in her voice.

He said, "Miss Walker has no more reason to be disturbed about this than about Mrs. Caldwell's taking relief money. It's just as impersonal."

This was gratuitous and he looked at Mrs. Folger to see how she took it. She was very bitter, but she had nothing to say. There had not, he thought, been malice in her comments. It was only that her loyalty of commitment to Miss Walker, and by extension to Mrs. Bradley, was very deep. Loyalty was a virtue.

"And you'll tell the two ladies about the money? You'll tell them that Mr. Simpson and I will make no difficulty about its being paid back?"

She did not speak an answer, did not even nod one, only looked at him with her clear, blue, intelligent eyes full of understanding and dislike for him. She knew he was seeing all there was to be seen and she held her look boldly, returning his, and then he saw something fade and change in her eyes and knew that she was looking at him with less dislike and no small respect. He thought how difficult it was to get along with people and how many different ways one had to use, and he began to sink into the full tiredness of the events of the last twenty-four hours.

12

The funeral was held the next day at ten o'clock. Laskell came to the Crooms' before going to the church because Arthur had asked him to—Arthur wanted as many friends around Nancy as possible. Nancy's eyes that morning were deeply ringed and her face was pinched and drawn. The death of the child had shaken her terribly. She moved with a touch of the somnambulism of the bereaved, almost as if the dead child were somewhat hers. But she could not, after all, go to the funeral, although she wanted to. There was no Eunice to stay with Micky—the terrible event had made Miss Walker's need of Eunice immediate and Nancy had been told that morning that she could not have the full respite of four days that had been promised her.

Kermit and Maxim wore white linen jackets and Kermit was disturbed that they did not have clothes more proper for the occasion. He was casual about his dress, but some deep ritualistic propriety made it seem very wrong to him to attend a funeral in a white linen jacket. But he had no other; he looked with envy at the dark suits that Laskell and Arthur wore.

When the four men were already on their way, Nancy came out to the road and called after them, and when they stopped and turned, she said, "John, wait a minute!" She went back toward the house. Laskell walked back, leaving the others waiting for him, and when he came to the house he found Nancy at one of her flower beds. On the whole, Nancy's flowers had not done well that summer. She had planted rather too late and she did not have, as she herself said, liking the country phrase, a green thumb. But the cosmos, an easy flower to grow, had done fairly well and so had a bed of purple and white asters. With a kitchen knife Nancy was rapidly cutting the flowers of the cosmos, taking every one of them,

and when she had finished doing that, she stripped the bed of
asters. The two kinds of flowers made a very large bunch when
Nancy gathered them up. The colors went happily together, and
because Nancy had cut low on each stem, there was a great deal of
green. It was a wild and beautiful profusion and Nancy gave it to
Laskell with a sudden impulsive gesture. She had cut every flower
and every bud and she had cut low and now the beds looked star-
tlingly bare. As Laskell held the big bunch and was not quite able
to turn away from her ravaged look, she said, "The stems—they
aren't even. Let me cut them." In her hurry, she had pulled at a
few of the stalks so that the whole plants had come up with their
roots; Laskell held the bouquet for her to trim it as she wished. She
cut with a feverish haste and an excess of concentration, and suddenly she cried out and thrust the thumb of her left hand into her
mouth.

"You've cut yourself!" Laskell said.

She shook her head vigorously, angry at herself and refusing to
pay any attention to her hurt. Laskell put down the flowers and
took Nancy's hand from her mouth.

"It's nothing," she said. "I'm so damned clumsy."

It certainly was nothing much of a cut, but Laskell took his
handkerchief and wiped away the little flow of blood. "Go put
some iodine on it," he said.

"It's nothing. Don't pay any attention to it. Go along, John,
you'll be late."

"Put some iodine on it," he said.

He picked up the flowers and left her. The other men had begun to walk back in impatience, and they stood in the road just
before the house. Laskell said, "Arthur, why don't you stay with
Nancy? She'd like you to, I think."

Arthur took the suggestion with a kind of relief. "I think I'd
better," he said.

So Laskell, Maxim, and Kermit set off to the funeral without
either of the Crooms. But they had not gone far when Arthur
caught up with them. "She doesn't want me to stay," he explained.
"She insisted I come."

The coffin stood on a pair of trestles before the communion-
table, and Laskell, seeing it, was for some reason surprised that it

was the very same one that he and Kermit had selected yesterday. He had somehow never supposed that the coffin—the casket—they had bought after having all its advantages lucidly explained by the undertaker would actually figure in the burial of Susan Caldwell. He was startled that it was white after all—the undertaker had explained that white was appropriate for a child, that in fact the only caskets of proper size were white. Neither he nor Kermit had quite liked it, they would have preferred dark wood, but they had yielded to exigency and to what the undertaker had assured them was local custom.

A sheaf of delphinium had been laid on the coffin, and on pedestals set at the four corners there were vases of flowers. Laskell did not know what to do with the bouquet he had brought, and he was sitting at the end of a pew, awkwardly holding it, when Glenda Parks turned, saw him, and came over. "Would you like me to take those?" she said, and Laskell gave the flowers to her. Then she saw that they were loose, and she said, "I'll fix them." She went away and came back shortly with the flowers tied with a string. She showed this to him, nodding and smiling, and then she went forward and laid them on the coffin. On her way back she smiled to him and he nodded and smiled his thanks. He thought it very kind of her.

There were about fifty or sixty people in the church, and Laskell saw that almost everyone who had been at the Bazaar was here now. They sat without impatience, as people do at funerals; they have come promptly at the time appointed even though they know that they are sure to have to wait for the service to begin. Miss Walker came in, attended by Mr. and Mrs. Folger. She took a seat in the first pew and the Folgers sat behind her.

They did not have very long to wait. Presently Mr. Gurney came down the aisle followed by Emily Caldwell and the two women who flanked her. Laskell recognized one as Mrs. Gurney, whom he had met yesterday when he and Kermit had called on the minister. The other was no doubt Mrs. Bradley, the half-sister from Hartford, who, with Miss Walker, was said to be so vexed with him. She looked vexed now but in a forbearing way. Emily wore a black dress and a black hat. This strange apparel made her seem alien and, to Laskell, almost frightening.

Mr. Gurney led the women down the center aisle and to the first pew. As Emily was about to enter the pew, Miss Walker rose and stepped out into the aisle and put out a hand, ineffectually, not so much giving support as indicating that she would be willing to give it. At this there was an exchange of glances among a few of the congregation, those who were interested in the old quarrel, and Glenda Parks turned and looked at Laskell as if this were a matter that would especially interest him.

The minister took his place beside the coffin. In his hand he held a little black book. It was called *The Pastor's Helpful Funeral Guide.* Laskell knew the book, for yesterday, when they had gone to see Mr. Gurney and had been asked by his wife to wait in the dining-room, the book had been lying on the table and Laskell had read in it. It contained all that a minister might need to know about the conduct of a funeral. It began with the near approach of death, instructing the pastor in how many times he should call on a family when bereavement threatened. The book contained three services—Episcopal, Presbyterian, and Methodist, although Mr. Gurney himself, it had turned out, was of the Congregationalist Church. All three faiths lived very comfortably in the small black book and Laskell thought how many passions had died, how much belief had attenuated, to make this possible. The book contained all the scriptural texts that were relevant to the occasion, and prayers, and poems, and lines of poems that could be quoted to advantage.

Mr. Gurney began the service by reading a sentence from the book, "I am the resurrection and the life," and then several other scriptural sentences. He ended with the sentence, "He shall feed his flocks like a shepherd: he shall gather the lambs with his arm, and carry them in his bosom." After this he spoke an invocation and then the Lord's Prayer. The congregation repeated the prayer softly with him, and Laskell was startled to hear Maxim saying it out beside him in a loud full voice. He had not, like Kermit Simpson, doubted Maxim's conversion to religion, but he was not prepared for devotion. Kermit was repeating the prayer in a quiet decorous voice, Arthur was not saying it at all. Both turned their eyes to Maxim in his fervor. But Maxim refused to be aware of any surprise he may have caused his friends.

Then the minister read a Psalm and then he read from Corinthians. Mr. Gurney must have had some sense of Susan's strangeness, or perhaps of Emily's, for he chose to read: "But the manifestation of the Spirit is given to every man to profit withal. For to one is given by the Spirit the word of wisdom; to another the word of knowledge by the same Spirit; to another faith by the same Spirit; to another the gifts of healing by the same Spirit; to another the working of miracles; to another prophecy; to another discerning of spirits; to another divers kinds of tongues; to another the interpretation of tongues: But all these worketh that one and the selfsame Spirit, dividing to every man severally as he will." He also read the texts about there being both celestial bodies and terrestrial bodies, both having their own glory. "There is one glory of the sun, and another glory of the moon, and another glory of the stars; for one star differeth from another in glory." Laskell found this emphasis on diversity very relevant. He liked being reminded of the difference of gifts and of glories. He had been brought up without religious belief and the words had no force of childhood reminiscence; he knew them only from having read St. Paul the year he had studied philosophy. Yet they had considerable force. When the minister read appropriate sentences from Mark and Matthew about little children and the kingdom of heaven, they did not seem to have nearly so much to do with Susan.

And now Mr. Gurney seemed to commune with himself. He looked inward, and when he looked outward again it was to convey the idea that he meant no one any harm. He was about to make an address, to say a few words. Laskell wished Mr. Gurney had chosen to say nothing in his own person; the old things from the Bible that were available to say were still the best things because they were old and had always been said. Looking through the *Helpful Guide* at the minister's house, he had especially studied the "Hints for Sermons." The hints were actually outlines. The one for the funeral of a child opened with the text from Isaiah, "And a little child shall lead them," and then it had gone on: "Power of a little child . . . Infant fingers pluck sweet music from heart-strings . . . What it means to be as a little child . . . 'Heaven lay about me in my infancy.'—Wm. Wordsworth . . . 'Tis better to have loved and lost than never to have loved at all.'—Lord

Tennyson." The outline had not promised well for the sermon Mr. Gurney might deliver. Yet Mr. Gurney not only delivered a sermon similar in kind—he delivered, as Laskell recalled at every point, this very sermon. And perhaps all the rest of the congregation knew the sermon too. Perhaps it was the same address the minister made whenever a child died, and therefore his words, so far as this community went, were as traditional as anything he had read from the Bible.

The cemetery was a short distance from the church, up the road to the right, in a direction Laskell had never taken. Here Laskell saw Emily's face—saw it across the open grave in which the coffin lay. It was flushed and dry, like the face of a woman who has just come out of surgical anaesthetic. It was terribly composed. When Laskell saw it, his stomach contracted with fear. He found it frightening to know that the face which, on the river bank, should have been so eager and warm with the knowledge of love should now be so rigid with the knowledge of death.

The service at the grave was shorter than the service in the church. Mr. Gurney's good heart surely must have wished that his small community could have afforded the grieving mother the kind of protection from the harsh physical facts of death that modern thoughtfulness had devised. He must have wished that instead of the trestle of boards across the grave, which made a scraping and hollow sound as they were removed, and the creaking ropes, there could have been one of those contrivances which noiselessly lower the coffin into the grave, giving the effect of a process being carried out by unseen hands. And he must have wished too that the raw red earth could have been covered with blankets of artificial grass. But he did what he could. He omitted, as it was his option to do, the old phrase, "earth to earth, ashes to ashes, dust to dust." He had thoughtfully provided a little handful of flowers—they chanced to be a few of Nancy's asters and cosmos—which, rather than earth, he gave to Emily to throw into the grave. She took them obediently, and obediently threw them upon the coffin. But then she knelt, as if in obedience this time to some old memory or instinct, and gathered up a handful of earth. She crumbled it fine with her fingers, took out two or three small pebbles, and let it fall into the grave. Mr. Gurney said the Lord's Prayer again; at the first words, Maxim knelt down. Laskell did not know whether in the ritual of any of the faiths one knelt for the Lord's Prayer, but there was Maxim on his knees, asking for his daily bread, and for the kingdom to come, and for forgiveness for his trespasses, and for deliverance from evil. Everyone looked at him in surprise.

Laskell had not yet made plans for his departure. Until Susan's death, he had vaguely thought that he might continue in the country for another two weeks. But walking away from the cemetery he realized that his time here was up, and when he went to the Caldwell house that afternoon he knew his visit was one of farewell. And even if he had not been leaving, Emily was. Mrs. Folger had told him that Emily Caldwell was to be "taken away" by her family and that seemed expectable enough. But even if she had been staying, he would have had nothing else to say to her except good-by.

Good-by was virtually all he said. The half-sister was there in the tiny ingenious room, not particularly hostile but thoroughly on guard. The family, it was clear, had suffered enough from Emily's vagaries; the death of Susan, under such circumstances, they seemed to regard as a last slur on their Hartford respectability. The half-sister sat there in black, not unkind, but conspicuously appointed to see that, at least while she was present, things should be as they should be. Beneath the middle-aged capability of her face was the resentment of her compromised position in being so closely related to the wife of a man who had killed his child, a man who was himself in jail.

"I've come to say good-by," Laskell said. With the half-sister listening, it was the most personal communication he could make.

"Are you leaving?" said Emily politely.

"Well, soon," said Laskell. "Soon. I heard you were going away."

"Yes, I'm taking Emily home for a while," said Mrs. Bradley. She said to Emily, "Do you want some more tea?" There was a teapot on the table and an untasted cup of tea before Emily. Laskell had the impression that the half-sisters had been sitting there quite a long time without saying anything.

"No, thank you," said Emily, and shook her head.

Laskell repressed the impulse to say, "Try her with coffee." He remembered what it was to her—nectar and ambrosia.

It was very hard to believe that only a few days ago there had been passion between them. Nothing in their temperaments, nothing in their fates, existed to show that they were matched. Perhaps they could not have spent an evening happily together—Laskell, who in his illness had been able to project a long-continuing relationship with Paine, had never projected anything for his relationship with Emily. She sat there with her face made intelligent by grief, which, because it subordinates all facts to one fact, is so like an act of intelligence that it gives to the face of sorrowing people, for a short time, the look of wisdom. Laskell could not say that she had made him happy. Indeed, wondering what he would have said in farewell if the half-sister had not been present to prevent his saying anything, he had to ask himself what the word "happy" meant. He thought that perhaps he should speak of the dead Susan—that subject could not be forbidden. But this he was not able to do. As he called the child to mind, she ceased to be the Susan Caldwell her mother knew—she became, poor thing, the abstraction of her own grace and of her own desire to have things as right as possible. But Emily had known Susan in all a child's troublesomeness and cross-grained tempers, not as an idea, however lovely a one. Before she had taken the lumps out of the handful of earth she had strewn on Susan's coffin, she had taken the lumps out of Susan's cereal and mashed potatoes.

So he did not speak of the child. He only said, "Good-by," and then added, because something had to be added, "If I can help in any way, please—" He heard a rustling as the half-sister moved remonstratively in her chair. He remembered Mrs. Bradley's vexation. Mrs. Bradley, although she had not yet made any attempt to remove the cause of her annoyance, and would not make the attempt, was seeing to it that she would not have occasion to be vexed again.

"Thank you, I will," Emily said, not wholly mechanically. "But there's nothing, really." And she smiled to him, with difficulty, but sweetly.

He ventured, half-sister or not, to look at her face. But no, there was no connection between them. There was only the empty air between them. He hoped that at least there was as much purity in the airy emptiness as there seemed to be.

But this was not, after all, the last time that he saw her. That was his great good luck.

Kermit planned to leave the next day and it hastened Laskell's thought of departure when Kermit offered to drive him to Westport and to put him up for the night. Laskell accepted the suggestion and told Arthur. He was sitting in the trailer when suddenly Nancy appeared. Arthur had told her their plans. She had come over to try to persuade them not to leave so soon. "When things happen, one wants one's friends about," was the way she put it, shyly. Maxim was there too, with Laskell and Kermit, and it was unmistakable to Laskell that Nancy's glance as she made her request included him. They all agreed, of course, to stay. The child's death had hit Nancy very hard indeed. She had preferred not to say "died" and she had jibbed at the idea of death, but when it came to the actuality, she was taking its full force. That the person who had died was a child made the matter worse for Nancy. "Such a little thing," she would say. "Such a little thing," although Susan, for her age, had not been little, but rather tall. And Nancy had more to deal with than the fact of Susan's death. The Folgers had in effect told her that this was not her place, that another outlander, Miss Walker, one with more power than poor Nancy had, was much more at home here than she. Worst of all, however, as Laskell could guess, was the difficulty of having to cope with what Duck Caldwell had done. Laskell would catch her looking both at him and at Maxim in a curious and distracted way, and he knew it was because she remembered that the two of them had spoken against Duck when she herself had valued him so highly.

The next day the weather turned wet and cold. The Crooms spent most of their time about the fireplace, the one that drew so well because of Duck's skill. Simpson and Maxim sat with the Crooms most of the day, for the trailer made close quarters. Laskell came and went, was in and out of the house according as he needed company or could not endure it.

It had at last broken in on Kermit that Maxim was really religious. The loud voice in which Maxim had said the Lord's Prayer the first time and his kneeling to say it the second time had been conclusive. Kermit put his discovery before Maxim. He presented it cheerfully, but Maxim said coldly, "I have been trying to tell you, Simpson, what it is that I really believe. But you have refused to understand me."

Kermit shook his head amiably, as if to remark what strange and interesting manifestations of the human spirit could exist in a democracy. Arthur could not take it that easily. "My God!" he said. Then he stopped, not exactly in embarrassment but because the interjection in the context had suddenly turned out to mean something different from what he had intended. He went on, "Have you lost your nerve to that extent?"

"It may be that I have lost my nerve," Maxim said. He had the quiet of a man who, though under attack, knows that he has won the advantage for the first time—he has at last made his opponents take him seriously. "But nerve, you know, is not really enough to live on. It is not really anything to live on at all."

"I don't know what you mean when you say a thing like that," Arthur said. "Why isn't nerve a thing to live on?"

"Because life is not an adventure," Maxim said. "If you say to me that I have lost my courage, I'll tell you that you are wrong. But at least I know that we are being serious with each other. But when you tell me that I have lost my nerve—then I say, yes, you may be right, but it doesn't interest me."

"But Giff"—Arthur fluctuated these days between Maxim's last name and his first—"you can't *possibly* believe all that business."

"What business?" Maxim spoke the word "business" as if it were the habit of theologians everywhere to employ it in their most learned discussions. "Now, Reverend Father, as to this business of transubstantiation," they might say to each other. If Arthur wanted to talk about religion, Maxim was quite willing to talk about it in any language that suited Arthur.

"You know what business."

"You mean, in general, the unseen. It is not so very hard. I am practiced in believing doctrine that is full of mysteries. I have, you know, been dealing with free-will and predestination and foreknowledge, in original sin and redemption, all under different names and with a different outcome for a good many years now."

Arthur looked puzzled, then he impatiently understood. "It's not the same thing at all," he said rather harshly.

Maxim raised his eyebrows in question. "It's not so different as you think. We all have a passion for faith in the unseen. It is really the only thing we have faith in. You, for example, have a profound faith in what our clerical friend, Mr. Gurney, calls the Research Magnificent, the Great Experiment. You believed me when I brought you good news of it. Now that I bring you bad news of it, you not only will not listen to me, but you fear me and call me names. I am sure that you will say that I have no proof. But I had no proof before. You believe as you want to believe."

"I believe where reason and the facts permit belief."

Arthur's replies were of this kind, defensive but so fiercely said that they served as attack. Laskell had never heard Arthur so stubborn and fierce.

It was Maxim's strategy to draw Arthur on to attack an established position. Maxim was good in defense—it would not take many months for him to be very good indeed. But his faith was still somewhat new. He had no doubt begun to formulate his religious beliefs at the same time that he was doing his "special and secret" work. He could not have given very much time to the refining of his homiletics, and he now had to work hard on the spot. But he did it very well. His line of defense—not, of course, a new one—was based on the assumptive nature of all human life, on the awareness of complexity and mystery in the world. It referred to the conceptualism of modern science—not the science of the nineteenth century but contemporary science—and claimed for the moral and spiritual life the same rights of concept that were granted to science.

Maxim handled his argument skillfully. In the main it was Arthur who answered him. Nancy sat silent, Kermit said very little. Arthur did not say much but he said it stubbornly and with anger. He chiefly said, "I don't see that," or "It seems to me that that kind of talk means nothing at all."

Suddenly Laskell got up and said, "I'll see you all later." He took his raincoat and left before they had a chance to protest. It was late in the afternoon and the heavy, drizzling sky brought twilight in early.

It was not that the subject of their conversation had disturbed him. It was a subject proper to all men, especially when the heart was sore and grieving, as his now was. But he was utterly weary of his friends. His mind drooped under its knowledge of them. He saw them in their wills—Nancy's fierce and Arthur's stubborn, both perhaps temporarily checked and baffled but soon again to be released, and Maxim's subtle and masked in talk of mysteries and the charity of these mysteries. It was not their wills that wearied him but the necessity they shared to make their wills appear harmless.

In the midst of his disenchantment with his friends, Laskell knew that he would not feel as he did were he not disenchanted with himself. He walked home—that is, to his room at the Folgers'—in the chilly drizzle, through the mud of the road. There was a lamp lighted in the Caldwell house, the afternoon was as gray as that. He hurried by. The light, and the thought of what went on around that light, in Emily's heart, between Emily and Mrs. Bradley, made him wholly desolate. There was nothing he could do for Emily—he did not love her enough to dare to do anything.

In his room he lit both lamps and tried to read. But he was cold and restless. He got up for a package of cigarettes from his dresser and his eye fell on Emily's bowl. He took it up to look at it once more, for it could be thought of as the sad monument of his summer.

Especially in the light of the lamps, it seemed, with its heavy colors, to be very dark in its conception. He did not know what part of Emily Caldwell had given it this character, for, although it synopsized in some uncomprehending way so much of the recent art of the Western world, it must also have some particularity of the individual who had made it. In his knowledge of Emily, Laskell had never seen in her anything that he could think of as the source of this unhappy design in which, although the intention had been to show the angles and curves moving at their freest, there was something claustral and desperate. There were, it seemed, depths below the bright humanistic surface that he did not know about, except as the bowl now suggested them. He had seen Emily in many aspects—for an instant as Demeter in the pride and grace of her maternity, then as the partisan of an outworn rebellion, as the ambitious mother scheming for middle-class advantages for her daughter, and as a tender and responsive woman on the river bank. Now, looking at the bowl she had painted, he saw her deep awareness of nullity, her knowledge of darkness. He no longer saw the ineptness of the design, but only what it suddenly and darkly spoke of.

But then as he looked at the bowl, the awkwardness of the design appeared to him again, and he thought of the pride that Emily had taken in her work. It had led her to raise—actually to double—the price she had put upon the bowl. Laskell did not love her. But he loved her natural foolish pride which had led her to place this large valuation on the thing she had created and which he knew was connected with the warm generosity of their meeting together on the river. As he thought of that meeting, he remembered the spiritedness with which she had asked him whether he was supposed to hate death, the authority with which she had spoken. He knew, now that he thought he understood the meaning of the abstract design of the bowl, at what cost that spiritedness had been won and on what her authority was grounded. He did not love her, not in any sense of that word as it is used between men and women. He felt no community of passion with her. But in that moment, in all the empty world, she was the one person who existed for him in love. And he remembered with despair the words and habits that had separated them, the accusations that had been made by his divided mind and the severe judgments of his demanding and critical heart.

It rained again the next day. Once more they all sat around the Crooms' fire. There was not much to talk about today and they were bored. The cigarette smoke and the wood smoke made their eyes smart and their heads ache. Micky was cross from being kept indoors and also, no doubt, because he sensed some trouble in his mother's mind. All their nerves were strained. But late in the afternoon there was a break in the weather. The rain stopped and then, almost suddenly, the sun began to shine. They tumbled out of the house like Laplanders seeing the first light of the year. Nancy put rubbers on Micky and turned him loose on the lawn. The others stood about, breathing deeply and stretching their legs.

Had it not been for what had happened they would not so

quickly have heard and taken notice of the clink of her pails at a distance. But they did hear the pails clinking and they waited for her to appear, a little tensely, as if they felt some fear. And actually Laskell's heart was pounding in his chest.

"She shouldn't have to go that extra distance to get her water," said Nancy in a low voice. "There's no reason why she shouldn't get her water from us." And she said with determination, "I'll tell her."

Nancy started toward the road and so did Laskell. Arthur followed, and Kermit and Maxim followed him, so that they were all trooping rather absurdly over the lawn toward Emily Caldwell. They stood waiting on the muddy road, and she came up to them.

"Oh, thank you," she said when Nancy made the suggestion about the water. "But you see, I've been used to getting it at the Korzinskis' always. But thank you just the same."

"If there's anything I can do—" Nancy said.

"It's kind. There's nothing." She looked down at her feet. "Only," she said, "only you'll not have any feeling about Duck working for you again, will you?" The question was addressed to the Crooms. "He'll be back in a day or so."

"Back?" Nancy gasped. She should not have been surprised. She had heard the men agree that the coroner would not hold Duck, not for slapping his child in the face—for he had not killed his child if two reputable medical men from Hartford could testify, as of course they could, that the child had had a serious condition of the heart. Nancy had heard this but apparently she had not listened. All she knew was that Duck had killed Susan. And she said again, "Back?"

"Why, yes," said Emily, looking up sharply. "It was not a crime. Not even manslaughter. He didn't mean it. He didn't want to do it. He was a little under the influence of alcohol. And then Susan's heart was weak—very. It was always a danger for her. Everything was dangerous. Two doctors told me. Duck didn't know about it. They say he didn't do anything that a father might not do. It wasn't his fault. He was just—the—the—"

"Just the agent of fate," said Kermit to help her out, and then seemed surprised that he had said it.

"Yes," she said. "Just the agent."

Arthur said, "Don't worry about Duck working for us. It will be all the same as it was."

"If it was anybody's fault," Emily said, "it was mine. I'm to blame—I didn't tell him about her heart condition. I had no right to keep it to myself. If he had known, he would have been careful of her. It's my fault."

She still had some of the first hysteria of grief, and it was threatening to break through, so she turned and walked on as fast as she could.

"Emily," Arthur called after her. "Don't worry, Emily. It will be all right."

To Laskell it was unendurable that she should go. And when she was at the end of the stone wall that separated the Crooms' property from the road, he ran after her. She must have heard him running through the mud, but she did not turn. But when he caught up with her, she stopped. Then she looked sharply at him. "You're crying," she said simply.

And it was true, although he had not known it until she told him.

"Don't," she said.

"No," he said. "No, I won't."

She put down her pails and took a handkerchief from her short sleeve and wiped his cheeks vigorously. She did it without any hesitation or sorrow. And he understood that she felt she had a right to do so because they had been lovers. He had the full conception of her spirit when he understood that she had no desire to blot out that incident on the river bank. Her grief did not destroy her moment of passion. She did not think, as many another woman might have thought, in the superstition of early grief, that her moment of passion had been paid for by the death of her child. She did not have to make believe that her relationship to Laskell, short as it was, had never existed. She scrubbed once more at his face and smiled to him wanly. "There!" she said.

Then she said, "You have been very good."

He shook his head.

"Yes," she said. "To me you were very good. And to Susan. I'm happy she liked you so much—she was happy when she was with you. And I'm glad you paid for the funeral. You had a right to."

And then she said, but it took more courage, "And you were good to him. I know about how you ran after him. I know why you did it. He knows too. When I saw him in Hartford and told him about the heart, he said, 'So that's why he ran after me.' You have been very good."

She leaned toward him, touched with the tips of her fingers one of the cheeks she had just scrubbed of tears and put her lips lightly to the other cheek. He closed his eyes against what she was doing. She picked up the pails and went on her way to the Korzinskis', leaving him there on the road.

He did not know why her word "good" struck him like an accusation, so that what with the force of that emotion and the force of what he felt from her touch and her kiss, he put his hands to his face as if in some distraction. His friends had seen the meeting and what Emily had done. Laskell knew they saw, but he did not care. When he returned to them—they had all gone into the house—they gave no sign that they had seen anything.

To lighten the mood of all of them, Kermit suggested dinner at a road restaurant he knew of about fifteen miles away. They would have gone had it not been that Nancy had Micky to think of.

"But you all go," Nancy said.

"Unthinkable," said Kermit and made another proposal, that they all drive to Hartford to buy lobsters which he would broil outdoors. It would be a change. It was a change—they were not a very gay company, but it was better than sitting about. They bought the lobsters and a case of beer, and when they returned Kermit made cocktails and broiled the lobsters. They ate outdoors beside the trailer, for the weather had turned soft and bright. Nancy did her best, but she was still brooding. She had been absent-minded as she advised Kermit about the selection of the lobsters, she was silent on the drive back and all through dinner. And after dinner, over the plates of empty lobster shells, what was troubling her came out as well as she could say it.

She turned to Arthur and said with a simple decisiveness, "We can't have him here."

Arthur said, "Who? Oh—you mean Duck?"

"Yes, we can't have him back. I couldn't stand it."

But it was not only this that was troubling Nancy, for she suddenly burst out, "Oh, I don't know what to do—I don't know what to think. It's not his fault—it's *not*. But I couldn't stand having him around me. I'd think of it all the time. I couldn't stand seeing him. And yet it's not his fault, it's not."

Laskell saw the light leap into Maxim's eyes as Nancy moaned out her dilemma. But Maxim veiled the light with lowered lids and did not look at Nancy but poked at a lobster claw as he said softly, "Why isn't it his fault, Nancy?"

Nancy began to reply. But then suddenly she was struck by the absurdity of his asking that question of her, for although Maxim had not in actual fact inducted her into her philosophy, he had once been so important in it that he was, in effect, her teacher. She said stiffly, "You surely know why it isn't his fault."

He spoke as if he were indeed still her teacher. "Perhaps I do. But you explain to me why."

"Nancy means," Arthur said when Nancy did not immediately speak, "that social causes, environment, education or lack of education, economic pressure, the character-pattern imposed by society, in this case a disorganized society, all go to explain and account for any given individual's actions."

Maxim was annoyed by Arthur's interference. "Is that what you mean, Nancy?"

"Yes," she said. "We can't say he's to blame personally, individually. But," she said with great unhappiness, "I can't stand the idea of having him around me. Not that I'd be afraid, but I'd always be thinking that this man killed his child."

"You're upset," said Arthur. "Naturally you're upset. When you get calmer—"

"Who *is* to blame, Nancy?" Maxim said.

"I told you—Arthur told you. Society."

"Are you a member of society?" Maxim had the Socratic manner.

"Yes, of course I am," said Nancy, submitting to the *elenchus* that was clearly to come.

"Are you to blame for what Duck did? I mean are you to blame in part?" And Maxim, having asked the question, glanced slyly at Laskell.

"Nancy's not part of society in that sense," Arthur said. And then, because it sounded like a defense of his wife's good name, he said, "Nor is any of us."

"Is that true, Nancy? Do you agree with that? That you are not part of society in every sense?"

"Well, I'm against the bad in society. If you mean, do I have any share in what Duck did—no, I don't."

"Only the bad part of society does have a share?" Maxim insisted.

Arthur interrupted again. "But he didn't do anything bad—he didn't really kill the child, he meant just to smack her. Even Emily says that. You heard her say that."

"Let Nancy speak for herself, Arthur," Maxim said peremptorily. "Nancy thinks he did something bad. That is the source of her dilemma. And she is right, deeply right. You are right, Nancy. For that man is bad, and everything he does is bad, even if he wants it to be good."

"Oh, come, Giff!" said Kermit. "What is this, Calvinism?"

"His will is a bad one," said Maxim, in answer to Kermit's expostulation, but addressing Nancy to confirm her in her perception. "His will is a bad one and what he does is bad." Maxim spoke like a medical professor summarizing a case to the assembled students. "Nancy's dilemma is an inevitable one. She refuses to say that Caldwell has any responsibility, any blame or guilt. And then she refuses to allow him to come near her." Nancy was both the case and the students. "Let me show you the advantage of my system, Nancy. You won't believe it, you won't agree, you won't even hear it, so there's no danger in listening." He paused. "You see, Nancy," he said, "I reverse your whole process. I believe that Duck Caldwell—like you or me or any of us—is wholly responsible for his acts. Wholly. And for eternity, for everlasting. That is what gives him value in my eyes—his eternal, everlasting responsibility. His every act, to me, involves the whole universe. And when it breaks the moral law of the whole universe, I consider that his punishment might be infinite, everlasting. And yet in my system there is one thing that yours lacks. In my system, although there is never-ending responsibility, there is such a thing as mercy."

Maxim was not finished with what he had to say, but he paused here for a moment to let the word have its full weight. He went on. "Duck can be forgiven. I can personally forgive him because I believe that God can forgive him. You see, I think his will is a bad one, but not much worse, not different in kind, from other wills. And so you and I stand opposed. For you—no responsibility for the individual, but no forgiveness. For me—ultimate, absolute responsibility for the individual, but mercy. Absolute responsibility: it is the only way that men can keep their value, can be thought of as other than mere *things*. Those matters that Arthur speaks of—social causes, environment, education—do you think they really make a difference between one human soul and another? In the eyes of God are such differences of any meaning at all? Can you suppose that *they* condition His mercy? Does He hold a Doctor of Philosophy more responsible than a Master of Arts, or a high school graduate more responsible than a man who has not finished the eighth grade? Or is His mercy less to one than another?"

None of them had ever heard language like this, although they may have read it, and they did not know how to respond. Laskell had no impulse to respond to it. He was thinking that Maxim was not long for Kermit Simpson and *The New Era* and that when Maxim left Kermit, he would not religiously retire from the world but would go where worldly power lies waiting for men to pick it up. He had been seeing the great executive force that lay behind Maxim's expression of his view of the nature of guilt and responsibility. It seemed to him that the day was not very far off when Maxim's passions would suit the passions of others. The idealism of Nancy and Arthur, which, raised to a higher degree, had once been the idealism of Maxim himself, had served for some years now the people who demanded ideas on which to build their lives. It had presented the world as in movement and drama, had offered the possibility of heroism or martyrdom, made available the gift of commitment and virtue to those who chose to grasp it. But Laskell saw that the intellectual power had gone from that system of idealism, and much of its power of drama had gone. The time was getting ripe for a competing system. And it would be brought by the swing of the pendulum, not by the motion of growth. Maxim was riding the pendulum.

This perception, rather than the course of the argument, had been filling Laskell's mind. He was not prepared to answer when

Kermit, whom the silence oppressed, said, "John, what is your feeling about this?" To Kermit a difference of opinion was a difference of opinion and showed that liberalism still flourished. Yet Laskell, called upon, had an answer. He said, "Is it really a question, Kermit? I can't see it as a question, not really. An absolute freedom from responsibility—that much of a child none of us can be. An absolute responsibility—that much of a divine or metaphysical essence none of us is."

He hesitated, and then, because it seemed at this moment ungenerous to be shy, even about a new and untried thought, he went on, "I cannot absolve the world or society or God or my parents or nature from all blame from what I am or do. I didn't make myself and I don't dare cut my connection with all the things in the world that made me. I cannot hold myself free of these things. I will blame them when they injure and reduce me, as they do every moment of the day. And for that matter, I cannot avoid my gratitude to them."

There was a deeper silence than had fallen any time during his summer visit, although many silences had fallen during that visit. It was a deeper silence than had greeted any of Maxim's speeches, for Maxim was contributing to it.

Then Maxim said, "Neither beast nor angel!" It was the first time Laskell had ever heard Maxim sneer. "You're not being original. Pascal said it long ago."

"Yes," said Laskell. "I remember he did."

"But his position was more mine than yours."

"In some ways," said Laskell.

"Like any bourgeois intellectual, you want to make the best of every possible world and every possible view. Anything to avoid a commitment, anything not to have to take a risk."

"Certainly there's a good deal of shilly-shally in what you've just said, John," said Nancy.

"And a good deal of name-calling and motive-attributing," said Arthur.

"No, Arthur," Kermit said. "I don't think that's true."

"Childish—he said our position was childish, that we were trying to evade responsibility."

They were very angry. How angry they were Laskell could tell from the distress on Kermit's face. Considering Maxim's intellectual habits, it must indicate the loss of a good deal of temper for Maxim to have begun his rebuttal by announcing that his antagonist was not original.

He knew why they were angry at him. It was the anger of the masked will at the appearance of an idea in modulation. The open will does not show that anger; only the will masked in virtue shows it. His idea, which he now saw as nothing much of an idea, had affronted them. They were staring at him as silently as the great mural figures that once had flanked Gifford Maxim when he talked of politics and the future. He could see their stern faces in the early twilight.

"They are very angry with me, Kermit," Laskell said.

"I don't think so," said Kermit positively. "Why should they be?" Kermit was a little annoyed that Laskell should have seen anger where none properly should be.

But Laskell's remark broke their hostile stare and Nancy said in a way which was not very different from any she might have used a month ago, "Yes, I am angry with you—I don't like to see you trying to be above the battle that way. And you are trying."

He knew he was not, so he said nothing more than, "No."

"No," said Maxim. "No, you are not." His voice had lost all its anger. "No," he said turning to Nancy, "he is not above the battle."

Laskell did not know what magnanimous intention had prompted this. He did not care to find out. He wanted to leave, but he did not want to go while the drama was still so high. To make a commonplace on which he could quietly depart, he got an empty carton and began to clear the table of its untidy debris of lobster shells. But no one spoke while he did this and the tension of the drama did not relax. It even increased, for Maxim, by watching Laskell in every move he made, indicated that he was not finished, that he was going on to say more.

When Laskell had cleared the table, Maxim said, quite abolishing the interruption, "No. John is not above the battle. He will not cease from mental fight."

And as he said this, very tenderly, Laskell knew how intense this last struggle with Maxim was going to be. It seemed that Maxim liked always to have a reminder of death to make his work easier. Laskell put his hands on the back of one of the metal chairs and leaned on it and waited.

"John," said Maxim, "you were right in what you said. I'm sorry I got angry—but you can have the satisfaction of knowing that my getting angry shows how right you were. But you were right too late, or too early. You were right for yourself, perhaps, at that moment. What you said showed your moment of happiness, and I suppose I got angry out of envy. But you were not right for the world. I know why you spoke as you did—you spoke as a forgiven man, because of what happened on the road this afternoon between you and Emily Caldwell."

Nancy said, "Oh, *no!*" her sense of fair-play terribly offended. Maxim looked at her to take in her meaning and then went on as if such delicate considerations would count as little with Laskell as with himself. "Yes, you were right. The Crooms and myself are at hopeless extremes. The child and the metaphysical essence—you put it very well. You could have said, the foetus and God, *causa sui,* the cause of himself. And you spoke up for something between. Call it the human being in maturity, at once responsible and conditioned. You could understand that and want that because for that moment in which you spoke you were moving in an atmosphere of love. You were without guilt. I don't know what she said to you, but I saw what she did, and I know what you believe happened."

Maxim's eyes left Laskell's face and dropped to Laskell's hands which were gripping the back of the chair. Laskell thought: He is looking to see if my knuckles are white, he should not doubt that they would be, he should have more confidence in his powers. He said nothing.

"You spoke with courage and the intelligence of courage because you felt forgiven. It was a frightening thing to be, wasn't it? Which is why, as I think, you put your hands to your face. What a blow—to be kissed on the cheek and forgiven!"

"Giff! For God's sake!" said Kermit.

"You were freed from guilt—from the immediate guilt of not having loved Emily Caldwell, though you had made love to her, for having valued her low, though you liked her and got pleasure and help from her. And from the general guilt of other people's sins, or of their suffering, or of their death. Perhaps you were freed from your guilt of your own death. Does that sound crazy?"

"Yes!" Kermit cried. "Cut it out, you don't know what you are talking about."

Maxim glanced at Kermit and then turned again to Laskell, conveying that this was a matter between Laskell and himself, two men who could face the truth.

"I sometimes think," he went on, "that we feel guilty at the idea of our own death. Why is that? I don't know. I think we do not fear extinction, not extinction of our whole being but the part of our being that keeps everything else in check. As if we feared the death of conscience in ourselves, or the death of the State, or as if we were killing our parents—whatever it is that keeps in check every filthy impulse in ourselves that would overwhelm us." He shrugged. "It's just an idea. It's not important. All I want to say is that this afternoon poor Emily Caldwell gave you what you think was forgiveness, and now you feel that being human is permissible. That's why you spoke out of the old knowledge of what the human fate is. It wasn't shilly-shally, as Nancy says. But it's the *old* knowledge—you've had it too late. It won't last with you yourself, John. It can't. Your uncertainties will come back, your former guilts, the same ones that oppress us all. In a short time you will not even be able to remember what you felt when you felt free of it. You stand there now, thinking that you know us all, and disapprove of us all, and yet do not hate or despise us. You are being proud of that flexibility of mind. But it won't last, John, it's diminishing now. It is too late for that—the Renaissance is dead. You could have kept that kind of mind up to fifty years ago, vestigially even up to ten years ago. But now it is dead and what you feel is only a ghost. You know it as well as I do—the day for being human in the way you feel now is over. Gone. Done for. Finished. Maybe it will come again. But not for a long time, John, not until the Crooms and I have won and established ourselves against the anarchy of the world."

"The Crooms and you!" said Arthur, and was too outraged to say more.

"My God!" said Nancy.

Laskell wondered if any man had ever made an attempt on another man such as Maxim was making upon him.

"I'm sorry, Arthur. I'm sorry, Nancy." And Maxim's expression of regret was scarcely ironic. He really seemed to apologize for the alliance he insisted on. "I'm sorry—but we must go hand in hand. Let it be our open secret. You will preach the law for the masses. I will preach the law for the leaders. For the masses, rights and the freedom from blame. For the leaders, duties and nothing but blame, from without and from within. We will hate each other and we will make the new world. And when we've made it and it has done its work, then maybe we will resurrect John Laskell. But resurrection implies—" And he shrugged.

"Giff, I swear I think you're crazy," Kermit said earnestly. "I swear I do."

"He is crazy. He's insane," Nancy said.

"No," said Laskell. "He's not."

Maxim pointed his finger at Laskell. "Remember it!" he said to the others. "It is the last time that you will see it." He spoke gaily, as if the conversation had been the brightest, most successful nonsense among friends. "The supreme act of the humanistic critical intelligence—it perceives the cogency of the argument and acquiesces in the fact of its own extinction."

"You have been very clever, Maxim," said Laskell. "Cleverer than I thought a man could ever be. But you are wrong on one point—I do not acquiesce."

"Yes," said Maxim, still in his gay, bright excitement. "Of course I was wrong. You cannot possibly acquiesce. But it does not matter, John," he said kindly, "whether you do or not."

"It matters," Laskell said. "Oh, it matters very much. It is the only thing that matters. The world is full of open secrets, Maxim, and one of them is the ferocity—"

"If you had said 'tenacity,' the tenacity of your kind of mind, that might have made sense. But if you defend yourself with ferocity, John, we have won—we take you into camp. Better wait for the resurrection, John."

"Most fortunately I lack that kind of historical perspective, Maxim."

"Oh, what are you two talking about!" Nancy cried and brought their cold exchange of taunts to an end.

Laskell came the next morning to say that he was leaving in the afternoon. He told Kermit first. Kermit was troubled, for he had undertaken to drive Laskell home; he would have set out with the trailer at once, but he had promised Nancy to stay two days more. "But let me drive you to the station," he said.

"Thank you, but I'd like Arthur and Nancy to drive me."

"Of course," said Kermit.

Maxim came out of the trailer while they were saying good-by. He looked drowsy and below himself, as if he had been on a debauch.

"John's leaving today," Kermit explained.

Maxim blinked in the sunlight. "I'm sorry I talked the way I did last night. I had no right—"

"You had your inspiration and you had to yield to it."

"Sometimes he just talks," Kermit said.

"Not usually," Laskell said.

Maxim's eyes creased and he grinned at Laskell. Neither of them offered to shake hands in farewell.

The Crooms, when Laskell told them that he was leaving that afternoon, expressed surprise at the suddenness of his departure. But they did not protest it—it was so very clear that the visit was over.

"Kermit offered to drive me to the station," Laskell said. "But I'd rather if you two took me."

"Yes, of course, naturally!" they cried.

On the way back to the Folgers' to pack his bags, he met Duck Caldwell. Duck must have been watching from his window, for he came lounging out of the door just as Laskell was about to pass the house. He looked a little pale, but not otherwise different.

"You leaving us, Mr. Laskell?" He must have had that news from Mrs. Folger, whom Laskell had told early that morning.

"Yes, I am," Laskell said. He looked at the man, letting come whatever emotion might come. But none came. He had dreaded this meeting.

"You feel all well now?" Duck said solicitously.

"Yes, I think I do."

"That knife I pulled on you—I didn't know why you came after me." It was meant for apology and reconciliation, as far as Duck could go, which was to his next remark. "I'm not speculating, mind you, how you knew about my own kid when I didn't. I'm not in a position to do any speculating."

Again Laskell waited for an emotion. But none came even now, not guilt, not anger, not pity.

"I hear you're in the building trades in New York," Duck said. "Do you think you could get a clever man a job?"

"Possibly."

"I'm thinking of getting out of these parts." Duck pointed backward to the little green house as showing reason enough for not wanting to stay. And indeed the house looked desolate. "Should I look you up if I make up my mind to change?"

"You can think about it."

Laskell nodded to Duck, who coolly nodded back, and he continued on his way.

As he settled his accounts with Mrs. Folger, he saw that she had forgotten not only that he had once been a naughty boy but also that she had ever had a moment's dislike of him—he was out of connection, merely a summer boarder ready to leave. He paid her the small sum of money he owed her and shook hands and thanked her for her kindness to him. She said, "It was a pleasure to have you. You were no trouble at all." He asked her if Mr. Folger would be back so that he could say good-by to him. She said she was sure he would be, but Mr. Folger did not return.

He did not pack the test tube in which he had been boiling his urine. He tossed it into the trash-basket, doing this with a certain dryness—the gesture made him feel somewhat insincere, as any intelligent person is likely to feel who performs a symbolic action. He brought the bags down and put them on the porch. When he came down again, with his rod and creel and the wooden bowl, which would not fit into either of his bags, old Mr. Folger was on the porch. The old man said something which must have had reference to Laskell's departure, and Laskell shouted back an answer, "Yes, I'm leaving. Have to get back to the city." The chickens were on the lawn and the hounds were lying on the path with their tongues out. They were very lazy and on hot days they gasped and looked at the world with suffering eyes, but they really had a very easy life and were well fed and much petted. Mrs. Folger came out and sat down and crossed her hands over her apron. For all his desire to be away, Laskell had the inevitable twist of the heart at leaving any part of life.

The Crooms came in good time, and Arthur jumped out and insisted on carrying the bags to the car. Laskell shook hands with Mrs. Folger once more. They all got into the front seat, Nancy between the two men, Micky on her lap. It was not a comfortable arrangement for any of them, but on neither side did they want further separations.

They had to wait for the train. They sat on the bench where Laskell had had his terror. He could scarcely remember just what had happened, although he knew it had been something quite devastating. He saw the shabby little station, the three red gas-pumps not far off, but these seemed elements of safety, not of threat.

Nancy said that the summer was nearly over, and one could see all around that she was right, although it was very hot. She asked when Labor Day was, and they told her it was ten days off. Laskell asked them how long they were going to stay, and they told him that they would stay a week beyond Labor Day. They agreed that they would have dinner together as soon as the Crooms returned to the city and were settled. It was the conversation that any friends might have, waiting for the train that one of them is leaving on after weeks in the country together. There was a touch of bleakness in it, but all such conversations near the end of the summer are a little melancholy, even though the separation is only for a matter of days. Other people in similar situations must have had their conversations touched with unhappiness, perhaps greater that year, if they were intelligent, than the year before because of the growing knowledge that intelligent people had of the danger in the world. But the Crooms included Laskell among the dangers of the world, and Laskell included the Crooms. This made them very attentive and courteous to each other.

Laskell got up as if to stretch his legs and to see if the train was coming. Then he stood before them as they sat on the bench. "It was good of you to have me up. I really—" He was about to say, conventionally, "enjoyed it." But he could not say that, for it was not true. "—had great benefit from it," was what he said. And as he heard the stiff little phrase, he thought that in some difficult way it was true. He said, "I'm sorry that we seemed to get into so many disagreements."

Arthur began to brush this aside, but Nancy said, "We did, didn't we? Why did we?" And she rose and stood facing him to make the question real.

He wanted very much to be able to answer her. He was on the point of saying, "Because we are parts of history, elements in the dialectic." But it would have been a wry joke. He said, "I don't know."

"It has been sad and—and awful. What Maxim said last night— you don't believe that, do you? About him and us being together against you. As if that could ever be true."

"I hope it's not true," said Laskell.

They heard the whistle of the train and Micky had to be held against his excitement or fear. They remembered that it was the first time that Micky had ever seen a train, and Arthur held him so that he could both see and be safe, and Nancy held his hand and told him what was coming, talking to him to make sure that he would feel her presence and not be frightened at the locomotive. When the train had come to a stop, Arthur gave Micky to Nancy so that he could help Laskell with the bags. Laskell protested, but Arthur insisted. He picked up the bags, looked for the emptiest and least shabby of the four cars and started toward it. Laskell gathered up what was left for him to carry. He shook Micky's hand. Nancy put out her cheek and he kissed it. Arthur already had the bags in the car and on the luggage rack. They shook hands and Arthur left, and Laskell saw him take Micky from Nancy. They all three stood waving at him, Nancy showing Micky how to wave. Laskell waved back. Nancy blew a kiss and showed Micky how to blow a kiss and then the train left.

Laskell put the rod up with the bags and he tried to put the creel up too. The creel was coming back without having held a single fish, but this was not the first time it had done that. The creel would not fit on the rack with the bags, nor would the bowl, so he kept these on the seat beside him.